T0284276

"No!" Ner'zhul raced toward the portal. He was still several feet away when the shimmering curtain of light flickered, contracted, froze—and then exploded. Stones and dust erupted from the archway. Ner'zhul was tossed into the air like an old bone, and struck the earth hard. Dentarg let out an angry bellow and rushed to his master's side, scooping him up as if he weighed nothing. The old shaman lay limp, head lolling, eyes shut, a trickle of blood along his right side. For a wild moment energy screamed and shrieked about them all, howling like angry spirits. Then as abruptly as they had come the lights vanished, the curtain disappearing utterly, leaving only an empty stone portal behind.

The Dark Portal had been severed.

Gratar stared at that stone archway, and at all the Horde warriors who had escaped back through it one last time. Then he glanced over at Dentarg, and the elderly shaman cradled in the ogre's surprisingly gentle grasp.

In the name of the ancestors . . . what would they do now?

WORLD OF WARCRAFT®

BEYOND THE DARK PORTAL

AARON ROSENBERG
&
CHRISTIE GOLDEN

© 2022 Blizzard Entertainment, Inc. All rights reserved. Warcraft, World of Warcraft, and Blizzard Entertainment are trademarks and/or registered trademarks of Blizzard Entertainment, Inc., in the U.S. and/or other countries. No portion of this book may be reproduced or transmitted in any form or by any means without written permission from the copyright holders.

This book is a work of fiction. Names, characters, places, and incidents are either products of the author's imagination or are used fictitiously, and any resemblance to actual persons, living or dead, business establishments, events, or locales is entirely coincidental.

Blizzard Entertainment does not have any control over and does not assume any responsibility for author or third-party websites or their content.

Library of Congress Cataloging-in-Publication Data available.

ISBN: 978-1-956916-05-8

First Pocket Star Books paperback edition July 2008
First Blizzard Entertainment printing October 2022

10 9 8 7 6 5 4 3 2 1

Cover art by Glenn Rane

Printed in China

*To my family and friends and especially my lovely wife,
who help me hold back the tide.*

*For David Honigsberg (1958–2007)
Musician, writer, gamer, rabbi, and friend extraordinaire.
Teach Heaven to rock, amigo.*

PROLOGUE

"Throw down!"

"Shut up!"

"Throw *down*, damn you!"

"Fine!" Gratar growled, half-rising, his powerful shoulder muscles bunching. One arm whipped forward and down, fist descending in a blur—and his fingers opened, the small bone cubes spilling from them to clatter upon the ground.

"Hah!" Brodog laughed, tusks jutting up as his lips pulled back in a grin. "Only one!"

"Damn!" Gratar sank back down onto his stone, sulking as he watched Brodog again gather the cubes and shake them vigorously. He didn't know why he kept throwing against Brodog—the other orc practically always won. It was almost unnatural.

Unnatural. A word that had nearly stopped having any meaning for Gratar. He glanced up at the stark red sky that filled the horizon, the sun a burning globe of the same shade. The world had not always been thus. Gratar was old enough to remember blue skies, a warm yellow sun, and thick green fields and valleys. He'd swum in deep, cool lakes and rivers, blissfully ignorant of how precious a thing water would one day become. One of the most basic needs of life, uncontaminated water was now brought in in casks and stingily parceled out.

Rising, Gratar kicked idly at the ground before him, watching the red dust puff upward, parching his mouth, and he reached for the waterskin and drank sparingly. The dust covered his skin, dulling the green hue, lightening his black hair. Red everywhere, as if the world had been drenched in blood.

Unnatural.

But the most unnatural thing of all was the reason he and Brodog were stationed here, whiling away the dusk-clogged day with idle games of chance. Gratar looked past Brodog at the towering archway just beyond them and the shimmering curtain of energy that filled it. The Dark Portal. Gratar knew that the strange mystic doorway led to another world, though he had not passed through it himself—none of his clan had. But he had watched as proud Horde warriors had entered the portal to win glory over the humans and their allies. Since then, a few orcs had returned to report the Horde's progress. But lately there had been nothing. No word, no scouts; nothing.

Gratar frowned, ignoring the clattering sound of

Brodog's tossing of the bones. Something about the portal seemed . . . different. Gratar stepped closer to the towering gateway, the hairs along his arms and chest tingling as he approached.

"Gratar? It's your turn. What are you doing?"

Gratar ignored Brodog. Squinting, he stared at the rippling veil of energy. What was going on beyond it, on that strange other world?

As he watched the curtain's undulating shimmer grew and became more translucent, allowing Gratar to see through it as if through murky water. He squinted his eyes, peered intently—and gasped, staggering back.

Playing out before his eyes, as if he were watching a ritual enactment, was a fierce and violent battle.

"What?" Brodog was beside him in an instant, the game forgotten, and then he was gaping as well. They both stared for a second before Gratar regained his wits.

"Go!" he shouted at Brodog. "Tell them what's happening!"

"Right—the commander." Brodog's eyes were still glued to the scene before them.

"No," Gratar replied sharply. He had a gut feeling that what was about to happen would be more than his commander was prepared to handle. But one orc he knew might be. "Ner'zhul. Get Ner'zhul—he'll know what to do!"

Brodog nodded and took off at a run, though not without glancing back a few times. Gratar heard him leave, but still his gaze was riveted to the battle that was so violent but so oddly veiled. He could see orcs, some of whom he thought he recognized, but they were fighting strange figures, shorter and more narrowly built but more heavily armored. The strangers—they were called "humans," Gratar remembered—were quick and as numerous as gnats, swarming over the beleaguered orcs and overpowering them one by one. How could his people be suffering such a defeat? Where was Doomhammer? Gratar saw no sign of the massive, powerful warchief. What had happened on that other world?

He was still watching, sickly enraptured, when he heard the sound of approaching feet. He tore his gaze away to see that Brodog had returned with two others. One was a massive figure, larger by far than any orc and much stronger, with pale milky skin and heavy features. An ogre, and a mage, by the cunning Gratar saw glinting in his small, piggy eyes. More important than this towering figure was the orc who accompanied him, pushing his way forward right up to the portal itself.

Though his hair was gray and his face heavily lined, Ner'zhul, chieftain of the Shadowmoon clan and once the most skilled shaman the orcs had ever known, was still powerfully built and his brown eyes were as sharp as ever. He stared at the portal and the vaguely glimpsed disaster unfolding behind its shimmer.

"A battle, then," Ner'zhul said as if to himself.

And one the Horde is losing, Gratar thought.

"How long has—" Ner'zhul began. Suddenly the space framed by the Dark Portal shifted, its energies swirling violently. A hand thrust from the curtain as if it were rising from water, gleams of light and shadow clinging to green skin as it breached the barrier. A head followed, then the torso, and then the orc was through. His war axe was still in his hand but his eyes were wild as he stumbled, then caught himself, racing past Ner'zhul and the others without even looking.

Behind him came another orc, then another and another and another, until there was a flood of them, all racing to pass through the portal as fast as their feet would carry them. And not just orcs—Gratar saw several ogres emerge, and a group of smaller, slighter figures with heavy hooded cloaks bridged the gap as well. One warrior caught Gratar's attention. Too tall and bulky to be a full orc, his features brutish enough to have some ogre blood in him, this one did not run with the air of panic the others did, but with purpose, as if he was running to something rather than from it. At his heels loped a massive jet-black wolf.

An orc shoved past this warrior as they stepped from the portal, snarling at the obstruction. "Out of the way!" the orc snapped, but the warrior merely shook his head, refusing to be baited at such a time. The wolf, however, snarled at the orc before the warrior silenced it with a sharp hand gesture. The wolf fell silent, utterly obedient, and the warrior dropped a huge hand on the black head with affection.

"What has happened here?" Ner'zhul demanded loudly. "You!" The shaman pointed toward one of the unfamiliar creatures. "What manner of orc are you? Why cover your face so? Come here!"

The figure paused, then suddenly shrugged and stepped closer to Ner'zhul. "As you wish," he said in a cold voice that had a slightly mocking tone to it. Despite the heat of the land's baked, lifeless soil, Gratar shivered.

A mailed hand slid the hood back, and Gratar could not help crying out in horror. Perhaps the being's features had once been fine and regular, but no longer. The skin was a pale grayish green, and had burst open at the juncture where ear met jaw. A thin trickle of ooze glimmered. Swollen, cracked, purple lips drew back in a smile as the eyes glowed with malevolent humor and a fierce intelligence.

The thing was obviously dead.

Even Ner'zhul shrank back, though he rallied quickly. "Who—what are you?" Ner'zhul demanded in a voice that shook only a little. "And what do you want here?"

"Don't you recognize me? I am Teron Gorefiend," the figure replied, chuckling at the shaman's obvious discomfiture.

"Impossible! He is dead and gone, slaughtered by

Doomhammer along with the rest of the Shadow Council!"

"Dead I am indeed," the creature agreed, "but not gone. Your old apprentice Gul'dan found a way to bring us back, and into these rotting carcasses." He shrugged, and Gratar could hear the lifeless flesh creak in slight protest. "It suffices."

"Gul'dan?" The old shaman seemed more shocked by that revelation than by the sight of the walking corpse in front of him. "Your master still lives? Then you should return to him. You forsook me and the shaman tradition to follow his lead and become a warlock when you lived, abomination. Serve him now that you are dead."

But Gorefiend was shaking his head. "Gul'dan is dead. And good riddance. He betrayed us, halving the Horde at a crucial moment and forcing Doomhammer to pursue him instead of conquering a human city. That treachery cost us the war."

"We . . . have *lost?*" Ner'zhul stammered. "But . . . how is that possible? The Horde covered the very plains, and Doomhammer would not go down without a fight!"

"Oh, he fought," Gorefiend agreed. "Yet all his might was not enough. He killed the humans' leader but was overpowered in turn."

Ner'zhul seemed stunned, turning to look at the panting, bloodied orcs and ogres who had rushed through the gates moments earlier. He took a deep breath and straightened, turning to the ogre who had accompanied him. "Dentarg—summon the other chieftains. Tell them to gather here at once, bringing only weapons and armor. We—"

The wave washed out of the portal with no warning, a massive energy burst that slammed all of them to the ground. Gratar gasped for breath, the wind knocked out of him. He stumbled to his feet, only to be greeted by a second explosion, more violent than the first. This time hunks of stone had been snatched up by the energy that powered the portal and came flying past them, chips and slabs and slivers and sheets. The curtain wavered, becoming opaque.

"No!" Ner'zhul raced toward the portal. He was still several feet away when the shimmering curtain of light flickered, contracted, froze—and then exploded. Stones and dust erupted from the archway. Ner'zhul was tossed into the air like an old bone, and struck the earth hard. Dentarg let out an angry bellow and rushed to his master's side, scooping him up as if he weighed nothing. The old shaman lay limp, head lolling, eyes shut, a trickle of blood along his right side. For a wild moment energy screamed and shrieked about them all, howling like angry spirits. Then as abruptly as they had come the lights vanished, the curtain disappearing utterly, leaving only an empty stone portal behind.

The Dark Portal had been severed.

Gratar stared at that stone archway, and at all the

Horde warriors who had escaped back through it one last time. Then he glanced over at Dentarg, and the elderly shaman cradled in the ogre's surprisingly gentle grasp.

In the name of the ancestors . . . what would they do now?

CHAPTER ONE

"Ner'zhul!"

Gorefiend and Gaz Soulripper strode into the village as if they owned it, booted feet moving swiftly over hard-packed dirt. Curious villagers poked their heads out of the doors and windows of their simple huts, only to shrink back inside as the interlopers fixed them with a baleful stare from unnaturally glowing eyes.

"Ner'zhul!" Gorefiend called again in a voice that was both cold and commanding. "I would speak with you!"

"Don't know who you are," a voice growled behind him, "and don't much care. You're trespassing on Shadowmoon territory. Leave or die."

"I need to speak with Ner'zhul," the death knight replied, turning to face the powerful orc warrior who had stepped threateningly behind him. "Tell him Teron Gorefiend is here."

The orc looked unsettled at the name. "Gorefiend?

You are the death knight?" He grimaced, showing his tusks, glancing at Gorefiend and his companion, then obviously mustering his courage. "You don't look so dangerous."

"Dangerous enough," replied Soulripper. He turned and nodded at something the orc could not see. Several more beings, their faces hooded but their glowing eyes visible, emerged from the very shadows of the village's huts and stepped up beside their two fellow death knights. Gorefiend chuckled, and the orc swallowed. "Now fetch your master, lest your arrogance bring you swift death instead."

"Ner'zhul sees no one," the orc stated. He was beginning to sweat, but he obviously had his orders.

Gorefiend sighed, a strange whistling sound as air was taken into and then expelled from dead lungs.

"Swift death then," he said. Before the orc could even form a reply, Gorefiend extended a mailed hand and murmured something. The warrior gasped, doubling over and then dropping to his knees. Gorefiend tightened his fist and blood suddenly burst from the hapless orc's nose, eyes, and mouth. Gorefiend had already turned away by this point, having lost interest in tormenting the annoyance.

"Dark magic!" one of the Shadowmoon warriors shouted, grabbing up the axe beside him. "Kill the warlocks before they can afflict any more of us!" he bellowed, and his fellows responded by readying themselves as well.

Gorefiend whirled, glowing eyes narrowing. "If you all die so be it; I will speak with Ner'zhul!" This time he extended both hands, and darkness formed at his fingertips. It exploded like a glowing black flame, knocking back the orc who had hurled the axe as well as his fellows. They lay where the blast had blown them, screaming in agony.

"*Stop!* There has been enough killing already!" The old orc's voice rang with authority. Gorefiend lowered his arms and his companions fell back, watching their leader.

"There you are, Ner'zhul," Gorefiend drawled. "I thought that might get your attention." He turned to regard Ner'zhul, mildly surprised to notice that the old orc's face had been painted white—almost like a skull, Gorefiend mused. As their eyes met, Ner'zhul's widened.

"I . . . have dreamed of you," he murmured. "I have had visions of death, and now here you are." Long green fingers reached to touch the skull painted on his face. Small bits of white flaked off at the gesture. "Two years have I been dreaming of this. You have come for me, then. For us all. You have come to take my soul!"

"Not at all. I've come to save it. But—you are partially right: I have come for you, but not the way you think. I wish to see you lead."

Ner'zhul looked confused. "Lead? Why? So that I can destroy more of the Horde? Haven't I done enough?" The old shaman's eyes were haunted. "Nay, I

am done with such things. I led our people once—
straight into Gul'dan's plots, straight into schemes that
have doomed this world and a battle that nearly destroyed us. Seek a leader elsewhere."

Gorefiend frowned. This was not going as expected,
and he couldn't simply slay Ner'zhul as he had the
shaman's clansmen. He tried again. "The Horde needs
you."

"The Horde is dead!" Ner'zhul snapped. "Half our
people are gone, trapped on that horrible world, and
lost to us forever! You want me to lead that?"

"They are not lost forever," Gorefiend replied, and
the calm certainty in his tone brought Ner'zhul up
short. "The portal was destroyed, but may yet be restored."

That got Ner'zhul's attention. "What? How?"

"A small rift remains on Azeroth," Gorefiend explained, "and this side is intact. I helped create the Dark
Portal, and I can still sense it. I can help you widen the
rift until the Horde can pass through it."

The shaman seemed to consider this for an instant,
then shook his head, folding in on himself almost vis-
ibly. "What good would that do us? The Alliance is
too great a foe. The Horde will never win. Our people
are as good as dead already. All we have left now is
the manner of that death." Again his fingers touched
the painted image on his face, almost of their own
volition. His weakness disgusted Gorefiend. It was
hard to believe that this wreck, obsessed with death,

his own and that of others, had once been so revered.

And unfortunately still so necessary.

"Death is not the only option, not if we rebuild and use the portal," Gorefiend countered, forcing patience. "We don't have to win—we don't even need to battle the Alliance again. I have quite another plan for the Horde. If I can get ahold of certain artifacts—there are things I learned about from Gul'dan that—"

"Gul'dan and his twisted schemes—they reach out and destroy lives even from beyond the grave!" He scowled at Gorefiend. "You and your plans! And how much power would you gain from success? Power is all you Shadow Council bastards care about!"

Gorefiend's patience, never great, had evaporated. He seized the old shaman's arms and shook him angrily. "Two years since the portal collapsed, and you have been hiding in your village while the clans slaughter each other. All they need is guidance and then they will be powerful again! Between your supporters and my death knights, we can force the clans to obey you. With Doomhammer dead or imprisoned on Azeroth, you are the only one left who can lead them. I have been examining the portal, assessing the damage, and I told you I have a solution. I've assigned several death knights to the site already. Even as I speak to you, they are working spells, preparing it for its reopening. I am sure it can succeed."

"And what is this solution?" Ner'zhul spat bitterly. "Did you discover a way for us to return to Azeroth and win the war we lost two years ago? I think not. We are doomed. We will never win." He turned away, and took a step back toward his hut.

"Never mind the war! Listen to me, old man!" the death knight shouted after him. "We do not need to defeat the Alliance *because we do not need to conquer Azeroth!*"

Ner'zhul paused and glanced back. "But you said you could reopen the portal. Why do that if not to return there?"

"Return, yes, but not for battle." Gorefiend closed the gap between them again. "We need only to find and claim certain magical artifacts. Once we have those, we can leave Azeroth and never return."

"And stay here?" Ner'zhul waved a hand, the gesture encompassing much of the stricken landscape around them. "You know as well as I that Draenor is dying. Soon it will not be able to sustain even those of us left."

He had not remembered the shaman as being so slow-witted. "It will not have to," Gorefiend assured him, speaking slowly as if to a child. "With these artifacts in hand, we can leave both Azeroth and Draenor behind and go someplace else. Some place better."

Now he had Ner'zhul's full attention. Something like hope flickered across the white-painted face. For a long moment, Ner'zhul stood poised either to reenter his hut and resume his self-pitying seclusion, or to embrace this new possibility.

"You have a plan for this?" the old shaman asked finally.

"I do."

Another long pause. Gorefiend waited.

". . . I will listen." Ner'zhul turned and stepped back into his hut.

But this time Teron Gorefiend—warlock and death knight—came with him.

CHAPTER TWO

"Look at this place!"

Genn Greymane, king of Gilneas, gestured at the citadel towering over them, the same massive structure whose front gates they were striding through as he spoke. Though a large, burly man, Greymane was dwarfed by the edifice they were entering, the arch of its front gate more than twice his height. The other kings nodded as they too passed through, admiring the thick outer walls with their heavy block construction, but Greymane snorted, and his frown showed he did not echo their approval.

"A wall, a tower, and a single keep," he rumbled loudly, glaring at the half-completed buildings beyond. "This is where our money's gone to?"

"It's big," Thoras Trollbane pointed out, the terse Stromgarde ruler as usual wasting as few words as possible. "Big is expensive."

The other kings grumbled somewhat as well. They

all grieved at the costs involved. Especially since they, the Alliance leaders, were sharing the expenses equally.

"How great a price do you put on safety?" commented the tall, slim young man near the front of the group. "Nothing worth having comes cheaply." Several of the others ceased their grumbling at the subtle admonition. Varian, the recently crowned young king of Stormwind, had known safety, and been robbed of it. His realm had suffered greatly at the hands of the orcs during the First War. Much of the capital city in particular had been reduced to mere rubble.

"Indeed—how does the rebuilding go, Your Majesty?" a whip-thin man in green naval garb asked politely.

"Very well, thank you, Admiral," Varian replied—though Daelin Proudmoore was ruler of Kul Tiras, he preferred to use his naval title. "The Stonemasons' Guild is doing an excellent job, and I and my people owe them our gratitude. They're fine craftsmen, with skills to rival those of the dwarves themselves, and the city is rising higher and higher every day." He grinned at Greymane. "Worth every copper, I'd say."

The other kings chuckled, and one of them, tall and broad with graying blond hair and blue-green eyes, caught Trollbane's gaze and nodded approvingly. Terenas, ruler of Lordaeron, had sponsored young Varian when the prince and his people had sought refuge from the Horde, and had taken the youth into his own home until such time as Varian could be restored to his father's throne. Now that time had come, and Terenas and his old friend Trollbane were well pleased with the results. Varian was a clever, charming, noble young man, a natural leader and a gifted diplomat for one so young. Terenas had grown to think of him almost as a son, and he now took nearly a father's pride in admiration of the way the youth had controlled the conversation and distracted the other rulers from their previous complaints.

"In fact," Varian continued, pitching his voice slightly louder, "there's the miracle worker himself." The king indicated a tall and powerfully built man speaking animatedly with some dusty-looking workmen. The man in question had black hair and dark green eyes that sparkled as his head turned toward them, having clearly overheard the words. Terenas recognized Edwin Van-Cleef, the head of the Stonemasons' Guild and the man in charge of both Stormwind's restoration and the construction here at Nethergarde Keep.

Varian smiled and beckoned him over. "Master Van-Cleef, I trust the work continues apace?"

"It does, Your Majesty, thank you," VanCleef replied confidently. He banged a heavy fist against the thick outer wall and nodded proudly. "It'll hold against all comers, sire, I promise you that."

"I know it will, Master VanCleef," Stormwind's king agreed. "You've outdone yourself here, and that takes some doing."

VanCleef nodded his thanks, then turned as another

man somewhere by one of the unfinished buildings called for him. "I'd best be back to work. Your Majesties." He bowed to the assembled rulers, then turned and hurried off toward the shouts.

"Nicely handled," Terenas said softly to Varian as they fell into pace together. "Defusing Greymane and flattering VanCleef at the same time."

The younger king grinned. "It's an honest compliment, and he'll work all the harder because of it," he pointed out just as quietly, "and Greymane only complains to hear the sound of his own voice."

"You've grown very wise for your age," Terenas said, laughing. "Or perhaps just wise in general."

Of course, Varian's hidden reprimand could not shut Greymane up for long. As they crossed the wide courtyard Gilneas's king began grumbling again, and soon those rumblings in his thick black beard formed words once more. "I know they are working hard," he admitted grudgingly, glaring at Varian, who grinned in reply, "but why all these buildings?" He waved a large hand at the single completed keep they were entering as they passed beneath the portcullis and up the stairs. "Why go to so much trouble—and cost—to create such a vast citadel? It is only here to maintain watch over the valley where the portal once stood, is it not? Why would a simple keep not have sufficed?"

Khadgar, archmage of Dalaran, exchanged tired but still slightly amused glances with his fellow wizards as Greymane's strong voice carried to them even before they entered the large meeting room.

"It is good to hear Greymane is his old self," Antonidas, leader of the Kirin Tor, commented dryly.

"Yes, some things never change," Khadgar replied, stroking his full white beard. He turned, his youthful quickness giving a seeming lie to his lined visage, to face the kings. "You want to know what your money has bought you, then?" he said to the newcomers, nodding a brief greeting to them but otherwise treating them as equals—for such they were, as Khadgar, a member of the Kirin Tor, was a ruler in his own right.

"Well, I'll tell you, and you can thank me. Nethergarde Keep is large, yes. It has to be. Quite a few people will be living here—the magi we brought here from Dalaran, as well as the soldiers who watch for more mundane threats. The valley below us was once the site of the Dark Portal, the Horde's entrance into our world. If they ever return, we'll be ready."

"That explains the warriors," Proudmoore agreed, "but why these magi you spoke of? Surely a single mage would be enough to monitor the situation and alert you of any danger?"

"If that were all that was required, yes," Khadgar agreed, pacing the room. His strides were that of the young man he truly was. Khadgar was only a handful of years older than Varian, but he had been aged prematurely by the magic of Medivh just before the Magus's death. "But Nethergarde is quickly becoming more than just a watch post. You can't possibly have missed the reason for our concern as you rode up. Something drained the life from Draenor, from the very land itself. When the Dark Portal was opened that lifelessness touched our world as well, killing the land around it and spreading outward. When we destroyed the portal, we thought the land would heal itself. It did not. In fact, the taint continued to spread."

The kings frowned and looked at one another. This was news to them all.

"We began to study the situation, and discovered that, even with the portal gone, a small dimensional rift remained." That brought gasps from the assembled rulers.

"Did you find a way to stop the taint from spreading?" Proudmoore asked.

"We did, though it took several of us working together to do so." A frown crossed his lined face. "Unfortunately, we were unable to restore the land that had been damaged. This area was once the Black Morass, and we managed to protect the northern half and keep it in its former state. There are rumors that some orcs are still hiding out there, but we've not seen anything concrete. But the southern half—for whatever reason, we could not breathe life back into it." He shook his head. "Someone took to calling it the Blasted Lands, and now the name has stuck. I doubt this land will ever be able to support life again."

"Still, you stopped the taint and saved the rest of the

world's soil," Varian pointed out. "That is incredible enough, given how rapidly the effect spread."

Khadgar inclined his head, acknowledging the praise. "We have done more than I had dared hope," he admitted, "though less than I might have liked. But a full contingent of magi must remain here at all times, to watch the area and make sure we lose no more of Azeroth to this strange taint. The magi also monitor the rift itself at the same time. And *that*, good majesties, is why Nethergarde had to be so large, and is costing so much."

"Is there really any risk that the rift might reopen?" Trollbane asked, and the others turned back to Khadgar, clearly awaiting his answer but worried about what it might be. He could read their thoughts on their faces; the idea of reliving what had happened eight years before, when the portal had opened and the orcs had come pouring through, unnerved them all.

Khadgar began to answer, but was interrupted by a shrill caw from just outside the meeting hall. "I think the final member has just arrived by gryphon and landed on the wall walk," he said. The woman who entered the meeting room a few moments later was tall and almost unspeakably lovely. Worn-looking green and brown leather clung to her slim form as she strode toward them. Her golden hair was tousled and she brushed it absently back from long, pointed ears. Exquisite and delicate she might seem, but everyone present knew well that Alleria Windrunner was a formidable ranger, scout and fighter and wilderness expert. Many of those present had fought in battle alongside her—and owed their lives to her sharp eyes, quick reactions, and strong nerves.

"Khadgar," she said bluntly as she stepped up beside him, tall enough to almost look him eye to eye.

"Alleria," he replied. Affectionate nostalgia made the single word warm. They had been comrades in arms not so long ago, good friends fighting a good fight. But there was no warmth in her green-eyed gaze, nor on a face that, while beautiful, might have been carved from stone for all the animation it displayed. Alleria was courteous, but that was all. Inwardly, Khadgar sighed, stepping back through the door and gesturing for her to follow.

"This had better be good," she said as she entered the room proper and nodded briefly to the various kings. Despite her willowy build and youthful golden looks, Alleria was easily older than any of the human rulers, which made her immune to—and often mocking of—their majesty. "I was hunting orcs."

"You are always hunting orcs," Khadgar countered, more sharply than he intended. "But that is part of why I wanted you here for this."

He waited until he had her full attention and that of the various kings. "I was just explaining that we've noticed a dimensional rift in the area where the Dark Portal once stood, Alleria. And recently the energies emanating from it have increased dramatically."

"What does that mean?" Greymane demanded. "Are you trying to tell us it's getting stronger?"

The young-old archmage nodded. "Yes. We think the rift is about to expand."

"Has the Horde found some way to restore the portal?" Terenas asked, just as shocked as the rest.

"Perhaps, perhaps not," Khadgar answered. "But even if they cannot create a stable portal again, once the rift alone is large enough, the orcs will once more have access to our world."

"I knew this would happen!" Greymane all but shouted. "I knew we hadn't seen the last of those monsters!"

Beside him Alleria's lips curved, her eyes growing bright in—was that anticipation?

"How soon?" Trollbane asked. "And how many?"

"How many, we cannot say," Khadgar replied, shaking his head. "How soon? Very. As little as a few days, perhaps."

"What do you need?" Terenas asked softly.

"I need the Alliance army," Khadgar answered bluntly. "I need the entire army here in case the rift does begin widening. It's quite possible we could have a second Horde pouring out into that valley." He smiled suddenly. "The Sons of Lothar must step forward once again."

The Sons of Lothar. That's what they had taken to calling themselves, the veterans of the Second War. Victory had been bought, but at a dear cost—the death of the Lion of Azeroth, Anduin Lothar, who had been the man all were willing to follow. Khadgar had been there when he fell, slain by the orc chieftain Orgrim Doomhammer. And he'd been there when his friend Turalyon, now the general of the Alliance forces, had avenged Lothar by capturing Doomhammer. Lothar's protégé, coming into his own, carrying on a heroic legacy; and thus in blood had been born the Sons of Lothar.

"You're sure about this rift?" Terenas asked carefully, clearly reluctant to offend a wizard. Which, Khadgar mused, was hardly ever a good idea. But in this case, he wasn't offended at all.

"I wish I weren't. The energy level is most definitely rising. Soon that energy will be enough to widen the rift, allowing the orcs to pour forth from Draenor onto our world." He felt suddenly tired, as if sharing the bad news had emptied him somehow. He glanced again at Alleria, who noticed the gaze and lifted an eyebrow, but said nothing.

"We cannot afford to take chances," Varian pointed out. "I say we rally the Alliance army and make ready for war, just in case."

"Agreed," Terenas said, and the others nodded their approval.

"We'll need to contact General Turalyon," Varian continued. Alleria stiffened slightly, a flicker of unreadable emotion crossing her face, and Khadgar's eyes narrowed. Once, the elven ranger and the human paladin had been more than comrades in arms. They'd been good for each other, Khadgar had always thought. Alleria's age and wisdom strengthened Turalyon's spirit, and his youth and innocence softened the somewhat jaded elf. But something had happened. Khadgar had never known what, and was discreet enough not to ask. An alarmingly cold distance had sprung up between Turalyon and Alleria. Khadgar had felt sorry for them at the time; now, he wondered if this distance would cause problems.

Varian appeared not to have noticed the subtle change in Alleria and continued, "As commander of the Alliance army, it's his job to gather our soldiers and prepare them for what lies ahead. He's in Stormwind now, helping us rebuild our defenses and train our men."

An idea occurred to Khadgar, one that might solve two problems at once. "Alleria, you could reach Turalyon more quickly than anyone else. Take the gryphon and head to Stormwind. Tell him what's happened, and that we'll need to reassemble the Alliance army immediately."

The elven ranger glared at Khadgar, her green eyes flashing fire. "Surely another could accomplish the trek as easily," she stated, her tone sharp.

But Khadgar shook his head. "The Wildhammers know and trust you," he answered. "And these fellows have their own arrangements to make." He sighed. "Please, Alleria. For all our sakes. Find him, tell him, and bring him here." *And maybe you two can settle your differences . . . or at least decide to work together,* he thought.

Alleria's glare hardened into that implacable, expressionless mask. "I will do as you have requested," she said almost formally. Without another word she turned and stalked back across the hall and out the front doors.

"Khadgar's right," Terenas said as they watched her walk away. "We'll each need to rally our troops and gather supplies, and right away." The other kings nodded. Even Greymane was quietly compliant—the thought of the Horde returning had shocked any griping clean out of him. Together they moved toward the doors, heading back into the courtyard and from there toward the massive front archway they had first passed under not an hour before.

"Aye, go," Khadgar whispered as he watched the kings depart. "Go, and rouse the Sons of Lothar. I just pray it is not too late."

CHAPTER THREE

The axe shrieked as it arced downward, catching the light and glinting brightly, thirsting for blood. Its wielder laughed in a manic harmony, opening his black-tattooed jaw almost impossibly wide in the scream that had given him his name. Long black hair whipped behind him as he moved, red eyes glowing, slashing at the imaginary foe again and again, honing his moves so that in a real battle, his enemy would be so much raw meat. Grom Hellscream grunted and whirled and turned, sheer power tempered by skill, until the sound of his name being called pulled him from the red haze that descended at such times, even in a mere exercise such as this.

"Grom!"

Grom Hellscream lowered Gorehowl, panting only slightly from the vigorous exertion, and glanced up to see an older but imposing figure stomping toward him.

"Kargath," he replied, waiting until the Shattered

Hand chieftain had reached him. They clasped hands—right hands; Kargath's left hand had been severed long ago and replaced with a wicked-looking scythe's blade.

"Well met."

"Well met to many, it seems," the older chieftain said, nodding to where more orcs were gathering. "Ner'zhul sent emissaries to every clan, or so I was told." Grom nodded, his black-tattooed jaw setting into a grim line. Some of those emissaries had been his, sent at the old shaman's request.

"He is planning something." Grom shouldered the massive axe and together the two leaders turned and walked across the valley, toward the ruins of the Dark Portal, passing warriors from both clans. Glares and sharp words were flying here and there, but at least no one was fighting. Yet. "But what?"

"It doesn't matter," Kargath replied. "Anything is better than this!" He ran his fingers absently along his scythe's edge. "These past two years we've sat and done nothing. Nothing! And why? Because the Alliance defeated us? So what? Because the portal was destroyed? Surely they can craft another! There has to be someone we can fight, else we'll sit and molder like so much rotten meat!"

Grom nodded. Kargath was a creature of combat, pure and simple—he lived to fight and to kill. Grom could appreciate that, and what Kargath said had merit. They were a combative race, the orcs, and constant struggle honed their wits and strengthened their limbs.

Without that they grew soft. He had kept his own people sharp by warring against the other clans, and he suspected Kargath had done the same, though their two clans had not skirmished. Still, one could attack patrols and scouting parties only so often before it led to true war, and warring against his own kind did not interest him. When Ner'zhul had formed the Horde, he had united the clans into a single massive unit. And even after all this time Grom still thought of them that way. When his Warsong warriors fought the Thunderlords or the Redwalkers or the Bladewinds, they were battling their fellow warriors, orcs they should have been fighting alongside instead of against. During combat he still felt the same bloodlust, the same pure joy as Gorehowl tore a shrieking path through his foes, but afterward he felt empty, hollow, and slightly unclean.

What had happened? he wondered as they approached the ruins and the figure standing before them. Where had the Horde gone wrong? They had outnumbered the blades of grass that had once covered the plains and the drops of water comprising the ocean! When they marched, the thunder of their footsteps shattered mountains! How could such an army fail?

It was Gul'dan's fault. Grom was sure of it. The lifeless plains that had once been covered in grain and grass, the trees that had withered and blackened, the skies that had grown dark and red as blood—all that had been caused by the warlocks and their quest for powers never meant for orcish hands. But it was more than that. They had doomed Draenor, all of them, but Gul'dan had been behind the warlocks' every move. And it was his fault that the Horde had failed to conquer that other world and claim it as their own. After all, the wily warlock had convinced Grom to stay behind on Draenor during the first battle, instead of taking his rightful place at the vanguard.

"We need you here," Gul'dan had claimed. "You and your Warsong clan are some of our finest, and we need to hold you in reserve, just in case. We also need someone to stay here on Draenor and protect our interests, someone powerful, someone we can trust. Someone like you." Grom had been a fool, letting the warlock's flattery lure him from his path. He had watched as Blackhand and Orgrim Doomhammer led the Horde through the portal into that strange place called Azeroth. And he had watched as reports came back, reports of their initial successes and then of their ultimate failures.

Grom growled softly beneath his breath. If only he had been there! He could have turned that final battle around, he was sure of it—with his help Doomhammer could have conquered that human city by the lake and still sent forces to crush the traitorous Gul'dan and his cohorts. Then they could have claimed Lordaeron and spread out from there, sweeping across the land until no one was left to stand against them.

Grom shook his head. The past was past. Blackhand was dead, his old friend Durotan was dead, Doomhammer was captured, the Dark Portal was destroyed,

Gul'dan was gone, and the Horde was a shadow of its former glory.

But perhaps some of that was about to change.

He and Kargath had reached the portal now, and he could see the waiting figure clearly. Ner'zhul's hair was completely gray now, but otherwise the Shadowmoon chieftain and former Horde leader looked as powerful as ever. Then he turned in Grom's direction.

The Warsong clan leader growled and jerked in surprise as he got his first good look at the shaman's face. White paint adorned Ner'zhul's cheeks, upper lip, nose, brow, and forehead, turning them white as bone. And that was clearly the intent, Grom realized. The old shaman had masked his face to resemble a skull.

"Grom Hellscream and Kargath Bladefist!" Ner'zhul called out, his voice still strong and clear. "Welcome!"

"Why have you summoned us?" Kargath said bluntly, wasting no words.

"I have news," the shaman answered. "News, and a plan."

Grom snorted. "For two long years you have hidden away from us. How can you have news?" he said, anger and doubt in his voice. He gestured at Ner'zhul's painted face. "You let Gul'dan supplant you, you refused to drink from the chalice, and you sulk like a marmot in its burrow. Now you announce you have a plan, and emerge from your seclusion wearing the face of the dead—I do not think I want to hear what sort of plan that involves."

He could hear the pain in his own voice. Despite all that had happened with Gul'dan, despite his distrust of advisers and shaman and warlocks alike these past few years, he wanted Ner'zhul to still be the shaman Grom remembered from his youth, the strong, stern, wise orc who had forged the fractious clans into a single fighting unit. Despite his scathing words, Grom wanted to be proven wrong.

Ner'zhul touched the white skull on his face and sighed deeply. "Long have I dreamed of death. I have seen him, spoken with him. I have seen the death of my people, the death of all I have loved. And this—this image I wear to honor that. I did not wish to come forth, but I now believe that I owe it to my people to lead them once more."

"Lead as you did before?" Kargath cried. "Lead us to betrayal? To defeat? I will send you to that death which you are so enamored of with this very hand if you attempt to so lead us, Ner'zhul!" He brandished his scythe-hand at the shaman.

Ner'zhul began to reply but stopped as he spotted something behind them. Turning, Grom saw a hulking figure approaching, an ogre judging by the way it towered over the orcs it passed.

"What news, Dentarg?" Ner'zhul called out as his assistant crossed the clearing that separated the portal ruins from the orcs milling about. "I sent you to locate the other clans and summon them here—as I told you two to do as well," he reminded Grom and Kargath.

"Yet I see only Shadowmoon, Warsong, and Shattered Hand in this valley. Where are the rest?"

"Lightning's Blade said they would attend," Grom assured him. "They have a long way to travel, so it may take them another day or two." He shook his head. "Neither Thunderlord nor Laughing Skull listened, however." He growled. "They were too busy slaughtering each other."

"This is precisely why we need to act!" Ner'zhul cried. "We are killing ourselves and each other if we sit and do nothing!" He bared his teeth in a grimace. "All the work we did—all that I did—to forge the Horde is crumbling away, the clans splintering off and fighting with one another. If we do not act soon we will be reduced to the old ways once more, with the clans meeting only in battle save the yearly gatherings—if that!"

"What did you expect to happen while you hid away for two years?" Grom snapped. "We understand that you were wounded by the explosion. But then, even after your wounds had healed, you never came out. Long we waited for your counsel, but it never came. Of course we went our own ways! Of course we began fighting with one another. You abandoned us so you could dream your dreams of death, Ner'zhul. And this is the result."

"I know," Ner'zhul said softly, in pain. Grom's further angry words died on his lips in the face of that grief and shame.

"The Bladewind clan will join us," Kargath

continued, breaking the uncomfortable silence. "But Redwalker refused. They said the Horde is nothing but a memory now, and each clan must look out for itself instead." He snarled. "I would have slaughtered their chieftain then and there, if you had not ordered otherwise."

"You would have been killed in return," Ner'zhul pointed out, "or you would have slaughtered the entire clan making good your escape. I did not want to risk you, or lose them when there was a chance they might be persuaded." He pursed his lips. "We will deal with them soon, however, never fear." He glanced around. "What of the others?" His eyes narrowed. "What of the Bonechewers?"

That brought a snarl to Grom's lips. "I sent emissaries to Hurkan Skullsplinter," he said curtly. "He sent back assorted limbs."

"They would be a great asset in battle," Kargath mused, idly stroking his scythe. "The Bonechewers are a powerful force on the field." Then he shook his head. "They have grown even wilder since the portal fell, however. They cannot be controlled, or trusted."

Ner'zhul nodded. "What of the Whiteclaw clan?" he asked Dentarg.

The ogre frowned. "Dead, most of them," he replied. "Mostly wiped out by other clans before the truth about Gul'dan and his warlocks came to light. Even after Durotan's exile and death, the Whiteclaws never hid their sympathy for the Frostwolves, and it

made them a target. Those who survived are scattered."
He shook his head. "In truth, it is a clan no more."

Ner'zhul felt a shiver of guilt at the mention of
Durotan. He had warned the now-dead leader of the
Frostwolves once, seeking to undo some of the dam-
age he had done, but in the end, it had been no use.
Gul'dan's Shadow Council had found Durotan, and
slain one of the noblest orcs Ner'zhul had ever known.

But regret and self-pity would not serve. He focused
again on Dentarg's words, and let himself grow angry.

"The Whiteclaw clan was one of our oldest and
proudest! Now they are little more than clanless sav-
ages? Is this what our race has fallen to? No more! We
must rebuild the Horde and renew the bond between
all orcs! Only as a united race can we have any hope of
survival, of honor, and of glory!"

Dentarg dropped to his knees. "You know I live to
serve you, master," he said simply.

Grom gazed at the elderly orc, his brow knitting.
"Tell us this plan of yours, Ner'zhul," he stated, making sure his words carried to the orcs beyond the clearing. "Tell us—and if it is sound, we shall follow you."

Kargath inclined his head. "I cast my word with
Hellscream's," he said.

Ner'zhul regarded the three of them solemnly for a
moment, then nodded. "We will wait until the Lightning's Blade and Bladewind clans arrive," Ner'zhul said.
"Then we will go to the others again, the Thunderlord
and the Laughing Skull and the Redwalker and even

the Bonechewer clans. Our people must be united."

"What if they refuse still?" Kargath growled.

"Then we will persuade them," Ner'zhul replied, his grim tone leaving no doubt as to his meaning. Kargath roared his approval, raising his scythe high so it caught the light. Ner'zhul turned to Grom. "And you, Grom," he said softly. "While we wait for the other clans, I will tell you my plan, and set you to a task."

Grom's red eyes glittered. "Tell me what you would have me do, and why."

Ner'zhul smiled, the death mask on his face making it a rictus.

"There is something I need you to find."

CHAPTER FOUR

"Warsong, attack!"

Grom held Gorehowl high, letting the sunlight play along its blade. Then he leaped forward, swinging the axe in a great arc, the hollow space behind the haft shrieking as the blade cut through the air. Behind him his warriors waved and swirled and swung their own weapons, creating the unsettling shrieks and whistles and whoops for which the clan was named. Many began to sing as well, chanting tunes that were less about the words than about the rhythms, the pulse-pounding beats that fired their blood and at the same time made their enemies quail.

Except that, this time, the enemy wasn't quailing—in part because many of them were too unaware to do so.

The first foe came within range, bellowing something inarticulate. Gorehowl caught him in the neck, slicing smoothly through flesh and bone and tendon.

The head flew off, mouth still open in a shriek, the foam at its lips now joined with bloody spittle. The green body collapsed, though it made a feeble attempt to swing its hammer even as it fell. Blood spattered on Grom's face like warm red rain. He grinned, his tongue snaking out to lick it from his lips. One less Bonechewer to worry about.

All around him the Warsong warriors were carving into the Bonechewer clan. Normally the Bonechewer orcs were crazed enough to strike fear into any heart, but Grom had prepared his warriors. "They are like wild beasts," he had warned them. "They are strong and know no fear or pain. But they have no sense, either, and they do not coordinate or even consider. They simply attack on instinct. You are the better fighters. Focus your minds, watch your flanks, work with your brothers, and we will sweep through them like a wind through the grass, laying waste to all before us." His people had cheered, and so far it seemed they were remembering his words. But he wondered how long they could go before their own bloodlust took control, pushing aside all rational thought and causing them to abandon strategy just as their Bonechewer cousins had.

He felt it himself, that sweet hot feeling that quickened his pulse and made him thrum with energy. As Gorehowl split a charging Bonechewer from shoulder to hip, Grom felt the joy and rage swirling within him, dulling his mind, charging his senses, threatening to sweep him away on a tide of raw exultation. He wanted to surrender himself, to give in to the song of combat, to lose himself in the thrill of death and destruction and victory.

But he would not. He was Grom Hellscream, chieftain of the Warsong. He had his duty. And he would require a clear head to fulfill it.

A flurry of activity caught his eye. A massive orc lifted one of his warriors and hurled him bodily at a cluster of Warsong, then grabbed one of the fallen and wrenched an arm free to use as a gore-dripping club. This was the one Grom sought. Swift as thought, he closed the distance between them, cutting down any Bonechewer in his way and shoving his own warriors aside as well. At last he was facing the crazed orc with only a single body-length between them.

"Hurkan!" he bellowed, swinging Gorehowl in front of him both to clear a space and so its shrieking would cut through the combat sounds all around them. "Hurkan Skullsplinter!"

"Grom!" the Bonechewer chieftain shouted back, holding high the limb in his hands. It still spasmed slightly. "Look, I have one of your orcs! Part of him, anyway!" Hurkan laughed uproariously, spittle flying from his mouth.

"Call off your warriors, Hurkan!" Grom demanded. "Call them off or we will kill every last one of them!"

Hurkan raised the severed arm high in response, and around him many of his warriors stilled to hear what their leader had to say. "Do you think we fear death?" Hurkan asked with surprising calm.

"I know you don't," Grom replied. "But why throw your lives away here, fighting your own kind, when you could instead spend them slaughtering humans on Azeroth?"

That made the Bonechewer chieftain tilt his head. "Azeroth? The portal fell, Hellscream—or don't you remember?" He grinned, a nasty expression that revealed his many broken teeth. "Not that you were ever allowed to set foot on that other world, of course."

Grom's head pounded and his vision turned red for a moment. He desperately wanted to wipe that sneer off Hurkan's face, preferably with Gorehowl's blade. But he knew his fellow chieftain was deliberately goading him, and used that knowledge to help resist the fury that so wanted to boil to the surface.

"You weren't either," he retorted, though he had to grit his teeth not to shout the words or simply spit them. "But now we will get our chance. Ner'zhul says he can open the portal again. The Horde will return to that world and conquer it at last."

Hurkan laughed, a rough sound that started low and rose to a shrill cackle. "Ner'zhul! That withered old shaman! He gets us into this mess, then runs off and hides—and now he wants us to dance at his command, all over again? What do we gain from it all?"

"The chance to kill humans—many of them," Grom answered. "The chance to win glory and honor.

The chance to claim new lands, lands still rich and fertile." He gestured around them. Nagrand was still lush and green, unlike most of Draenor, perhaps because the battle-crazed Bonechewer clan had not bothered much with warlocks. Even so, Grom knew the Bonechewer clan was as desperate for new foes to conquer as any orcs would be.

"What would we have to do?" Hurkan asked. He was still holding the severed arm of one of Grom's warriors. Grom narrowed his eyes. Perhaps this was a break of sanity in the storm of madness that whirled around the Bonechewer leader. He had lost a few good warriors today, and if he could bring Hurkan in line without losing more he would be well pleased. He would see no more of his people ripped to pieces if he could help it.

"Two things. First, pledge yourself and your clan to Ner'zhul," Grom replied. "Follow his orders, and fight alongside the other clans rather than against them."

Hurkan grunted. "Give us something else to fight and we'll leave the rest of you alone," he promised.

"You'll have more than enough foes to keep you busy," Grom assured him. He shifted his grip on his axe; he didn't think the next request would be so will-ingly granted. "There is one other thing. Ner'zhul wants that." And he pointed.

Hurkan looked down, puzzled, but his expression changed to a frown when he realized Grom was indi-cating the skull hanging around his neck. An orc skull, bleached from years of exposure. Deep gouges were visible in the bone.

The Bonechewer chieftain scowled. "No. He cannot have this." He rested one hand protectively over the ornament. "It is not just any skull. It is Gul'dan's skull!"

"Are you so certain?" Grom replied, hoping to plant the seed of doubt. "I was told he died on Azeroth."

"He did," Hurkan said. "Torn apart by demons, they say, on an island he raised from the sea itself. Killed by his own power and pride." He guffawed. "But at least one of the warlocks with him survived. He escaped the temple they had found there. On his way out, he found Gul'dan's remains—ripped to shreds, he said." The Bonechewer leader shrugged. "Even dead they had power, or so the warlock thought. Especially the head. So he took it with him." He laughed. "Looks like Gul'dan got to return to Draenor after all!"

"How did you get it?" Grom asked.

Again Hurkan shrugged. "A warrior killed the warlock and took it from him. I killed the warrior and claimed it myself. Or perhaps there were others in between. No matter. Once I saw it and learned whose skull it was, I knew it must be mine. And it is." He grinned again. "And I will not part with it. Not for Ner'zhul, not for anyone."

Grom nodded. "I understand."

His attack was sudden and swift, Gorehowl already slicing the air as he leaped forward. But Hurkan was an experienced warrior and for once he was thinking clearly—he dove to the side, the axe shrieking past his shoulder, and then spun, his massive fist catching Grom across the cheek. The blow sent a jolt of pain through him, but Grom ignored it. Hurkan grabbed a warclub dropped by one of the warriors he'd killed and swung it toward Grom. Grom danced aside, the club narrowly missing his chest, and lashed out again. Gore-howl caught Hurkan across the upper right arm, carving open the flesh.

Grom was vaguely aware of the gathered orcs watching, waiting to see who won. He knew more than just his own life hung upon the outcome of this battle, but he could spare no more than a passing thought for such a thing if he were to be the victor.

Hurkan was proving to be a worthy foe. The big Bonechewer chieftain was as large as Orgrim Doomhammer had been and almost as fast. And when he was thinking, Hurkan was no fool but a wily old warrior, one who could read an opponent and anticipate his moves. He proved that as he ducked another swing and came up beneath it, slamming both hands into Grom's chest and sending him stumbling back several paces.

But the moment of clarity had passed. Already Grom could see his foe's eyes beginning to roll back, and foam flecking his lips. Hurkan's breathing was becoming labored, his strikes more powerful but also less controlled. Grom easily ducked or blocked the wild swings, although his arms strained with the effort. Grom bared his teeth in a wicked grin, feeling the bloodlust rise within him. It wanted to control him, as it controlled Hurkan. But Grom would not let it. He was the master, not it. It was time to end this. He ducked beneath Hurkan's latest swing, filled his lungs, and thrust his head forward into the Bonechewer's face.

His black-tattooed jaw opened almost impossibly wide and a violent, gut-wrenching scream pierced the air. Hurkan's own scream was a bass counterpoint as he clapped huge hands to his bleeding ears and dropped to his knees in agony. Blood spurted from his nose and eyes and dripped from his open mouth. Grom's legendary war cry mutated into a laugh of triumph as he swung Gorehowl in a smooth arc, separating Hurkan's head from his massive shoulders.

The body continued to move, its arms flailing for a moment. For a second it paused, as if listening with some other senses, then pitched forward to the ground. It lay there, twitching slightly.

Grom stared at it, grinning, then kicked the body over. Fortunately, the prize he had come for was undamaged. He looked at the skull for a long moment, remembering Gul'dan, remembering Ner'zhul. Remembering all that had happened over the last few years. Then he pulled a thick cloth bag from his belt and dropped it over Gul'dan's skull, scooping the grisly item up safely. Teron Gorefiend had spoken with Grom before he left, and the death knight had warned Grom not to touch the skull directly. While Grom disliked and distrusted the death knight, an unnatural thing somehow returned from death and wearing a human corpse for flesh, he did heed the warning. Gul'dan had been dangerous enough in life that Grom could easily imagine the warlock's remains still having power in death.

Straightening with Gorehowl in one hand and the bag in the other, Grom looked out over the assembled orcs. "Who now speaks for the Bonechewer clan?" he demanded loudly.

A tall, powerfully built young orc pushed his way forward. He wore a belt fashioned from orc spines and bracers carved from the spine segments of an ogre. A heavy spiked club rested across one shoulder. "I am Tagar Spinebreaker," he announced proudly, though his eyes shifted uneasily to Hurkan's body before returning to Grom. "I lead the Bonechewers now."

Grom gestured with the bag. "I have taken the skull. Now I will ask you, Tagar Spinebreaker: Will you join with us, or will you join Hurkan?"

The new Bonechewer chieftain hesitated. "Before I answer, I have a question for you, Grom Hellscream. You ask us to follow Ner'zhul. Why have you chosen to do so? You once said he created all our troubles!"

So, the brute wasn't as stupid as he looked. Grom decided he deserved an answer. "He did create all our troubles," Grom replied, "by handing control to this traitor"—he gestured with the bag—"and letting Gul'dan do whatever he chose without obstruction. But before that Ner'zhul was wise, and advised the clans well. And he first forged the Horde, which is a great thing.

"I follow him now because he has sworn to reopen the Dark Portal. I should have been there before, slaughtering humans on Azeroth, but Gul'dan prevented it. Now I will have my chance." He laughed. "Ner'zhul has told me that Gul'dan's skull is a necessary ingredient in the rite to open the portal. Sweet it is to me that Gul'dan, who denied me before, will now be the key to my opportunity. That, Bonechewer, is why I follow Ner'zhul.

"Now—the choice is yours. Rejoin the Horde. Or"—he raised Gorehowl again, and spun it so it sang, an undulating dirge of blood and chaos—"we slaughter you all, down to the last suckling babe. Right now." He tilted his head back and roared, the pounding overtaking him. Behind him, his warriors started to chant, stomping their feet and swinging their weapons to add to the rhythm, until the very plain shook with the sound.

Grom licked his lips and raised his axe, then met Tagar's wide eyes. "Which will it be?" he growled. "Gorehowl longs to shriek again. Shall it taste human flesh . . . or Bonechewer?"

CHAPTER FIVE

"A what?" Turalyon, General of the Alliance forces, paladin of the Silver Hand, stared in utter bafflement at the tiny figure who sat before him. "A rat problem!" the gnome exclaimed.

"When you said there was an issue with wildlife that was threatening to derail the entire tram construction project," Turalyon said slowly, "I assumed you had run into difficulties with the subterranean lake, or perhaps the creatures in . . ." Turalyon's voice trailed off. "You did say 'rat'?"

"Indeed!" Tinker Gelbin Mekkatorque, head of the project to construct a mechanical transportation system that would eventually link Stormwind and Ironforge, shuddered.

"Horrible things, those vermin. Some bodies we've found were *this big*!" Mekkatorque spread his hands about six inches apart. Granted, on that tiny frame, that was a substantial amount, but still . . . the engineer had called an emergency session with the general of the Alliance over a rat problem?

Turalyon still wasn't quite sure what to think of the small beings who were good friends with the dwarves. If Mekkatorque, who had come to Stormwind a few years ago with the full endorsement of the dwarven king Magni Bronzebeard himself, was any indication, they were a curious bunch. Mekkatorque talked fast and used terms that Turalyon was utterly unfamiliar with, and struck him as a jovial fellow. The gnome representative didn't even reach Turalyon's hip when standing, and was all but swallowed by the large chair in which he was now ensconced. The table was level with his bright eyes, and at one point, Mekkatorque let out an exasperated huff and simply climbed atop it to point at the blueprints he had unfolded within two minutes of his arrival.

"They've completely infested the prototype, chewing through the wiring here, here, and here," Mekkatorque continued, stabbing a tiny finger down at the blueprints. "We can't extract it or even get in to repair it without losing more good people to those vile creatures. The last team we sent in after it . . . well, it wasn't a pretty sight." His large eyes looked solemn.

Turalyon nodded. The idea of a tram had struck him as brilliant when it was first proposed shortly after the Second War. Progress on rebuilding Stormwind was being made, but slowly—it was a long and dangerous trek from Ironforge to Stormwind, and King

Bronzebeard had chafed at the delay in getting supplies to his allies. Turalyon felt out of his depth at the time, and still had that reaction every time Mekkatorque came to him with updates or problems. He was a paladin, a warrior by fate and a priest by training. He knew little enough of simple construction, and this "tram" was quite beyond him. Especially when Mekkatorque talked so fast.

Turalyon had discovered that gnomes were fiercely if eccentrically intelligent, and he was willing to believe it if this . . . contraption that Mekkatorque proposed did even part of what he claimed it would do. He remembered their first conversation.

"How safe will it be?" he had asked.

"Er . . . well, we *are* on the cutting edge technologically with it, you must understand," Mekkatorque had said, running a hand along his muttonchop whiskers. "But I'm willing to bet it will eventually be as safe as the safest gnomish creation ever!"

Something in the sound of his voice had warned Turalyon that that might not be particularly safe at all. But he wasn't a builder, or an engineer. Still, it was coming along.

Until this rat problem.

"I understand that rats are proportionately much larger, and therefore much more threatening to your people than to mine," Turalyon said as diplomatically as he could, although he wondered why Bronzebeard hadn't handled the problem on the Ironforge end. "And we can't have them chewing through the wiring. I'll send some of my men back to Ironforge with you. They'll, er . . . hunt the vermin down and help you effect repairs."

Turalyon might have been Greatfather Winter himself the way Mekkatorque reacted. "Thank you, thank you! This is excellent. It will be back on track in a jiffy. And then we can finally tackle that pesky underwater problem." The gnome slipped off the chair and reached up a small hand to Turalyon, then pumped it vigorously.

"Go speak to Aramil," Turalyon said, referring to a former guard at the keep who now served as Turalyon's assistant in all things nonmilitary. "He'll take care of the arrangements."

Turalyon watched the gnome depart, and turned back to his correspondence. Dozens of letters, from so many people, all wanting something from him. He ran a hand through his short blond hair and sighed. A walk would do him good.

The air was clean and clear as he stepped outside, although clouds lowered. He walked up to the canal, gazing briefly at his reflection in the now-cleared water. Turalyon had never been to Stormwind until the day he and his men had entered the city two years ago, and so he had not had the additional horror of knowing what the city had been like before it fell. It was horrific enough as it was. These famous canals had been clogged—with stones and lumber, with dirt . . . with defiled corpses. The dead had been respectfully buried, the rubble cleared. Now the canals ran freely again, connecting the various parts of the city. Turalyon lifted his gaze to the white stone, gray now in the dimming light, and the red roofs. The Dwarven District housed many of Bronzebeard's hardworking men, sent along with Mekkatorque, and nestled next to that area was the cathedral.

Thunder rumbled as he approached. He fixed his eyes on the glorious building, one of the first to be completed in its entirety. The orcs had damaged it badly, but even then it was a place of safety—the enemy had not realized that the cathedral had vast rooms and catacombs beneath it. Dozens had huddled there, sheltered by its stone while terror raged above them. It was one of the few buildings large enough to house the refugees in the initial stages of reconstruction, and even now, people flocked to it when they were ill, or injured, or even just in need of a little reminder of the Light.

Like Turalyon.

"Oof!" He stumbled forward, so lost in thought that he hadn't seen the pair of children until they'd slammed into him.

"Sorry, mister!" the boy cried. The girl gazed up at him with solemn brown eyes. Turalyon smiled and patted her hair as he spoke to the boy.

"With an attack like that you'll make a fine soldier one day," he said.

"Oh yes, sir, I hope so, sir! You think all the orcs will be dead before I'm old enough to kill them?"

Turalyon's smile faltered. "I'm sure you'll be able to serve the Alliance well," he said, evading the question. Revenge. The fiery need and anger it kindled in the heart had cost Turalyon someone he loved. He would say nothing to foster blind hatred in a child. Keeping his hand on the girl's head, he murmured a soft prayer. Light glowed around his hand and for a brief moment, the child was enveloped in radiance. Turalyon lifted his other hand and blessed the boy as well. Awe shone in both pairs of eyes that regarded him.

"Light bless you both. Now, you two had best be getting home. Looks like rain."

The boy nodded and grabbed his sister's hand. "Thanks, Mister Paladin!" The two ran toward their home. It was not far; Turalyon realized they lived in the building adjacent to the cathedral. The orphanage.

So many orphans. So many lives lost.

Thunder rumbled again, and the heavens let loose. Rain began pouring down in sheets. Turalyon sighed, pulling his cape around himself and running lightly up the steps to the cathedral, getting soaked even in that short distance. The smell of incense and the soft, barely audible sound of chanting coming from somewhere in the building soothed him at once. He had become used to giving orders, to fighting battles, to emerging from them covered in his own blood or that of the orcs. It was good to come back to the church, and to remember his origins as a simple priest.

A soft smile curved his lips as he beheld his brethren, his fellow Knights of the Silver Hand, doing their duties here as surely as they had on the battlefield. Archbishop Alonsus Faol had created the order three years ago, and it was by his decree that the paladins now served humbly in the communities that had been so devastated by the war. Even as he looked around, Turalyon saw his old friend Uther, whom he himself had given the title "Lightbringer." Turalyon was used to seeing the powerfully built man in full armor, swinging his weapon, his ocean-colored eyes afire with zeal as the Light came to him in the form of powerful attacks. But Uther now was clad in simple robes. He was attending to a woman who looked exhausted and drained, gently wiping her forehead with a damp cloth and cradling something in his free hand.

As Turalyon drew closer, he saw that the bundle Uther held so gently was a newborn, its skin still mottled from birth. The new mother smiled tiredly but happily and reached for her child. Its lusty, healthy wail was the sharp, sweet song of hope. Uther rested his hand on the woman and blessed her and her child, as Turalyon had done with the orphans earlier. Turalyon realized that although Uther was obviously at home on the battlefield, using the Light to take the lives of those who would slay him and those he served, he was equally at home here in the cathedral, bringing a new little life into the world. Such was the dichotomy of paladins; they were warriors and healers both. Uther glanced up and smiled, rising to greet his friend.

"Turalyon," he said in his deep, gruff voice. The two paladins clasped hands. "Good to see you. About time you found your way down here." Uther cuffed the younger man playfully.

"You're right," Turalyon agreed, chuckling. "It's good to be here. It's too easy to get caught up in all the things that need to be done but can never quite be finished. Like a rat problem."

"Eh?"

"I'll tell you later. For now, how can I help?" This was what mattered, he thought. Not staying holed up in the keep pushing paper.

Uther's eyes narrowed slightly as he looked over Turalyon's shoulder. "I think you've got some of that unfinished business right here," he said.

"Oh?" Turalyon said casually, turning around.

It was like seeing a ghost, a moment wrenched out of its proper place in space and time and incongruously reenacted. She stood before him, face and hair and clothing wet, emerald eyes fixed with his eyes. She had gotten caught in the rain, looking almost as she had that night nearly two years ago, coming to him now as she had come to—

Alleria Windrunner's eyes narrowed, as if she, too, recalled that night, and found it an unpleasant memory. Turalyon felt a chill sweep over him that had nothing to do with his wet clothing.

She bowed, stiffly, first to Uther, then to him. "Light-bringer. General."

Ah. This was how it was to be played, then. "Ranger." He was surprised at how calm his voice sounded. He had half-expected it to crack with emotion. "What brings you here?"

"Tidings," she said, "of the worst sort." Her eyes flickered to Turalyon's, then back to Uther's. "Little else would."

Turalyon felt a muscle twitch in his cheek and gritted his teeth. "Then pray deliver them."

The elf looked around, slightly contemptuously. "I wonder if I have not come to the wrong place for aid. I did not expect to find generals, knights, and holy warriors tending to babies in a church."

Turalyon welcomed the anger; it chased away the heartsickness. "We serve where we are called, Alleria. All of us. I feel certain you didn't come all the way here just to insult us. Speak."

Alleria sighed. "A short time ago, I met with Khadgar and several of the Alliance leaders, including your own king. It seems that there is a dimensional rift where the Dark Portal once stood. Khadgar believes that very soon, orcs—perhaps an entire second Horde—could come through again. He sent me on gryphonback at once to inform you."

She had their attention now, and they listened in silence as she repeated what she had learned. Not for the first time since the Lion of Azeroth's death, Turalyon wished Anduin Lothar were here. He often found himself wishing that when faced with a difficult decision, or impending combat, or simply the need to talk to someone. Lothar would have responded instantly, calmly but decisively, and others could not have helped but follow. While the veterans of the war had begun calling themselves the Sons of Lothar, Turalyon himself—Lothar's lieutenant—was not comfortable with the term. He did not feel like a son of the great man, although he would defend Lothar's ideals to his last breath. He was still thinking when Alleria finished talking and turned her eyes expectantly upon him.

"Well?" she demanded.

"What say the Wildhammers on all this? What does Kurdran think?"

"I doubt he knows," Alleria admitted, the blond ranger having the grace to at least be embarrassed by that statement.

"What? You flew all this way to inform me—on one of their gryphons, no less!—and no one told the Wildhammers' leader what was going on?"

She shrugged again, and Turalyon bit back a curse. During the Second War the Alliance had all fought together, elves and humans and dwarves—both the Wildhammers and their Bronzebeard cousins—side by side. But in the past year it seemed the human rulers had been distancing themselves from their nonhuman allies. The elves still participated in the defense of Nethergarde, but that was as much from their fascination with all magic as from any desire to help humans. The Bronzebeard dwarves had an ambassador, Muradin Bronzebeard, at Lordaeron, and so they maintained close ties with King Terenas. And there was cheerful little Mekkatorque and his assistants here in Stormwind. Turalyon felt the heat of shame rush through him at the recollection of his amusement at the gnome's expense earlier, when Mekkatorque and his people were performing an invaluable service to strangers.

But for all the Wildhammers' loyalty and bravery and skill, many humans seemed to think the gryphon riders little more than beasts.

"Will you wait for the dwarves to give you instructions? Or perhaps Lothar's ghost?"

Turalyon frowned. Color rose in Alleria's cheeks and she glanced down, realizing she had gone too far.

"The Wildhammers have been staunch allies," Turalyon said in a soft yet sure voice. "They are as much a part of the Alliance as anyone. I will see to it that they are informed as soon as possible."

"We must go immediately," Alleria said. "The gryphon will bear you to Lordaeron. I will make my own way there."

She wouldn't even deign to ride with him, then. Turalyon didn't answer at once. He glanced at Uther, who was bridling on his behalf. Their eyes met for a moment. The bigger man nodded and turned back to the young mother and her child.

"You will bring the members of your order, yes?" Alleria said, almost perfunctorily, as if she knew the answer already. When Turalyon shook his head, her jaw dropped. "What? Why not?"

"The Archbishop wishes them to stay here and in Lordaeron. To tend to the people who need them."

"You haven't even asked!"

"I know without asking. Don't worry. If the need is great enough, they will come. But need can take many forms. Come. Let us talk for a bit."

"We should—"

"Five minutes will change nothing." She frowned. He realized she was shivering. A drop of rain slid from her wet hair down her face, looking like a tear, but it was nothing nearly so soft. At that instant, he wanted to pull her into his arms so badly. This coldness, this acerbic venom that poisoned her words and turned her lovely face ugly with hatred—he knew what it was. And he knew why she carried it.

And the knowing was like a knife in his heart.

"I wrote. You never answered," he said quietly.

She shrugged, pulling her cloak about her slim frame automatically, although what she needed was dry clothing. "I have been traveling. On patrol. Our most recent task was a patrol through the Alterac Mountains," Alleria said. "There were rumors of orcs hiding among the peaks there." She allowed herself a grim smile. "We found ten of them." Turalyon didn't have to ask what she and her rangers had done with the discovered orcs. He wondered if she'd started taking trophies. He'd seen her once crouching over a body, a twisted grin on her face, and had been stunned by the glee she took in the killing.

"Alleria," he said quietly, "I've been writing you and you've never answered. You owe me nothing. I understand that. But if . . . what happened between us means you can no longer work with me, I need to know that now. I'm your commander. I—the Alliance—can't afford to find out on the battlefield that you're not listening, or not obeying." He waited until she looked at him. "Do you have a problem with that?"

"There is no problem," the blond elf answered sharply. "The Alliance wants every orc dead. So do I. We can work together on that."

"That's all we are to you now—a means to an end. A way to kill more orcs more quickly."

"What else is there?" she answered. "Khadgar only found me because my band and I were hunting orc renegades in Alterac. I agreed to meet with him at Nethergarde because his messenger said it involved orcs, and I agreed to bring his summons to you for the same reason." She frowned. "And the sooner we reach Lordaeron, the sooner I can seek out more of those orc abominations and kill them!" Her voice rose with passion and her eyes flashed. Some heads turned in their direction. "I will see them dead, every last one of them. Even if it takes me a hundred years!"

Turalyon felt a shiver run down his spine. "Alleria," he began, pitching his voice low, "you're serious."

The smile that curved her lips was a cruel one. "I am. This is nothing more than exterminating vermin."

He realized with a shock that she honestly believed her words. She really didn't see the orcs as sentient people. She saw them as abominations, as monsters, as . . . rats. Turalyon knew he had slain his fair share of them—had done so at times with great anger in his heart at what they had done to his people. But this . . . Alleria didn't want justice. She didn't want the orcs to pay for the crimes they had committed, she wanted to hurt them. Every last one of them, if she could.

He took a step toward her, reaching out a hand, hoping to connect. "You've lost so much. I know that."

Alleria knocked his hand away. "Hah! A human speaks of loss? What do you know of it? Your lives are so brief you never learn what it means to truly love someone!"

Turalyon felt the blood drain from his face. For a moment he couldn't respond. She stared at him, breathing quickly, daring him to speak.

"Just because you live longer doesn't mean you feel more," he said. "Trust me on that one." He gave her a lopsided smile. Her face only hardened the more.

"So, you are better than me because you live for *this* long?" she challenged, snapping her fingers. "Or are you better than me because of your precious Light?"

"Alleria, I want to see justice done. You know that. But you're not talking justice, you're talking vengeance. And I see what it's doing to you. The Light isn't mine, it's everyone's. It's about healing. It's—"

"Don't you dare lecture me!" she warned, her voice dropping to a steely hiss. "Your Holy Light didn't stop the orcs from tearing open a way into our world, did it? The Light can't restore my ravaged homeland, or give me back my—"

She closed her jaw with a snap. Turalyon stared at her for a long moment, then sighed deeply.

"Ranger," he said formally, "here are my orders. For the moment, you will stay here in Stormwind, along with half of my troops and myself. Send for your rangers, have them gather here. The city has just started to get its feet underneath it. I won't leave it unprotected."

Her jaw tightened. "So we're just going to wait out the war here, *sir*, like cowards, *sir*?"

Turalyon did not rise to the bait. "I will request reinforcements, and when they come, we'll leave. But until then, we stay here."

She nodded. "You'll protect a city when it's your own. I see now. Permission to leave to gather my rangers, *sir*?"

Alleria's words were designed to get under his skin, and they had. But Turalyon was more concerned about what had happened to Alleria—or more correctly, what she was doing to herself—to cause her to speak them. She had changed so very, very much. Sadly he recalled first their initial reactions to one another—he stammering, awestruck first by her grace and beauty and later by her consummate skill, and she amused, intrigued, slightly supercilious. He had lost some of his awe—not all of it; he would never lose all of it, but some—and she had grown to respect him. To like him. To seek out his company, to want him by her side in battle and, he'd once believed, in a more intimate way.

But there seemed little of that woman left. And all he could do was be saddened and worried by the changes, and wonder if she'd let her hate for the orcs get in the way of her judgment. By the Light—if she died because of this recklessness of hers—

He realized he was staring, and nodded. He did not trust himself to speak past the lump in his throat. Alleria inclined her head, the barest gesture of required respect, and strode past him.

Turalyon watched her go, wondering if he'd made the right decision. What would Lothar have done? Would he have waited until reinforcements came, or would he have charged into battle? Was he wasting time or being smart? Was it enough, to send his second-in-command Danath Trollbane and half his men to Nethergarde right now?

He shook his head, clearing it. He couldn't afford to second-guess right now, and his decision felt like the right one. He'd need to send some messengers. One to the Wildhammers, letting them know the situation. One to Lordaeron.

And one, he thought with a small, sad little smile, to Mekkatorque, to let him know that unfortunately, the men intended as ratcatchers for the tram would not be coming after all.

Alleria did not head back to the keep, as she had said she would. Instead, once she left the cathedral, she started to run, her feet swift and almost completely silent as they carried her along the streets toward the great gates of the city. She ignored startled glances as she ran, permitting the gawking stares to fuel her anger, and raced through the gates into the wooded area beyond. She ran until she found a small stream and there, beneath the boughs of the sheltering trees, she sank down on the sodden earth.

She was cold and soaked to the skin, but she ignored the discomfort.

It had gone worse than she had feared.

How was it that a mere human could rattle her so? He was a child beside her, a rude, loud child who—even as she thought the words, she knew that they were wrong. Turalyon was shockingly young compared with her, but he was reckoned a man among his own people, and he was kind and wise and smart.

And at one point, so long ago it seemed now, she had thought she loved him.

Alleria growled and put a clenched hand to her

heart, as if warning it not to soften. Her fingers touched the wrought silver of a necklace that held three precious stones. It had been given to her by her parents; it was a link with a world that had once been. A world of grace and beauty and balance. A world the orcs had forever ruined.

The trees here were not those of the forests of Eversong, those beautiful, golden-leafed patriarchs whose branches had held her and her sisters and— She squeezed her eyes shut, and whispered a name: "Lirath . . ."

Her youngest brother. She remembered him now the way he had looked the last time she had seen him. Beautiful, laughing, dancing beneath the golden leaves as a piper played a sprightly tune. Young, so young. He wanted to be a ranger, like his sisters, but in this moment she had frozen forever in her mind, Alleria watched him simply enjoy being alive.

The orcs had slaughtered him, snuffing out his bright life like a flame pinched between a cruel thumb and forefinger.

Had slaughtered so many, too many other kin— cousins, aunts, uncles, nieces . . . had slaughtered friends she had known longer than Turalyon had been *alive*—

And they would pay. Her hand tightened on the necklace. They would suffer, as gentle young Lirath had. As her people, her city, her land had. They would taste a thousandfold the pain they had inflicted upon her. It would be sweet—sweet as the blood she had once tentatively licked from her hand after a kill. Turalyon had almost caught her that time. Now, she told herself, he must not know.

He must not stop her.

He must not soften her heart, as he had come perilously close to doing once before.

Whatever the cost, Alleria Windrunner would have her revenge.

Rain pounded down outside, but the stables were dry, if steamy. The scent of horses and leather filled the moist air. The beasts whickered, pawing at the hay-covered cobblestones beneath their hooves as their riders saddled them. They were trained warhorses, and had not seen battle in some time. They seemed as anxious as Danath Trollbane was to depart.

Danath's men, though, were greener.

His own horse had been saddled and ready quickly, and now he moved among his soldiers. "Make haste," he glowered at one who was having trouble with the stirrups. "This is no pleasure outing!"

Turalyon had let him choose half among all the military left in Stormwind. He'd chosen cavalry units he knew would be able to cross the miles quickly and form ranks again soon after. They needed to move fast—but they had to be careful not to wear out the horses. He suspected they wouldn't have the luxury of a rest to reorganize and regroup. But most of the men he'd fought with were scattered now over the human territories, and there was no time to summon all the veterans home.

"We don't want to miss the fight, do we, sir?" a soldier said with a grin as he grasped his mount's reins. He was little more than a boy, really, too young to have fought in the Second War—one of the many who had joined after the war's end, to help fill out the ranks so badly decimated by the fighting.

Danath shook his bald head and ran a hand through his silvering beard, trying to recall the boy's name. Farrol, that was it. "You've not faced orcs before, have you, Farrol?" he rumbled.

"No, sir!" Farrol replied with a wide grin that showed how young he really was. "But I'm looking forward to it, sir!"

"I'm not," Danath replied, making the soldier gasp and stare.

"You're not?" the boy asked, his voice faltering a little as he noted his commander's grim expression. "But why not, sir? We're going to trample them, aren't we? I heard that there weren't many orcs left anymore, and they're hiding in the woods and the mountains like wild animals!"

"The ones who got left behind when the portal closed, that's true," Danath agreed. "But that's not what we're dealing with here. They think the Dark Portal's going to reopen. Do you know what that means?" The soldier gulped, and Danath raised his voice to make sure the soldiers saddling their mounts around them could hear him as well. "It means we won't be facing a ragtag group of orc survivors, boy— we'll be facing the Horde, the largest fighting force ever seen. And that force has never been defeated, not in truth."

"But we won the war, sir!" one of the other men— Vann, Danath recalled—protested. "We conquered them!"

"That we did," he agreed. "But only because some of their own forces turned on them and we were able to crush them at sea. What we fought at Blackrock was only a portion of the true Horde, and even then it was a close thing." He shook his head. "For all we know, there could be as many as a dozen more clans back on the orcs' world, just waiting to break through again." He heard the muttering and gasping that swept through his men. "That's right, lads," he announced loudly. "We could well be heading toward our deaths here."

"Sir? Why are you telling us this?" Farrol asked quietly.

"Because I don't believe in lying about our chances," his commander answered. "You've a right to know what you'll be facing. And I don't want you going in thinking this'll be easy. Expect hard fighting, and stay sharp," he said, his tone shifting from advice to order. "Go in expecting trouble, and you're more likely to survive." He grinned suddenly. "And then you can call yourselves Sons of Lothar."

All around him men nodded, more sober now. These

were good men, if not as seasoned as he might wish. He already regretted the deaths he knew would come if the portal did indeed reopen. But they were sworn to defend the Alliance, even at the cost of their own lives. He just hoped they wouldn't be dying for nothing. Even though precious time was ticking past, Danath permitted himself a few moments to look at them, to memorize faces, summon names to mind. He had no children of his own; while they were under his command, he was father to these boys. Even if they all were Sons of Lothar. The thought made him smile slightly.

"Mount up, lads!"

Two minutes later, they were galloping down the cobblestone streets of Stormwind and out the main gates.

"Listen, do you hear that?"

Randal laughed. "You're getting jumpy, Willam," he told his friend. "It's just the wind." He glanced around, looking across the blasted landscape, and shivered. "Nothing to block it out here."

Willam nodded but still seemed uneasy. "Maybe you're right," he admitted, rubbing his face with one gloved hand. "I hate this detail. Why've we got to guard this thing, anyway? Isn't that what the magi are for?"

Both soldiers glanced behind them. If they squinted they could make out a shimmer in the air, just beyond a pile of old rubble. The distortion was narrow, perhaps the width of a man but twice as tall. They had been told that rift was all that remained of the Dark Portal, and that their task was to keep watch over it.

"Dunno," Randal replied. "You'd think if anything did happen the magi'd know before we did." He shrugged. "At least it's an easy job. And our shift's over in another hour."

Willam started to say something else, then stopped, his eyes wide. "There!" he whispered. "Hear that?"

"Hear wh—"

Willam shushed him frantically. They sat stone-still for a moment, ears straining. And then Randal heard it. It was like a low moan, then a high whistle, as if the wind were sweeping across a wide plain before cutting through the valley around them. His eyes went back to the rift—and he gasped, almost dropping his shield and spear. It was wider now!

"Sound the alarm!" he told Willam frantically, but his friend was frozen in fear, eyes riveted on the sight before them. "Willam, *sound the alarm!*"

As Willam hurried to obey, the rift shimmered again, growing brighter, colors leaking out along its expanding edges. It seemed to split open, like a mouth ravenous for food, and shadows billowed forth. They spread rapidly, and Randal blinked, unable to see the rift or the rubble below it anymore. Even Willam had vanished, though he could hear his friend blowing on the horn, alerting the other guards.

Randal swiveled this way and that, trying to peer through the sudden darkness, his spear and shield at the ready. Was there something there? Or there? He strained to listen.

Was that a sound? A thud, as if something had rolled over—or dropped? Was that another?

Yes, he was sure he'd heard something now. He turned in the direction he thought it had come from, raising his spear slightly and hoping it wasn't Willam. Those definitely sounded like footsteps, heavy ones— and many of them.

"Hold!" Randal shouted, wishing his voice weren't shaking. "Who goes there? Stand and identify yourself, in the name of the Alliance!"

The steps grew closer, and he spun, trying to pinpoint their source. Were they behind him? Off to his side? Right in front of him? He turned slightly as the ground shook beneath his feet, raising his shield instinctively—

—and cried out as something heavy crushed it like paper, the impact shattering his arm as well.

Blinking away the pain, Randal thrust his spear forward, but something caught the weapon's long haft and wrenched it from his grip. A face appeared out of the darkness, inches from his own—a wide, heavy face, with a looming brow, squat nose, and two sharp tusks jutting up from the lower lip.

The horrifying face leered at Randal, and he had a brief glimpse of something else rushing toward him from the shadows, something wide and flat and curved. . . .

★ ★ ★

The other guards rallied, alerted by Willam's horn, but it was too little too late. The darkness filled the valley, preventing them from even seeing their foes, and while the humans blundered about in confusion, orc warriors and death knights poured out of the newly expanded rift, crushing everyone in their path. It was more of a slaughter than a true battle. Within minutes every human defender was dead or dying, and the orcs controlled the Azeroth side of the Dark Portal.

CHAPTER SIX

Whispers.

Soft susurrations, barely heard unless listened for. The flutter of a bird's wings in flight, the sound of a leaf drifting toward the earth . . . these were louder than the whispers that teased at Ner'zhul's ears.

But he heard them.

He held the skull in his hands, gazing deeply into empty eye sockets, and heard Gul'dan's voice. It sounded to him as it had in life—sycophantic, anxious for approval, eagerly answering questions and offering solutions; and yet simultaneously barely hiding a vast contempt and lust for power.

Gul'dan, in death, hoped to lull his former master into the same false sense of security he had when he lived. But Ner'zhul would not be duped a second time. Inadvertently Ner'zhul had betrayed his people with his gullibility, and this orc whose skull rested in his gnarled hands had risen to power by thinking he had ground the old shaman into the dirt.

"Who is alive and in power, and who is dead, eh, my apprentice?" he whispered to the skull.

He blinked suddenly, startled out of his conversation with the skull as light flooded his traveling tent. A figure stood silhouetted against the daylight that knifed through the gloom of the tent's interior.

"We control the portal!" Grom Hellscream announced.

Ner'zhul smiled. Thus far all had gone according to plan. He absently caressed the yellowed bone as he might a pet fawning for his attention. Fitting and just, that Gul'dan's skull should help him reopen the rift.

Ner'zhul waved Grom and his companion, Teron Gorefiend, inside. He had appointed them his seconds, Gorefiend overseeing the death knights and ogres and Grom conveying his orders to the various clans. And there were many clans now. The Thunderlord, Laughing Skull, and Bonechewer clans had joined them, leaving only the Redwalker clan—what was left of it. All the other clans had united under his leadership once more, making the Horde nearly as strong as it had been before the first attack on Azeroth. Nearly.

"I am well pleased," he said. "And now—you know what you must do next."

"Oh, I know what to do," Gorefiend assured the old shaman. "But are you sure you can maintain the rift by yourself?" Even with the skull's aid and suggestions—

not that all of those had proven valuable or even reasonable—it had taken several death knights working in tandem to help Ner'zhul sufficiently widen the rift.

Arrogance! He should not speak so to you, came the soft whisper from the relic.

No. He should not.

"I can manage," Ner'zhul replied shortly, feeling the power coiled within him, more power than he had felt in years. It was as if tapping into the skull's energies had awakened something deep within him, something he had never even realized he had been missing. And it felt . . . good. "Once the framework is rebuilt there, the portal will maintain itself. Be off about your duties, Teron."

From within the darkness of his hood, the death knight's eyes flickered slightly. Then he nodded curtly and turned on his heel, his cloak billowing behind him as he slipped out of the tent.

Ner'zhul turned to Grom, who nodded. "I am ready, Ner'zhul. More than ready."

"Very well—the sooner you begin, the sooner we can achieve our goals." Grom raised his axe in salute, then followed Gorefiend. Ner'zhul lingered for a moment in the darkness, then emerged from the tent just in time to see orc and death knight stride up to the portal and step through it into that other world, a place he had never set foot upon himself.

He stared at the rift, his fingers idly stroking the smooth surface of Gul'dan's skull.

And now, you will never need to see this Azeroth. Soon, a greater glory will be yours! came the skull's eager, dead voice.

Yes, mused Ner'zhul, *very soon.*

"What news?" Teron Gorefiend demanded of Gaz Soulripper as his booted feet strode on Azerothian soil. The other death knight had led a handful of their brethren through the rift once it had opened, and was now in charge of the work on this side of the portal. While the orcs provided the labor that would rebuild the portal from the rubble that was strewn about the area, it was the death knights who would make that portal more than a physical gateway. With their dark magics, they would be able to widen and stabilize the rift so that it would be of better use to the Horde.

"They died almost too easily," Soulripper replied, laughing. "With the darkness they never stood a chance." He gestured behind him, to where Gorefiend's altered senses could pick out the framework despite the magical shadows filling the valley. "We're progressing well on the framework. It should be up within the next day or two."

Gorefiend grunted, studying the work. A simple stone archway at the top of a short ramp had held the original Dark Portal. When the portal had collapsed, the archway had fallen as well. The orcs they had pressed into service for this task had already cleared all those remains out of the way and were busy assembling the stone blocks they had lugged through from Draenor. This framework would be more functional than decorative, with only a few orcish runes hastily carved on it, but as long as they could utilize the framework to stabilize the portal he didn't care.

"What of the other clans still on this world?" he asked.

"We spoke to them through dreams and visions once we'd secured the valley," Soulripper replied. "No idea how long it will take for any of them to reach us, though."

As it turned out, it was mere hours later that Gorefiend heard the sound of approaching footsteps. He rose from the boulder he had been leaning against, noticing that the portal was already nearing completion, and paused. The unnatural darkness still held—it would prevent the humans from mounting a counterattack too quickly, and would keep them guessing—but it did not much slow down either orcs or death knights, and the footsteps drew steadily closer.

At last a band of orcs marched into view. They were battered and worn, barely three dozen, but they held their heads high and their weapons ready. Before them strode an older orc, his body still powerful despite advanced years, his head turning constantly. As they drew closer, Gorefiend recognized him and realized why he moved his head so—the orc had only one eye. The other was a mass of scar tissue, and Gorefiend remembered the many rumors of how Kilrogg

Deadeye had lost that orb—and what he had gained in return.

Gorefiend moved forward to meet the Bleeding Hollow chieftain. "Kilrogg," he called as he approached. It was not a good idea to approach Kilrogg without warning.

The chieftain's head swiveled about until his one eye was locked on Gorefiend. "Gorefiend," he called in return, stepping up and gesturing for his warriors to spread themselves out behind him. "I had a vision you were here."

The death knight nodded. He watched Kilrogg's gaze track past him to the almost completed Dark Portal.

"So it is true," the chieftain said softly. "The portal has been restored!"

"It is true," Gorefiend replied. "We came from Draenor. And you can return there."

"Has the land been restored to life?"

"Draenor is still dying," Gorefiend acknowledged, "but Ner'zhul has a plan."

That only made Kilrogg's scowl deepen, however. "Ner'zhul? That old fool? What is his involvement here? I saw him too in my vision, but thought that merely an image from the past."

"An image of our future, more like," Gorefiend responded. "Ner'zhul has taken control again, and has reforged the Horde. He has united all the remaining clans on Draenor"—he conveniently ignored the Redwalker clan, which was barely alive now anyway—"and reopened the rift. And he has a plan that will ensure the survival of our people, if not our world."

Kilrogg scratched the scar tissue beneath his missing eye. "He has done all this? This plan—you think it sound?"

Gorefiend nodded.

"Hmm. Perhaps he's finally shaken off the weakness and doubt Gul'dan inflicted upon him, then. If he is anything like the Ner'zhul of old, I would gladly follow him." He shook his head and lowered his voice. "And, in truth, I would happily forsake this world for our own, even in its current state. We have been trapped here too long."

Gorefiend nodded. "Go then," he urged the Bleeding Hollow chieftain. "Ner'zhul and the others await you beyond the portal, and I know your experience and wisdom would be of great value to them. But first tell me, what of the other orcs still here?"

"Aside from the Frostwolves, who will have nothing to do with the rest of us, there are only two other clans not in captivity," Kilrogg said. "The Dragonmaw and the Blackrock." He grimaced. "The Dragonmaw remain hidden in the mountains somewhere, safe from human eyes, and they still control the red dragons. They formed an alliance with the Blackrock a year ago. Rend and Maim Blackhand lead the Blackrock, and have claimed Blackrock Spire as their own." He shrugged. "I'd not want the site of Doomhammer's defeat as my base, but then the brothers never cared for him."

This was not good news. "Will they return to the portal, and to Draenor, do you think?" Gorefiend asked.

Kilrogg shook his head. "Nay, they seem content to remain on Azeroth," he replied. "I'd not expect them."

Gorefiend scowled but nodded. "My thanks, Kilrogg. Now go—Draenor awaits."

Kilrogg nodded and turned away, leading his warriors up the ramp to the restored portal, which shimmered even in the darkness. "Onward to Draenor!" he bellowed, pointing, and the first warrior strode through the portal without hesitation, followed by the rest. Kilrogg himself went last, then he glanced back at the valley and at Azeroth. He lifted his weapon.

"A warrior retreats . . . but only to regroup. I will return," he vowed. "This world and its people will know my wrath." Then he too stepped through, and was gone.

Grom Hellscream watched the Bleeding Hollow warriors vanish through the portal. He was pleased to see that Kilrogg still survived—the older chieftain had always been one of the canniest of the Horde leaders, and one of their finest tacticians. He was sure Kilrogg's expertise would prove valuable very soon.

Turning back to the orc who had just approached, Grom nodded for the warrior to continue.

"The humans have not been idle. A large fortress stands to the north," the scout reported. "It guards the pass out of this area. There is no other way past."

Grom grinned. "Perfect," he said slowly. "That's our target. We take the fortress and we can hold this valley indefinitely, no matter what this human Alliance throws against us." He nodded to the scout. "Tell the others to prepare. We will march at once."

The scout nodded, but before he could move away Grom held up a hand for silence. He paused, listening closely. It sounded like footsteps, but faster, harder, and with a strange echo. More like a beast than a man, but if so it was a heavy beast, with solid hooves rather than soft paws. He had heard about the humans and their strange steeds—"horses," they were called—and guessed that was what he was hearing.

"Humans approach!" he shouted immediately, raising Gorehowl and whipping it around overhead. "Dispel the darkness!"

He didn't know where the death knights were, or even which ones had been maintaining the unnatural shadows that covered the valley, but they heard him. The darkness began to fade, light seeping through a wisp at a time, color washing across the valley even as the dark ebbed away, until at last he could see the place clearly. There stood the Dark Portal, fully restored. Up to the north he spotted stone towers—the fortress his scout had mentioned. But now, through the narrow pass from that direction came a force of men, astride beasts with gleaming hides and long flowing manes and tails. At the front of the wave of warriors was a man who wore metal across his chest, dark blue but with a pattern like twinned flames outlined in gold. He waved a sword overhead, driving his horse forward without pause. This, then, was their leader.

Grom grinned and raised Gorehowl again. With the darkness gone its blade shone silver in the daylight. He swung it in a slow arc, his grin widening as the weapon sang its war song of approaching death. Several of the humans faltered.

"For the Horde!" he shouted, and charged forward. His warriors were right behind him.

The humans hesitated, thrown off by the strange darkness they'd just seen slip away, surprised to find a mass of orcs now charging toward them, and terrified by the shrieks and howls arising not just from the approaching orc warriors but from their very weapons. And for the first rank of humans, that hesitation proved deadly.

Grom struck first, Gorehowl slicing the leading rider from shoulder to opposite hip. The top half of the corpse slid from the horse even as the bottom half toppled the other way. Grom never saw it fall; he was already on to the next targets, spinning to remove the legs of two more warriors as he stepped between them.

The orcs strode between the beasts, slicing into steed and rider alike, sending some horses careening back into and even over many of the Alliance foot soldiers. The force that had marched into the valley was sizeable but nothing to compare with the clans Grom had brought with him, and the orcs had surprise and focus on their side.

The humans fought bravely, Grom would grant them that. And some showed skill at arms. But they lacked an orc's size and strength, and he found it an easy matter to overpower a human fighter and carve him open right through the strange metal shirt they all wore. For a sweet time he let the bloodlust take control, hacking and slashing wildly about him, caring for nothing more than the spatter of blood, the reek of death, and the cries of the wounded and dying. How glorious to again kill without concern or guilt! No fellow orcs fell beneath Gorehowl, only the humans, one after another after another, and their fear and screams were intoxicating.

His blood pounded in his veins, his vision had strange spots of color around the edges, and he was gasping for breath, but Grom had never felt more alive. Good. It was good. There came a momentary lull in the fighting, and he glanced around. Everywhere he looked he saw human corpses. Dozens of them, their eyes staring, fear twisting their features, blood still pumping from . . .

Grom frowned, the bloodlust starting to retreat. Yes, dozens of corpses, but the human he had noted, the one with the golden chest plate—where was he?

He growled and shook his black head, forcing the bloodlust back so he could listen to his warrior's instincts. Ignoring the shouts and cheers of his warriors,

Grom ran toward the edge of the valley. Then he stopped and listened. Yes, he could definitely hear hoof-beats, and they were receding fast. Someone had survived, and had the sense to ride away.

Back toward the fortress.

Returning to the battlefield, Grom found Gorefiend. Seizing his arm, Grom shouted, "One of them escaped! Their leader, I think. He is headed for the fortress!"

Gorefiend nodded. "Follow him," he replied, yelling as Grom had been to hear over the din, "and keep the Alliance forces in that fortress busy. We need to get to the artifacts. We should be back in a matter of days."

Grom nodded. "You need not worry," he promised. "I will do my duty. See to it you do yours."

The death knight laughed and turned away without further reply, dismissing the Warsong clan leader. He extended his mailed hands, and a bolt of darkness exploded from them to flatten two horses and their riders. Grom ground his teeth together. He disliked Gorefiend, and all the death knights, in fact—they had already lived their lives and had returned from death itself, trapped now in human bodies. How could such unnatural creatures be trusted? But Ner'zhul had approved Gorefiend's plan, and so Grom had no choice but to go along with it. He just hoped the death knight was right, and that these strange items they were so doggedly hunting really would allow Ner'zhul to save their people.

In the meantime, he had orders he was only too happy to obey. "A handful of you, stay here," he instructed his warriors. "The rest of you, and the other clans, come with me." He grinned and raised Gorehowl high. "We have a fortress to take!"

CHAPTER SEVEN

Muradin Bronzebeard, brother to King Magni and ambassador to the human realm of Lordaeron, hurried along the corridors of the royal palace. "All these twists an' turns an' nooks and crannies," the dwarf muttered to himself. If he remembered correctly, the spiral staircase that would take him up to the king's private apartments and balconies was around here somewhere. He seemed to recall that if he ducked through this armory hall, he'd—

"Hoy!"

Muradin jumped slightly even as he realized the voice belonged to a child. His grin was hidden by his thick, bushy beard as he peered around a corner to see young Arthas standing in front of a suit of armor on a small pedestal. The prince was all of twelve now, a right bonnie young lad, all smiles and golden curls and rosy cheeks. At the moment, though, Prince Arthas looked very serious and had a wooden sword pointed at the throat of a suit of armor.

"Think you to pass here, vile orc?" Arthas cried. "You are in Alliance lands! I will show you mercy this once. Begone and never return!"

Although Muradin was hungry, and although he was late, he found himself watching, smiling. This was what they'd all fought for, was it not? He and Magni and their brother Brann, and the humans Lothar, rest his soul, and young Turalyon—they'd fought together against the orcs to save Ironforge toward the end of the Second War. And then Muradin and Brann had gone with the humans to the Dark Portal, to watch its destruction with satisfaction. Keeping the wee ones safe. Buying a future for all of them.

Arthas stiffened. "What? You will not depart? I have given you a chance, but now, we fight!"

With a fierce cry, the young prince charged. He was wise enough not to actually attack the ancient suit of armor, which would no doubt incur his father's disapproval, but set to his imaginary foe with vigor a few paces away. Muradin's grin faded. What was this? Who in the world had been *teaching* this boy? Look how wide and uncontrolled that pretend parry was! And the grip—ach, wrong, all wrong. He frowned terribly as after a particularly energetic swing, Arthas lost his grip on the wooden sword and it flew across the room to clatter loudly on the floor.

Arthas gasped and looked around, to see if the

sound had drawn attention. His cheeks turned bright pink as he met Muradin's gaze.

"Um . . . Ambassador . . . I was just . . ."

Muradin coughed, as embarrassed for the boy as Arthas himself was. "I'm lookin' fer yer father, boy. Can ye direct me? This infernal place has too many turns."

Arthas pointed to a stairway on his left. Muradin nodded and hurried up the twisting steps, anxious to be away from the scene.

He arrived just in time to hear Thoras Trollbane bellowing—which, he mused, was hardly anything new.

"Trade? With you? You're double damned, no-good Horde sympathizers!"

What was going on? Muradin burst onto the balcony, expecting to see . . . well, he wasn't sure what, but it certainly wasn't a small green being with large, bat-like ears and eyes that were currently wide with apprehension. He was completely bald and wore trousers, a crisp shirt and waistcoat, and a monocle that had popped out and was now swinging wildly from a chain attached to his person.

"No, no no no!" the green creature gasped in a strained, shrieking voice, waving his hands frantically. He stood about eye level with the breakfast table at which Trollbane and King Terenas were seated and fumbled with the monocle. "You've got me all wrong! It's not like that at all!"

"Isn't it, Krix?" The mildness with which Terenas

uttered the words told Muradin that nothing of real threat was going on. The king reached for a piece of bread and began to butter it.

"No!" Krix exclaimed, looking offended. "Well. One trade prince, yes. Did. That." He coughed slightly. "Allied with the Horde. But! Only one very foolish prince, and even he came to his senses after the Second War. But the rest of the goblins have come to realize that it's much better to remain neutral. Much better, for you, for us, for everyone! Free trade thrives that way and we all benefit!"

Muradin scowled. He knew what manner of creature he was facing now—a goblin. "What's this wee green moneygrubber doing at our breakfast table, Terenas?" Muradin asked, shouldering past the creature.

Before the king could answer, the goblin burst out, "Krix Wiklish, pleasure to meet you. I see you're a dwarf!"

"Brilliant observation," Trollbane growled.

"Perhaps your people would like to enter a trade agreement! These two humans don't seem so keen on it. I mean—think about it!" Krix smiled ingratiatingly, the effect marred only by the sharpness of his teeth. "You like to mine—why, *we* like to tear down trees! It's a perfect business relationship! Our shredders can clear land—"

"Thank you, Krix, that will be enough," Terenas interrupted. "Now that Ambassador Muradin has arrived, we have business to attend to. I'll talk again with you later this afternoon and look at the papers you promised me."

"What?" Muradin scowled at Terenas. "This wee bugger does deals with both sides, Terenas. I'd sooner trust a—hey!"

Krix froze, the apricot scone he had snagged halfway to his mouth. He smiled weakly. Muradin glared. Within a month of his arrival the dwarf had been on a first-name basis with every one of the palace chefs, and he had gone to extra efforts to secure the friendship of the pastry chefs. Such overtures were now bearing sweet, delicious fruit, if the scones were any indication. And now this goblin was about to devour *his* pastries!

"King Terenas asked ye tae leave," he said. Krix nodded. The monocle fell out again. He popped the scone into his mouth, bowed low, and scurried off.

"Ruddy parasite, that one is," growled Muradin.

"But amusing," Terenas said. "And his ideas do have merit. But now that you are here, Ambassador, I fear we must talk of less amusing things. Such as the situation with King Perenolde."

"King! Bah. The word sits ill in my mouth. It's an outrage!" Trollbane cried. He slammed a fist down on the table, making cups and flagons and plates jump. "He betrays us all, damn near destroys us, and this is all he gets?" His long face set in a deep scowl. "I say prison, if not outright execution!"

"Aye, I'd not be keepin' traitors in gilded cages

meself," said Muradin. He did not mince words; he said what was on his mind outright and didn't worry about whom it might offend. Muradin knew that some of the Alliance rulers found that combination distressing, but he also knew that both Terenas and his old friend Trollbane found it refreshing.

The three sat at a small table on one of the palace's higher balconies that overlooked the lake just beyond the city, with the mountains forming a backdrop beyond. It was a stunning view, but it also served to ground their discussion, for it was through those same mountains that Orgrim Doomhammer had led his Horde, thanks to the treachery of Alterac's ruler, Aiden Perenolde. After the war Terenas had led Alliance troops into Alterac, declaring martial law and taking Perenolde, the fellow Trollbane had been ranting against, into custody. But Terenas had simply placed the former king under house arrest, confining him to his palace and the rest of his family to close watch. Nothing more had been done with them since then.

Trollbane, for one, was not satisfied. As Perenolde's closest neighbor, he had long been forced to weather the Alterac king's wily schemes, and it had only been Trollbane's quick thinking and equally quick action that had sealed the mountain passes and cut off a portion of the orcish Horde. Otherwise the entire force would have flowed down onto the plains and across the lake toward Capital City itself, and most likely the city would have fallen.

"I agree, he deserves a far worse fate," Terenas said carefully, clearly trying to soothe his friend's temper. Muradin reached for a scone and a hard-boiled egg. "But he is, or at least was, a sovereign king," Terenas continued. "We cannot simply exile him, or imprison him—not without making every other king worry that we will do the same to them if they disagree with us on anything."

"We will, if they turn traitor like he did!" Trollbane argued, but he soon settled down. He was far from stupid, Muradin knew; that gruff exterior hid a sharp mind.

"Aye, it's a tricky issue," Muradin said, deciding to help himself to another pastry. "Ye canna be dropping him off a cliff, for it'll lose ye the trust of yer other fellows, but ye canna leave him to get away with it, either."

"We need to force him to abdicate," Terenas pointed out yet again—this was not the first time they'd had this discussion. "Once he's no longer king, we can try him and execute him as just another Alliance noble." He tugged at his beard. "The problem is, he's refusing."

Trollbane snorted. "Of course he is! He knows that means his death! But we have to do something, and soon. Right now he's got too much freedom, and that's bound to cause trouble."

Terenas nodded. "It has certainly sat for too long," he agreed. "Something must be done about Alterac, especially with these new problems brewing." He sighed.

"The last thing we need is to fight another war while worrying about betrayal again."

"And what of the lad?" Muradin asked, flicking a stray crumb from his majestic bronze beard. "Will he no be tryin' for the throne?"

"Aliden, you mean?" Trollbane replied. He snorted. "Cut from the same cloth as his father."

"I don't care for young Aliden much myself," Terenas admitted. "He was far too pampered as a youth—he has never known hardship or travail, and has never faced danger. I fear he has no leadership skills, either. Yet what grounds have we to deny him the throne? He is Aiden's heir, Alterac's crown prince—if his father does abdicate, the crown falls to him."

"There's no proof he knew of his father's treachery," Trollbane said grudgingly. "Not that being ignorant is much better than being underhanded, but at least he has that in his favor."

Just then a servant appeared at the door. Muradin frowned, fearing that the pesky goblin wanted to talk to them. Instead, the servant had good news. "Lord Daval Prestor wishes an audience, Your Majesty," he told Terenas.

"Ah, send him up, by all means, Lavin," Terenas said. He turned to Trollbane and Muradin. "Have you both met Lord Prestor?"

"Aye, and it's a fine man he is," Muradin replied. "And much to his credit that he's survived as well as he has, with all he's faced." Trollbane nodded his agreement.

Lord Prestor had been dealt a harsh hand by fate, Muradin reflected as he bit into the egg. He'd never heard of the man until recently, of course—he didn't much follow all the twists and turns of human nobility—but from what he'd been told, Prestor had been ruler of a tiny domain deep in the mountains of Lordaeron. He could trace his ancestry back to the royal house of Alterac and was a distant cousin of Perenolde's. Prestor's entire realm had fallen to a dragon attack during the Second War, and he and a handful of close family alone had escaped. The first anyone had heard of the man or his realm had been a shocking introduction—Prestor had staggered all the way to Capital City without servants or guards, indeed with little more than the clothes on his back and his good name. His lineage had earned him admittance into the noble circles and his engaging personality had won him friends, the three at the table among them. It had been Prestor's suggestion to pass martial law in Alterac, and not only Terenas but the rest of the Alliance had agreed at once that it was a fine albeit temporary solution.

The man in question stepped onto the balcony a moment later and executed a graceful and deep bow, his black curls gleaming almost blue in the warm early light. "Your Majesties," Prestor murmured, his rich baritone carrying easily across the small space. "And noble Ambassador. How good to see you all again."

"Indeed it is," said Terenas jovially. "Sit and join us. Would you care for some tea?"

"The apricot scones are particularly fine today," Muradin offered, covering his mouth with his hand as he inadvertently sprayed some crumbs. Something about Prestor's characteristic tidiness always made the dwarf feel a bit . . . rustic.

"Many thanks, my lords." Prestor seated himself gracefully, though not before using his napkin to quickly dust off his seat, and poured a cup of tea. Muradin offered him the plate of scones, but Prestor smiled, holding up a manicured, uncallused hand in polite refusal. "I hope I am not intruding?"

"Not at all, not at all," Terenas assured him. "In fact, your timing is excellent. We were just discussing the matter of Alterac."

"Ah yes, of course." Prestor took an appreciative sip of tea. "No doubt you have heard about young Isiden?" He seemed surprised at the blank looks he received in response. "One of Lord Perenolde's nephews, little more than a youth still."

"Ah, yes. Ran off to Gilneas, didn't he?" Trollbane asked.

"Indeed he did, shortly before you declared martial law throughout Alterac. Rumors say he is hoping to rally support there for his own bid for the throne."

"Greymane mentioned something of that," Terenas recalled. "But he has not met with the boy, or encouraged his suit in any way."

Prestor shook his head. "He is noble indeed, King Greymane," he mused softly, "to overlook something which could so easily work to his benefit. All he would need to do is back Isiden for the throne and Gilneas would gain a direct stake in Alterac's welfare—and no doubt favored status through the kingdom's many mountain passes."

Muradin scratched at his beard. "Aye, that'd be a hard one ta pass up," he agreed.

Terenas and Trollbane exchanged glances. Greymane was canny enough not to miss such an opportunity. Yet he claimed he'd not spoken with the boy. Had he lied? Or was he playing a more subtle game?

"What do you think should be done with Alterac?" Terenas asked Prestor.

"Why do you ask me, sire?"

"An outsider's perspective is useful, and we value your opinion."

Prestor colored slightly. "Truly? You honor me, thank you. Well . . . I think you should claim it for your own, Your Majesty. You are the leader of the Alliance, after all, and took the brunt of the costs for the last war. Surely you are due a reward for all your efforts?"

Terenas chuckled. "No thank you," he said, holding up a hand in mock horror. "I have more than enough to handle here in Lordaeron—I've no desire to double my troubles by taking on a second kingdom!" Muradin knew he had considered the idea, of course, and from some vantages it held merit. But the troubles it would cause, not least of them among his fellow rulers, would far outweigh the benefits, at least to Terenas's mind.

"How about you then, Your Majesty?" Prestor suggested, turning to the Stromgarde king. "Your quick action stopped Perenolde's treachery. I well know you lost many men defending those mountain passes from the orcs." A shadow of pain flickered across the young noble's face, and all three of his companions winced slightly, knowing exactly where his thoughts had led him. Maybe that was why he was so meticulous about his person. If he'd been forced to flee a city that had been destroyed by dragonfire, walking for ages in the same filthy clothes, Muradin mused, maybe he'd be a bit of a dandy now too.

Trollbane frowned thoughtfully, but before he could speak, Terenas interjected gently, "Neither Thoras nor I could claim Alterac. It is not simply a matter of one kingdom invading another. We are all part of the Alliance, and must all work together to protect our world and our lands. The Alliance *as a whole* defeated the Horde and won the war. That means any spoils of war, including Alterac, must fall to the Alliance as well." He shook his head. "If any one of us tried to annex Alterac, the other Alliance rulers would feel slighted, and rightly so."

"Aye," Muradin agreed. "It must be decided by all, or not at all." He grinned. "Though presentin' a fine idea to the rest could ease the matter somewhat."

Prestor nodded and set down his cup. "My apologies if I spoke out of turn," he said, "or if I offended you in any way." He offered them a small smile. "I can see I still have much to learn before I can hope to match your wisdom or diplomacy."

Terenas waved the apology aside. "No harm done, dear boy. I asked for your opinion and you gave it. Part of the reason we three were meeting here was to discuss this very matter, in the hopes of finding some way to satisfy everyone involved and still keep Alterac safe and active." He smiled. "Our friend Muradin is right— if we can present a good plan to the rest of the Alliance, it could save much time and argument."

"Of course. I only hope my small contribution has been in some way helpful." Prestor stood and bowed deeply. "Now if you will excuse me, I will leave you to these weighty deliberations, which I fear are far beyond my own ability." He waited for Terenas's nod of permission, then graced them all with a smile and exited the balcony.

Trollbane watched the young lord go, frowning. "Prestor may be naive," he said, "but he has a point. Maybe Alterac should pay reparations."

"With what?" Muradin scoffed. "They're bled dry, just like all of us. Besides, that sounds too much like blood money, which is the same as saying vengeance."

"Most of our money is going toward rebuilding," Terenas pointed out. "We added Alterac's treasuries to the Alliance's once we took control of the kingdom."

"Aye, and the orc internment camps are no cheap either," Muradin added. "With all the money goin' ta those and ta repairs, and ta that fine new fortress by the portal, what's left for reparations?"

Trollbane sighed. "You're right. I just feel they should pay, somehow. Alterac's betrayal cost so many lives."

_"*Perenolde's* betrayal," Terenas corrected gently but firmly. "We must remember that. Very few of Alterac's citizens even knew of their king's treachery—Perenolde simply ordered them away from certain passes and made those trails accessible to the Horde. It was less a question of Alterac helping the Horde than of its king granting the orcs free passage and keeping his own citizens out of the way."

"True enough," Trollbane agreed. "I've known many from Alterac over the years, and most are fine folk, not like their snake of a king." He shook his head, drained his flagon, and wiped his beard and mustache with the back of his hand. "I'll give the matter more thought," he promised.

"As will we all," Muradin assured him, snatching up one last scone as they rose from their seats. "Dinna worry—we'll find a solution yet."

"I'm sure we will," Terenas agreed. "I just hope we can do so before we're forced to set the matter aside for more pressing issues." His two companions knew what he meant. They had received Khadgar's warning only a few days before, and now were waiting on word from Turalyon. If the Horde did attack again, if the portal did reopen, all questions about Alterac would quickly become moot. As long as Perenolde was under house arrest and the kingdom under Alliance control, they could worry about other details later—if they survived.

Muradin thought somberly of young Arthas swinging away at a suit of armor, and hoped that the prince would not get a taste of war just yet.

CHAPTER EIGHT

Clouds hung low over Stormwind, brushing the tips of the city's many towers. A chill wind tugged at the guards' cloaks as they huddled at their posts outside Stormwind Keep, shivering. Inside, their commander Turalyon and his advisers were still awake, poring over maps in one of the armories in the keep, now the Alliance command post. The guards had nodded to the beautiful elf who had accompanied their commander and was currently in the room with the other strategists, though anyone with eyes could see the tension between the two.

They shivered, but paid no real heed to a particularly cold breeze that wafted through the city, danced in through the keep's gate doors, and then drifted up the wide central hallway and veered to the left. Up it swirled, through another corridor and across a small courtyard open to the cloudy night sky.

A pair of guards stood to either side of the entrance to the royal library. They shivered as they felt the breeze brush up against them, and squinted as the shadows around them seemed to deepen.

Suddenly a stronger wind sprang up, whisking the shadows away and revealing several figures in their stead. Four of them seemed to be human, at least in size; they all wore heavy hooded cloaks and strange wrappings around limbs and torso, but their eyes glowed a fiery red. The last figure, however, towered over them, and even in the near-dark his skin gleamed green.

One of the guards inhaled to cry out an alarm as he drew his sword. He never got the chance. The orc stepped forward, already swinging a massive axe. The guard fell in two pieces. His companion was able to raise his shield and block a blow from one of the strange wrapped figures and thrust with his spear. To no avail; another of the intruders caught the spear haft and chopped it in half, then spun and delivered a sweeping blow to the guard's neck just above the shield's edge. The man fell without a sound, his head nearly severed, and the figures stepped over the two twitching corpses, pushed the doors open, and entered the royal library.

"Be quick," Gorefiend instructed. "We must not be discovered." His death knights nodded, as did Pargath Throatsplitter, the orc who had so quickly dispatched the first guard. Gorefiend had wanted a Bleeding Hollow warrior with him, since they knew this world better than any other Horde member, and Pargath had impressed him as one of the smarter and quieter warriors available.

All five of them spread out, combing the library for their prize. After several minutes, Pargath cursed. "It's not here!" he whispered.

"What?" Gorefiend joined the warrior next to an empty glass case. "Are you sure?"

In response Pargath gestured at the case, and at a small tan card stuck in one corner. Gorefiend had access to his host body's memories and skills, and after a second of concentration he could make out the writing: *Book of Medivh. Not to be opened without express permission from the king or from the Alliance commander.*

"It *was* here," Gorefiend mused, studying the case's deep velvet interior, which had clearly been weighed down by something large, heavy, and rectangular. "But where is it now?"

"Over here," one of his death knights called softly, and Gorefiend hurried toward him, Pargath and the other two death knights right behind him. "It looks as though someone else was thinking along the same lines we were." The death knight pointed at a small reading alcove—and the body within it. The corpse wore the armor of an Alliance guard, a dagger hilt protruding from the narrow space between the helm and breastplate.

"Alterac," Pargath whispered, staring down at the dead man. "That insignia, there." Pargath pointed to the markings on the dagger hilt. "That's the Alterac crest."

Gorefiend's own host memories confirmed it. "So Alterac has the book," he mused. Despite his betrayal during the previous war, Lord Perenolde still ruled Alterac, at least for now. And the book was valuable to the Alliance—Alterac could use it as a bargaining chip. Yes, it did make sense.

"But why leave behind such an obvious clue?" he wondered aloud. "That's a careless assassin."

"Perhaps he was sending a message," Pargath suggested. "Showing the Alliance that Alterac and its king are still in the game. Or," and he grinned, his tusks showing, "maybe he was just a careless assassin."

"Well, we shall not be so careless," Gorefiend said. "We need this book—and so we must go to Alterac. Take the dagger—I'd just as soon the Alliance didn't have the same clue we did. The corpse is fresh—let the guards think all three were slain by the same hand, when they come across them on the morrow."

Pargath obediently knelt and tugged free the deadly weapon. "To Alterac then?"

"Yes . . . but not just yet. We need to keep to our original plan as much as possible. We're still going to Blackrock Mountain. We need Rend, Maim, and the red dragons they control."

Pargath nodded. "Blackrock is on the way to Alterac," he pointed out.

"Exactly." Gorefiend grinned. "And with a red dragon at our disposal we could be there and back in hours, and still return to the portal ahead of schedule." He nodded. "But first we must leave here as quietly as we came." He beckoned them to him. The shadows crept closer, the temperature in the library dropping. A moment later, a chill wind slipped through the doors, past the cooling bodies and the pools of blood around them, back down the corridor, and out of the keep, where it quickly escaped into the night.

A day later, Gorefiend and his band reached Blackrock Mountain. Their small group had grown. He had contacted Gaz Soulripper, and his fellow death knight had sent Fenris Wolfbrother of the Thunderlord clan, Tagar Spinebreaker of the Bonechewer clan, and several of each's finest warriors. The orcs had met up with Gorefiend and the others at the base of the mountain range as commanded. Their expanded group was as large a force as Gorefiend felt they could assemble without being spotted by the Alliance; he hoped it was large enough to get the attention of the sons of Blackhand.

They climbed openly up the mountain, making sure the orc sentries hidden nearby could see them clearly. Gorefiend did not want even the suggestion that they might be attacking or sneaking in. Finally they reached the top, where rocks had split open and magma flowed through natural channels like a glowing red river beneath graceful bridges. A massive stone keep stood against the spire itself, carved from the same glossy black rock which gave this place its name, and Gorefiend's lips curled in wry memory. This had been where Doomhammer had established his base, and where the Horde warchief had introduced Gorefiend and the other death knights to the assembled clans. And it was below here, in the valley at the mountain's feet, where Doomhammer had fought the Alliance leader Lothar and won, only to then be bested by Lothar's second, Turalyon. Defeat and victories both had their ghosts here. He did not waste much time recollecting; he had the present to think of, and his own advancement.

With a gesture he instructed his group to halt at the entrance. Sure enough, a moment later four armed guards, large and powerful, appeared, looking more than eager to strike.

"We come to speak with the sons of Blackhand. Tell them Teron Gorefiend has news and a proposal for them." He stepped forward and let the hood fall from his face. The guards paled slightly. One of them whispered something to another. The second orc listened, bowed, and disappeared into the darkness. He returned a few moments later. The commander listened, then turned to Gorefiend and his group.

"Stay close," he warned, and led them into the keep himself. Gorefiend followed as they went ever deeper into the heart of the mountain, his glowing red eyes taking everything in. The keep was clearly in heavy use, and they saw several other orcs marching past here or there. All stopped to study them as they passed, obviously surprised to see a death knight here on Blackrock Spire, but none of them dared say anything.

Finally they reached the wide chamber Gorefiend remembered as Doomhammer's throne room and war council. The figure who now lounged in the heavy black chair carved from the mountain rock was shorter than Doomhammer, more brutish in appearance, with heavier features and an unkempt mane of brown hair. Medals and bones dangled from his hair, nose, ears, and brow, and his armor was heavily adorned, as was his massive, razor-sharp sword.

"Rend," Gorefiend said as he stopped just beyond the sword's reach.

"Gorefiend," Rend Blackhand, co-chieftain of the Blackrock clan, replied. His ugly face split in a grin that made him look even uglier. He shifted his position, flinging a leg over the arm of the throne. "Well, well, well. What brings you here, dead man?"

"Yeah," came a higher-pitched voice. Gorefiend's eyes shifted to where Rend's brother, Maim, crouched beside and just a little behind the throne, half-hidden in the shadows. "You got some nerve coming all the way in to see us."

"The Dark Portal has been restored," Gorefiend began, but Rend waved that away with a snort.

"I saw it in my dreams," the orc leader replied. "I knew it had to be one of you warlocks causing it." A frown crossed his broad face. "What about it?"

Gorefiend frowned. This conversation was not going as he'd hoped. "Ner'zhul leads the Horde now," he said. "I have been sent to bring you back into the fold, you and your Blackrock clan. We need the Dragonmaw clan as well, and the red dragons they command."

Rend glanced over at Maim, and the two brothers laughed together. "After two years where nothing happens, you come marching back up here, into *my* keep, a handful of fresh warriors trotting behind you, and you expect me to get all excited about kneeling before a withered old shaman? And by the way, I should also hand over not only my own warriors but my dragons as well?" He laughed again, though his eyes blazed with fury. "Not damn likely!"

"You must," Gorefiend insisted. "We need your strength, and your dragons, to carry out our plan!"

"I don't care what you need," Rend replied coldly. He rose, and Gorefiend realized that despite his childish attitude, Rend Blackhand was very dangerous. "That's your problem, not mine. I don't give a damn about whatever old Ner'zhul might be planning. Where was he when we fought the Alliance? I was here. Where was he when Doomhammer fell? I was here!"

"Me too," echoed Maim.

"Where was he when the portal was destroyed and we got stuck here?" Rend continued. "Where was he when we were hunted for two long years, and slowly rebuilt our forces with whatever orcs had survived and could make their way to us? I'll tell you where—he was safe and snug on Draenor, not lifting a finger to help!" Rend snatched up his sword and slammed it down on the throne's arm so hard the stone splintered. Maim jumped, then laughed with an echo of mania in his voice.

"But I was here! I pulled these orcs back together! I

rebuilt the Horde, not over on Draenor but here on Azeroth, right beneath the Alliance's nose! I am warchief now, and no used-up old shaman is going to take that away from me!"

Gorefiend longed to smear the boy into paste, but refrained. "Please," he said through clenched teeth. "Please, I ask you to reconsider. Without your aid, Ner'zhul will—"

"—fail," Rend finished bluntly. Maim looked gleeful. "He's got no experience with real war. He's got no head for tactics, no understanding of combat, and no real leadership skills. The Alliance will crush his little pretend Horde, and then"—he grinned—"I will pick up the pieces. We will gather all the survivors to us, Maim and I, just as we have been doing all along, since the last war ended."

Maim crept closer, and Rend let his hand fall on his brother's head as he might a pet dog's. "And with the Horde, the *real* Horde, even larger, and with the dragons at our side and me in command, we're going to sweep across the face of Azeroth." Rend grinned directly at Gorefiend. "And then, dead man, you'll serve me."

Behind Gorefiend, Tagar stiffened. "You coward!" he howled at Rend. "Traitorous dog, I'll cut you down like the cur you are, and take your throne for myself! Then your people will follow my orders and take their place in the Horde once more!"

"Oh yeah?" Rend replied lazily. "You want to attack me now?" His grin widened, and Gorefiend turned to rest a hand on Tagar's shoulder.

"He has guards nearby—many of them," he warned the Bonechewer chieftain quietly. "If you attack him they'll kill you, and then we're short one chieftain." He shook his head. "Now is not the time."

Tagar grumbled but stepped back a pace. Rend looked disappointed.

"One final time—will you join us?" Gorefiend asked Rend softly.

"Oh, wait, let me think—no," Rend retorted, smirking. Maim chuckled.

"Very well." Gorefiend bowed. "Then there is nothing more to say."

Rend laughed. "Go on," he instructed. "I can't wait to get news of your gory destruction." He and his brother laughed again, and the sound echoed through the chamber and into the halls and corridors beyond as Gorefiend led his dispirited group out of the keep and back down from the spire itself.

The sun had already set and the sky was fading from dusk to true dark. Gorefiend glared at the dancing orange and yellow campfire. Things had not gone according to plan, and he was deep in thought, pondering his next move. The others were wisely silent, and the only sound was the crackle of the flames and the occasional soft grunt of quiet conversation. A sudden noise in the darkness made them all leap to their feet, the tension strung taut as a bow.

"Human! Kill him!" came the cry from the orc sent to keep watch. The death knights stayed silent, but the orcs roared, happy to have a target for their frustration. Gorefiend could see the human now, wandering boldly up to their very encampment. Tagar charged him, bringing down his club in a blow that would crush the human's fragile skull.

What happened next stunned them all. Gorefiend watched as the human reached upward, almost languidly, caught the club, and twisted it from the orc's grasp. Tagar gaped at him, then he and the others prepared to lunge again.

The human cried, *"Hold!"*

Even Gorefiend doubted he could move against the human, such was the power in that single word. Who *was* this man? Gorefiend watched, curious and not a little concerned, as the human entered the ring of firelight. He would be handsome among his people, Gorefiend thought; tall and well-built for a human, with lustrous black hair and strong yet elegant features. Fine clothing draped his frame and an untouched jeweled sword hung at his side. He grimaced slightly and brushed something from his sleeve.

"I know you'd like nothing better than to attack me again, but you've sullied my clothing enough for one night. I don't fancy getting your blood on it." He smiled, a slow, dangerous smile that revealed perfect teeth. "I'm not quite what I seem, you see." His shadow flickered behind him, then suddenly seemed to rise up, growing monstrous in size and shape, great shadow-wings spreading all around them.

"Who are you?" Gorefiend demanded.

"I've been known by many names." The grin widened. "One of them . . . is Deathwing."

Deathwing! Gorefiend's mind reeled. He didn't question the statement, bizarre as it sounded; he'd already felt the faintest hint of Deathwing's power. Gorefiend had heard of the mighty black dragon, perhaps the single most powerful creature on Azeroth. They had seen black dragons a few times during the war, and Gorefiend had always wondered why the Dragonmaw clan hadn't captured them instead of the reluctant red dragons. He had suspected they were either too difficult a target or that doing so would awaken Deathwing's wrath.

Gorefiend tried to speak, but could not, so stunned and horrified was he. He tried again. "Wh-what do you want with us?"

Deathwing waved a beringed hand airily. "Calm yourself," he replied, slightly contemptuously. "I have not come to slay you, else you would be mere ash already." His eyes glowed from within for an instant, hinting at the vast fires that lurked beneath that human façade. "Quite the contrary. I have been watching you, and I like what I see." He spread a kerchief on a nearby rock, then settled himself beside the fire and motioned for them to do the same. They obeyed, slowly. "You have great strength and impressive focus." He grinned at them. "I would very much like to behold the world that gave rise to such a fierce and determined people."

Gorefiend studied their uninvited guest. Was Deathwing asking to visit Draenor? Why?

As if reading his mind, Deathwing turned to meet Gorefiend's gaze, and nodded. His dark eyes were hooded, the power within banked, and for the moment he seemed merely a self-assured human. "I know of your meeting with the one called Rend Blackhand," Deathwing said softly. "Idiots, he and his brother both. But not without their own power. And I know you desired the red dragons the Dragonmaw clan has . . . captured." The corners of his mouth turned up at that last word, as if the very idea delighted him. "Substandard beasts, in my opinion. I don't know why you're bothering with them."

Gorefiend wasn't sure how to respond. "Dragons are powerful beings," he began cautiously.

"Indeed we are. You wish for allies? Then I have an offer for you. My mighty children shall lend you their aid, and willingly rather than under duress."

One of the orcs, obviously anxious to please the unexpected guest, hesitantly offered Deathwing a mug of ale. The great creature frowned terribly, glaring at the orc. "Take that putrid stuff away!" Cowed, the orc retreated. Deathwing composed himself, turning his banked-fire eyes to Gorefiend. "Where was I? Oh yes. I will lend you the aid of my children. In return, I demand safe passage through the Dark Portal, and aid in transporting some cargo through there as well."

"You want to go to Draenor?" Tagar burst out. "Why?"

The smile Deathwing turned upon the Bonechewer

chieftain froze any further interruptions in the orc's throat. "My plans are my own, orc," the dragon-man said quietly, his voice almost a hiss. "But don't worry. It will not hinder your own plotting."

Gorefiend considered the offer. He needed dragons, whatever their color, for their plan to work. If he accepted the bargain, he would not need to deal with Rend again after all, though he might pound some humility into the self-styled warchief later if he had the chance. He didn't know what Deathwing was up to, but as long as it didn't interrupt their own plans he didn't see a problem with granting the dragon's request.

"Very well, Deathwing," he said finally.

"*Lord* Deathwing." He smiled without humor, and there was an edge to his voice. "Let's observe the proprieties, shall we?"

Gorefiend inclined his head. "Of course, Lord Deathwing. I agree. We will give your—people and cargo safe passage. But first I have a mission to accomplish in the north. I need to retrieve some cargo of my own."

"Very well," Deathwing agreed. He rose gracefully to his feet. "I will speak to my children and inform them of this bargain. When I return, I shall help expedite this task of yours." He dusted his hands off, although he had touched nothing, and without another word he strode into the shadows.

"Right," Gorefiend said after a moment, when he was sure the dragon was gone and not about to leap out at them from the darkness. "Let's pack up. We need to get moving, and we don't have much time." The others hastened to obey, all of them clearly happy to focus their attention upon breaking camp rather than on the strange figure who had just allied himself with them. Gorefiend just hoped Deathwing really was an ally—if he proved otherwise, there was nothing they could do to stop him.

Two figures, male and female, turned at Deathwing's approach as they waited, not far from the orc's encampment. The man was powerfully made and wore a short dark beard and neat mustache, while the woman was petite and had pale skin and long flowing straight hair. Both had glossy black hair and features similar to those Deathwing sported in his human guise.

"What news, Father?" the woman asked, her voice like silk over iron.

"They have agreed, as I knew they would, Onyxia," Deathwing replied. He stroked his daughter's cheek and she leaned her face into his hand, smiling up at him. "Soon we shall have two worlds at our disposal instead of one." He kissed her pale brow, then turned to her brother. "But I have another task for you while I am gone."

"Name it, Father," the man replied, "and it shall be done."

Deathwing smiled. "There are still orcs within Blackrock Spire. They have severed ties with their kin, and refuse to rejoin the Horde. That leaves them ripe for the plucking." His smile widened as he reached out to clasp his son by the shoulder. "When I return, Nefarian, I want this Rend Blackhand. You two will take control of the mountain and the orcs living in it. They will become our servants."

Nefarian grinned, his expression a mirror of his father's. "Little could be easier. We'll have the orcs and their mountain fortress waiting for you," he promised.

"Excellent." Deathwing regarded his children for a moment, then nodded. "Now I must return to our new allies, and aid them in their little tasks, that they may the more quickly turn to mine."

As their father returned the way he had come, Onyxia bared her teeth in a feral smile. "Well, brother, shall we go see to our new home and our new subjects?"

"Indeed we shall, sister," Nefarian replied with a laugh. "Good sport ahead, I think." He offered his arm, which she accepted, curling delicate, pale fingers around his powerful bicep, and together they vanished into the shadows.

A heartbeat later, the sound of great wings flapping overhead blended into the evening breeze.

CHAPTER NINE

"Faster! *Faster,* damn you!"

Danath lashed the reins against his steed's neck. His horse whickered in protest, its mouth flecked with foam, but obeyed.

Danath didn't hear the sound of the horse's increasingly rapid hoofbeats on hard-packed earth. He heard only the sound of weapons striking home, the grunts and howls of brutality, the cries of his men as they fell, taken by surprise at that strange darkness that had abruptly dropped to reveal the orcs waiting for them. They'd been led right into a trap. There was no time to strategize, no time to do anything but fight, and too many were so taken aback they didn't even have time to swing before the green tide had washed over them.

Danath closed his eyes, but he still saw them fall. Horses and men both, going down beneath the on-slaught that was as efficient as it was brutal and barbaric. He'd been looking right at Farrol, about to cry out a warning, when a huge orc had literally barreled into the boy's horse and unseated him. The boy went down at once. Danath didn't see Farrol die, but he thought he'd hear his screams for the rest of his life. Farrol, all afire with a desire for battle and glory, wanting to go kill his first orc. He hadn't even had a chance to strike a blow.

Danath had realized at once, sickened, that they would fail.

His men had seen it too. And they'd known what must be done.

"Commander! Get to the fortress!" Vann had urged him, even as he struggled with a much larger opponent wielding a club. "Tell them! We'll cover you!"

Other soldiers had added their voices in monosyllables, agreeing. Danath hesitated, feeling ripped in two. Stay here and fight with his men, or flee to perhaps save them?

"Go!" Vann cried, turning his head to shout at his commander. Their eyes met. "For the Sons of Lo—"

The orc had struck in that second of inattention, his club descending with deadly force. Danath had wheeled his horse around before Vann fell, and had spurred it on, screaming insanely at the beast, galloping away from the carnage and toward the fortress. Away from Farrol, and Vann, and all the others he had led here to their deaths.

Danath bit his lip hard enough to draw blood.

They'd been right, of course. Someone had to warn Nethergarde, and he had the authority and familial connections to make himself heard. His experience and leadership skills, too, could not afford to be lost.

But by the Light, he'd never done anything harder in his life than leave his men behind. He cursed softly, shook his head to clear it, and yelled at the horse again.

The trail twisted and turned in the life-drained land. Red dust rose beneath his horse's hooves. Danath clung like a burr and glanced up at one point to see the vast stone walls of Nethergarde Keep. Already he could see guards atop its parapets, pointing down at him and no doubt alerting others to his approach.

"Open the gates!" he shouted as loud as he could, holding his shield high before him so they could see the Alliance symbol emblazoned there. "Open the gates!"

The heavy timber and iron gates slowly parted, and he galloped on through without slowing. Once inside Danath slipped from his saddle and turned to the nearest soldier. "Who's in charge here?" he demanded, realizing he was gasping for breath.

"Sir, state your name and business, please," the soldier replied.

"I don't have time for this," Danath growled, grabbing the soldier by his breastplate collar and drawing him close. *"Who's in charge?"*

"I am," a voice said from behind him. Danath released the soldier and spun around, to find himself facing a tall, broad-shouldered man in the violet robes that marked him as one of the Dalaran wizards. The man had long white hair and a matching beard, but behind the lines on his face his eyes were young and alert.

"Danath Trollbane, isn't it?" the mage asked. "I thought you were with Turalyon?"

Danath nodded, both in confirmation of the man's statement and in recognition of Khadgar's identity, and sucked in air to speak. "Close the gate and arm your men! The Horde is here!"

Khadgar's eyes widened, but he did not argue. He signaled with his hand and men rushed to obey his silent commands. The gate was closed as someone came to take Danath's poor overworked mount and another approached with a waterskin. "What's happened?"

"Turalyon sent me with half the men we had at Stormwind." Danath gulped down water, warm but wet, and nodded cursory thanks to the man who'd brought it to him. "We left as soon as he received your message. He'll follow with the rest." He shook his head, wiping his mouth. "We were too late. The orcs have already rebuilt the portal, and they were waiting for us there. My boys . . . never stood a chance."

Khadgar nodded, his eyes somber. "I am sorry for their loss, but your warning gives us time to prepare. If the Horde plans to invade Azeroth again they will have to get past us first. And Nethergarde was built for this. They will not find this keep so easily taken."

"How will you defend it?" Danath asked, sufficiently

recovered from his ride to glance around. "Doesn't look like you have that many soldiers, and I don't see any ballistae or other siege engines along the walls."

"We do not have many soldiers, it is true," Khadgar agreed. "But that does not mean we are without defenses, or weapons. You will see."

"I suppose I will." Danath bared his teeth in a smile. "And when they come, I will be waiting."

The orcs arrived an hour later.

They swept up the path, filling the trail like water roiling down a narrow chute, elbowing each other aside in their haste to reach the keep's sturdy outer walls. Danath and Khadgar stood upon one of the taller parapets, watching the scene below.

"Damn . . . there are hundreds of them," Danath whispered, watching the Horde literally fill the plain before the keep and advance in a great sheet of flesh and weaponry. In the thick of the battle, he had not been able to notice the sheer numbers.

"Indeed," Khadgar said. The young-old mage did not seem concerned. "Not as many as during the Second War, though—either they lost much of their strength in those battles or they are withholding part of their full force now." He shrugged. "Not that it matters. We will deal with whatever they throw at us. You inquired about the keep's defenses? Watch."

He pointed, and Danath made out splashes of color all along the walls. Men and women stood there, clad in violet robes much like Khadgar's own. The arch-mage nodded then, and all the magi raised their hands as one. Danath felt his hair stand on end, and heard a faint hum. Then lightning arced down, destroying the first wave of orcs and scattering many of those behind them.

"Impressive," Danath acknowledged, his ears ringing from the accompanying thunderclap. "But how many times can they do that?"

Khadgar smiled. "I expect we're about to find out."

Turalyon crouched low over his horse, urging it on to greater speed. Even though he knew that waiting for reinforcements in the form of Alleria's rangers had been wise, something inside him insisted that they might be too late—that something was already happening at Nethergarde. He wasn't sure if it was a soldier's instinct or his own insecurities, but the paladin, normally gentle with beasts, kicked his horse again and again.

Beside him rode his men, Alleria, and her rangers. Alleria threw him a curious look, noting his spurring of the mount, but stayed silent. He glanced over at her, wanting to explain somehow, but all that came out was "Something's happening already."

She opened her mouth for a quip, but closed it when she saw the look on his face. Instead, she simply nodded, and bent over to whisper in her horse's ear. He realized she believed him, and for a moment, the worry and fear abated before a quick warmth.

The ride seemed to take forever. Through the meadows and rolling hills of Goldshire and the little town of Darkshire, through the gray land that was aptly named Deadwind Pass, near where Medivh had lived in Karazhan, into the muddy, malodorous Swamp of Sorrows. But now the land was changing, and Turalyon felt a lurch inside him as he noticed it. The foliage, though decomposing and unpleasant-smelling, was at least a sign of life. The ground beneath them was starting to turn red and dry, almost desertlike.

Alleria frowned. "It . . . feels dead," she said, shouting to be heard over the thunder of horses' hooves. Turalyon nodded, unable to spare breath. They pressed on through the bare landscape, cresting a small hill. There, rising like a white peak above the blood-red surroundings, was the keep. He drew his horse to a halt, straining to see what it was that nagged at his mind, and murmured, "Something's wrong."

Alleria shielded her eyes from the glare of the sun. She could see better than he, and when she gasped, Turalyon knew he'd been right.

"It's under attack!" she cried. "The Horde—Turalyon—it's like seeing the force from the Second War all over again! There must be hundreds of them!" The tone in her voice was half horror and half glee, and the cold-hot smile of hate and rage had twisted her face again. He recalled their conversation upon her arrival in Stormwind. It certainly looked like Alleria was going to get the chance to exterminate a lot of "vermin." He hated to see her so hungry for death—and feared that that hunger might make her reckless.

"We're almost upon them," he said, to her and to his commanders, who had drawn up beside him. "We'll strike from behind, pinning the orcs between Nethergarde and us. Once we've defeated them we'll enter the citadel and fortify its defenses in case they attack again. Let's go."

They raced toward the last rise. Right before they crested it, Turalyon again called a halt. Just beyond them the trail climbed a final time, past boulders and up a short incline, and then the plateau opened before them. From here, they could see it all.

Orcs, hundreds of them, were battering at Nethergarde's walls, though the keep thus far seemed to be weathering the attack with ease. Here and there were orc bodies. Turalyon saw at least one with an arrow through its neck; several others were badly charred, but some corpses seemed unharmed. He glanced up, spying the violet-robed figures upon the fortress's parapets, and despite the direness of the situation, he smiled slightly as he understood.

"We need to strike before they realize we're here. Rally the men and charge upon my command." His commanders, including Alleria, nodded and moved off to their own units, passing orders quietly. Weapons were drawn, straps were tightened, shields and visors were lowered, and the army advanced. Turalyon and the others crept forward, covering the last distance before the plateau, their horses' feet muffled by the dust; thank the Light, the orcs were too busy shouting and cursing and grunting to hear their approach.

It was time. They had gotten as far as stealth would take them. Turalyon took a deep breath and raised his hammer high over his head.

"Sons of Lothar!" he shouted, the power of the Holy Light magnifying his voice so it carried to everyone under his command. "For the Alliance—*for the Light!*"

His soldiers roared behind him, and several hundred throats uttered their own battle cries. Turalyon swung the hammer down and forward, and the charge began.

Some of the rearmost orcs heard his shout and turned, only to be trampled by the surging horses. Others were taken unawares, slain before they could even see the threat racing up from behind. From the fortress men cheered as Turalyon and his forces swept forward, laying about them with hammers and axes and swords. Alleria and her rangers fired arrow after arrow, drawing and nocking with inhuman speed, their aim unerring, their horses never breaking stride. In a surprisingly short time Turalyon had won through to Nethergarde's enormous front gates, which swung open as he approached. Turalyon hesitated, looking back over the battle. His eyes met Alleria's. He gestured toward the gate. She frowned slightly—she was as reluctant as he to leave the thick of battle, but they were the leaders of their units and she knew, as he did, that they should speak with the commander of the keep as soon as they could.

When she nodded, Turalyon spurred his steed through the narrow gap, crushing an orc that tried to follow. Alleria was beside him, close enough that her leg brushed against his, and then the gates shut again behind them.

"Ah, good, Alleria—you've brought Turalyon to us just in time." Turalyon turned toward the speaker and smiled as he recognized Khadgar. Roughly they embraced; Turalyon had missed the friend he'd grown to so like and admire as they worked together through the Second War. He wished they were not reuniting under these circumstances. Alleria gave the mage a curt nod.

"I came as fast as I could," Turalyon said. He spied another man he recognized, and he smiled in relief. "Danath," he greeted his second-in-command. "I am glad to see you're safe." He glanced around. "But . . . where are your men?"

"Dead," Danath replied curtly.

"By the Light . . . all of them?" Turalyon whispered. Danath had taken fully half the warriors of Stormwind. Danath gritted his teeth at the words.

"The orcs had a nice little trap ready for us when we reached the valley. They slaughtered my boys before they could react." Danath's voice cracked ever so slightly. "My boys," he had called them. Turalyon realized Danath blamed himself for the deaths. "They sacrificed themselves that I might reach here and warn Khadgar of the Horde's approach."

"They did the right thing. And so did you," Turalyon

assured his friend and subordinate. "It is an awful thing, to lose the men under your command, but alerting Nethergarde was the first priority." He frowned. "Khadgar—we need to figure out why they're attacking now."

"It's obvious—they need to get past us to reach the rest of Azeroth," Khadgar replied, but Turalyon shook his head.

"No, that doesn't make sense. Think about it. They lack the numbers to take this keep, and they must know it. I'm willing to bet this is not the entire Horde—it can't be. So where are the rest? Why attack with only a partial army?"

Khadgar's white brows drew together over his youth's eyes. "You raise an excellent point."

"One way to find out," Danath said brusquely. "Bring me an orc, and believe me, I'll get out of him what we want to know." The way he said it and the set of his jaw made Turalyon flinch. He saw in Danath's face an echo of Alleria's single-minded hatred of the orcs. For all their brutality, for all the pain and damage and hurt to this world they had caused, he could not help but pity whatever captive Danath Trollbane took it upon himself to question. He only hoped the orc would speak quickly—for its sake, and their own.

They were waiting for his approval. He nodded reluctantly and turned to Alleria, but before he could speak she had hurried up one of the towers, anxious to be doing something, anything. She called down the order, waited for the reply, then grinned fiercely.

"It will not take long," she said. Turalyon expected her to climb back down. Instead she stayed where she was, nocking an arrow to her long, elegant bow, taking aim, and joining in the battle from that vantage point.

The elf was right. Not three minutes later a cry went up outside: "We've got one!"

The massive gates were again opened. A pair of Turalyon's men rode through, half-dragging an unconscious orc between them. They dumped the body on the ground at their general's feet. Blood covered its bare green head, and its eyes were closed. It didn't stir as it hit the ground.

"One orc, still alive, sir!" one of the two men reported. "He took a good hit to his head, but he'll live. For a while at least." Turalyon nodded, dismissing them. Both men saluted before wheeling their horses about and charging back out the gate, diving once more into the fray.

"Let's see what we have here," Danath muttered. He bound the orc's hands and feet with heavy rope, then splashed water on the monster's face. It awoke with a start, grimacing, and then frowned and started to growl as it noticed the restraints.

"Why are you attacking us now?" Danath demanded, leaning down over the orc. "Why hit Nethergarde when you aren't at full strength?"

"I show you strength!" the orc warrior roared, struggling against his bonds. But they held fast.

"I don't think you quite understand," Danath said

slowly, drawing his dagger and idly waving it mere inches from the orc's face. "I asked you a question. You'd best answer it. Why attack Nethergarde now? Why not wait until the entire Horde is here?"

Blood and spittle spattered Danath's face. He jerked back, surprised, then slowly wiped the spit off. "I'm tired of playing with you," he growled, and leaned forward with the dagger.

"Wait!" Turalyon ordered. He deeply disapproved of torture, and he was beginning to think that even if he permitted Danath to continue, the orc would say nothing of use—orcs had a high tolerance for pain—and chances were he'd pass out, or die, before speaking. "There might be another way to find out."

Danath stayed his hand. He felt Alleria's eyes on him, angry, wanting to see the creature hurt. But that would solve nothing.

Turalyon closed his eyes and slowed his breathing, reaching for the quiet, still pool deep inside him, the center where no matter what was raging in his head or heart, he was at peace. From that place of calmness, he asked for aid, for the Light. He felt a tingling along his skin as the Light responded, granting him its power and its unspeakable grace. He heard gasps from his friends and a frightened cry from the prisoner, and inhaled deeply, opening his eyes to see the familiar shimmering along his hands, his arms. Danath and Khadgar stared at him, their eyes wide in shock. And as for the orc, it was a huddled ball of green at his feet, whimpering incoherently. When he spoke, Turalyon's voice was completely calm and controlled. There was no place here for hate or the heat of anger. Not when one stood fully in the Light.

"Now, by the Holy Light, you will answer our questions and do so truly," Turalyon intoned, reaching out and resting his palm against the orc's forehead. There was a sudden, blinding flash of light. He felt a spark leap from flesh to flesh. The orc shrieked, and when Turalyon removed his hand there was a dark handprint there, as if it had been burned in. The orc shivered and groveled, weeping. Turalyon hoped he had not scared it senseless.

"Why attack now?" he asked yet again.

"To—to distract you," it sobbed. "From the thefts." It had been stubbornly silent before; now it apparently couldn't speak fast enough. "Ner'zhul needs things. Artifacts. He ordered us, attack the keep. Alliance stay busy here, and not see anything else."

Khadgar was stroking his full beard. He'd recovered faster than Danath, who was still staring at the young paladin. Turalyon risked a glance up at Alleria to find her, too, looking at him with an expression of stunned disbelief. When their eyes met, she colored slightly and looked away.

"A simple plan, but simple plans are often the best," Khadgar offered. "What artifacts, though? And why would he need any such thing from our world and not from his own?"

22222222222

The orc shook his head, trembling. "He doesn't know," Turalyon said. "He'd tell us if he knew." With the Light upon him so, the orc could not lie.

The gates creaked open just enough for two elves to squeeze through before it shut again. Turalyon glanced up as they approached him, his eyes narrowing as he realized they both looked exhausted. "What news?"

"Stormwind, sir," one of the elves replied. "Someone broke into the royal library. The guards found the bodies of the two men stationed outside the door and the one inside. Looks like one died by an orc axe, sir."

"Orcs? In the royal library?" Turalyon whirled to stare at Khadgar, then at the orc, who cringed away. "Artifacts . . . ," he murmured, putting the pieces together.

"The perfect distraction," Khadgar was forced to admit. "Damn it. I'd say that simple plan worked very well indeed. We were busy here fighting the orcs, and someone made off with—" He turned to the elves. "What exactly *did* someone make off with, if anything?"

Now the elven scouts looked even less happy. "Unfortunately, you are right, Lord Wizard—one thing was indeed missing."

"And that was?" Turalyon prompted.

The elf cleared his throat. "The, uh . . . the Book of Medivh."

"By the Light," Turalyon whispered, feeling a knot form in the pit of his stomach. The Book of Medivh? The spellbook of the greatest mage in all the world, the man who had helped the orcs create the original portal? The book containing all the brilliant wizard's many secrets? In the hands of the orcs?

Beside him Khadgar seemed stricken as well. "Turalyon . . . I need that book! To close the portal!"

"What?" Turalyon cried.

"Medivh and Gul'dan created the thing. That spellbook could tell me how to close it! Not only that—if the orcs have it, they can use it against us in any number of ways. This is bad. This is very, very bad."

Turalyon shook his head, reaching for the calm place inside himself. "I understand. But we can't worry about it right now—we've got orcs outside, and distraction or not, they're still a great danger. Our job is to protect this keep, and prevent them from spreading past it. Once that's done, then . . . well, we'll go from there."

He eyed his friends, who nodded slowly. He glanced up at Alleria, thinking he saw a hint of approval glimmer in her green eyes before she again lifted her bow to resume firing.

"You're right, General," Khadgar said, inclining his head. "We have a keep to defend. We can't solve a puzzle if we're not alive to do so."

Turalyon gave a weary, worried grin, climbed back atop his mount, and rode again into the maelstrom that was battle.

CHAPTER TEN

"We'll divide into two groups," Gorefiend instructed Fenris, Tagar, and his death knights. Around them was the bustle of a camp being broken as swiftly as possible. "I need—"

He glanced up as the sounds stilled abruptly. Deathwing had rejoined them, looking as perfectly human as he had before. He caught Gorefiend's eye.

"What, did you think I would not return?"

"No, of course I did."

Something about how he said it obviously displeased the great dragon, whose black brows drew together. Gorefiend realized the words could be interpreted as arrogance and hastened to add, "I completely trust your word, Lord Deathwing."

The dragon looked mollified. Gorefiend continued, "We need to travel to Alterac, and from there to Dalaran. May we ask you for the aid of your children in this?"

"You may. I will summon them now." Deathwing tilted back his head, his mouth opening far wider than any true human's could, and uttered a strange rippling cry that teased at the ears, creating phantoms of other sounds and generating a cool breeze that reeked of old death. Some of the orcs shrank back, and even Gorefiend was hard put to keep his face calm as the earth itself shook and rumbled beneath his feet, as if replying directly to the black dragonlord.

Finally, Deathwing closed his mouth and his face assumed its normal proportions. "There we are," he said, grinning in obvious delight at the discomfiture of both orc and death knight. "They will come."

"Thank you." Gorefiend bowed. He turned toward the two orc chieftains. He was not looking forward to what he had to ask of them, and feared they might balk; but it had to be done. "Your task will be challenging, but vital. I must ask you to go to the Tomb of Sargeras."

Tagar growled uneasily, and even the sturdier Fenris looked upset. "You send us to our deaths then!" Fenris snapped.

"Not at all. There is an artifact there that Ner'zhul requires. I will send along Ragnok to aid you and explain what—"

"Gul'dan—the powerful Gul'dan died there!" Fenris interrupted. "We have heard the stories—of how Gul'dan raised it from the ocean bed, only to be attacked by the monstrous things guarding that horrible place. We have heard how only a few escaped and that most died there, screaming in pain. . . . Evil lives in that darkness, Gorefiend!"

The death knight spared only a moment to be amused at the comment; he well knew that the humans on this world thought the orcs themselves monstrous, evil things.

"Do you think I would send you and one of my own knights if I believed you would not be successful?" They had no answer for that and exchanged uneasy glances. Gorefiend graced them with his death-rictus smile. "That's better. As I was saying, you must retrieve a certain artifact. Ragnok will explain everything. Once you've found it, return to the Dark Portal as soon as possible and we will meet you there. The Warsong clan won't be able to keep the Alliance distracted and busy forever."

Both chieftains nodded, looking more confident. Gorefiend regarded them for a moment. Tagar was a powerful fighter, but he had no subtlety and little intelligence. Fenris, however, was clever and subtle enough for both of them, and his bearing told Gorefiend he would keep the young Bonechewer chieftain in line. Satisfied, Gorefiend turned to the dragonlord. "Great Deathwing—can you bear them to the tomb?"

The dragon-man nodded. "We know this island of which you speak," he said. "And here are my children— enough to accommodate both groups, I think."

Even as the words left Deathwing's lips, Gorefiend

heard a sharp flurry of noise, as if a heavy rain were striking, its pellets slashing through the air and into the rock and earth all around. Looking up, Gorefiend did see dark streaks against the stars, but they were most certainly not raindrops. Beneath his feet, he felt the earth rumble again. Suddenly he saw specks of bright orange as the streaks increased in size, swelling and becoming diamond-shaped. His eyes widened as he realized the orange glows he had seen was fiery magma in the beasts' huge jaws, and the increasingly loud noise was the beating of gigantic wings.

Gorefiend watched, awestruck, as the dragons swooped down. The very earth shook as the mighty creatures landed, liquid fire dripping from their mouths to steam, glowing and sullen, on the earth. They were beautiful in their deadliness. Their scales gleamed in the starlight, a glossy black like a midnight pool, and their claws seemed like polished iron as they perched on the earth or on giant boulders, seeming to Gorefiend's eyes a living, lethal extension of the earth upon which they stood. When they had all come to ground, the dragons folded their great leathery wings and watched the orcs closely, their ebony eyes staring, their heads swiveling and tails flicking slightly. Gorefiend was reminded of a cat analyzing its prey before it casually dispatched it, and shivered slightly.

"Here are my children," Deathwing announced, the pride evident in his voice. "The finest of all the creatures of Azeroth!" He pointed to a particularly large dragon nearby, two great horns jutting up from its brow. "Sabellian," Deathwing announced, and the dragon lowered its head as its name was announced, "is my lieutenant in all things. He and a few companions will bear your orcs to the island you spoke of. And as for your jaunt to Alterac, I'll take you there myself."

"I am honored," Gorefiend started to say, but Deathwing silenced him with an impatient wave of his hand. His eyes glittered like banked coals as he continued, "Don't get too full of yourself, death knight. I do not do it to show you respect, but to ensure success. My plans will come to naught if you fail. I suggest you don't, not if you wish to remain alive—well, at least as alive as you are now."

Deathwing smirked slightly. Then he began to laugh, the sound rising from an ordinary human laugh to mutate into something much darker and much more frightening. He threw his head back and lifted his arms, the gesture stirring up a wind that buffeted Gorefiend and the others against the rocks behind them. What was he doing? Gorefiend wondered for a frantic moment if this whole thing had been some sort of dreadful joke, and that at last Deathwing had tired of the game. The flames of their dying campfires flickered and swayed in the sudden gust, casting grotesque dancing shadows. Behind the maniacally laughing man, Deathwing's own shadow swelled and grew, twisting as if it were a living thing itself, changing form as it rose behind him, vast wings spreading out across the mountain range, engulfing all his dragons and much of the surrounding land as well. For a third time that night, the earth trembled, and this time many of the orcs fell hard to the ground. Sudden fissures split open, scalding steam rippling the space above them, red-orange magma in their depths echoing the liquid flame that dripped from the dragons' mouths.

Even as his shadow rose and took on more detail, Deathwing's human body contorted. Its edges grew indistinct, as if it were being absorbed into the shadows behind him. Only his eyes remained clear, growing longer and more slanted, taking on a reddish cast from the reflected glow of the flames but then outshining those thin fires.

Still the shadow grew, as did the shifting, blurring body that cast it. It seemed to have its own substance now, and was somehow pushing away from the rocks. The body elongated and increased in bulk, changing rapidly to match its shadow. A black dragon, yes, but more—*the* black dragon, the mightiest, most powerful, most dangerous of them all; the father of the flight.

Gorefiend thought he would be the most perfect specimen of his kind, but as the shape before him grew more distinct, the death knight realized that Deathwing lacked the dark beauty of his children. Giant plates made of gleaming metal ran along the dragon's spine from the tail to the back of the long narrow head. Beneath them Gorefiend caught glimpses of red and gold and white in radiating lines, as if molten fire were somehow . . . breaking through. As if the metallic plates fastened onto Deathwing's spine were physically holding him together. The effect was disjointed, disharmonious, and suddenly Gorefiend realized why Deathwing was so meticulous about his appearance in human form—his dragon form was flawed.

Red eyes blazed now from a reptilian face. Deathwing spread his wings wide, their great leathery surfaces as dark as a starless sky and as wrinkled as an old crone. Power pulsated from the dragon in waves, like heat from a raging fire.

"Come, little death knight, if you dare," Deathwing commanded, his voice now a deep rumble. He lowered his head almost to the ground, and Gorefiend actually found himself frozen in place for a moment before he forced his body to obey. Trembling, he clambered up onto the dragon where his neck met his heavily armored shoulders. Fortunately, the unnatural metal plates provided easy handholds. The others emulated him, and soon all Gorefiend's band were astride the dragons.

With no warning, Deathwing launched himself into the air with a powerful kick and a downward sweep of his wings, lifting them up into the sky by sheer muscle alone. Gorefiend clung tightly as the ground fell away, and then Deathwing's wings beat down and back, and again, and they were soaring, the air supporting them as if the massive dragon were as light as a stray leaf. Sabellian and his chosen followers split off, racing forward and disappearing into the night, while Death-wing banked to the right, that wing dipping so low Gorefiend thought it might scrape the ground, and headed for Alterac.

Aiden Perenolde, king of Alterac and prisoner in his own palace, awoke with a start. He had been dreaming, and still remembered vague flashes of something large and dark and reptilian looming above him and . . . laughing? Perhaps, he thought bitterly, it was a metaphor for his fate.

He rubbed his face, chasing away the nightmare, but sleep would not return. Muttering, Perenolde rose from his bed. Perhaps some wine would help. He poured himself a glass of the dark red liquid—red as blood, he mused—and sipped it slowly, thinking about the choices that had led him here.

It had seemed so easy at the time. So wise, so right. The orcs were going to destroy everything in their path. So he'd negotiated with them to save his people. He frowned into his glass as he remembered his conversation with Orgrim Doomhammer. It was going to work just fine—except somehow it hadn't. His so-called "treachery" had been discovered, and the orcs had failed to do the one thing they apparently excelled at—destroy things. Stupid great green oafs.

The doors to his bedchamber suddenly burst open. Perenolde started at the noise, spilling the wine all over his sleeping clothes, as several large figures charged in.

For an instant he simply gaped, caught up in the sensation that he was still in a reverie as the great green oafs he'd just been brooding about charged into his private chambers. Things got even more surreal as the orcs— what were orcs doing in his palace?—seized him and shoved him to the door. Recovering his wits slightly, Perenolde tried to twist away. Without breaking stride, one of them hoisted the king over his shoulder like a sack of grain and they continued. They stalked through the palace, past the bodies of Perenolde's guards, and out the front doors. Then the orcs set Perenolde on his feet again.

"No! Please, I—" His cries died in his throat. A vast creature, large as the palace itself, loomed above him, a mass of black scales and gleaming plates and leathery wings. The long head, easily as big as he was, swiveled to study him, the red eyes glowing.

"King Perenolde." The dry voice did not seem to emanate from the dragon's long fang-filled mouth, and with a start Perenolde realized the creature was not alone. Someone sat astride its neck, up against its shoulders. Or perhaps some*thing*, Perenolde corrected himself, noting the rider's glowing eyes, hooded cloak, and strange wrapped limbs. Hadn't he heard of such creatures during the Second War? As agents of the Horde?

"King Perenolde," the rider said again. "We have come to speak with you."

"Yes?" Perenolde replied, his voice little more than a squeak. "With me? Really?"

"During the war, you formed a treaty with the Horde."

"Yes?" Perenolde made the connection. "Yes!" he said quickly. "Yes, I did. With Doomhammer himself! I was an ally! I am on your side!"

"Where is the Book of Medivh?" the strange rider demanded. "Give it to me!"

"What?" The incongruity of the question momentarily banished Perenolde's fear. "The book? Why?"

"I have no time for debate," the rider snapped. He muttered something else, gesturing with one hand, and suddenly Perenolde was racked with pain, his entire body spasming. "That is but a taste of what I can do to you," the stranger informed him, the words reaching Perenolde as if from a great distance as the pain washed across him. "Hand over the spellbook now!"

Perenolde tried to nod but could not, and fell to his hands and knees instead. Then the pain was gone. He stood slowly, his limbs still trembling, and eyed the two powerful creatures before him, the dragon's burning gaze searing deep into his soul. Somehow that stare seemed less troubling than it had before. The pain had helped clear Perenolde's head and focus his mind. This could be an opportunity if he could just keep his wits about him.

"I have the book," he admitted. "Or rather, I had it stolen from Stormwind and I know where it is." He brushed absently at the wine stain on his sleeping clothes. "I thought I might need it as a bargaining chip.

The Alliance has claimed my throne and my kingdom because I helped your kind in the last war." He studied the rider—a death knight, he thought, suddenly remembering the term. Yes, clearly he was a death knight, which meant he held some importance in the Horde.

Perenolde considered. "I will give you the book . . . for a favor." The rider did not speak, but something in his bearing indicated he was still listening. "The Alliance has stationed troops here in my kingdom, to watch me and to control me. Destroy them, and the book is yours."

For a second the rider did not move. Then he nodded. "Very well," he replied. "It shall be done. We will return afterward and you will tell us where to find the book." The death knight whispered something to the black dragon and it leaped skyward, his wings carrying him aloft. A rustling all around startled Perenolde, followed by the sight of several more dark shapes taking flight.

Perenolde stared as the black dragons flew from sight, and then he started to laugh. Could it be that simple? Trade an old spellbook—one he could not use himself—for his freedom and his kingdom's independence? He continued to laugh, aware of the manic quality the peals held.

"What's going on?" came a voice. Perenolde started, then realized it was his eldest son. "That . . . that was a dragon . . . and I think a death knight!" Aliden continued in a shocked tone. "What did you say to them? How did you convince them to leave?"

Perenolde laughed on, unable to stop himself. "Damn it, Father!" Aliden burst out, punching his father in the jaw hard enough to send the older man sprawling. "Two years I've spent trying to overcome the stigma you've cast on our family name. *Two years!*" Aliden glared down at his father, tears streaking his face. "You stupid, selfish bastard, you've ruined everything!"

Perenolde shook his head and rose to his feet, but froze mid-motion as he heard a new sound over his son's recriminations. What was that? It sounded like— yes, like a ballista releasing its payload, the rush through the air and the sudden release of the cargo, then the dull whump of the impact. He heard it again, and again, and realized the sounds were coming from over the rise, on the far side of the city. Near the barracks the Alliance forces had commandeered. He knew then what the sounds must mean, and began laughing again.

The dragons had begun their attack.

Aliden stared at him, then toward the sounds, then back at him again, comprehension and horror slowly washing across his face. "What have you done to us, Father?" he demanded. *"What have you done?"*

But Perenolde could not control himself enough to answer. Instead he slumped to the ground and sat there in a heap, shaking with mixed chortles and sobs, as he listened to the sounds of death and destruction.

He had never heard anything so lovely in all his life.

"Over there." Sabellian circled, then settled gracefully onto the ground. "Boats."

"Boats?" Tagar had asked when Ragnok had explained the plan, clinging to the great black dragon's neck as they flew through the night. "I thought the dragons were flying us to this island."

But the death knight had shaken his cowled head. "It is too far for them to fly directly," he had explained. "They'll take us to Menethil Harbor, and we will obtain boats there to complete the journey."

Fenris had frowned. "Menethil . . . that is the name of a line of kings of this world," he had said quietly.

"Yes . . . it is an Alliance outpost," Ragnok had admitted. "But it is the closest port to the island."

Fenris had disliked the idea, but he supposed it could not be helped. The dragons had set them down on a stretch of hilly land close to the harbor, separated from it by a small body of water. Fenris slipped off the dragon and gazed over the dark inlet speculatively. It looked quiet, but there were lights here and there. The harbor likely would be guarded. He motioned to his warriors, pointed at the harbor, and lifted a finger to his lips. As silently as he could, Fenris slipped into the water and began to swim as the dragons, their task discharged, took to the skies. The dragons had flown as close as they dared; even those in a little town, deep in slumber, would be roused by several dragons landing right next to them.

Most of the orcs were not armored and swam quickly, but those who had bits and pieces of plate, mail, or leather armor had a harder time of it. The orcs emerged dripping and chilled. Fenris glanced at them. Their green faces loomed pale in what light there was, and he frowned. He scooped up a handful of dirt and began to smear it on his face.

"Coat yourself with mud," he instructed both Tagar and the other orcs as quietly as possible. "We will need to move quickly, quietly, and without being seen." The rest of them complied. Fenris felt a quick stab of wistful memory as he watched his companions smear their faces with mud. Once, his skin had been this color; once, all orcs had been this shade of brown. Had things been so bad then? Had what they'd gained since that time been worth losing their world for? Sometimes, he wondered.

He shook off the melancholy and focused his attention on his companions, nodding as he saw they were all but invisible now in the darkness. "We only need a few boats. We'll take those three there, closest to the water's edge. Move quickly, and kill anyone who gets in your way." He glared at Tagar. "And *only* those in the way. Tagar, keep your warriors in line. Silent kills only—we don't want anyone to sound the alarm."

"Let them!" Tagar blustered. "We will strew the water with their bones!"

"No!" Fenris's sharp hiss cut him off. "Remember what Gorefiend said! We get in and get out, that's it!"

Tagar grumbled, but Fenris glared at him until the Bonechewer chieftain nodded.

"Good." Fenris gripped his axe, a narrow-bladed affair with a short haft and wicked edges. "Let's go."

They crept forward, moving silently across the moist earth, weapons at the ready. The first orcs had just reached the wooden piers when a dwarf walked past, clearly on patrol. He had not seen them yet, but he would any second, and Fenris nodded to the two warriors in front. One of them darted forward, grabbed the dwarf's head, and yanked his axe across the dwarf's exposed neck, severing his head completely. The body dropped with only a soft thud, the head rolling a short distance away, its expression revealing just the beginnings of surprise.

They advanced upon the boats Fenris had selected. Another guard approached, this one human, and one of Tagar's warriors dropped him with a single crushing blow to the head. Fenris nodded his approval. He'd been worried about the Bonechewer orcs, but perhaps they were not as unruly and undisciplined as he had always thought. He moved on, then heard a strange crunching sound—and a short, breathy wail. Fenris whirled around. The orc was still crouched over his recent victim, and he was making the crunching sound—but not the wailing. Then, even as Fenris realized what the Bonechewer was doing, the wailing drew out and became words.

"Ah!" the guard cried, shrieking in pain. "My legs! It's eating my legs!"

A cry went up and lights were lit in buildings. Humans and dwarves poured forth from seemingly nowhere, and Fenris realized they weren't going to be able to escape without a fight. He attacked fiercely, hoping to end it quickly. His orcs rallied around him, and soon cleared the immediate area of humans. But Fenris knew the docks would be overrun before long.

"To the boats!" he shouted, raising his axe high. They clambered into the three boats, one Bonechewer dropping his victim's remains back on the pier, hacked free the anchor lines, and cast off. It was clumsy, but the orcs managed to get all three boats pushed away from the docks and out into the bay beyond. Even as they left the harbor behind, however, a beacon fire flared to light.

"This is Baradin Bay," Ragnok said, "and the fleet of Kul Tiras patrols it regularly. They will see the beacon and be here within minutes."

"Then we should be gone before they arrive," Fenris replied grimly. He pulled a pair of oars from the long case set between the benches lining the boat and tossed them to the nearest warrior. "Row!" he shouted, grabbing more oars and distributing them as well. "Row with all your might!" The other boats followed his lead, and soon they were skimming across the water, their powerful arms lending the boats speed.

But it was not enough, Fenris realized as he saw other, larger boats racing toward them. "Kul Tiras

naval vessels!" Ragnok confirmed, studying their out-
lines. "Admiral Proudmoore hates orcs—he will stop at
nothing to destroy us!"

"Can we fight them?" Fenris asked, but he knew the
answer even before the death knight shook his head.

"They are trained for ship-to-ship battle. And they
can outrun us as well. We do not stand a chance!"

Fenris glanced up at the star-pocked sky and nodded.
"Perhaps we don't. But then again, perhaps we do. Keep
rowing!"

Their boats moved quickly, but as Ragnok had predicted, their pursuit was faster. The human boats drew
closer, until Fenris could make out the grim men clad
all in green who stood ready at the taller ships' railings.
Many of them had bows ready, while others had short
swords and axes and spears in hand. He knew his warriors could defeat a larger number of humans if they
were on land, but here at sea they were at a serious dis-
advantage.

Fortunately, they had not come alone.

Just as the first human boat came close enough for
Fenris to make out the men's faces, a dark shape
dropped out of the sky between them. Massive wings
flapped hard enough to drive the boat back and knock
the men off their feet. Then the dragon's jaws opened
wide and fire shot forth, engulfing the ship's prow. The
tar-coated wood caught at once, and soon the entire
boat was alight. The sounds of screaming and crackling fire lifted Fenris's heart.

But the humans did not flee. Again their boats closed in, and again a black dragon intercepted it and charred timbers and crew alike. A third time the humans tried, their weapons bouncing off the dragons' tough hides, and a third boat was reduced to ash and bone. After that the human ships fell back, letting the three orc-captured boats pull away. A cheer rang out from the orcs.

"They're giving up!" Tagar cried from the prow of the boat beside them.

"They're no match for the dragons and they know it," Fenris corrected. "But I would not think they are giving up."

"Any sign of smaller fires on the other ships? Controlled ones?" asked Ragnok.

Fenris studied the retreating vessels. "Yes, I see a signal fire, and smoke," he said finally.

"They're warning the rest of their fleet," Ragnok said. "They'll be waiting for us."

Tagar laughed from the prow of the boat beside them. "The warnings will come too late," he proclaimed, licking blood from his axe blade. "By the time the humans have gathered their courage to come after us again, we will be long gone with our prize."

Fenris nodded. For the first time, he hoped that the Bonechewer was right, and that he was wrong.

CHAPTER ELEVEN

Antonidas, archmage and leader of the Kirin Tor, sat in his study examining a recently arrived scroll. The news was grave indeed: Admiral Proudmoore reported that a group of orcs had stolen several ships from Menethil Harbor. Worse, when he'd pursued them, Proudmoore's ships had been driven back . . . by dragons. *Black* dragons. Antonidas felt a vein throb in his temple and rubbed it. During the Second War the Horde had somehow enlisted the aid of the red dragons, and now that the portal had been restored it seemed they had allied with the black dragons as well. It was almost unbelievable. Two dragonflights? How could the Alliance hope to stand against that?

A soft tap came at his door. "Enter, Krasus," Antonidas called out, his magical skills already telling him who was calling at this late hour.

"You left word that you wished to see me?" the other mage asked as he entered and closed the door behind him, keeping his delicate features deliberately bland. Antonidas suspected it was to stop him from losing his temper, but if so it did not succeed.

"Yes, I left word," Antonidas replied, all but spitting the words through his long gray-streaked beard. "Months ago! Where have you been?"

"I had other business to attend to," Krasus answered evasively, perching himself on the edge of Antonidas's desk. Lamplight caught the hints of red and black lingering in his silver hair and turned the whole into fire and gleaming metal.

"Other business? You serve on the Kirin Tor, Krasus, a fact I should not have to remind you of," Antonidas pointed out, frowning. "If you cannot make time for such duties, perhaps it would be best if another was appointed in your stead."

To his surprise, the slender mage bowed his head. "If that is truly what you wish, I will step down," Krasus stated quietly. "I would prefer to remain, however, and I promise you that Dalaran and the Kirin Tor currently have my utmost attention."

Antonidas studied him a moment, then finally nodded. He didn't really want to lose Krasus—the enigmatic mage had surprising stores of both power and knowledge. And despite the man's occasional evasiveness, Antonidas did feel his colleague had all their best interests at heart.

"Take a look at this," he said, thrusting the scroll into the other man's hands. He watched as Krasus read, shock and growing horror on his face.

"The black dragonflight!" Krasus whispered when he had finished, rerolling the scroll and placing it carefully on the desk as if the very words might attack. "My research leads me to believe the red dragons have no love of battle or bloodshed, and only served the Horde under duress. But the black! That pairing seems more logical and deliberate—and much more dangerous."

"I agree," Antonidas said. "Krasus, you are our resident expert on dragon lore. Do you think there is any way to stop them, or at least limit their effectiveness?"

"I—" A sharp keening cut through the still night air. The two wizards locked eyes for a moment. They knew what that sound meant—it was an alarm. Krasus stayed silent while Antonidas tried to identify it. Which of the old spells was it—was it that one, or . . .

"The Arcane Vault!" he said at last, eyes widening. "It's been breached!"

Krasus looked as frightened as he felt. The Arcane Vault stood near the heart of the Violet Citadel and was protected by the strongest magics the magi could devise. It held many of the city's most powerful artifacts, as well as some items the magi could not use themselves but could not risk allowing to fall into anyone else's hands.

Standing, Krasus held out his hand. Antonidas grasped it and without a word the two teleported to the Arcane Vault.

The world around them blurred, the book-lined walls of Antonidas's cozy study disappearing to be replaced in a blink with a large stone chamber. The

floor and walls were roughly hewn from the earth itself, and the ceiling was vaulted. The room had no windows and only one door. Except for the space around
that lone exit, the rest of the room was lined with
shelves and boxes and bookcases, all of them full.

Standing amid the dust and the artifacts were several
men. At least, Antonidas thought they were men. Then
his senses detected the rippling black aura around each
of them, and even before they turned, revealing glowing eyes gleaming in the shadows of hoods, he knew
what manner of creatures had pierced their defenses.
Knew, and quailed from that knowing.

Death knights.

Human corpses animated by dead orc warlocks,
they reeked of dark power. Enough to make Antonidas
blanch with horror; enough to pierce even the powerful wards that had been erected here. And so they had
come to this highly protected place—

—for what?

This place housed artifacts galore—easily enough
weapons for the death knights to win the war once and
for all. Yet they did not move to take the priceless ob-
jects. They stood in a circle around a central figure,
who bore something clutched in his hand. Antonidas
concentrated on the item. It was extremely powerful,
and the taste of its magic felt familiar. But it wasn't
until the lead death knight shifted, raising the object he
held slightly, and light reflected off its facets and cast
violet rays around the room that Antonidas realized

what single treasure would be great enough for the death knights to ignore everything else.

"He has the Eye of Dalaran!" Antonidas shouted, raising one hand to cast a mystic bolt while with the other he summoned the rest of the Kirin Tor. Only a handful could fit into the Arcane Vault, but at least he and Krasus would have reinforcements when they invariably fell victim to the crushing fatigue that often accompanied a wizardly duel.

This was no formal duel, however, Antonidas thought as his mystic bolt caught one of the death knights in the torso and slammed the creature into the far wall, smoke rising from the hole in his chest. One of the other death knights raised his truncheon, the jewels along it winking in the candlelight, and Antonidas felt as if something had gripped his heart in ice-cold hands and started to squeeze. He clutched at his chest with both hands, pressing hard to push away the pain that knifed through him. He managed to mutter a spell and a violet glow sprang up around him, dissipating the cold. He could see the attack spell through his mystic senses, looking like a colossal hand shaped from smoke, and slapped the thing away, sending it careening back into its master. The death knight went sprawling.

Another of the Kirin Tor teleported in beside him, an elven woman with long black hair. One slender, pale hand went to Antonidas's chest while the other gestured at the terrifying intruders. Antonidas was dimly aware of other figures materializing in the room. He gasped for breath as his lungs expanded and his heart beat once more, blessed warmth flowing through him even as he saw two death knights begin to writhe in pain. Flame suddenly licked at their limbs, torsos, and heads. Two other death knights suddenly stepped back. Antonidas's eyes widened in shock as he realized that they were attempting to escape. Distorted shadows cast by the flames of their dying brethren suddenly took on a life of their own, wrapping about the death knights and absorbing their flesh until they were nothing but wispy memories.

Although they would not survive—if such a term could be used—the beleaguered death knights would not go into death's final embrace alone. Still weak from the attack and his attempt to combat it, Antonidas could do nothing but watch helplessly as the two death knights turned, their bodies still blazing, and attacked the woman who had saved Antonidas. Sathera's pale face contorted, her head falling back and her black hair cascading around her like a shroud as air was forced from her lungs. Antonidas heard a crack as the increasing force collapsed her chest and crushed her bones.

"Sathera! No!"

Antonidas turned to see Prince Kael'thas, his handsome features contorted with rage at the death of his friend and colleague. The elf raised both hands and drew them apart. Across the room one of the death knights jerked and then shrieked as his body was literally torn limb from limb. The sight shocked Antonidas back to his senses.

"Kael'thas!" he shouted into the tumult as he struggled to his feet. "Kael'thas!" On the second attempt the elf turned and fixed Antonidas with his powerful stare.

"Don't let them teleport!" Antonidas shouted, fending off an attack with one hand by erecting a quick shield upon which the deathbolt shattered. The elven prince shook his head as if to clear it, then nodded. He turned the full fury of his gaze upon the intruders and moved his hands to work the spell.

The leader snarled at Kael'thas. "Death knights, to me!" he shouted, holding the Eye high above him. The few who remained obeyed, forming a tight circle and facing away from the center to protect him and his prize. Even as Kael'thas murmured the incantations and the spell neared completion, the shadows about the intruders writhed once more, this time taking on a purplish cast as the Eye shed its light all around them, and the death knights' forms grew indistinct. They had escaped with barely a heartbeat to spare. Kael'thas swore in his native tongue.

The prey was gone—but they could be followed and trapped at their second location. Antonidas murmured a teleport incantation, adjusting it slightly so that he would rematerialize in the same place as the death knights. In an instant Antonidas found himself standing on a wide balcony. He recognized it as one of the Violet Citadel's upper floors. The death knights were all clustered together off to one side, their leader standing proud and tall among them, the Eye in his mailed hand. Krasus, Kael'thas, and others followed.

This time, Kael'thas and Antonidas were prepared, the spell already in their minds and on their tongues, and they were successful. The death knight leader whirled to give Antonidas a baleful stare, and the archmage permitted himself a slight smile.

"You were swifter in the vault, but we are swifter here. This balcony is warded against your teleportation spells. There is nowhere to run," Antonidas called out, staring right at the death knights' leader. They would now be able to capture or kill the death knights, keeping one alive for information. Then they would know a good deal more about the new Horde's leaders and their plans.

"Perhaps not," the lead death knight said softly, his words carrying nonetheless. "But why should we run when we can fly?"

At his words a wind sprang up behind him, from past the balcony, strong enough to make Antonidas stagger. A whistling noise accompanied it, growing louder and louder, and then a piece of the night sky dropped down alongside the balcony. The darkness slowly divided into several long, sinuous forms that hovered in the air just past the balcony railing, their cruel eyes staring out of their gleaming black faces. Antonidas could already feel the heat beating at him, and his shirt was quickly soaked with sweat.

"Foolish human, did you believe we had come alone?" the death knight leader said, laughing. The largest dragon Antonidas had ever seen swooped in closer to the balcony until its long barbed chin rested over the railing.

Antonidas saw Krasus go pale and caught a single whispered word: "Deathwing."

At the sound of his name, the mighty dragon swiveled his head and fixed Krasus with an intent gaze. The mage did not cringe from that scrutiny, but Antonidas staggered.

Deathwing? *Here?*

The death knight stepped up onto the railing and then across to Deathwing's back. "I have what I have came for. Let us be off!"

Antonidas recovered enough to hurl a lightning bolt at the fleeing figures, but it bounced off their shields. Teleporting was out of the question—they were moving too quickly and too closely together. Kael'thas and the other magi shook their heads. They were simply not fast enough to strike at the death knights without possibly hitting and angering a dragon that would happily incinerate the entire citadel.

As if to punctuate that threat, two of the dragons flanking Deathwing suddenly flew closer, opening their mouths wide. The magi could barely put up shields in time. Streams of molten red and gold burst from their wide-spread jaws, striking the balcony and igniting curtains and scrolls in the room behind them. Antonidas cursed under his breath as he watched the other death knights climb onto the dragons' backs and then soar up into the sky, disappearing from view. He knew the mighty creatures would tear right through the wards he had enacted—he had never built them to withstand giants.

Antonidas felt a stab of despair. He and the rest of the Kirin Tor were charged with protecting the city and its people, and tonight he had failed them. He had always said that every mage should know his limits, and tonight, Antonidas knew that he had met his. He stared up at the sky, searching for any sign of the invaders, but they were gone. And they had the Eye of Dalaran, one of the city's most powerful artifacts.

I have what I came for, the death knight had said.

Antonidas knew what. The question was, why?

CHAPTER TWELVE

Fenris stared up at the clearly old edifice, confused. He had not been sure what to expect from the Tomb of Sargeras, but it was not this. What he had at first thought were carvings were in fact the shells and bones and spines of various sea creatures, attached to the building's outer walls from years of submersion. It was like seeing the bottom of a deep ocean, only raised up onto land and fashioned into a habitable structure. And the door to this odd building hung wide open.

"This is where that artifact awaits?" Fenris asked, frowning. He was having a hard time reconciling this place's lumpy appearance with the earth-shattering item Ner'zhul had said would be here.

The death knight had no such doubts, however. "It is here," Ragnok insisted. "I can sense it, deep inside."

"Then let's go!" Tagar shouted. "Why are we standing around? The sooner we go in the sooner we come back out!"

Fenris often found himself at odds with the Bonechewer chieftain, but he was right on that count. Fenris was anxious to be done with this job of courier. He signaled to his orcs and they followed Ragnok, Tagar, and Tagar's Bonechewer warriors inside. Everywhere he looked he saw signs that the building had spent hundreds, perhaps even thousands, of years under water. Edges and corners were rounded, both from constant friction with the water and from moss and coral and shells that had attached themselves there. The floor was covered with mold and seaweed. Any decorations along the wall were either destroyed by all those years in the water or covered by just as many years of accumulation. Here and there some water had remained pooled, and was now long since stagnant. No light penetrated here—the strange building had no windows—but that was not a concern. Ragnok raised his hand and a burst of yellowish illumination appeared above him. It cast disturbing shadows about the corridor but at least allowed them to move steadily inward.

As they progressed deeper, Fenris noticed that the walls here were cleaner than they had been nearer the entrance, and not just less grimy but less degraded. The carvings that decorated every surface had not been worn away to the same degree, and he caught glimpses here and there of what this temple must have been at its height. It would have been magnificent, filled with a beauty and an elegance he had never even imagined possible, and Fenris felt rough and bestial treading its halls. He could see that the rest of his clan felt the same way. Tagar and his Bonechewer orcs seemed unaffected by the temple's beauty, but then they seemed to have little appreciation for anything beyond death and destruction. Ragnok appeared utterly focused on the task at hand.

Which might have been why it was Tagar who suddenly stopped and pointed at a spot on the wall near where it met the floor. "Look there!" the Bonechewer chieftain said. Fenris followed his gesture and saw a smear of something dark across the carvings. It looked like—"Blood," Tagar confirmed. He knelt by the smear, sniffed at it, and then touched his tongue to it. "Orc blood," he clarified, rising to his feet again. "Several years old."

"Likely the blood of Gul'dan or his warlocks," Ragnok said. "We're getting close!"

It was not a pleasant thought, even if it did mean that the end of their quest was at hand. "Be on guard," Fenris said to his orcs, and they nodded somberly.

"Are you scared, Fenris?" Tagar mocked, stepping up and shoving his face close to Fenris's. "Afraid of what we might find?"

"Of course I am, you idiot!" Fenris snapped, his tusks scraping the younger chieftain's cheeks. "Gul'dan was a traitor and a fool, but he was still the most powerful warlock the Horde has ever seen! And something in here killed him and all his followers. You'd have to be insane or stupid not to be afraid!"

"Well, *I'm* not afraid!" Tagar replied, drawing smiles and laughs from several of Fenris's warriors. Fenris himself just shook his head and wondered yet again why he'd been sent with such an idiot. But that's why, he answered himself. Because someone has to be smart enough to know what to do and when—and someone else has to be foolish enough to go on anyway, even when it's near-suicide.

"Fine," Fenris said, allowing himself a small grin. "You go first, then."

Tagar smiled and whooped, his war cry echoing down the hall. He strode forward, leading the way without a moment's concern. The others followed.

The condition of the walls and floor continued to improve as they descended farther into the temple. Its glory was breathtaking. At one intersection of corridors Ragnok stopped, apparently confused. He turned first one way, and then the other. Fenris frowned.

"What's wrong?"

"Nothing. I—" The death knight hesitated again, then nodded to himself and strode firmly down one of the halls. Fenris shook his head, but followed.

The hallway ended in a wide room. The walls here were blank, surprisingly enough—clean and smooth and bare—and the sudden contrast made the room seem stark and dignified. At the far end a massive vault door of plain black iron filled most of the wall.

"This is it," Ragnok breathed. He swung the door open.

And froze in utter terror.

Beyond the door lay an almost impenetrable darkness, as if night had been condensed and hidden here where the light would never find it.

Standing in that darkness, just past the doorway, was a creature from a nightmare.

It towered over them, standing so tall it was forced to hunch within the room beyond. Its skin was scaled and covered in bumps that seemed to ripple, as if somehow its surface were fluid like water. Spikes jutted from the shoulders, the forearms, the chest, and various other places. The overlong arms ended in huge hands with long claws. The face was too narrow at the bottom and too wide at the top, with eyes that glowed a smoky, roiling yellow and a tiny mouth somehow filled with an insane number of razor-sharp teeth. A long tail whipped about behind it.

In one of its clawed hands it held a long rod, almost a spear, with a wooden haft and worked silver ends. The top was a mass of spikes clustered around a large gem that glowed with a brilliant white light of its own, and it was that radiance that held the darkness in the tomb partially at bay. Small flickers of lightning burst from the gem as well, only to fade into the darkness again.

The Scepter of Sargeras—the artifact Ner'zhul had sent them to retrieve.

All they had to do was take it from what Fenris was absolutely sure was a demon.

"You will not pass," the creature hissed, its voice rolling over them in oily waves. "This tomb has already been defiled by mortals once! It shall not happen again!"

"We don't want to pass," Fenris replied, biting back the fear and bile that leaped up his throat. "We just want that scepter you're waving about."

The demon laughed, a low chuckle like bone grating on bone, and stepped forward, its long clawed feet digging deep furrows into the marble floor. "Then you may try to take it from me," it offered. "And after you fail, I will shred your bodies and sup upon your souls."

"I'll crack your bones with my teeth and drink out the marrow!" Tagar bellowed back at the demon—this was the kind of language he understood. Then he charged, his axe held high.

And, though he cursed Tagar for a fool and himself for a worse one, Fenris raised his own weapon and leaped into the fray beside his fellow chieftain. The other thirty or so Thunderlord and Bonechewer warriors were right behind them.

Even so, it was a difficult battle. The demon was strong, stronger than any one of them by far, and faster as well. Its long claws cleft skin and bone and muscle with ease, tearing through the orcs as if they were dried leaves. The scepter it held was heavy enough to crush an orc's skull without taking a dent. Even the demon's tail was a weapon. Tagar shrieked in outrage as the creature struck one of the Bonechewers with it.

The long barb at the end went easily through the hapless orc's chest and emerged, dripping blood, from his back.

But the worst, the most frightening attack it possessed, was its bite—that unbelievable mouth stretched wider than should have physically been possible, exposing row upon row of teeth. Fenris watched the demon bite off half a warrior's head, and even through his own battle rage he felt sick.

It was that battle rage that saved them. Under normal circumstances Fenris disapproved of the bloodlust, but now it was a boon. Without it, many of the orcs—including himself—would have run away in abject terror. But with their heads pounding and their vision blurring and their blood humming, they attacked and continued to attack. Yes, the demon was faster, but with so many warriors attacking on each new assault, a few hits got through. The demon was stronger, but severing its limbs still crippled it.

At the last, with the demon's tail and one arm and part of a leg gone, and the other arm so shattered it writhed like a snake, Fenris and Tagar struck as one, their axes slicing into its thick neck. The blows came from opposite sides, delivered with all the force their respective masters could muster, and both chieftains took thin cuts along their fingers where the other's blade had nicked. But the demon toppled to the ground, his neck cut clean through from both sides, the head landing at Ragnok's feet.

Fenris bent down and picked up the scepter. It was lighter than he had expected, but he could feel a faint thrum of power through it.

"We have what we were sent for," he said, turning back. "Let's go."

"What?" Surprisingly, it was Ragnok who protested. "But this is the Tomb of Sargeras! And you just killed its guardian!"

"That was one guardian," Fenris replied. "There will be others, you mark my words." He held the scepter up so it caught the light. "Fortunately, we don't have to go any deeper into this pit."

"You don't understand," Ragnok continued. He stepped up closer to Fenris. "We got the scepter; we should get the Eye of Sargeras as well. Do you remember when I was confused earlier? It was because I was sensing both artifacts! It took me a moment to realize what was going on. But I know exactly where the Eye of Sargeras is now—down that other corridor. That was the artifact Gul'dan sought, and now it's within our grasp!"

Ragnok's glowing eyes narrowed in fury. "Pitiful things. I could destroy you with a mere thought! You will come with me to retrieve the Eye or—"

"Or what?" Fenris spat. "Go ahead. Kill us where we stand, and go back alone for the Eye. Either way, we will be dead." He was mostly sure that the death knight was bluffing, but he stood by his decision. Ragnok might kill them in a fit of anger. But whatever was sure to be guarding the Eye would most definitely kill them.

Ragnok lifted his hands and for a moment Fenris's heart stopped. But then the death knight sagged; he had been bluffing after all.

"You are fools," Ragnok growled, but his voice was laced with defeat.

"Maybe," Fenris agreed, "But we are fools who will live to see another day." Without another word he turned. His clan followed him, as did Tagar and his orcs. It was only with the smallest satisfaction that a few moments later, he noticed that Ragnok had again joined them.

"Do you have it?"

Fenris dismounted, sliding off the dragon's back and planting both feet solidly on the cracked ground, then met Gorefiend's stare as the death knight hurried toward them. The dragons had been waiting for the orcs when their boats had reached land again, and had quickly carried them back into the Blasted Lands to rejoin Gorefiend and the others.

"Yes, we have it," Fenris confirmed, holding up the long cloth-wrapped scepter. He handed it to Gorefiend, happy to be rid of it. "What now?"

"Now we make haste back through the portal," Gorefiend answered. Fenris suppressed a shudder as Gorefiend's hands closed about the bundle protectively. "Our tasks here are finished. Azeroth is no longer important to us. We'll leave this world to the humans and their allies, and good riddance."

Fenris started to ask for more detail, but a loud rumbling stopped him. Glancing over his shoulder, he saw several large carts rolling into the valley, orcs guiding each one. Remembering the discussion back in the Blackrock Mountains, he realized those must contain the cargo Deathwing had asked them to allow through the portal. He wondered idly what could be so important the black dragon wanted it moved to another world, but resigned himself to likely never knowing.

Another orc, though, was more curious than Fenris. He started to approach one of the carts. Before Fenris could even draw breath to shout out a warning, a dark shape swooped from the skies. The orc screamed and dropped to the ground, clutching at his face. Blood dripped from between his fingers.

"Get back!" Fenris cried. "Stay away from the carts!"

The dragons that had borne the orcs here now took to the skies to defend the cargo, some of them not waiting to make sure their riders had completely dismounted.

"Gorefiend!" came a voice Fenris recognized. That scream could belong to no one other than the Warsong chieftain. Grom Hellscream had clearly been with the forces harassing the Alliance troops at Nethergarde Keep and had just returned with them. He was still halfway across the valley, but they heard him clearly. "Did you bring these creatures?"

"I did!" Gorefiend replied, not raising his voice but his words carrying nonetheless. "The black dragons are our new allies!"

Grom ducked as a black dragon's claws slid by dangerously close to his head, and scowled. "Some allies!" he shouted. "Do something about your winged friends before they cause a panic—or kill us all!"

The death knight glanced up at the dragons, studying them a moment. Then he nodded. "Deathwing!" he called. "I swear to you that I will defend those carts and their cargo! Please pull your dragons back to the valley's edge!"

Fenris couldn't pick the dragon elder out among all the shifting, gliding shapes, but a moment later the dragons wheeled and made for perches along the cliffs ringing the valley floor.

"Better," Grom grunted, approaching them. He nodded at Fenris, who nodded back—the two of them had always gotten along. Fenris considered Grom one of the finest chieftains in the Horde, and a superb warrior as well.

"Did you get what you needed?" Grom asked them both.

"We did," Gorefiend replied. He didn't say anything further. Grom peered at the carts.

"What are those?" Grom asked.

"Cargo," Gorefiend replied shortly. Each cart was made of sturdy wood beams, had high sides, and was completely covered with a thick tarp. Fenris could see from the way the tarp shifted that the carts were full, but could discern nothing more.

"I thought all we had to retrieve were those artifacts," Grom said.

"There has been a change of plans," the death knight answered. "Nothing to worry about." He raised his voice and must have worked some magic as well, because suddenly it echoed across the valley. "Those carts are under my personal protection, and anyone who interferes with them—or tries to look in them—will answer to me." Several orcs glanced up, startled, and two who had been approaching the rear cart hastily backed away.

Fenris shrugged. His task was done, and if Gorefiend wanted to play some other game that was between him and Ner'zhul. "How soon can we go through?" he asked instead.

"I need some of your clan to stay behind and defend the portal for a short time longer. You and the rest can go through now, if you like," Gorefiend answered. "Tagar, you too. I need some of your Bonechewers."

Fenris frowned, but nodded. He had hoped all his clan would be allowed to return, but he understood Gorefiend's reasoning.

"What of us?" Grom was asking Gorefiend, but Fenris turned away. The Warsong's orders were not his concern right now. Instead he signaled his second, Malgrim Stormhand, and together they selected twelve orcs to stay behind under Malgrim's command. The orcs did not protest. They were Thunderlords; they served the Horde as asked.

"To the portal!" The rest of the Thunderlord clan marched across the valley floor and approached the towering new Dark Portal. Just ahead of them were the covered carts, and Fenris saw several death knights detach themselves from the forces positioned around the valley and step up beside those mysterious vehicles. Gorefiend was there as well, near the front.

Fenris heard Tagar yelling at his Bonechewers, trying to divvy them up, and the roars of ogres as they were promised combat. "I smash!" one of them cried gleefully. The entire Warsong clan, too, would stay, judging from the comments he heard. The portal would be amply protected. Part of him thought he should remain as well, but another part of him was deeply weary and longed for home. Later, perhaps, he would return with fresh orcs to relieve those he had stationed here.

Fenris hastened up the ramp and faced the Dark Portal itself. The portal still made him nervous, with its strange rippling energy. It disturbed him that something so small—he could easily walk around the portal; it wasn't even as wide as the thick stone columns framing it—could form a bridge between two separate worlds. He kept half-expecting the portal to fail somehow, to collapse and tear apart anyone caught within it. The thought made him pick up his pace, and he ran through it, feeling the strange jarring sensation he'd noticed when he'd left Draenor, as if his body were being shunted a great distance. A cold prickle ran across his skin and a brief flash crossed his eyes, then he was staring at the familiar red skies of Draenor again. Fenris breathed a sigh of relief and continued on away from the portal, stopping finally to allow the rest of his clan to catch up.

Behind him he saw some of the other clans filing through as well, and Gorefiend had already departed with those carts. Fenris had done as ordered, and now he would simply wait until Ner'zhul had new instructions for him. Until then, the Thunderlord warriors would return to their home. He had had enough of intrigue and deception and plotting to last him a long, long time.

CHAPTER THIRTEEN

Khadgar was in the meeting hall, one of the few completely finished structures in Nethergarde. He had wanted to stay on the parapet and continue lending a hand against the Horde but Turalyon had convinced him to rest for a few minutes and eat something. "Archmage or not, you're no good to us if you're fainting from hunger or fatigue," his friend had pointed out. It was sound advice, and so Khadgar had let himself be led over here and had dutifully eaten the bowl of stew someone had placed in front of him. He remembered that much, and now he supposed he must have fallen asleep. He was dreaming, and the dream was bittersweet. For in the dream, Khadgar was young.

He turned his clean-shaven face to the night sky, and let the moon bathe it, the wind tousling his hair that was dark save for single streak of white. He lifted his hands, marveling at how young and strong they looked, ungnarled and unspotted. He strode across Lordaeron like a giant, each step carrying him whole leagues, his head brushing the clouds. It was night, yet he walked surely and without hesitation, his feet knowing the way. He found himself heading toward Dalaran, and forded the lake in one step to stand beside the mage-city. Light poured from a single room in the Violet Citadel, despite the late hour, and Khadgar focused his attention there. He began to float upward, growing smaller as he approached the room. As his feet touched down on the balcony, he was his normal size again. The door was open, and he entered, pushing aside the gauze curtains that kept out bugs but allowed moonlight.

"Welcome, Khadgar. Come and join me." Khadgar was not surprised to see Antonidas there, and to realize that these were the Kirin Tor leader's own chambers. He sat in the proffered chair and accepted a glass of wine from the other archmage, amused that for once Antonidas, with his long brown beard just beginning to gray, actually looked the senior—normally it was Khadgar whom strangers thought the elder mage, thanks to his snow-white beard, even though in reality Antonidas had several decades of experience over him.

"Thank you," Khadgar said quietly, after they'd both sipped at their wine a moment. He gestured at his boyish face, his powerful, slim youth's body. "For this."

Antonidas looked a bit uncomfortable. "I thought I would make this as pleasant as possible."

"I've missed it. Being young. I wouldn't change a

thing—Medivh had to be stopped—and most of the time I don't mind. But sometimes . . . I miss it."

". . . I know."

Khadgar changed the subject. "I take it this is no ordinary dream?"

Antonidas shook his head. "No, unfortunately not. I have grave news to impart. The black dragonflight has allied itself with the Horde."

It took a great deal of will not to choke on his wine. "The black dragonflight?" Khadgar repeated. "But what of the red?" The two dragonflights were mortal enemies.

His host shrugged. "They have not been seen for some time. It may be that they have finally broken the Horde's control." He frowned. "But the orcs have found new allies, and it seems to us willing ones this time."

Khadgar shook his head. "Are they heading toward Nethergarde?"

"We don't know," Antonidas admitted. "Perhaps. They have already been here, and to Alterac as well." His frown became a full-fledged scowl. "They stole the Eye of Dalaran, Khadgar."

"The Eye?" Khadgar knew well what kind of a blow that was to Dalaran. "But what does the Horde want with it?"

"I know not, but they were here specifically to steal it," Antonidas confirmed. "A handful of death knights managed to get past all our defenses, take it, and use the dragons to escape. Dragons that shortly thereafter slaughtered the Alliance forces watching Alterac, no doubt at that traitor Perenolde's command."

Khadgar made a face. "I wonder how Perenolde managed that."

"Yet another mystery. I know how much you are dealing with already, Khadgar. But I thought you should know."

"Thank you," Khadgar told him, and meant it. "Yes, I'd rather know." He frowned thoughtfully, reaching to stroke his beard and momentarily nonplussed to find only his bare chin. "And perhaps I can even find out why these things happened. First the Book of Medivh, now the Eye of Dalaran. Why these specifically?" He set his wineglass down on Antonidas's desk and stood, reluctantly. "I should be getting back."

Back to being a boy in an old man's body. Back to watching Alleria and Turalyon enact a painful drama of denial and hurting and solitude when any fool could see they would be stronger and happier together. Back to fighting orcs and closing portals and bearing the weight of the world on his artificially aged shoulders. He sighed heavily.

"As you wish. Good luck, my boy." Antonidas waved his hand, and Khadgar awoke, sitting up at Nethergarde's meeting room table. He was back in his elderly body now, and felt a wistful pang as he regarded his withered hands and long white beard.

Rising, Khadgar left the dream and the meeting hall behind. He spotted Turalyon and a few others at the main gate. They were clustered around a new prisoner. They looked up as he approached and stepped back. The archmage suppressed a shudder as he saw the creature's rotting, once-human face and glowing red eyes.

"Khadgar!" Turalyon called as he noticed his friend. "I was just about to send for you."

"I assume you needed my help with this one? Was the Light ineffective?"

Turalyon looked frustrated. "Quite the contrary. His reaction was so extreme I was afraid I was going to kill him. I thought perhaps you—"

"Of course." Khadgar sank down to a crouch beside the prisoner, meeting his fiery gaze. "Do you have a name, death knight?"

The creature merely snarled, writhing against his bonds. They held fast, however.

"If that's the way you want it," said Khadgar, shrugging. He summoned power to him, then focused that power into a tight beam. The spell easily pierced the Horde creature's defenses as Turalyon's Light probably had, but although the death knight stiffened, he was not so maddened by agony he could not speak. And speak he would.

"Your name?"

The death knight glared at him, murder in his eyes, but his mouth opened and formed words of its own accord. "Gaz Soulripper."

"Good. Now, how did the Horde reopen the portal?"

Khadgar demanded, as Turalyon and the others crowded close behind him.

"Ner'zhul," it replied. "Ner'zhul used the Skull of Gul'dan to force the rift open again."

"Is such a thing possible?" Turalyon asked.

"Entirely," Khadgar said. "It's starting to make sense now. We know Gul'dan created the Dark Portal in the first place, working together with Medivh. It's likely that his remains would still have a link to it, and therefore could be used to gain greater control over the rift. Just like the Book of Medivh."

Ner'zhul had needed Gul'dan, or at least his skull, to open the rift again. And without that skull, Khadgar couldn't shut it either, not completely. Now he understood why the rift had remained before. Without using Gul'dan's skull, Khadgar would never be able to seal the rift for good. And without the book, he wouldn't be sure he was using the right spell.

He felt a tap on his shoulder. Glancing up, he saw Turalyon gesturing him to step away. Puzzled, Khadgar complied.

"Good news," Turalyon said. "Our forces are driving the Horde back toward the Dark Portal. We also had word from Admiral Proudmoore. Other groups of orcs are running, too. Apparently a band of Horde orcs—backed by black dragons, if you can believe it!—stole several boats from Menethil Harbor recently."

Khadgar sighed, remembering his dream conversation with Antonidas. "I can believe it. I—wait. You said 'boats'?"

"Aye. They headed southwest, into the Great Sea."

Khadgar gripped Turalyon's tunic. "Southwest? Damn it!"

"What is it, Khadgar?"

"They're not running. The boats—they were heading for the Tomb of Sargeras! Gul'dan tried that once, and it killed him!"

"Why would the orcs do that? Medivh is dead and Sargeras is gone. The tomb's empty." His eyes widened slightly. ". . . Isn't it?"

It all clicked into place. "Sargeras is gone," Khadgar said slowly, "but that doesn't mean the tomb is empty. We know the orcs are seeking artifacts—what if Sargeras left something there? The tomb was shielded so that no creature of Azeroth could enter—but the orcs were never from here! The wardings would mean nothing to them now, just as they meant nothing to Gul'dan when he—that's it. That's got to be it!"

Khadgar turned back to the death knight and dropped to his knees beside the creature.

"Why did Ner'zhul send orcs to the Tomb of Sargeras?" he demanded. Gaz Soulripper laughed, foul breath from dead lungs caressing Khadgar's face. He'd pulled tightly into himself in the few moments of respite and was not about to say anything. Khadgar frowned. He extended his magic once again, this time without any effort at finesse, and the illumination of his spell was like a lance to the creature's forehead. Soulripper arched in agony, but stayed silent.

"Tell us!"

"We—care nothing for your world!" Soulripper grunted, his hands clenching.

Khadgar made a subtle move with his fingers, and this time Gaz Soulripper cried out. "I need better than that."

"Ah!" The dead thing bit its lip in pain, teeth sinking easily through rotted flesh. "Our destiny—greater than you can imagine, human!"

Khadgar's heart sped up. These half-truths, these hints . . . What was the reality? Sweat dotted his forehead, but not from exertion. He tightened his grip, and the death knight convulsed.

"Khadgar . . ." said Turalyon, wincing a little.

"I can keep this up all day, Soulripper," Khadgar said. When there was no response, Khadgar lifted his left hand to join his right.

"An artifact!" the death knight screamed. "From the tomb. The Scepter of Sargeras."

"That's better. What about it?"

"W-with that, the Book of Medivh, and the Eye of Dalaran, Ner'zhul can—no!"

Khadgar was surprised at the level of resistance the death knight could put up. He shared Turalyon's distaste of torture, but they were so close. . . .

"What can he do? *Tell us!*"

"He—he can open portals from Draenor to other worlds."

Khadgar immediately ceased tormenting the death knight, who flopped over, groveling in recovery. He sat, stunned for a moment, then looked up at Turalyon. He saw his own horror mirrored in the youth's face.

"Other . . . *worlds?*" Turalyon said, his voice faint with shock. "Azeroth and Draenor . . . aren't the only ones?" He stared down at the death knight, his mouth working for a moment before anything came out. "Worlds . . . more than ours. Worlds without end, innocents without number falling before them . . . Light save us."

Khadgar nodded. "I know it's difficult to grasp. The Horde we've faced was half-crazed with desperation and hunger. Their world is dying, and they needed to take ours. Now they're going to open portals to countless other worlds as well. This same scenario will be repeated again . . . and again and again."

Turalyon barely heard his friend's words. They seemed to fade away, smothered by the thudding of his own heart in his ears. The hideous visage of the death knight, too, was fading, drowning in a slow but steady glow of white light that seemed to be coming from inside the paladin's own head.

He burned to protect his people—the Alliance—all life on this world from the havoc that the ever-hungering orcs had chosen to wreak. That seemed daunting enough, but now—*worlds!* Just how many were they talking about, anyway—one? Two? Two million?

Hysteria bubbled up inside him as he sat in the white, empty space and danced on the verge of madness as he tried to comprehend the incomprehensible. The innocent were his charge. He had to protect them. But how could he possibly do so? So many who—

The pounding of his heart suddenly paused.

And in that place of pure, brilliant light, he saw a figure that was light—the Light—itself. It hovered and glowed, gleaming as if its form was hard and crystalline but also soft, unspeakably soft, as soft as a tear, as soft as forgiveness, as soft as Alleria's pale skin. Golden strands draped the being, and Turalyon could not tell at first if they were leading from or to the creature— and then he understood, it was both. All that was, was this being, and this being, was everything. Awe flooded him and he drank in the sight of this beautiful, luminous being, feeling it fill him with hope and calm as if he were an empty vessel.

Do not despair, came a voice like bells, like chimes, like the sigh of the ocean. *The Light is with you. We are with you. No matter how vast the darkness, Light will scatter it. No matter what world, no matter what creature, the Light is there, in that place, in that soul. Know this, and go forward with a joyful heart, Turalyon.*

As if it sang in response, Turalyon's heart began to beat once more. He realized it had never stopped; that the long, frozen, rapt moment had been less than the blink of an eye.

Khadgar gave Turalyon the space to let it sink in. Finally, Turalyon lifted his head. His eyes were focused, clear, and his face was resolute.

"We have to stop them," Turalyon stated firmly. "We can't let other, innocent worlds have this . . . this . . . unleashed on them. It ends here. On Azeroth. No one else should have to suffer as we have. The Light shines on other worlds than ours, and it needs our help. It will have it."

Khadgar heard some resentful murmurings from some of Turalyon's men. Turalyon heard it too, for he stood, frowning.

"If you have something to say, say it clearly," he ordered. The soldiers who'd been talking exchanged glances, then one stepped up.

"Sir . . . why don't we just let them go? If they have fresh worlds to take, maybe they'll just go away and leave us alone."

"Even if it were that simple, we can't let that happen. Don't you understand?" Turalyon said. "We have to stop them. We can't save our world at the expense of countless innocent lives!"

"Besides," came Alleria's clear voice as she strode up to them, dusty and sweaty and spattered with blood too dark to be her own, "what is to stop them from returning once they have gotten fat off plunder? With her sharp sense of hearing, of course, she'd heard everything. Khadgar thought her a trifle paler than usual, but she was almost eerily composed. Would you like to battle a Horde twice the size of the one we faced during the Second War, completely united, and with the ability to open portals to Azeroth from anywhere?"

Khadgar saw the disappointment in Turalyon's eyes. The paladin had hoped the men would understand his point. And more, he'd hoped Alleria would. But it seemed that Alleria was still consumed with hatred for the orcs. She did not really care about other worlds. She wanted to hunt the orcs down and kill them herself; she had no wish to let others share that particular cruel delight. She turned to Turalyon, and color rose briefly in her face, then subsided.

"Sir, while we were fighting, I saw something I think you should be aware of. We noticed a group of . . ."

Khadgar was barely listening to her musical voice. Something else was nagging at his thoughts . . . something was not right. He gasped as understanding burst upon him.

"I'm an idiot!" Khadgar cried, cutting Alleria off in mid-sentence. "They're not losing!" he shouted. "They're retreating! They've found all the artifacts they needed and they're returning home to Draenor! The entire invasion was just a feint to distract us, and now they're done!"

Gaz Soulripper glanced up at him, shock and fear in his glowing eyes. The death knight surged to his feet, snapping the stout ropes that bound his hands and feet and chest. Terror lent him magical strength as well— from somewhere deep inside, Gaz shunted aside

Khadgar's mental lance and raised fresh shields that blocked the archmage's reflexive attempt to regain control.

"You will not interfere!" Gaz roared, leaping atop Khadgar and wrapping mailed hands around the archmage's throat. "You will not thwart our destiny!"

The death knight began to squeeze, and Khadgar gasped for air, struggling to push the creature away even as his vision swam. Blackness crept in along the edges of his sight, framing wild colors flashing before him. He couldn't push the hands away, he couldn't think to summon a spell.

And suddenly, through the insanely swirling palette of colors came a flash of pure white. Even as it seared Khadgar's eyes, it wrapped him in reassuring warmth and a sensation of peace sharply at odds with the pain of hands crushing his windpipe and cutting off blood. Briefly he wondered if he was already dead but hadn't gotten around to noticing it yet.

The light swelled, then faded. The dead hands around Khadgar's throat tightened convulsively before the pressure suddenly disappeared. Khadgar swayed, blinking, dazzled from the white light, coughing and gasping at the same time, his lungs struggling to bring air back into his body.

"You all right?" It was Turalyon, his hands, still glowing softly, helping Khadgar to rise. Glancing down, Khadgar noticed that his violet robe was now dusty gray—all that was left of Gaz Soulripper. He looked at

Turalyon, stunned again by the young general's power. Turalyon read his glance and smiled sheepishly. Khadgar clasped his friend's arm. "Thank you."

"It was the Light, not I," Turalyon said with his characteristic modesty.

"Well, your damned Light killed him too fast," Alleria growled. Even Khadgar blinked at the venom in her voice. "We could have asked him about the carts I saw."

"Carts?" Khadgar asked. "Explain."

She turned to him, clearly more comfortable speaking with the mage than with Turalyon. "I saw some of the orcs going through the portal. Black dragons accompanied them. There were carts, several of them, all covered. They were taking things back to their world."

"They came to get artifacts, not souvenirs," grunted Khadgar. "What would they need carts for?"

Alleria shrugged. "I know not, but I thought you should know."

"Another puzzle piece. Just when I thought we'd figured it out." Khadgar brushed disgustedly at his robe, then looked up at them. "We've got quite the task ahead of us. We need to send an expedition into Draenor. We have to find and kill Ner'zhul before he can open any more portals, retrieve those artifacts— especially the Book of Medivh—and Gul'dan's skull, and destroy the Dark Portal for good."

Turalyon nodded, summoning a scout with a quick gesture, every inch the military commander. "Send word to the Alliance kings," he said quickly. "The Horde is—"

His words were cut off as a shadow passed over the sun. Shielding his eyes from the glare, he glanced up, then began to laugh as the shadow broke apart into several winged forms that circled down toward them. These were not arrow-straight like dragons; they were broader, stouter, and softer, covered in tawny fur and feathers of gold and white.

"What took you?" Turalyon called back, laughing with Khadgar as Kurdran Wildhammer, leader of the Wildhammer dwarves, shook his head and managed to look embarrassed from atop his gryphon.

"Bad winds," the dwarf admitted, bringing Sky'ree in for a landing. The great beast landed gracefully and cawed, flapping its wings one final time before its rider dismounted. Despite the direness of the situation, Khadgar found himself smiling. It was good to see hale, gruff Kurdran.

"Your arrival is most timely," the archmage said, stepping forward to shake the dwarf's hand and permitting his own to be enthusiastically pumped up and down. "We've a message to be delivered, and quickly."

"Aye? As long as ye promise me an' me boys we'll get a crack at those orcs, we'll take a message for ye." He waved at some of the other Wildhammers, who hastened forward and stood at attention.

"We'll need to dispatch several messages to the various leaders," Turalyon said, the grin fading. Khadgar wondered if Turalyon really knew just how no-nonsense he could look when he had to. "Tell them this: The orcs are retreating to Draenor, but they have found a means to open new portals to other worlds."

The dwarves' eyes widened, but they didn't interrupt. "They are taking with them cartloads of something they obviously value, we do not yet know what," Turalyon continued. "We intend to pursue them through the Dark Portal, and stop them from opening those portals. By any and all means necessary."

"Are ye sure, lad?" asked Kurdran quietly. Turalyon nodded. Everyone stood silently for a moment, knowing that Turalyon spoke what had to be done, but even so rendered mute at the reality.

"Now hurry," Turalyon said. "Make that gryphon earn her dinner." The scouts nodded, saluted, mounted their gryphons, and took to the skies. Turalyon turned to his friends.

"And now," he said somberly, "we prepare to leave our world behind."

CHAPTER FOURTEEN

The rest of that day and evening was crammed with chaotic planning. Who should go? Who should stay behind? What provisions should they take? How long should they wait? Debates went from discussion to argument to even shouting, and at one point Turalyon thought Alleria and Kurdran might come to blows over how best to utilize the gryphons.

Finally a plan was drafted that all could be satisfied with. Some, including Alleria, wanted to head out right then. "My rangers can see as well or better than the orcs at night," she pointed out, "and even you humans have the moonlight."

"No," Turalyon had said, putting his foot down. "We don't all have your vision, Alleria. And we're exhausted. The orcs would definitely have the advantage at night. You'll notice they're not attacking right now."

Her eyes had narrowed. "No, they're probably

resting up so they can be fresh in the morning to have at us then."

Turalyon let her words hang there for a moment. Once she realized she'd made his arguments for him, she scowled, but stayed silent.

"Turalyon's right," Khadgar said. "We're exhausted. Dead on our feet. The purpose here isn't to kill as many orcs as possible and go down shouting battle cries, it's to get to the other side with as many as we can so we can stop something bigger than the handful that's at the gates right now."

Turalyon suspected the comment wasn't particularly directed at Alleria, but it struck home nonetheless. She'd turned first red, then white as a sheet, and stalked from the room. Turalyon automatically moved to follow, but Khadgar's hand closed on his arm.

"Let her go," he said quietly. "Talking to her now will just make things worse. She's as exhausted as the rest of us right now and isn't thinking clearly at the best of times. Let her come to you."

Let her come to you. Turalyon wondered, as always, how much the young-old mage knew, and if the phrase had been calculated or casual.

"Verana, a moment," said Alleria as she and her second-in-command left the meeting room for their assigned barracks. She indicated that the other elf follow her outside onto the walkway, underneath the moon and the stars. Wordlessly, Verana obeyed. There had never been any question but that Alleria would be among those going through the portal at dawn tomorrow. Verana and a few others would remain behind, to aid the Sons of Lothar in case something went wrong. Verana turned inquiringly to her commander.

"I have a special task for you. One that goes beyond your military duties," Alleria began. "It is not maudlin to think that I might not return. That none of us might. We do not know what we face on the other side."

Verana looked troubled; they had been friends for decades. But she nodded. "Of course."

"If I do not come back . . . do not come home . . . bear a message for me to my family. Tell them I took the fight to the orcs' own world, to avenge Quel'Thalas and to keep our people safe from future attacks." She thought of Turalyon's impassioned, implacable words—that they could not release the horror that was the Horde on other, innocent people. A lump suddenly swelled in her throat. "Tell them," she continued, her voice rough, "tell them I went to try to save other worlds as well. Others who will, I pray, never know the pain of what we underwent. Tell them I chose to do this of my own free will, and that whatever happens to me . . . my heart is with them."

She fumbled in a pouch and emerged with three small necklaces. Each was graced with a glowing, beautiful gem: an emerald, a ruby, and a sapphire. Verana gasped and looked up, clearly recognizing the stones.

"Yes. They're from the necklace my parents gave me,"

Alleria confirmed. "I had the necklace melted down in Stormwind, and three lockets made from it. I will keep this one." She selected the emerald and fastened it about her throat. "I wanted to give the other two to Vereesa and Sylvanas when I—" She bit her lower lip. "Please. Take these home with you, when you are able to return. Give them to my sisters. Tell them this way, no matter what happens . . . we'll always be together."

Verana's eyes shone with tears that slipped down her cheeks. Alleria envied her the ability to weep. The other ranger studied the inscriptions, which Alleria knew by heart: *To Sylvanas. Love always, Alleria. To Vereesa. With love, Alleria.*

"You will return, my lady, and give these to your sisters yourself. But for now I will keep them safe until you do. This I swear."

Verana hugged her tightly, and Alleria stiffened. She had not allowed anyone to touch her in other than a perfunctory manner since—

Alleria let her arms go around her friend and hugged Verana back for a long moment, then dismissed her. Verana saluted, wiped her face, and hurried back to their barracks. Alleria lingered, letting the fresh air calm her. An ear twitched as she heard soft steps. Quickly she faded into the shadows, frowning to herself as she recognized Turalyon. He walked to the wall and leaned against it, his broad shoulders bowed in the moonlight. Her sharp ears heard her name whispered; her sharp eyes caught a glitter of tears. She turned and vanished, moving silently the way she had come. The talk with Verana had unnerved her sufficiently. To speak with Turalyon now could undo everything she had worked so hard to create over the last two years. She would not risk it.

The general of the Alliance forces stood alone in the moonlight. Despite his advice to his troops, he had found himself unable to sleep. Khadgar's words and Alleria's expression had haunted him, and his mind went back, as it had countless times before over the last two years, to the night when his whole world had changed.

He barely heard the soft whisper above the pounding of the rain on the field tent, and at first Turalyon thought it was merely wishful thinking when he heard Alleria's voice whisper, "Turalyon?"

He lifted his head and in the dim orange glow of the brazier saw her standing just inside the tent. "Alleria! By the Light, you're drenched!"

Turalyon leaped up from his cot, clad only in a pair of light linen breeches, and rushed to her. Shivering, the elf gazed up at him silently, her eyes wide, her glorious golden hair plastered to her skull. A thousand questions crowded Turalyon's lips. When had she gotten back? What had happened? And most important, why was she here, in his tent, alone at this hour?

All of that would wait. She was soaked and chilled, and as he reached to undo her cloak he found it to be as wet as if she'd fallen in a lake. "Here, he said, tossing the sodden thing away. "Stand close to the brazier. I'll get you something dry to wear."

His matter-of-fact tone seemed to hearten her and she nodded, stretching out small hands to the warmth of the glowing embers while he rummaged through his trunk. He found a shirt, breeches, tabard, and cloak. She'd swim in them, but they were dry. He turned to see that Alleria hadn't moved. Something was very wrong indeed.

"Come on," he said, gently, and led her to the trunk, sitting her down on it. Usually so self-controlled, almost haughty, at this moment Alleria looked like a despairing child. Biting his lip against the questions, Turalyon knelt and drew off her boots. Almost an inch of water was in them, and her feet were icy to the touch. He rubbed them briskly, noting how delicate and pale they were, until they warmed somewhat, then rose and helped her to her feet.

"Here are some dry clothes," he said, steering her back toward the brazier. "Change into those and I'll get something hot for you to drink. Then we'll talk."

Turalyon pressed the clothes into her hands and turned his back, blushing a little. He heard a soft rustling behind him and waited for her to tell him she was ready for him to turn around.

He inhaled swiftly as he felt a pair of small hands slip around his waist from behind, and a slender figure press against his back. Turalyon did not move at once, then, slowly, took the cold hands in his, lifted them gently, and pressed them to his heart. It was racing. He shivered as he felt chilled lips press a soft kiss onto his shoulder, and closed his eyes.

How long had he wanted this? Dreamed of it? He'd realized early on that he'd fallen head over heels in love with Alleria, but until recently he had never expected the emotion to be returned. Over the last few weeks, however, it seemed to him she had sought out his company; had contrived to touch him more often, though still in a teasing manner. And now . . .

"I'm c-cold," she whispered, her voice thick. "So cold."

Unable to bear it any longer, Turalyon turned around in her embrace, sliding his hands up her bare back, in awe of how silky her pale skin was beneath his callused, war-roughened hands. The dim light of the brazier caught the gleam of three gems on a necklace that encircled a long, swanlike throat and turned her skin warm and golden. His vision blurred as she turned her face up to him, and he blinked back tears of an emotion so profound it shook his very soul.

"Alleria," he whispered into her long, pointed ear. Suddenly he tightened his arms around her, holding her close, pressing her against him. "Let me warm you," he said, brokenly. "Let me take away whatever it is that's hurting you, that's frightened you. I can't stand the thought of you in pain."

He would do no more, ask for nothing more. He was terrified that at any minute she would recover, tell him she was simply playing with him, and retreat to a respectable distance to discuss tactics or strategy with him. Turalyon would let her, if that was what she wanted. If that was what she needed to recover, to get the light and life back into her eyes, to banish this terrifying stillness.

She did not pull away. Instead she reached to touch his face.

"Turalyon," she whispered, and then in her native tongue, "Vendel'o eranu."

He cupped her face in his hands in turn, feeling the delicate bones of her cheek, realizing that for all her skill and energy and fire, she was fragile. She'd never let him see her fragility before. Water rolled down her cheek, and for a moment, he thought she wept. He realized an instant later that it was only a drop of rain from her sodden hair. Slowly, tentatively, he bent to kiss her. She responded at once, passionately, wrapping her arms around his neck. Turalyon felt dizzy as he drew back and she whispered, "Cold, so cold . . ."

He picked her up in his arms, astounded at how light she was to bear, placed her on the cot, and drew the furs about them both.

And they were warm.

Turalyon rubbed at his strained, tired eyes, blinking back what he insisted on thinking of as tears of exhaustion.

After their single night together, she had been gone the next morning. He'd emerged from his tent to news that shocked him to the core. Alleria and her rangers, of course, had returned from their scouting mission; he learned that gray morning, his eyes widening with compassion and pain, that the Horde had cut a dreadful swath through Quel'Thalas. And that Alleria had personally lost no fewer than eighteen kin of various degrees of closeness—cousins, aunts, uncles, nephews.

And among the dead was her younger brother.

He'd rushed to her, but when his hand closed on

her shoulder, she'd wrenched away. He'd tried to talk to her, but she'd brushed any words aside. It was as if they had never been lovers . . . as if they'd never even been friends. Turalyon felt something break inside him at that moment, something he'd since pushed aside and let scar over, because he was a general, he was a leader, and he could not afford to indulge his personal pain.

But when he'd seen her that day in Stormwind, soaked again to the bone, he'd thought—he'd hoped . . . well, he'd been a fool to hope. But a fool he would be, then, to the rest of his days. For despite everything, Turalyon knew he would always love Alleria Windrunner, and hold fast to their one night together as the brightest and most beautiful of his whole brief life.

"They come."

Rexxar's voice was deep and calm. Grom looked to where the half-ogre pointed and nodded.

"So they do," he said, and gripped Gorehowl as his eyes brightened in anticipation of the slaughter to come. It was no token force that was left behind as the rest of the clans departed Azeroth. The Alliance would face fearsome opponents this day.

His glowing red eyes narrowed as he saw the numbers flooding across the dead land. They had come in force indeed. Where was the leader, the one who had left his men to die to ride for a warning? Grom particularly ached to kill him.

Beside his master, Haratha whuffed in anticipation. Rexxar chuckled at his pet wolf.

"Come, little Alliance," murmured Grom. "Gorehowl is thirsty."

Turalyon reined in his horse as his group cleared the ring of hills that encircled a small basin and beheld the portal. If the orcs were indeed retreating, there were still plenty of them left behind. It was not going to be an easy canter to the portal. They'd have to fight their way through that ominous line of green-skinned beings and the huge, towering, pale things that fought alongside them.

Two warriors in particular drew his attention. Turalyon was not even entirely certain one of them was an orc. He resembled one, but his skin was yellowish-brown, not green, and he towered over the others. His build, too, seemed somehow different. Beside him stood a black wolf that Turalyon suspected was as deadly and focused as his master. A powerful warrior, yes, but not the leader.

There. That one. Larger than most, with a thick mane of black hair pulled into a topknot, a black jaw, glowing red eyes, and heavy bracers decorated with strange symbols, he stared boldly up at the superior numbers of Alliance warriors.

Their eyes met. Even as Turalyon watched, the orc leader lifted a mammoth axe in a salute.

"We're ready for you this time, you bastards," Danath

muttered. His eyes were bright and he was more than eager for battle. As was every soldier present.

"Sons of Lothar! Attack!" Turalyon cried. His troops let out a yell of their own and streamed down from all sides. The battle was on.

It was a simple plan—kill as many orcs as possible while heading straight for the portal. Turalyon fought fiercely, swinging his hammer left and right and beating back the snarling foes that surged up to block his path. Close by him fought Alleria, seemingly as grimly joyful in the slaughter as ever. Some sixth sense prickled at him and he looked up just in time to see the elven ranger bringing a sword down on one hapless orc while another loomed up behind her, lifting a brutal-looking club. She didn't seem to notice the threat—her face was alight with harsh glee as she pulled her sword free from the green corpse. She was too focused, too intent on her revenge—

"Alleria!" Turalyon cried, clapping heels to his warhorse and galloping toward her. As if in slow motion, Alleria raised her golden head, her eyes widening, her arm lifting the bloody sword to block the blow, but she was too slow, too slow, and he would never get there in time—

The prayer left his lips and he thrust his hands forward. White light shot forward and struck the orc square in the chest. He arched backward, the club tumbling helplessly from his grasp as he crumpled to the earth. For the briefest of instants, Turalyon's gaze locked with Alleria's, then she was on to the next orc, and he too had turned back to the fray.

His eye fell upon the orc leader he'd spotted earlier. He seemed to dance through the Alliance forces. The heavy axe in his hand shrieked as it cut air and flesh alike, and the sound rose above the screams and groans of his many victims. He paused now and then to shout and point.

But powerful though he was, he and his warriors were outnumbered, and by the look on his face he knew it. The wave of Alliance kept moving inexorably forward, to the portal. The orc seemed to make a decision. He turned and shouted something to a cloaked figure next to the portal itself, and the figure nodded. Then the leader bellowed something else, and all across the valley his orcs hastened to obey, backing away from the Alliance and retreating slowly but surely toward the waiting portal.

Another movement caught Turalyon's eye. A cloaked figure reached down and pulled something from beside the portal's rightmost pillar. Turalyon couldn't make out what it was, but it was metal and it glinted in the light. Something about the way he fiddled with it made Turalyon nervous and for some reason, his mind went back to his conversation with the gnome Mekkatorque.

How safe will it be?

. . . I'm willing to bet it will eventually be as safe as the safest gnomish creation ever. . . .

The orcs were suddenly trying to get through, whereas before they had fought. Khadgar had confirmed that they'd had the artifacts they needed and they were likely ready to—

"Damn it!" Turalyon cried. He hoped he was wrong. He looked over the sea of fighting men and orcs and saw Khadgar and another group of magi. He rode toward them, gasping out what he'd seen.

Khadgar frowned as he listened. "If I were them, I'd head for home too—but first I'd destroy the portal behind me so no one here could interfere."

"My thoughts too. I think it's something mechanical—like something the gnomes would make."

"Or the goblins," said Khadgar. Both men knew that, unlike the gnomes, who were firmly on the Alliance side, the recently encountered goblins happily sold their mechanical gizmos to both sides. "We destroyed the last portal. They can certainly destroy this one. And without Medivh's book and Gul'dan's skull, I doubt I could reopen it."

"Then let's go. I'll hold them off," Turalyon said, already wheeling his horse to charge the portal. Khadgar was right behind him. Turalyon battered away at the orcs, cutting a path through them like a man possessed. Khadgar bore down on the portal and the figure adjusting something beside it. Leaning over in his saddle, Khadgar slashed at the figure, who turned at the last second, though not fast enough to avoid a blow to the neck. It wasn't a strong enough blow to kill him at once, but the cloaked figure grunted in pain and dropped the device, his hands flying to his neck.

Swinging down from his horse, Khadgar ran over and grabbed up the strange machine. It was the size of a small shield, definitely mechanical . . . and it was making an odd ticking sound. He analyzed it quickly, but the construction was too alien. There was no way he could stop it. Whatever it had been intended to do, it was going to do it soon. Grunting, the mage lifted the package and threw it as far as he could, augmenting his physical strength with magic so that it arced out over the valley and looked like it might even glance off the cliff walls along that side.

The explosion rocked the entire valley.

Grom swore, ducking and covering his head, feeling stings along his back and shoulders where he had been peppered with small fragments of shattered rock. He looked up, rage burning inside him, and strode with dreadful purpose to the warlock. Kra'kul looked as shocked as Grom felt and cowered as Grom's fist descended.

"Traitor! You would kill us!"

"No! No, I swear, I was told it was a shield, a shield to protect us! I didn't know!"

Red swam before Grom's eyes as he lifted the cringing warlock with one hand and shook him. How he wanted to crush the orc's windpipe, to rip his head off and throw it as the elderly human had thrown the device that Grom had been told would protect them but instead had nearly killed them.

"Who told you this? Where is he, that I may tear his heart out!" Roughly he shook the warlock, curbing his bloodlust with great effort.

"I don't know—Malkor was sent to do it—he told me it was a shield—"

Cursing, Grom hurled the worthless wretch away and turned back to the fight.

Grom had been told the device was a shield, so that at the last moment, the Warsong clan could safely escape. He had been lied to. Someone in a position of power—Gorefiend? Ner'zhul?—had intended that the warriors left behind would not escape with their lives.

Grom vowed to survive this battle, unlikely as it seemed, so that someone would pay.

The explosion had rattled his people. The Alliance had recovered more quickly than the orcs, and Grom saw, furious and helpless, that they were being herded like beasts to the southwest. Yet he could do nothing about it. One group came from one side, a second blocked off the exit from another, forcing the orcs back and into a narrow valley mouth, away from the portal. Away from home.

"So be it," he growled. The Alliance might have this victory, but it would cost them dearly. He threw his head back, opened his jaw wide, and let forth a scream that froze two Alliance warriors in mid-swing. "Fight, my Warsong, fight like the orcs you are! Let your blood sing with battle lust! Tear them to pieces! *For the Horde!*"

★   ★   ★

"Someone has to stay here and watch this crew," Turalyon said, reining in beside Alleria and Khadgar and waiting for Kurdran to circle low enough to hear the conversation. "I'll station some men at the mouth of this valley to keep them from escaping again. Everyone else—"

He fell silent. Khadgar didn't envy him. No one really wanted to go through the Dark Portal—although he had to admit, a small part of him, the part that had led to him become a mage in the first place, was very curious about what lay beyond it.

"Well," Turalyon said. "We know what we need to do. Each of you, tell your units one more time that this is a volunteer expedition. I'll not force any soldier to cross worlds if he does not wish to."

Danath nodded and wheeled his mount away, bellowing orders. Alleria turned back to her rangers, and spoke softly to them in their musical language. Khadgar gave Turalyon a reassuring smile, but the paladin didn't return it. Quietly he said to Khadgar, "Alleria was almost killed today. I was barely able to save her."

"Turalyon," Khadgar said, equally quietly, "she's a trained warrior. She can outfight both of us, probably. You know that."

"That's not what I'm worried about. I know she can handle herself, normally. But . . . she gets careless. She gets—" His voice faltered, and Khadgar had to look away from the pain on the youth's face.

"She puts killing orcs before her own safety," Khadgar said. "She takes undue risks." Turalyon nodded miserably. "Well, now we take the fight to them, Turalyon. It could be good for her. For both of you."

Turalyon flushed slightly, but didn't answer. His eyes were on his troops now, and he guided his horse so that he was among them.

"Sons of Lothar!" he cried. "We have faced battle before. We have faced loss, and defeat, and known victory. Now we face the unknown." He caught Khadgar's eye and smiled slightly. "We take the fight to them. And we stop them—so they never trouble us, or other innocent worlds, ever again. For the Alliance! For the Light!"

He lifted his hammer and a cheer rose up as the hammer began to glow with a sharp, clear white radiance. Khadgar nodded to himself. This was what both he and Anduin Lothar had sensed in Turalyon when they had first met him. It seemed a lifetime ago, now. Both the Alliance commander and the mage had known even then that this priest-turned-holy warrior would rise to the challenge. Would blend his almost innocent and inherent decency with a fierce determination to protect his people. Would stand now, at the head of an army, rallying them to cross into a completely new world. Khadgar wondered if his friend saw, really *saw*, how much he inspired his soldiers. And how he inspired one in particular, who was looking at him now with an all-too-rare unguarded expression on her beautiful, elven face.

Turalyon turned his horse and spurred it up the stone ramp toward the Dark Portal itself. His steed shied, resisting, but Turalyon held the reins firm and forced it on. The swirling light beckoned, and he passed through it, its greenish glow overpowering his own white light for an instant before he vanished completely between the columns. Alleria and Khadgar were right behind him. The mage wrestled with his horse and felt a curious sensation as man and beast entered the rift, a ripple of cold and a tugging feeling, as if a strong current pulled at him. A chill swept over him, and for an instant he saw blackness and stars and swirls and flashes of strange colors all mingled together. Then he was emerging, and the hot air warmed skin that had grown inexplicably cold during the brief crossing.

Bright . . . it was so very bright. He automatically lifted a hand to shield his eyes from the glare. And hot, too, a dry, stifling heat that struck Khadgar as being almost physical. He blinked, letting his eyes adjust—and gasped.

He stood on stone, dwarfed by a version of the portal that was as huge and elaborate as the one they'd just crossed through was perfunctory and hastily assembled. Statues of hooded men towered on either side, and the stairs led down to a second courtyard flanked by enormous, sullenly burning braziers. Two pillars topped with fire stood on either side of a strangely made road and . . .

The cracked, red, barren plain that stretched before

them was somewhat familiar, evocative of the Blasted Lands. Even as he stared, in the distance the desiccated earth cracked open. Fire leaped upward as if a dragon were hatching, breaking through the earth as if from its shell. But Khadgar's eyes were fixed on the sky. It was red, the deep red of fresh blood, and high above shone an angry crimson sun, its heat beating down upon them. And, Light help him, the sky, too, was familiar.

"No," he said in a broken voice. "No," he whispered again. "Not here! Not like this!"

"What is it?" Alleria asked him. He ignored her. It was all as it was in the vision—the sky, the land— "Khadgar! What's wrong?"

He started, as if waking up, but the horrible scene before him did not dissipate. He shook his head and forced a wan smile. "Nothing," he lied. Then, realizing how transparent that falsehood was, he corrected himself. "I have had . . . visions of this place before. I hadn't expected—I didn't think I would have to face them so soon. I—it overwhelmed me for a second. My apologies."

Alleria frowned up at him, concerned, but saw that he was not going to explain further. "It is—" She closed her mouth, unable to find the words. She put a hand to her heart as if it physically hurt, and for a moment Khadgar roused from his own despair to pity her. She was an elf, a child of forests and trees and growing, healthy lands. She looked stunned, sickened—almost as sick as Khadgar felt. Out of nowhere, a wind kicked up. With no plants to anchor the soil, the greedy blast seized the dead, dusty soil and scoured them with it. They all coughed, and reached for something, anything, to cover mouths and noses and eyes.

This was it. Khadgar suddenly realized that in stepping through the portal, he had stepped forward into a destiny he had hoped would be a long time coming. In the vision, he looked as he had now—an old man. And now he was here. *Damn it, I'm just twenty-two. . . . Am I going to die here?* he thought sickly, trying to recover. *I've hardly even lived—*

The wind died down as quickly as it had come. "Ugly place," Danath Trollbane said, coughing as he drew up alongside them. Khadgar latched onto the steady warrior's matter-of-fact demeanor for support. "And is it me or do the Blasted Lands look a lot like this, as well?"

Khadgar nodded. It was good to have something else to focus on. "Their, uh—this world was leaking into ours through the rift. And whatever caused this damage—I suspect it was their warlocks and the dark magic they wield—began affecting ours as well." He forced himself to analyze their surroundings with a dispassionate eye. It was not just dead, it looked like this world had been sucked dry. What had the orcs *done* to this place?

"We managed to halt the process on Azeroth, thank the Light. But clearly the land here has suffered the same injury, only for much longer. I suspect this world was far more benign once."

Alleria frowned. "The road . . . it—" She went suddenly pale, then her lovely face contorted in anger. "Those . . . monsters . . ."

Turalyon had cantered up beside her. "What is it?"

"The road . . ." Alleria seemed unable to find the words. She tried again. "It's . . . it's paved with *bones*."

They all fell silent. Surely Alleria was mistaken. The road she indicated was no small path. It was a road proper, meant for dozens to ride abreast. For huge engines of war to traverse. It was wider than the bridge over the water that led into Stormwind, and so long that it trailed out of sight.

For it to be paved with bones would mean that hundreds . . . no, no . . . *thousands* of bodies had—

"Merciful Light," a young man whispered. He'd gone starkly white, and murmurs rose behind him. Even as the troops registered this horrific information, the enemy showed itself. Only a few orcs had been near the Dark Portal when they'd passed through. Khadgar had hoped they'd be the only ones they'd fight upon entering the orcs' world, but those few had had time to summon reinforcements. Along a ridge beyond the road of the dead, Khadgar could now see dozens of orcs, their weapons glinting in the harsh red light.

For the first time since this whole nightmare with the rift had started, Khadgar thought the soldiers might falter.

"It's a small army," he said softly. Orcs had been in his vision as well, orcs standing on a ridge, bellowing and snarling and cursing.

"We have an army of our own," Alleria said, looking at Turalyon.

"We do," Turalyon replied, emotion making his voice crack. He too had been shaken by their first sight of this world, but now he wore a look of passionate resolve. "An army that will stand between the orcs and those they would harm. That will not stand by and watch its own world suffer, as this poor place has." He looked back at his troops.

"Sons of Lothar," he shouted. "*This* is the fight we were made for! More than ever before, we fight for our world now! We will not permit them to do to us or others what they have done here!" His voice carried, clear and pure and strong, as bright and shining as the hammer he now lifted. "For Stormwind! For Lordaeron, and Ironforge, and Gnomeregan. *For Azeroth!*"

So be it, Khadgar thought, and followed his general into the fray.

CHAPTER FIFTEEN

N er'zhul sat upon his throne in Hellfire Citadel, the brooding, nightmarish fortress the Horde had built shortly after the clans united.

He loathed this place.

It was hideous, a disturbing, disjointed creation of jagged angles, dark stone, and corridors and walkways that twined in and over one another like a maddened snake. If it bore any resemblance to a traditional orc village, which was a collection of small buildings, huts, and short towers, it was only the most twisted distortion of such a wholesome thing, much as the orcs themselves had become twisted and distorted. Whereas orc huts were fabricated from green branches and covered in bark, these buildings were dark stone banded with rough iron. Strange support pillars rose around them, topped with gleaming steel spikes, as if colossal clawed hands were erupting from the cracked ground to grip the structures. The twisting, connecting paths extended from one roof to the next, more as if the buildings had melted and shifted than as if the paths were intentional. At the back rose a taller tower with a peaked roof. It was here that they had shaped a throne room for Blackhand, the Shadow Council giving a puppet ruler a pretend throne. Now that throne belonged to Ner'zhul, the new Horde leader in truth, and the rest of the abomination that was the stronghold with it.

Ner'zhul did not glance out through the arching windows toward the portal. He had no desire to be struck, again, by how desolate his once-fertile world had become. But really, there was no avoiding it, was there? Absently his fingers went to touch the white-painted skull on his face. Death. The death of his world, the death of his people, the death of his own idealism. Blood was on his green, gnarled hands; the blood of so many innocents. The blood of orcs who had trusted him, whom he had inadvertently led astray.

You must stop thinking of it that way, came a voice inside his head. He ignored it. It was easier to ignore the voice of the dead Gul'dan when he was not in physical contact with the skull. Yet even as he vowed not to give it heed, he cast a glance at it now as it sat on a small table. Torchlight danced off the yellowing bone. He found himself speaking to it, as if Gul'dan could hear him. Which, in a way, was true.

"We did much harm, you and I. Deathbringers, doom callers, both of us. But now we can try to save them.

And your skull, my old apprentice . . . your skull will be part of that. Dead you are better use to the orcs than you were alive. Back you have come, to your old master. Maybe together we can give them a new chance."

But that's not what you really want, is it, my master?

Ner'zhul blinked. "Of course it is! I have ever sought to aid my people! That I have become death to them . . . it sears me. It is why I wear this." He touched the paint on his face yet again. Skulls: the one before him, the one he adorned his face with. Death's heads.

Perhaps it once was, and Gul'dan's voice crept into his mind, soft, soothing. *But you are greater than that, mighty Ner'zhul. Together, we can—*

A scuffling sound drew his attention, and Ner'zhul reluctantly tore his gaze from the skull, leaving the latest debate with its owner unfinished. Gorefiend stood before him, along with a human Ner'zhul did not recognize, a tall, slender man with dark curls and a neat beard. The stranger wore sumptuous clothing and moved with the manner of a leader, all grace and confidence. There was something about him that did not ring true, and Ner'zhul frowned, sensing the power around the stranger.

"I have the artifacts," Gorefiend announced without preamble, holding up a large sack. Ner'zhul felt hope surge inside him and waved the death knight forward eagerly. Gorefiend approached the throne, pulling each of the items in turn from the sack and placing them in his ruler's lap.

Ner'zhul stared down at them, lifting each one to admire it. A large, heavy book, its red cover trimmed in brass and emblazoned with a raven in flight. A crystal the size of a man's head, its center faceted like a star and edged in deepest violet. And a long, slender scepter, silver and wood with a large white gem glittering at its peak.

"Yes," Ner'zhul whispered, resting his hands atop the three items. He could feel the power radiating from them, immense power—power enough to tear open the space between worlds. "Yes, with these we will create new portals. We will save the Horde. We must begin work at once! It will take some time to craft a spell of this magnitude, and everything must be exact." He allowed himself a smile. "But with these three things, we cannot fail."

Gorefiend bowed. "I told you this would work," he reminded Ner'zhul. He stepped back a pace and turned toward the human he had brought with him.

"We could not have retrieved the artifacts if not for the black dragonflight. Deathwing is their father and leader."

Deathwing! Ner'zhul's hands tightened on the arms of his throne. Skulls, death knights . . . and now before him a mighty being even named for death. Ner'zhul could see the dragon's true form wrapped around his human shell like wisps of smoke, and shivered inwardly. Deathwing's lips curved in a smile that was not at all warming, and he bowed with a hint of mockery. Ner'zhul tried to calm his racing heart. This, too, he had dreamed of—this shadow of death.

"He freely gave us the aid of his children in exchange for passage through the Dark Portal for himself, his kin, and certain cargo he provided," Gorefiend said.

"Cargo?" Ner'zhul found his voice, though he winced slightly at how treble it sounded in his ears. "What manner of cargo?"

"Nothing you need worry yourself about," Deathwing replied in the smooth, cool voice. It carried the subtlest hint of a deadly serious warning. For an instant the torches flickered as if a sharp wind stirred them, and the dragon's shadow rose up behind him, filling the room.

You see? Even now you fly with the dragon, all unwitting. You fly with the shadow of death, Ner'zhul. Will you not embrace it?

Ner'zhul wanted to clap his hands to his ears, but he knew it would be a futile gesture. He took a deep breath and forced himself to be calm.

"I thank you for your aid, Deathwing. We are grateful."

"*Lord* Deathwing."

"Of course—Lord Deathwing." The human-seeming dragon stood there, not acknowledging the subtle dismissal. "Is there anything else we could help you with?" Ner'zhul said. He wanted this creature gone.

The dragon-man considered, lips pursed, long fingers stroking his beard. Ner'zhul got the distinct impression that his pondering was feigned.

"That is generous of you to offer, noble Ner'zhul," he replied after a moment, managing to twist the words so that they sounded sarcastic. "And I would be lying if I said the skull you have over there did not intrigue me greatly." The words were polite, diplomatic, but they surged with barely restrained power, and the dragon's eyes glowed for an instant with a fire that put the torches to shame.

Ner'zhul gulped. Did Deathwing hear Gul'dan's voice too?

Deathwing chuckled softly and extended a well-manicured hand. A ring glittered in the light. "Come, good Ner'zhul. It's my understanding that with these trinkets I helped your friend Gorefiend obtain, you have all the power you need to achieve your goals. The skull is not necessary to you anymore. And I want it."

Ner'zhul fought back rising panic. While what Deathwing said was true, he did not want to hand over the skull. Gul'dan had been his apprentice, after all, and if there was any knowledge still locked in that yellowed relic, surely no one had a better right to it than Ner'zhul.

"I grow impatient," said the silky smooth voice of the dragon named for death. "I don't think you want me to be impatient, Ner'zhul. Do you?"

Ner'zhul shook his head and found his voice. "Please, take the skull, if you wish it. It is a trifling thing." A lie, of course, and both he and the dragonlord knew it. Deathwing smiled, showing sharp teeth, and strode to the skull. His eyes widened as it came into contact with his flesh, and for an instant Ner'zhul saw spikes and scales and metal plates where flesh had been, and smoldering red eyes in a long, triangular head.

"I must say, I'm pleased with our . . . partnership. It seems to benefit us both." The voice was warm, almost gloating. "Know that, if you should have need of us, you have but to call. I shall leave you for now. Several of my children will remain behind and heed all your commands as if they were my own." He nodded to both Ner'zhul and Gorefiend, then turned and exited the room, the skull in his hand, draped beneath a portion of his long cloak.

The orc shaman and the death knight watched him leave. "I wish he had not taken the skull," Gorefiend said after they were sure the dragon had gone. "Still, if we do not need it, it is a small price to pay for the artifacts he helped us acquire."

Ner'zhul took a deep breath, as if the air in the room was suddenly breathable again. "Do you have any idea what he wants it for?" he asked Gorefiend.

"None," the death knight admitted reluctantly. Their eyes met. In Gorefiend's glowing red depths, Ner'zhul saw something that alarmed him almost as much as the dragon's presence had: worry.

"Time grows short, and our window is narrow. Let us make all preparations as swiftly as we may." They needed to leave this dead world before it was too late.

CHAPTER SIXTEEN

Khadgar found he liked looking at the night sky in this world.

It wasn't red.

He sighed and adjusted his telescope, focusing in on a particularly bright star. It was a tiny bit closer to the constellation he'd dubbed Turalyon's Hammer. Now, if it would just—

"How much longer?"

Khadgar started, began to slip, and grabbed a handhold on the roof. "Damn it, Alleria, quit sneaking up on me like that!"

The beautiful ranger, peering at him from the window, simply shrugged. "I can't help it if I move quietly. And you're so focused you wouldn't hear an ogre trundling up here. How much longer?"

The mage sighed and rubbed his eyes. The tower whose roof he was currently perched atop was part of an outpost they'd named Honor Hold. It had taken months to lay the foundations for it and months more to

finish the outer walls and one or two buildings, including this one. During that time they'd had to fight off repeated Horde attacks, though fortunately most had been
little more than brief skirmishes. That the Horde was
out there was certain. That they were holding back was
also certain. Figuring out *why* they were holding back
was one of the reasons Khadgar came out, night after
night, to look at the stars.

The last several months had not been without their
challenges.

Since arriving and emerging victorious in that first
battle with the orcs on their native world, the Alliance
had held the portal. At least on this side. Shortly after
this expedition had come through, they had cheered at
the sight of more troops and supplies following them.
"Courtesy of the kings of the Alliance," they'd been told.
Particularly welcome had been a few kegs of ale. For that
little luxury, they had Magni Bronzebeard to thank.

But that hadn't lasted. When the second caravan of
supplies had failed to materialize on the appointed day,
a small group sent to investigate had returned quickly
with news that the orcs were currently in charge of the
Azerothian side of the portal. And so it had gone, the
supplies that made existence bearable—even possible—
coming only sporadically. Sporadically, too, came the
promised troops. Turalyon had optimistically predicted
being able to mount an assault within a month, but
with the portal changing sides so often, the promised
troops were unable to get through.

The orcs were based in a foul-looking fortress to the west of Honor Hold. It was huge and well-fortified in addition to being aesthetically repugnant, and any attack would take a lot of thought and preparation if it was to be successful.

"Soon," Khadgar told Alleria. "It will happen soon."

It had been a puzzle, at first. Shortly after they had arrived and building had begun on Honor Hold, the orcs had started attacking. That in itself was not surprising. What was surprising was that they kept attacking. Not daily, and not a lot of them. But enough. Also strange was that they seemed not to care about the portal anymore.

"Whatever else you can say about the Horde, they've never been stupid," Turalyon said one evening as he spoke with Danath, Alleria, Kurdran, and Khadgar. "So why do they keep just throwing themselves at us? Their numbers are too small to take the hold. And they're not after the portal."

"I do not think we are too late to prevent Ner'zhul from opening portals to other worlds," Khadgar mused. "Though why he has not done so, I'm not certain. He has the artifacts he needs. He must need something else." Khadgar had leaned back in the rough wooden chair, stroking his long white beard thoughtfully.

"Wouldn't it take massive amounts of power, and some very complex spellwork?" asked Danath. "Maybe he's spent all this time just working out the details."

"Doubtful," Khadgar said. "It's complicated, yes, but

I'm sure he was working on it while he was having the artifacts retrieved. Scepter, book, and Eye," he mused, thinking. "And what else? What could he be waiting for?"

They'd tried interrogating a few orcs they had captured, but none of them had told them anything useful. These were not death knights, but peons—cannon fodder, sent only to delay the Alliance while Ner'zhul waited for . . . whatever.

While knowing the need to travel light, Khadgar had nonetheless permitted himself to take a few items with him. One was a ring that enabled him to understand any language—and to be understood. It was what had enabled them to interrogate the orcs, who spoke only their own language. Among the other items were a handful of books—spellbooks and one book that had once belonged to Medivh. There was nothing magical about it, just notes about Draenor, its skies, its continents. Khadgar found comfort in gazing up at the skies at night; they were only red in the daylight, and Khadgar amused himself by identifying constellations while letting his mind chew on Ner'zhul's mystery. Comprehension came to him one night while he was so engaged, as if the stars had the answer. And it turned out they did.

"Scepter, book, and Eye!" he'd exclaimed to Kurdran as he rushed out of his quarters.

"Eh?" grunted the startled dwarf. "Lost yer mind finally, have ye, laddie?"

"Get the others. We need to talk." A few moments

later, the commanders of the various forces were in the tower. "Turalyon—you first. Get out there and look through the telescope. Tell me what you see."

Turalyon threw him a look of utter bafflement, but obeyed. Peering through the telescope, he said, "I see . . . stars. What am I supposed to be looking at?"

"Constellations. Groups of stars." Khadgar was so excited that the words tumbled out of him. "What do they look like?"'

"Well, one's kind of a square. The other's long and thin. I can't see any other distinctive shapes."

"No . . . you're not used to looking at them. One of Medivh's many areas of expertise was astronomy. He had books with star maps of constellations I'd never even seen. Constellations of this world."

"That's all well an' gud, lad, but I'm not about tae crawl up there without understanding why ye want me tae," Kurdran grumbled.

"Look at this." Khadgar shoved a book into the dwarf's hands. Turalyon continued to look through the telescope as Alleria, Danath, and Kurdran examined the book Khadgar had foisted upon them. "What do you see?"

"Constellation names," Danath said. "The Staff . . . the Tome . . . and the Seer."

"Scepter, book, and Eye," Alleria said slowly, lifting her fair head to stare at Khadgar with admiration. "So . . . Ner'zhul needed those artifacts because they corresponded with this world's constellations?"

"Yes—and no," said Khadgar, barely able to restrain his excitement. "There's much more. Once every five hundred and forty-seven years, there's a celestial event that involves these three stars. See that reddish dot in the middle of the book? That's the first thing that appears. In about a month you'll be able to see a comet streaking through the scepter. And at the next moon cycle, the moon will be full right smack in the middle of the Eye. Apparently it's quite the spectacle, according to these notes."

"So if Ner'zhul has items that correspond to these constellations," Turalyon said slowly, still peering at the stars, "and he uses the artifacts at a time when something extremely rare is happening in the skies to those three constellations—it augments his power, right?"

"The harmony so established, the sympathetic resonance—by the Light, Turalyon, I'm not sure it'd be possible to fail at any spell using that kind of energy."

Turalyon lifted his head from the telescope. "When?" was all he said.

"Fifty-five days. And the power will last for three."

They waited for more reinforcements, chafing at the delay. At least they knew precisely how long they could wait, and when they would have to attack regardless of their numbers. Khadgar sighed at the ranger who had interrupted his stargazing as he slipped back through the window. "We're one day closer than we were yesterday. I can't rush the stars, Alleria."

"Soon, soon; patience is a virtue," Alleria muttered angrily as Khadgar climbed back into the room. "I'm sick of the platitudes."

"For an elf, you're awfully impatient."

"For a human, you drag your heels. I want to be fighting, not holed up here."

Khadgar's irritation suddenly boiled over. "You don't want to fight, Alleria, you want to die."

She suddenly went very still. "What do you mean?"

"We've all seen it. You rush out there, on fire for blood. On fire for your revenge. You're reckless. You fight badly, Alleria, and you didn't use to. That's why Turalyon keeps ordering you to stay close, and sometimes not even go out at all. He's worried he's going to lose you."

Her gaze was haughty, cold, and angry. "I am not his to lose. I belong to no one but myself."

Khadgar knew he should just shut up. But he couldn't. He had held back all this time, watching Alleria and Turalyon, who obviously still loved each other, circle one another like wary dogs. He could take it no longer. "You don't even belong to yourself. You belong to the dead. Joining them won't bring them back, Alleria. There's a good, kind, intelligent man right here in this keep who could teach you a thing or two about how to live. You should try living for a change—opening yourself to something rare and wonderful instead of slamming doors."

She marched up to him until their faces were only inches away. "How dare you say such things to me! It's none of your business! Why do you care how I choose to live my life?"

"I care because I don't *get* to choose!"

The confession burst from him before he could stop it, and they both fell silent, staring at each other. He hadn't realized the truth himself, but there it was, out in the open now, naked and raw. "I know you think of our lives as shockingly brief. Our youths are even briefer. What, ten years to be young and strong, at the most . . . most alive we'll ever be? I didn't even get that. I became an old man at seventeen. Alleria, I'm even younger than Turalyon! Look at this face. I'm twenty-two—but what twenty-two year old girl would have this old man?"

He pointed angrily at his face—lined, framed by snow-white beard and hair. She gasped slightly and stepped back. Compassion softened her expression. Suddenly embarrassed, Khadgar looked away.

"I just—to watch the two of you throwing away something I'll never even get to taste—it bothers me, sometimes. And I'm sorry. I shouldn't have taken it out on you."

"No—I'm sorry. I didn't think."

The silence hung, heavy and awkward, between them. Finally Khadgar sighed. "Come on. Let's go find Turalyon and the others. We need to finalize our plans. Because, this is going to happen . . . well, you know."

"Soon," she said, and gave him an uncharacteristically gentle smile.

★　★　★

"The place is enormous," Alleria explained. Turalyon had asked her and her rangers to scout the citadel, and now the two of them, plus Khadgar, Kurdran, and Danath, were in the meeting hall discussing what they'd found. "The walkways on the walls alone support dozens of orcs. There are watch towers here." She indicated the places on the map. "We should attack from this area, here. While you're distracting them there, I can send rangers in and dispatch the sentries. Without an alarm being raised, the real fighting force will come in from the main gate—which we'll have opened for you."

"Good," Turalyon said. "We'll be attacking on two sides, one completely unexpected. We'll need to hit them hard. Box them in, don't give them room to escape, and then close ranks and cut down any orc still fighting."

"We'll be attacking from above," Kurdran pointed out, "keepin' them busy whilst you lads and lasses charge across tae finish the job."

Turalyon nodded, but Alleria shook her head. "You'll be busy with your own problems," she said. "They've got dragons, remember?" They had all seen the long dark shapes circling about the citadel, swooping and diving like great birds at play.

But Kurdran laughed. "Aye, but only a handful, lassie! We'll be killin' them afore you can blink, don't ya know?"

Turalyon couldn't help but smile at the Wildhammer leader's confidence. "Nonetheless," he said, "we'd best not assume any help from your gryphon riders, just in case." Kurdran nodded. He looked over at Khadgar. "Can you do anything to negate their warlocks, or the dragons?"

"I'm sure I can come up with something," Khadgar replied. He glanced at Kurdran. "I have some ideas that might give your gryphons even more of an advantage, and provide help for the soldiers as well."

Turalyon nodded. The plan was beginning to come together. Now for the part he dreaded. He took a deep breath. "We'll need someone to stay behind and be in charge of Honor Hold, in case we need to fall back. Alleria, I'd like that to be you."

"What?" She stared at him, openmouthed.

"It's key that someone I trust stay here. This is our base. We can't risk losing it if they split their—"

"You need me on the assault."

"I told you. I need you here. Send your rangers to take out the sentries."

She shook her golden head. "No you don't. Any soldier here would know how to hold this keep. My rangers answer to me. And I will not send them with you. Not if you order me to stay behind."

"Be reasonable," he began, but she interrupted him.

"Reasonable? I'm a veteran of more battles than you have years, Turalyon!"

"Alleria, you're—you're reckless," Turalyon said, hating to have to say it but seeing no other choice. "I've saved your life when—"

"And I've saved all of you, more than once!"

"Gentlemen," Khadgar said smoothly, clamping a hand down on Kurdran's and Danath's shoulders and steering them toward the stairs, "I'm sure you both want to see that celestial alignment I'm talking about."

"Och, aye," said Kurdran, and the three of them left the room quickly.

Turalyon was too focused on Alleria to notice that they'd been given a moment of privacy. "Alleria, you don't fight smart. Not anymore. I can't keep watching your back to save you from yourself!"

"I have a right to revenge! They butchered my family—my people—"

"You think Lirath would have wanted you to throw your life away? What kind of testament to his life would that be?"

It was the first time he had spoken of Alleria's brother, and the name stilled the hot words on her lips. Recklessly, Turalyon continued before she could speak again. "I know you're a good fighter. Just—not right now."

"Lirath . . . the others . . . I wasn't there with them. I might have been able to do something. But I wasn't *there*. I stayed safe while they died." Tears stood in her bright green eyes, and Turalyon inhaled swiftly. He had not seen her weep for her lost kinsmen before. "So I did the next best thing. I went after their murderers. And it helped. It kept pushing the pain away."

And suddenly Turalyon understood. "What you told me that night," he said, praying he was saying the right thing, "I had it translated." He hesitated, then whispered, "'Help me forget.'"

The tears welled and slipped down her angular cheekbones. "But I didn't want to forget. I don't want to let them go. If I don't grieve them . . . it's as if they're not really gone."

Tears stung Turalyon's own eyes. His heart was breaking for her. But she needed this. She needed to grieve, to mourn the dead. Killing orcs was no longer the panacea it once had been; it was no longer keeping the pain at bay, and she was starting to come undone with the holding-in of all of it.

"I can't stay behind. Don't ask me to. I stayed behind the last time. I won't watch someone I love go to his death while I—"

Suddenly her arms were around him, her head buried against his chest, and he held her tight. Her slender body shook with sobs too long held in check, and she clung to him like a drowning person. Turalyon pressed a kiss against her golden hair, inhaling her scent of pine and loam and flowers.

"I will never leave you behind," he vowed.

She turned her wet face up to his. "And I," she whispered as he bent to kiss her, "will never leave you."

CHAPTER SEVENTEEN

"Finished!" Ner'zhul sank back onto his throne and closed his eyes a moment, before glancing down at the scroll that lay unrolled across his lap. It had taken him months of research, planning, study, and concentration, but at last the spell was complete! Once the alignment occurred, he would be able to open portals to the other worlds, and his people could once more have a world—many of them, even—as vibrant as they were themselves. And it would all be because of him.

"Good," Kilrogg rumbled from his stance nearby. "A few more days until the alignment is complete, then we can finally abandon this forsaken place to the humans and begin the task of rebuilding our people!"

Ner'zhul regarded the one-eyed old warrior thoughtfully. Kilrogg had always impressed him, as much for his sharp mind and excellent tactical sense as for his fighting skills, and when the scarred Bleeding Hollow chieftain had limped back through the portal,

Ner'zhul had seen that sending him back out into battle would be a waste. Besides, there weren't many Bleeding Hollow warriors left—two years of hiding from humans and their allies had taken a heavy toll on the once-large clan. Ner'zhul had chosen to keep Kilrogg by his side instead, and to make the Bleeding Hollow clan his bodyguards. His own Shadowmoon clan had not been pleased with that, of course, but they were still numerous enough to be a force against the Alliance. Besides, Ner'zhul thought, he was warchief of the Horde now, not just chieftain of the Shadowmoon. He couldn't show favoritism.

"We have a journey ahead of us first," he told Kilrogg. He gestured at the citadel around them. "I cannot risk the spell failing. We have the skies cooperating with us; we must command the cooperation of the very land as well. I need to access the ley lines, as many as possible, so that Draenor herself will power the spell that releases us from her diseased grip." He sighed. "There is only one place that is ideal for such a task. The Temple of Karabor."

Kilrogg's one eye widened, but his expression did not change otherwise. "The Black Temple!" he said in a hushed tone.

Ner'zhul nodded. He did his best not to reveal the disgust he felt. He still remembered the war against the draenei with revulsion and not a little guilt, and the idea of entering their former temple sent chills down him, but he knew Kilrogg and the rest of the Horde did not share his sentiment. For them the death of the draenei was still a glorious victory, and the Black Temple a noble spoil. It was time for Ner'zhul to believe this also, if he were to lead them correctly. "If I perform the rite there, we cannot but succeed."

"I will make arrangements for us to depart at once then," Kilrogg said.

"Depart? Where are we going?" Kargath asked as he stomped into the throne room. The Shattered Hand chieftain had a broken arrow shaft protruding from his left shoulder. He reached up now and tore it out with a grunt. Ner'zhul had put Kargath in charge of the attacks against the Alliance stronghold, and the fool insisted upon leading many of the skirmishes himself. Most of the time they never even faced any of the humans directly—the Alliance archers rained death down upon them from above until Kargath got fed up and signaled the retreat. But at least it kept the Alliance occupied—and Kargath as well.

"I must go to the Black Temple when the stars align to cast the spell and open the new portals," Ner'zhul explained, rolling the scroll and tucking it securely inside the pouch hanging from his belt. He rose from his throne and patted it absently. It was not the most comfortable seat he had ever had, but it was certainly the most impressive. He would have a new one crafted on whatever world they went to next.

"I will gather the troops," Kargath replied, turning to go, but Ner'zhul stopped him.

"No," he said. "Not yet. Summon Dentarg and Gore-fiend instead. I will speak with the four of you here, and give you each your orders." Kargath hesitated, and Ner'zhul barked, "Now!" Kargath raised his scythe-blade hand in salute and hurried from the room.

"I will send word to Hellscream," Kilrogg said, and turned to leave.

"No."

Kilrogg turned slowly, eyeing Ner'zhul. "They are still on Azeroth. We need to give Grom and his clan orders as well."

"No, we do not. Grom Hellscream already has his orders. He is part of this plan as well." At Kilrogg's look of unease, Ner'zhul drew himself up to his full height. "You do not doubt my wisdom, do you, Kilrogg?"

The moment dragged out, heavy with tension, but Kilrogg eventually inclined his head. "Of course not, shaman."

"Go gather your warriors," Ner'zhul said to Kilrogg after Kargath had gone. "Tell them to make ready. We will depart shortly."

Kilrogg nodded and left as well, and Ner'zhul began pacing the room. He wondered if the bomb had worked as Gorefiend assured him it would. It must have; Grom had not charged through, red eyes blazing, demanding blood. That was well. Hellscream had always been a difficult one to manage, but he had served his purpose. He was no longer necessary.

Kilrogg returned shortly, a simple nod confirming

that his warriors would be ready. Gorefiend arrived a few minutes later, and both Kargath and Dentarg were right behind him.

"Good," Ner'zhul said when all his lieutenants were present. "I have completed the spell," he told Gorefiend and Dentarg, and the two smiled.

"I knew you could do it, master!" Dentarg said.

"You will be going to the Black Temple, then?" Gorefiend asked, and his smile widened to a grin at both Ner'zhul's and Dentarg's surprise. Ner'zhul realized he should have expected this. Gorefiend had been one of the most promising young shaman he had seen, in terms of ability and perceptiveness if not empathy, and he had grown into a powerful, confident, clever warlock even before his death. Since returning as a death knight, he had only grown in strength and cunning. He would become a danger soon.

"Yes. It is the ideal place to cast such a spell."

"I can have the Horde warriors ready by nightfall," Kargath reported. "We will leave behind a small force to man the walls here, and the rest will protect you along your way."

But Gorefiend shook his head. "The Alliance won't fall for our ruse much longer. And when they realize we have only been striking to keep them pinned up in their hold, they will attack with their full strength."

Ner'zhul nodded—he had already guessed as much himself. "You will remain here, with your clan," he instructed Kargath. "Hold off the Alliance forces when they attack, while we go ahead to the Black Temple." He frowned. "I will need time. You must delay them as much as possible. If you survive, meet us there."

Kargath paled slightly, then straightened and nodded. "The plains before these walls will be piled high with the bodies of their dead!" he promised, raising his scythe-hand. He nodded to the other three, and then turned on his heel and stalked off. They could hear him shouting orders once he'd left the room.

"They cannot win," Dentarg commented after a moment.

"They don't have to," Ner'zhul replied. "All he has to do is keep the Alliance from following us long enough for me to complete the spell." He shrugged. "This citadel is strong, and his Shattered Hand warriors are tough. They will put up a good fight, and the rest of our people will honor their memory on all the worlds we conquer in their name."

"Of course." Dentarg took the subtle rebuke with only a slight wince. "I do not doubt Kargath's loyalty, or the prowess of his warriors. He will fight to the end."

"Yes." Ner'zhul eyed the Shadowmoon ogre mage. "And you will fight with him."

"What?" This time Dentarg rocked back in surprise. "But master, you will need me at the Black Temple! My place is at your side!"

Sudden fury welled up inside Ner'zhul, hot and pure. "Your place is wherever I tell you it is!" He snarled, his voice deepening with his anger.

Dentarg's eyes widened. "Your face . . . ," he murmured, cringing back, fear and shock on his own visage. "The skull . . . !"

The moment passed, and Ner'zhul felt the fury leave him. He reached to touch his white-painted face; it felt the same to him as it always had.

"They have magi of their own, these humans," he said, his voice gentler. "Someone must be here to stop them, someone with enough magic to hold his own. Someone I can trust." He stepped forward, stretching his hand up to place it on the ogre's shoulder. Dentarg stepped backward, and Ner'zhul let his hand fall. "That someone must be you."

Dentarg glanced down at Gorefiend. "Why doesn't he stay?"

"I have far more knowledge of rifts and portals than you do," the death knight said. "Ner'zhul will need my help with the ritual, or I would stay here and teach those humans a thing or two about magic."

Dentarg's small, piggy eyes darted back to Ner'zhul.

"I do need him with me," Ner'zhul said in an avuncular, almost apologetic tone. "And while I would have you there as well, you can aid me far more by being here and lending Kargath your sorcerous skills."

The ogre finally nodded. "I will do as you command, master. I will stop the human magi. And if I survive, I will join you at the Black Temple." The desire to see that place and walk its halls was naked in his voice.

"Good." Ner'zhul nodded and turned away. They

both knew the chances of Dentarg's surviving were slim. "I will leave the black dragons here to help in the battle. Go now and coordinate with Kargath." From the corner of his eye he saw Dentarg nod, and listened as the ogre stalked out of the room. Once those thunderous footsteps had faded away, Ner'zhul turned back to Kilrogg and Gorefiend.

"Gather your warriors and your death knights," he told them. "We leave at once."

Less than an hour later, Ner'zhul was astride a wolf loping from Hellfire Citadel, surrounded by Kilrogg and his warriors. Gorefiend and his death knights scouted ahead on their reanimated steeds. Behind them, Kargath Bladefist and his orcs cheered from the citadel walls, chanting Ner'zhul's name. The Horde leader rested one hand on his pouch, making sure the scroll was still there, knotted the other in his wolf's thick pelt, and rode on.

He did not look back.

CHAPTER EIGHTEEN

Alleria had stayed with Turalyon that night. They had talked for a long, long time, and the chasm that had yawned between them had been bridged. When they could speak no longer, they let their hearts and bodies continue the healing. They had emerged from his quarters together the next morning, and if there were knowing grins from their friends, both knew there was also genuine happiness. Even though they faced death today, they would do so knowing that there was much joy waiting for them if they survived.

And they would survive. Turalyon was not about to let her go, not now that they'd found each other again.

He had kissed her hard, and she had slipped off in the predawn light with her rangers. They had discussed signals and such, and finally decided on a time.

"We will douse the lights for ten heartbeats, then relight them if we have taken the watch tower," she had said. "If we haven't taken them all by the time the sun is about to clear the horizon, come anyway," Alleria had said. "They will be able to see as well as you an hour later and this plan will have been for naught."

He'd nodded. Turalyon was at peace with her fighting out of his sight now; he knew she would take no unnecessary risks. She had returned to herself again.

Danath would lead the initial, decoy charge, while Turalyon would bring up the main offense once the Horde forces had engaged them in combat. Danath and his men would be outnumbered, but not for long.

"It will be harrowing for a while," Turalyon warned him. "You'll have to trust that all is going according to plan." He hesitated. "It might feel like the portal battle all over again, Danath."

Danath had regarded his commander with steely eyes. "No it won't. This time, we're the ones who are taking those bastards by surprise. I trust you, Turalyon. The ghosts of those dead boys will be fighting alongside us. They'll be at peace when we trap the orcs between two fronts."

Turalyon had shivered a little. "Danath . . ." he had begun.

Danath had waved it aside. "I've no death wish," he said, "don't worry about that. I want to get home one day, and to bring these boys home with me. I don't want to write one damned more letter that begins 'It is with deepest sympathy.' "

Turalyon had gripped his second-in-command's shoulder and nodded. Danath would hold the orcs long enough for the second force to crash upon them like a tidal wave.

Kurdran and his gryphon riders, along with Khadgar and some other magi, would be ready to be part of that wave. Turalyon would miss the mage's presence— they had been together throughout the Second War, and it would feel strange to go to battle without Khadgar by his side. But if all went well they would meet up and celebrate their victory.

Now he waited in the chill predawn for the signal. Danath's group had gone around and would be attacking from the rear with horses and loud shouts while Turalyon's group had moved carefully, quietly, on foot to a place close enough to see the signal but far enough away that the night still hid them. He gazed at the citadel, at the mile-long, solid wall that encased it. At intervals along that wall, huge braziers burned sullenly, casting just enough illumination to show the barest hints of the iron spikes that adorned the citadel. Jagged, powerful, dark—the building had a vivid presence. Turalyon somehow felt that not only would they need to defeat the orcs within its walls—the living ones and the death knights—but they'd have to defeat the citadel itself. It was an utterly hideous place, angular and organic at the same time, as if it were some massive beast whose flesh had melted in places to expose the sharp bones that had given it form.

He stared at the watch towers until his eyes ached from the strain. There . . . one of them had gone out.

And then been relit. Once the final light had been doused and relit, Turalyon heard the sound of human voices raised in a battle shout and the thunder of hooves. He wanted desperately to charge in, but he forced himself to wait. The rangers would need time and the opportunity to get to the gate, and that would only come when the orcs manning it had been called to fight Danath's men.

Every second was agony. Finally, when he heard the sound of weapons clashing and the bellow of orc war cries mixing with those of his men, he knew the moment had come. Turalyon lifted his hammer and raised it to eye level, where its dull metal head caught the early morning light.

"May the Holy Light grant us strength," he said quietly, and those gathered around him nodded, a murmur spreading among them as his hammer began to shine and then to glow from within. "May it guide us in this endeavor, leading us to victory, to honor, and to glory." For an instant the hammer seemed composed of white light. Then that light burst outward, washing across them all in a wave, and Turalyon knew the others felt the same strength and peace he did. A faint aura clung to the hammer and to each of them, outlining them against the red rock all around, and he smiled at this open sign of the Light's blessing.

Turalyon led his men at a fast lope toward the wall. The citadel loomed before them, and the closer they came, the more oppressive and mammoth it grew. He could see the gate now, looking like a mouth in a hideous face.

And then, right when he was wondering if he had mistimed the charge, the gate began to open.

"She did it," one of the men whispered.

"Of course she did," Turalyon said softly. "She's Alleria Windrunner." Light, how he loved her.

They were not the only ones who had noticed the gate opening, however. Even as Alleria and her rangers darted forward to join with Turalyon's group, a handful of orcs raced after them. Turalyon caught a glimpse of Alleria's golden hair in the faint light, and he sped up, breaking into a full run. His hammer rose almost of its own accord and began to glow again, a gleaming white light held high above his head. That caught one orc's attention, and the creature turned toward him instead of the rangers. It charged, and for a moment he thought it weaponless and mad—until he saw the scythe that served the creature for a hand.

"For the Sons of Lothar!" the paladin cried, tongue liberated as the need for stealth evaporated. He brought the hammer crashing down, crushing the orc's skull. Even as the first orc dropped, Turalyon hauled his weapon back around, striking a glancing blow to one in front of him before smashing an orc two paces over with his full strength. Another orc raced toward them, but an arrow suddenly protruded from its left eye and it toppled without a sound. A fifth snarled and swung the heavy club at its side, but Alleria leaped forward, ducked the blow, and thrust, her sword blade piercing the green creature's throat and emerging from the back of its head. Turalyon had spun and finished off the orc he'd stunned, and now he charged up the stairs at full speed, Alleria and her rangers and his men right behind him.

A troop of orcs met Turalyon as he rounded a bend in the stairs halfway up. They had the advantage of size, strength, and position, but he had momentum and determination. Holding his hammer before him, his hands gripping it just below the head, Turalyon used it like a small battering ram, slamming into one orc after another. The force of the impacts jolted him, and he had to fight not to totter back a step, but the orcs found themselves tossed aside and either slammed into the wall or toppled from the stairs, and fell to the ground below. The orcs that retained enough presence of mind to attack him in turn found themselves pierced with arrows, courtesy of Alleria and her rangers, and any orc Turalyon stunned but didn't kill the men behind him finished off as they raced up the stairs behind him.

In what seemed like minutes, but Turalyon knew had probably been longer, he reached the top. The citadel's ramparts stretched out before him, far longer than Honor Hold's but less even, more chaotic and oddly shaped. Some orcs stood here, heavy spears in hand, ready to hurl them down upon the approaching army, but most of the Horde had poured out of the front gates, Turalyon saw, and were running to meet the Alliance head-on. He also saw long dark figures circling above, and knew the black dragons were just waiting for the right moment to join the fight.

"Alliance!" Turalyon shouted, holding his hammer high and racing to the rampart's front edge. "Alliance!" From here he spotted Danath riding near the front of his group, and the warrior raised his sword in response. He was covered with blood and gore, but none of it was red human blood. Nor had he lost many men. The Light *was* with them!

Then what orcs were still up here reached him, and Turalyon was busy defending himself and clearing the ramparts of their defenders. The sounds of battle were everywhere: metal against metal, stone against plate, flesh against flesh, mixed with growls and roars and bellows and cries. The bodies were all mingled together, the orcs against the humans and their horses, with the gleaming sheen of armor and the dull luster of axes and hammers mixed in as well. At one point when he was able to spare a glance, Turalyon managed to pick out Danath again, and watched as the warrior impaled a charging orc upon his sword, yanked the blade free, and whirled to slice another's throat open.

Turalyon had just smashed down the last orc when he heard a loud shriek from above. Glancing up, he saw a cloud sweeping down toward the citadel, carrying a blast of hot air with it. He grinned at the sudden moist heat. The cloud had broken apart, forming a haze that settled over the citadel, blanketing it in fog that blurred edges and hid shapes and details.

The fog played tricks with sound as well, and so when a loud whoop sounded, Turalyon could not pinpoint its location. Neither could the dragons, it seemed, for they flew in circles, necks curling as they turned their heads this way and that, seeking the source of that sound. They didn't have to search for long—a small shape plummeted out of the fog, dropping like a stone toward one startled dragon. Just as they seemed about to collide the shape extended, long wings unfurling, and its rapid descent became a sharp wheeling dive. The gryphon—for such it had to be—banked around the surprised dragon. The dragon snapped at it, like a dog at an insect, but the half-lion, half-eagle creature was too fast. It darted beneath the dragon as the mammoth jaws closed right where it had been, and the dragon followed. It reared back and magma spewed in a long, fiery blast from its muzzle.

Again the gryphon and its rider were too quick. Over a dozen orcs shrieked in agony as the dragon accidentally incinerated its allies, too intent upon the swift gryphon to notice where it had directed its attack.

The dragon screamed in anger, slamming into the citadel and cracking the sturdy walls with a tremendous noise. Before it could gather itself and attack again, the Wildhammer atop the gryphon stood in his stirrups and hurled his stormhammer at the fearsome beast. As it struck the dragon in the eye, a thunderclap tore the fog asunder and brilliant sunlight streamed down. The Wildhammer whooped, his hammer returning to his hand as his gryphon soared back up, the sunlight gleaming on its feathers. Shocked, dazed, the dragon tried to fly, but the merciless Wildhammer dwarf led it on a merry chase, striking repeatedly at its wounded eye until, half-blinded and dizzy, it again slammed into the wall, which collapsed beneath the unintentional assault of the great beast. The dragon slid down to the earth, shaking it with its dead weight, a victim of its own violence.

The remaining dragons screamed their rage and hurtled toward the lone gryphon rider, who turned to meet their furious headlong flight. But just as they neared him, more gryphons burst from the remaining clouds above and descended upon the dragons. Each dragon was easily four times the size of a single gryphon, but the gryphons had speed and agility, wheeling about the larger beasts, luring them to the fortress, directing their fiery attacks or sending them careening into one another as they tried in vain to catch the elusive aerial dancers.

It looked to Turalyon as if Kurdran's earlier boast might in fact prove to be true. His Wildhammers were having enough success with the dragons already that they might well be done with those creatures soon enough to lend a hand with the main assault.

One of the gryphons broke away from the rest,

heading toward Turalyon. It bore two riders, one small and the other far larger, and the latter leaped down while they were still a short ways above the broad stone walkway, violet robes streaming around him. Turalyon felt his face stretch in a grin. Khadgar!

The mage waved his thanks to the Wildhammer who had carried him as the gryphon beat its wings and rose back up to rejoin the aerial fray. Then he turned his white head toward the main tower, eyes narrowing.

"I'll come help you when I'm done here," the mage said to Turalyon, gripping his staff in one hand and drawing the sword at his side with the other. "There's someone in there—an ogre mage. I need to deal with him first."

Turalyon nodded. He'd seen more than enough magic over the past few years to respect Khadgar's opinion on the matter. He turned as two men stationed by the far stairs came hurrying over, broad grins on their faces. Before Turalyon could ask why, he heard footsteps from that direction. And then heads appeared as several figures charged up the stairs and onto the ramparts. Figures wearing Alliance armor.

"Sir!" one of them called as they approached. "We have cleared the north wing!"

Turalyon nodded and returned the soldiers' salutes. "Good. I'll leave a few men here." He glanced at Alleria, who readied her bow. "The rest of you, come with me. We'll sweep the citadel to make sure it's clean, and then throw open the gates for the rest of our men."

They cheered, and he led them down the walkway Khadgar had just taken, turning off it halfway across to follow a narrower stair down. As he'd hoped, it led him into the heart of the orc stronghold, and soon Turalyon was too busy fighting off the orcs who had remained within to worry about Khadgar.

Khadgar paced the walkway slowly, his senses extended to study the area ahead of him. The ogre was still there, he knew, but did not seem to be doing anything—no spellcasting, no rituals. It was simply waiting.

Waiting for him.

The walkway ended at the tower, and Khadgar stepped inside. The room he entered was large and oddly shaped, not quite circular and with unevenly spaced angles, as if it had been carved from something rather than constructed. At the far end rose a monstrous chair that seemed to be pieced together out of colossal bones—he shuddered to think what beast might have yielded such specimens. Its high back reached almost to the arched ceiling above, and torches guttered to either side. But the throne was empty.

"My master is gone," a deep voice rumbled, as a massive figure detached itself from the shadows and moved to intercept him. Khadgar had seen ogres before, of course, but they had been down on the field and he had been back with the other magi, striking from a distance. This was his first encounter with one up close, and he found himself gulping as he stared up . . . and *up.* The creature's head nearly brushed the ceiling, and while its features were brutish, its deep-set eyes glittered with intelligence.

Then he registered what it had said, silently thankful for the ring that enabled him to understand it. "Gone?"

The ogre grinned, revealing surprisingly small, sharp teeth and large fangs. "Indeed," it answered. "He left here some time ago. Even now he is traveling to perform the ritual, while your Alliance is fighting its way past us." The creature scowled, then set its jaw. "We may die, but our deaths will ensure that the Horde lives on, and conquers worlds without end!"

"Damn!" Khadgar cursed, seeing what had happened. The orcs had tricked them! They'd allowed this attack simply so Ner'zhul could escape. "Nonetheless, if we're fast enough we can still go after him," he told the orc defiantly.

"You could," the ogre agreed. "But first, you must get past me." It raised its hands, each one larger than Khadgar's head, and they began to glow with a sickly green light that seemed to rise from beneath the skin. "I am Dentarg, of the Shadowmoon clan."

An honorable duel, then. "Khadgar of Dalaran," Khadgar replied. He raised his staff, and the tip began to shed a bright violet glow.

The ogre executed a clumsy bow. Then it struck. Both of its massive hands slammed forward, as if physically shoving Khadgar back. Green light erupted from them in a wave of energy that threatened to envelop and crush the human mage. Khadgar raised his staff, the violet light growing more intense, and the green wave split around him before bubbling away to nothing.

Next Khadgar struck, pointing the staff at the ogre's chest. The violet light lanced forward, stabbing toward the ogre's heart. But Dentarg batted the energy beam aside with his hands, the green still suffusing them, protecting him from any ill effect.

"We are well-matched," the ogre remarked, clapping its hands together. When it spread them wide, darkness billowed up between them, a great curtain of black that swept across the room.

"Perhaps," Khadgar replied. He did not move as the darkness fell, and within seconds he had vanished from sight, as had everything else. Through his other senses he could still locate the ogre, however, and knew that his opponent was searching for him. Khadgar waited another moment, unmoving, then slammed his staff down upon the floor. The shock wave split the darkness, cracking it as if it were blackened glass and leaving slivers and shards of it upon the floor, and threw the ogre from his feet as well. The crash Dentarg made as he fell was almost equal to the first shock wave, and the ogre groaned in pain.

Khadgar swiftly closed the distance between them. The light around his staff increased, until it was a beam of solid light, too bright to be violet though still tinged with that hue. He slammed the beam-encased staff

against the rising ogre's throat and held on as Dentarg
screamed, his flesh smoking where the staff touched it.

It was not a magical attack that saved the ogre then
but an instinctive one. He heaved Khadgar off bodily
and managed to regain his feet, though his neck bore a
charred black line across it. Dentarg snarled, showing
his fangs, and charged Khadgar, head down. But the
human mage sidestepped the attack and swung his
sword as the ogre stormed past, slicing the creature's
upper arm.

Dentarg's cry changed from one of rage to one of
pain. Green light rose again from his hands, though it
flickered here and there and flashes of crimson shot
through it. Bringing his hands together again, Dentarg
let the energy build between them, until he had a globe
of pure magic that writhed and roiled with hatred. This
he hurled at Khadgar, putting all his force behind it.

Khadgar studied the fast-approaching globe calmly.
Then he sheathed his sword and held out his hand,
palm outward. The globe connected with his flesh,
striking the palm squarely—and vanished into him, absorbed without a trace.

"Thank you," he told the astonished ogre. "I feel
much better now." He stamped one foot and a minor
shock wave toppled Dentarg again. The ogre landed
heavily on his knees, and bowed his head, knowing he
was in the presence of a superior opponent. Khadgar
spared him any further humiliation, drawing his sword
again and bringing it down upon the ogre's exposed

neck with all his might. Flesh and bone parted cleanly, and he stepped back as the ogre's head rolled across the floor, spraying blood in its wake.

For a moment he caught his breath, looking around the throne room, though he knew Dentarg had spoken the truth. He looked down at the ogre corpse, nodded, satisfied, and hurried back to find Turalyon. They would need to move quickly.

"Good news!" Turalyon shouted when he caught sight of Khadgar again. "We hold the citadel!"

"We were tricked," Khadgar said without preamble. "Ner'zhul is not here. He left well before the attack. He must have taken the artifacts with him. I wonder if he took the skull as well."

Turalyon stared at him. "It was all a diversion, then?"

"And we fell for it," Khadgar confirmed.

Turalyon frowned, trying to find the good in this. "Still—this was undoubtedly the bulk of their warriors. And we crushed them! We've also taken their citadel—even if Ner'zhul himself wasn't here, this was still their headquarters, and now it belongs to us. Their military might is broken for good."

"Aye, they'll not field another army again," Danath said, approaching them in time to hear the end of Turalyon's statement. His armor was battered in places, and he bore several cuts on his arms, legs, and face, but he seemed unfazed by the injuries as he reined in and dismounted beside them. Turalyon clapped him on the shoulder, happy to see that his lieutenant had survived.

"You did a fine job," he told Danath. "But Khadgar has discovered some ill news. Ner'zhul is not here—he knew we would attack, apparently, and stole away before we arrived. And we think he took the artifacts with him."

Alleria and Kurdran had joined them now, and Turalyon filled them in as well.

"Well, we'd best be after 'im, then, eh?" Kurdran replied.

"Do you know where they're going?" Alleria replied.

"I don't know," Khadgar said. "But I can find out." He smiled. "I know Gul'dan's magical aura from the war, and I know the Eye of Dalaran as well. I can trace both of them." The others stepped back as he closed his eyes, muttering something beneath his breath. The air around him seemed to shimmer slightly, and a wind appeared from nowhere, tugging at their clothes and hair. Then the mage's eyes snapped open. For an instant they glowed a brilliant white and showed strange images dancing within them. Turalyon shuddered, looking away. When he turned back his friend's eyes were normal once more.

"I found them," Khadgar reported, leaning slightly against his staff. "It wasn't easy, though. Turns out they're in two different locations."

Alleria shook her head. "The skull and the Eye aren't together? Why would Ner'zhul let either one out of his sight?"

"I don't know, but he has. The skull went north, but the Eye is headed southwest, through what I think they call Terokkar Forest. I sensed the Book of Medivh there as well, which makes me think that's the way Ner'zhul went. I'd assumed that he needed the skull for the ritual, just as I need the book and skull to close the portals. But apparently he sent the skull somewhere else, though I can't imagine why."

"And you need both? The skull and the book?" Turalyon asked.

"Yes," Khadgar replied. "I can't close the rift completely without them."

Turalyon nodded. "Then we'll have to go after both," he decided. He glanced at the others, weighing options in his head. "Danath, I think you'd like to kill a few more orcs."

"Indeed, sir, yes I would."

Turalyon sighed. It pained him to see those he was fond of so revenge-ridden. But who was he to judge—he had not seen his whole contingent slaughtered while he fled to get aid. Danath would have to make peace with his pain in his own way, as Alleria had finally done. He would need to learn that you could fight without hate in your heart—fight for something, rather than against it.

"Then you go after Ner'zhul. He's got a head start on us, so Kurdran, you and your gryphon riders scout ahead and find Ner'zhul and his companions. Attack them at once—kill them or at least slow them down and report back to Danath. He'll be following with ground forces."

"Take some of my rangers with you for scouting," Alleria said.

Turalyon smiled his thanks at her and said to Danath, "Your job is to destroy Ner'zhul and bring back those three artifacts."

"Consider it done, lad," Kurdran replied, and turned away to his gryphons. Danath nodded, saluted, and went as well, to gather the men and get them ready for travel.

Turalyon turned back to Alleria and Khadgar. "Getting that skull and closing the portal are my responsibilities. Khadgar, you're the only one who can trace the blasted thing. And Alleria . . ." He smiled softly. "I promised you I would never leave you behind."

"Indeed you did, my love. And do not think I won't hold you to it." He extended a hand, and she took it and squeezed it tight for a moment. There would be no more partings for them . . . until the final one.

And maybe not even then.

She grinned. "Let's go."

Together the three friends turned away from the conquered citadel and the portal in the distance. They would find the ghoulish relic that would seal that rift forever, or die trying.

CHAPTER NINETEEN

"They are gaining on us."

Ner'zhul glanced over at Kilrogg. "Then we move faster."

The Bleeding Hollow chieftain growled and shook his head. "We are already moving as fast as we can without killing our mounts and ourselves," he pointed out bitterly. "Any faster and my warriors will drop dead before the Alliance even reaches us. And who will protect you then?"

They had been marching for almost a week now, and the first few days had been uneventful. They had reached Terokkar Forest without any problem, and had stepped under those tall, twisted trees with a hint of relief. The forest was as dark and gloomy as ever, the dark clumped foliage of its trees high enough overhead that little sunlight could pierce their cover, the ground covered in fine dark moss and short scrub but otherwise bare. But after days of walking under the hot sun it was pleasant to find shade, and the forest seemed cool and peaceful.

Until one of Kilrogg's warriors, who had stayed far back from the rest to scout behind them, had come running to find them where they camped for the night.

"The Alliance!" the warrior had gasped, panting and sweating from his run. "They are right behind us!"

"They must have taken Hellfire Citadel faster than we'd expected," Gorefiend had said. "Damn Kargath! He was supposed to hold them!"

Kilrogg had remained calm, as always. "How many are there?"

The scout had shaken his head. "I could not get a clear count of them, but many. More than we have here, for certain. And they're moving at a frenzied pace."

"They're pushing themselves to their limits," Kilrogg had mused, idly stroking the scar below his missing eye. "Hate lends one speed."

"How long before they reach us?" Gorefiend had asked.

"They are perhaps two days behind us," the scout had answered. "But their leader drives them like a madman, and they are closing the distance rapidly."

"Rouse the camp," Kilrogg had decided. "Everyone up. We will march through the night to put more distance between them and us. Move!"

Within minutes they had been on the move again.

Since then they had taken only short breaks, stopping beside one of Terokkar's many glittering streams and rivers for water and to catch their breath. But still the Alliance came on, and the gap was lessening.

And now they faced an awful choice.

"We can stand and fight," Gorefiend suggested, but Kilrogg was already shaking his head.

"They outnumber us," the one-eyed orc pointed out, "by a significant margin." He scowled. "I hate to say it, but if we face them, they'll slaughter us. And while I will gladly die for the Horde, as will my clan, dying here will not get you to the Black Temple."

"And we cannot outrun them," Gorefiend offered. "I do not think that with their prey in sight, they will fall behind."

"We can take shelter in—" Ner'zhul began, but Kilrogg cut him off quickly.

"That is still days away," he interrupted hastily. "Surely we do not need to consider that just yet?" Sweat beaded across his brow and Ner'zhul was both surprised and amused to realize that Kilrogg Deadeye, a legendary figure known for his courage and sheer guts, was afraid.

This was not the time to be squeamish, however. "It is our only option," he pointed out, his tone sharp enough to prevent Kilrogg from breaking in again. "They are still gaining on us, and if we cannot run and cannot fight we must hide. And the only place in this forest we can effectively do that is—

This time the interruption came not from one of the two lieutenants before him but from above. Ner'zhul felt a change in the air, and the crackle of a possible storm, but unusually intense and concentrated in a tight line that bore down upon them. On instinct he dove for the ground. A heartbeat later something hurtled through the space where his head had been, trailing lightning behind it. He caught a glimpse of a dark blur that soared back up into the air and flew between the trees—to land solidly in the hand of a stout figure riding a winged beast that was bearing down upon them.

"Gryphons!" Kilrogg shouted, raising his axe above his head. "Take cover!"

Chaos erupted. Orcs ducked behind tree trunks and slid into the nearby river or hugged its banks. Everyone was stumbling and running and falling, scrabbling in the darkness to avoid the dimly seen figures up above.

A second lightning bolt streaked through the trees and seared Ner'zhul's sight, leaving nothing but a blinding white for an instant and flashing afterimages when that had faded. Then a thunderclap shook the forest, rattling the trees and throwing many orc warriors off their feet.

Clearly one of the Wildhammers' attacks had been successful.

The Wildhammers flew down upon their gryphons, hurling their stormhammers left and right. Some attacks missed their target, but those accursed hammers merely rose and returned to their owners, who loosed them again like vengeful spirits. Lightning split the air again and again, and the thunder was an almost constant roar. When they were not throwing their hammers, they were swooping in so close that the gryphons themselves could attack the orcs, slashing throats with claws the size of an orc hand, pecking out eyes and fracturing skulls with a single jab of a deadly beak. Between flashes Ner'zhul saw that some of the orcs had clustered together, assuming safety in numbers but in reality only providing an easier target. He watched a hammer blow scatter a dozen orcs at once. After the thunder and lightning only one of them even stirred, and that feebly.

"They're slaughtering us!" he hissed at Gorefiend, who was crouched beside him. "Do something!"

The death knight glared at him, and a slow, calculating grin spread across his rotting face. "This is but a handful of short human pretenders and overgrown birds. I thought the mighty Ner'zhul would be able to handle such a pathetic attack. But no matter. I can, if you are unable." He started to rise.

The impudence! Ner'zhul's mind shot back to the conversation with Gul'dan's skull.

Arrogance! He should not speak so to you.

No. He should not.

"You should not speak so to me, Teron Gorefiend," he said, his voice icy. Gorefiend blinked, surprised at his tone. "Nor will I permit it from you again."

Ner'zhul rose, fueled by his anger. He clenched his fists and concentrated on the earth beneath them and the air around them. His shamanistic magic had once made him one with this world, able to tap the elements themselves. But the elements no longer heeded his call—they had not since he had sworn allegiance to Kil'jaeden, as if the elements were disgusted by the demonic energy that now tainted all his race. But no matter. He had learned new skills since.

Whereas before the forest had been still, save for the cries of attack and the wails of the dying, now a wind erupted out of nowhere. A gryphon that had a moment before been diving smoothly for another pass, beak open in an angry shriek, claws extended, now cawed frantically as it was buffeted about as if by an unseen hand. Its rider struggled to maintain his seat, but failed and fell heavily toward the ground. The unburdened gryphon sought the skies. Ner'zhul gestured with both hands commandingly, and the wind snatched up dry gray sand and proceeded to scour both dwarf and gryphon with it. The Wildhammer cried out, not in victory but in agony as his skin was scoured from his bones. It was a sweet sound to Ner'zhul's ears. Its mount was no luckier. Feathers flew and droplets of blood were caught up in the whirlwind. Seconds later there was nothing but two piles of glistening flesh on the forest floor.

But Ner'zhul was nowhere near done.

A wave of his left hand, and rocks the size of his head dislodged themselves from the earth and shot upward as if hurled by the very ground rippling beneath them. Ner'zhul turned his attention to the rest of the Wildhammers. More rocks erupted from the ground, propelled into the sky, and the gryphons and their riders tried to dodge the suddenly animate stones. The attack against the orcs ended as the Wildhammers found themselves forced to concentrate on evading this new menace.

Ner'zhul turned to Gorefiend, a slightly superior smile on his lips. The death knight looked surprised, but recovered quickly. "Nicely done," Gorefiend said. "Now let me see if I can add to the confusion." Studying the forms darting about overhead, the death knight stood still a moment, eyes narrowed. "There," he said at last, gesturing toward one dwarf in particular. "I have seen that one before, during the Second War. He is their leader." Gorefiend stood up and raised his hands high. They began to glow with a pulsing green light, and then that energy shot upward, striking both gryphon and rider.

The gryphon squawked in obvious pain and plummeted, its wings furled tightly around it. At the same time, its rider convulsed as well and toppled out of his saddle. The gryphon managed to shake off its injuries and spread its wings just in time, turning a dead fall into a choppy glide and then beating hard to rise back up above the lower branches and into the shadows. Its rider was not so fortunate. The dwarf slammed into the ground and lay unmoving. Gorefiend was already sprinting toward the body, as was Kilrogg, and Ner'zhul joined them.

This was the first dwarf Ner'zhul had ever seen up close, and he studied the strange little figure intently, taking in the stout muscular build, the craggy features, the long braided beard and hair, and the tattoos that covered most of the dwarf's flesh. The Wildhammer was bleeding from several gashes, but his chest still rose and fell regularly.

"Excellent," Kilrogg commented, pulling a leather strip from his belt pouch and tying the dwarf's hands together behind his back, then doing the same to his feet. "Now we have a captive." He lifted the bound dwarf to his feet, and bellowed, "Begone, winged pests, or we will slaughter and devour your leader while you watch!"

The Wildhammers apparently decided they had had enough. The gryphons cawed and clacked their beaks, then wheeled and flew up beyond the trees, disappearing from view. Only Kilrogg's captive remained behind.

But that couldn't last. "We need to assess our losses," Kilrogg pointed out after the Wildhammers had gone. "And we should post scouts to check on the rest of the Alliance army."

Ner'zhul nodded. "Take care of it," he said absently. He would die before admitting it, but he found himself surprised by his own power. It had come so easily, and was so strong. And produced such impressive results. It felt . . . good.

"We lost a full quarter of our forces," Kilrogg reported some time later, stepping back up beside Ner'zhul where the shaman waited against one of the larger trees. "Those dwarves know how to attack quickly and effectively, and they used the trees to good advantage." Ner'zhul could hear the grudging respect in the aging chieftain's tone. Kilrogg was too good a strategist not to appreciate sound tactics, even if they were from the other side.

Then Gorefiend joined them. "The rest of their army is still racing toward us," he confirmed. "Clearly they sent the dwarves on ahead to wound us and slow us down." The death knight bared his teeth at their captive, who lay on the ground near Ner'zhul's feet. He had groaned several times but had not yet regained consciousness.

"How far behind us are they?" Ner'zhul demanded.

"Still a day, perhaps two. And in our current state we cannot stand against them."

Ner'zhul nodded. "Then only one course of action remains," he stated. "We must go to Auchindoun."

Kilrogg started, his eyes bulging, though he must have known this was coming. "N-no!" he stuttered. "We cannot! Not there!"

"Do not be such a whelp," Gorefiend sneered at him. "We are out of options! That is the only way we can hope to survive the Alliance army and reach the Black Temple!"

But the one-eyed orc shook his head hard. "There must be another way!" He grabbed Ner'zhul's arm with one hand and Kilrogg's with the other. "There must be! We cannot go to Auch—to there! It will be the end of us!"

"It will not," Ner'zhul replied coldly, pulling his arm free and staring at the orc. "Auchindoun is an unpleasant ruin, and a reminder of an ugly time in our past. Nothing more."

It was more, of course. Much more. Auchindoun had been well over a hundred summers old when Ner'zhul himself had been only a baby. It had belonged to the draenei then as always, hidden away deep within Terokkar Forest. The old shaman had told them that it was a sacred place where the draenei buried their dead and then returned to commune with their spirits, just as the orc shaman communed with their own ancestors. As youths Ner'zhul and his clanmates had crept through the forest to study the strange place, staring at its towering, chiseled stone dome. They had challenged each other to enter, to race through the tall doorway carved into the arching stone block that marked the dome's front, touch something within, and then return. None of them had dared attempt it. Ner'zhul had gone farther than most, creeping up to the entryway and running his hands along the rough stone that formed its massive doorway, but he could not bring himself to go farther. According to his clan's shaman, no one ever had. "The draenei dead protect their own," he had said.

Then the war had come. The orcs had banded together, setting aside their clan rivalries. As a single mass they had attacked the peaceful draenei and slaughtered them. Ner'zhul tried not to remember the part he had played in that destruction, or the fiery creature who had given the order to destroy those quiet, unthreatening neighbors. And when Ner'zhul had refused to subject his people to such an outsider's control, when he had resisted that stranger's grandiose plans, he had been replaced. His own apprentice, Gul'dan, had willingly given himself to the stranger, binding himself to the creature's will and gaining immense power in return. Gul'dan had fed the Horde's bloodlust, transforming the orcs into the brutes they were today. Then they had crushed the draenei and their entire culture. Only a few had escaped, and those had fled into Auchindoun, hoping the orcs would not pursue them there.

They had been mistaken. Gul'dan's lust for power knew no limits, and his new master had promised him untold might if he wiped the draenei from the face of the world. So Gul'dan had sent agents, a group of warlocks from his Shadow Council, which controlled the Horde warchief Blackhand from behind the scenes. They had marched into Auchindoun, confident in their victory and already imagining the power they would wield from the artifacts rumored to be buried there.

But something had gone wrong. They had found an artifact, to be sure, only to discover that it contained a strange entity—a being they had freed, though whether deliberately or through careless arrogance no one could now be sure. Because the creature's exultant escape had shattered Auchindoun itself, the great stone dome crumbling, the massive temple within it torn to pieces, and the countless underground tunnels that housed the draenei dead exploding outward into countless fragments. The impact had destroyed the forest for over a league in every direction, and littered the now-barren ground with bones from the draenei who had once lain at rest within Auchindoun's catacombs. Only a few of the Shadow Council members had survived and escaped, fleeing back to Gul'dan to report the grave-city gone but any draenei within assuredly killed as well. No one had ever returned there, and to this day orcs avoided the Bone Wastes, as the area around Auchindoun had been named.

Until now.

"We have no choice," Ner'zhul reiterated, fixing first Kilrogg and then Gorefiend with his gaze. "We must go there. Some of the tunnels must survive, at least for a short length, and within them we may be able to defend ourselves. Without such protection the Alliance forces will kill us all, and our race will die with us."

Kilrogg sputtered something unintelligible. Gorefiend stared at him contemptuously, red eyes narrowing. "Ner'zhul is right. We've no other choice. But we must proceed with caution. I've no wish to waken something we can't defeat."

"It is settled, then," Ner'zhul said. "Is it not, Kilrogg? I should hate to leave you behind."

The old chieftain swallowed hard and lowered his head. "Ner'zhul, you know I am afraid of nothing that lives. Nothing that I can fight and tear to pieces. But that place . . ." He sighed deeply. "The Bleeding Hollow clan will go where Ner'zhul leads."

"Good. Between us we will be more than a match for anything that waits within those walls. Now gather our warriors, and your death knights," he told his two lieutenants. "We must reach the Bone Wastes as soon as possible."

Kilrogg nodded and walked away. Gorefiend glared after him, then saluted Ner'zhul and followed, his fellow death knights clustering around him before he had gone far. Ner'zhul turned away as well, his hands clutching the bag at his side and feeling the rough shapes of the artifacts it contained. Despite his strong words, he wondered what they would find in Auchindoun. Did the draenei dead still linger there? Would they hold him responsible for the actions of his former pupil, or would they see that Gul'dan had betrayed Ner'zhul as well? Would the strange ruins prove a much-needed shelter from the Alliance army, or would taking his orcs there only expose them to even greater danger? He did not know. But he could not think what else to do, and so they would find out. Ner'zhul just hoped he was not making a grave error.

The Horde warriors came to a stop, staring. The trees ended just behind them, and before them stretched the gray soil and littered fragments of the Bone Wastes. Auchindoun rose in its midst, squat and ugly, the remains of its shattered dome jutting upward like broken teeth, the ruined temple nestled within it like a battered head half-buried in the dull ground.

Ner'zhul stared as well. He couldn't help it. The last he had seen of this place, the draenei's holy resting place, it had been ominous and intact. Now, with great gaping rents in the temple walls, with entire sections open to the sky, with the forest that had cradled it blasted away and bones covering the ground, he could barely reconcile it with the dreadful majesty of the monument that had so terrified him in his youth.

The ground seemed to shake all around him, and at first Ner'zhul thought it was merely the rush of blood pounding through his veins, his heart racing from the sight of the ancient grave-city. Then he realized the vibrations were coming from somewhere outside himself, and glanced around. His orcs stood still or quietly shuffling, some looking around as if searching for the same thing he was. Then he looked behind them, through the trees, and saw shapes flickering there.

"The Alliance is right behind us!" he shouted, his voice carrying easily here where the trees did not impede it. "We must take shelter! Into Auchindoun! Hurry!"

"Move it, you worthless cretins!" Kilrogg added, slamming his axe against a nearby tree so hard the entire trunk shuddered. The sound and the motion seemed to wake the warriors from their shocked trance, and they broke into a run, all heading for the draenei building's ruined doorway.

Passing through that massive, lopsided portal, Ner'zhul felt a shiver of fear race through him. Were there still spirits guarding this mass tomb, as he had felt there were when he had first approached it so long ago? Or had they fled with the building's ruination?

There was no time to ponder such things. He hastened deep into the demolished temple and down through a gaping hole into what remained of the labyrinth below, Kilrogg and Gorefiend beside him and several of Kilrogg's most trusted warriors before and behind them. Underground, Auchindoun was more elaborate than without, its carvings more intricate.

Some things, it seemed, had survived, at least to some degree. An elegant arch, now shattered, rose above the base of the stairs they had used, and above that Ner'zhul saw strangely graceful shapes that seemed less faithful than representative. Thick pillars had once supported a high roof directly beneath the temple floor, and portions of them remained, their rough unadorned surfaces a strong contrast to the decorated walls around them. Niches had been carved into those walls, row upon row of them, and hints of white and yellow within told him what he would find there. Bones. No doubt all the walls had contained such draenei remains, and it was their contents that were now strewn across the Bone Wastes, the draenei ancestors exposed to the elements where once they had rested in peaceful shade beneath heavy stone. The floor here was stone as well, small tiles intricately worked into a cunning pattern, and broad stairways connected different levels.

Glancing down Ner'zhul saw at least six floors below them, their centers ripped away by that fateful explosion, the remnants now exposed to open air. Then the others pulled him into a wide tunnel that ran off to one side from this central space.

"The walls here are still sound," Kilrogg was saying, glancing about and nodding in approval. Ner'zhul was pleased. Kilrogg had worried him earlier, with his almost debilitating fear. But now that he had made up his mind, Kilrogg was committed and calm.

"A few collapses, but most of the ceiling remains and the floor is still passable. We can group our warriors a bit farther back, where there seems to be less damage." He gestured toward the tunnel's back end, which stretched on into shadow. Ner'zhul saw that he was right—there was less rubble there and the ceiling seemed unbroken. "We can set up a strong defensive post here. The Alliance will have a hard time digging us out once we're set in."

"Some of the lower tunnels may still be intact," Gorefiend pointed out. "We should check those carefully before venturing forth. If nothing . . . else is there, they might provide an even better stronghold."

Kilrogg nodded and detailed some of his warriors to search the rest of this tunnel and several to search the tunnels nearby, though he warned them not to stray too far. The others he ordered to carry rubble to the tunnel mouth and to build a low wall across it as best they could. Then he, Gorefiend, and Ner'zhul settled in to wait and to discuss battle strategies.

A few hours later one of Kilrogg's scouts returned. The warrior's eyes were wide, but a faint smile played across his lips. "There is something you need to see!"

"What is it?" Ner'zhul asked, rising to his feet and dusting his hands against his thighs. He and Gorefiend had been working on a contingency plan that might ultimately save them all, but it was not yet finished.

"I—we found something, sir," the warrior replied. The smile was broadening into a grin now, and that lifted Ner'zhul's spirits. Whatever it was they had found, clearly this scout did not consider it a threat. Ner'zhul gestured for the orc to lead on, and followed him out of the room they had claimed for their project and down the long tunnel behind it. Other warriors were clustered there, and as Ner'zhul approached they fell back.

"By the ancestors!" Ner'zhul whispered, the words falling from slack lips as he gaped openly. Before him stood several figures. One was an ogre and the rest . . . were orcs! Ner'zhul did not recognize them, though, and their attire and adornment were wholly strange to him.

"Who are you?" he demanded, stopping only a few feet from these strangers. "And what are you doing here in Auchindoun?"

One of the orcs stepped forward. He was short and stout, much as Gul'dan had been, and indeed Ner'zhul saw much of his former student in the stranger's features and posture. The new orc's domed head glistened in the torches the warriors had placed along the hall, and his long fringed beard was black streaked with silver. Yet there was an aura of power around him as he stood there in strange rune-scribed black robes, an ornate staff in one hand.

"Ner'zhul?" he said softly, his voice rough. "Is that you? Where is Gul'dan?"

"Gul'dan is dead, the traitor," Kilrogg replied, snarling at the stranger and glowering down at him with his one eye. "He nearly saw the death of us all for his own twisted ambitions! Ner'zhul rules the Horde once more!"

The stranger nodded, apparently not shocked by this news. "Then I submit to your leadership, Ner'zhul," he replied, the words halting as if he had not spoken in some time. "I am Vorpil, once of the Shadow Council, though perhaps you do not recognize me."

"Vorpil!" Ner'zhul stared at the stranger, squinting in the dim light. Yes, it was Vorpil, whom he remembered as a promising young Thunderlord shaman. But that Vorpil had possessed a thick dark braid of hair that reached down his back, and his beard was short and black as well. What had happened to him, to age him so and give him such clear mystical strength?

Gorefiend stepped forward now, for he had also been part of Gul'dan's Shadow Council. "Vorpil?" he whispered. "How came you here, old friend?"

Vorpil hissed and jumped back, as did the others. Fear flitted across his blunt features as he got a good look at the death knight.

"Be easy," soothed Gorefiend, lifting his hands in a calming gesture. "It's me, Teron Gorefiend."

For a long moment Vorpil stared at Gorefiend, his eyes narrowing as he studied the death knight with more than mere sight. After a second those eyes widened. "Teron Gorefiend?" he asked. "It . . . yes, it feels like you, trapped within that rotting meat." The orcs lowered their weapons and looked uneasily at each other, but trusted their leader. Vorpil stepped forward hesitantly. "What has happened to you? What dead thing do you drape about your spirit like a cloak?"

"I inhabit the body of a creature called a human," Gorefiend answered. At the blank looks he received, he added, "It is one of the races we encountered when we went to that other world—Azeroth. The one Gul'dan created a portal to."

"Other world?"

Ner'zhul was growing impatient. "When our world was dying, Gul'dan was able to open a portal into another world known as Azeroth. It is there that we met these humans, and Gorefiend's spirit inhabits one of their corpses. More we will tell you later, but right now we would hear your tale, for that may aid us in our current plight."

"What plight?" asked the larger figure Ner'zhul had noticed earlier, stepping forward to join the conversation. "Are you in danger?" This creature was an ogre, as Ner'zhul had already realized, but not just any ogre, he saw as the torchlight revealed a second head atop those massive shoulders. Two-headed ogres were rare, and two-headed ogre warlocks—as the dark energies emanating from this one told Ner'zhul it was—were rarer still. Only two such had been part of Gul'dan's inner circle, he remembered: Gul'dan's own right hand, Cho'gall, and—

"Blackheart," Gorefiend whispered, having obviously reached the same conclusion. "Is it really you?"

The creature's two heads nodded. "It is," one answered. "Though not perhaps as you remember us," the second added.

That was certainly true. Ner'zhul had never had dealings with Blackheart directly—Gul'dan had recruited the ogre warlock personally, after taking control of the Horde—but he had seen the creature around more than once, a towering figure with long warrior braids and piercing black eyes.

Those eyes were gone now. One head had a strange metal patch over its right eye, evidently welded in place, and the other eye bore a sorcerous tattoo around it. The other head, which was covered in a close cowl, had only a single eye above its nose, twice the size of any natural orb. Strange runes covered Blackheart's flesh, a single massive sigil across his chest and two below a band on each arm. The ogre wore a loose robe draped across both shoulders and then down across its belly, a belt holding the fabric over its loins. Thick bracers covered both wrists, and it held a massive spiked hammer in one oversized hand. Blackheart's sheer size and strength had always been imposing, but now he presented a truly fierce figure.

"I ask again," the ogre rumbled, "what plight?"

"The Alliance is right behind us," Kilrogg said. "The humans we spoke of earlier, and other races they work with. We are outnumbered and cannot stand against them, not without aid."

"We cannot fall," Gorefiend added. "The fate of our people rests upon Ner'zhul reaching the Black Temple. He will perform a rite that will save us all." He did not explain further, but both Blackheart and Vorpil nodded.

"We have been here since Gul'dan sent us to Auchindoun to plunder it," Vorpil told them, "surviving within these tunnels and hoping to one day return to the Horde. Now the Horde has come to us. We know these ruins well, for they have been our home for years." The others behind him nodded. "We will fight these humans alongside you, and help you defeat them."

"I will crush any who stand against us," Blackheart agreed, raising his enormous hammer so the top spikes brushed the hallway's high ceiling. "We will rend them limb from limb!" his other head assured them.

"Our ancestors have smiled upon us, to restore you to us in this hour of need," said Ner'zhul. "Know that you are welcome in the Horde once more, and will share in our people's triumph."

The warriors around them cheered, chanting "Ner'zhul!" and "Vorpil!" and "Blackheart!" and "Horde!" loud enough for the walls to tremble, and Ner'zhul smiled.

He had been right to brave Auchindoun. With these newfound allies, he would surely make it to the Black Temple in time.

CHAPTER TWENTY

Danath slammed his fist into his other palm. "We have them!" he shouted. "Now all we have to do is go in and get them!"

"Yes, but not now," Talthressar replied. One of Alleria's rangers, he had somehow assumed the role of Danath's adviser during their pursuit of the Horde, and despite his aloof manner Danath liked him. Too, more often than not the elf was right. "We need to wait until morning."

"By morning they'll have dug in," Danath protested, glaring down at the slender russet-haired ranger and then across the bone-littered stretch of land to where the colossal ruins sprouted. "If we attack now we can take them before they've had a chance to settle and build up defenses!"

"Look around you," Talthressar urged. "You may be ready to fight, but your men are not. It is growing dark, and they are weary. Would you have them stumbling about underground, blind to danger and too tired to defend themselves from inevitable ambush?"

Danath turned an angry, anguished face to the elf. "They killed Kurdran!"

The news had shaken a group of men who were already exhausted from the brutal pace Danath had set them. When the Wildhammers had returned, making no effort to hide the tears in their eyes at the thought of their fallen—including their beloved leader—Danath had been forced to turn away himself. He'd lost so many, and now the bluff, jovial dwarf too—how many would have to die before these damned orcs were *stopped?*

"I know," Talthressar said quietly. "And you will not honor his spirit if you take men too exhausted to fight to avenge him. They will simply join him in death."

Danath scowled, but he knew the elf was right. He'd pushed his men hard all the way from the orcish citadel trying to catch Ner'zhul's forces in time. It was ironic that now that they had, they were too tired to do anything about it.

"One night," he said finally. "We'll camp one night, rest, and attack at first light."

"A wise choice," Talthressar agreed, and as usual Danath could not tell if the ranger was being sarcastic or sincere. And, as he always did, he decided to ignore the elf's tone and take his words at face value.

"Have the men fall out and set up camp," Danath instructed his lieutenant. "We attack at dawn." Then, trusting his subordinates to take charge, he dismounted and led his exhausted and thirsty horse down to the river to drink. He splashed water on his dusty, sweaty face and drank deeply himself, then headed back to virtually collapse in his tent.

A few hours later when Danath awoke, he was surprised to see not only other tents but also several tall posts outlining a large, rough square.

"What is all this?" he asked Herrick, one of his sergeants. "We're only here one night."

Herrick shrugged. "Some of the men mentioned this'd be a good place for a fort," he explained. "They wanted to set posts to mark it out. I didn't see the harm to it, so I said yes. It went fast—the elves helped."

"In light of the sacrifice of our dwarven friends, I thought it would be a good gesture," said Talthressar, stepping from the shade of a nearby tree and gliding over to them. "We are, after all, an alliance. How better to symbolize that than to start a stronghold together?"

Danath stared at the elf. "You're the one who was pointing out how tired my men were! And now instead of resting they're cutting and placing posts?"

Talthressar smiled. "It is but a few posts, and many hands make light work. See for yourself the results." Danath looked where he indicated. Dwarf, human, and elf stood together talking quietly. They still looked tired, but there were smiles on their faces, and one of Danath's men clapped the elf and dwarf on the shoulders as they spoke.

"Your men were right. Not only does it have strategic value, but this is the only place we have seen thus far on this planet that was not red and lifeless. This forest, at least, is still very much alive. If we some day return to these woods and complete what was begun here today, we shall name it the Allerian Stronghold. It is fitting—the orcs destroyed much of Quel'Thalas, and so in return we will claim this, the one green region left upon this forsaken world. And if not, these posts will stand as a reminder that the Alliance entered this forest and claimed it as their own."

Talthressar's voice had more passion in this short speech than Danath had ever heard from him before. Danath took another look at his men and nodded. "Let's get those orcs first, eh?"

He accepted the food Herrick pressed upon him, found a quiet place by one of the campfires to eat, and then stretched out his legs, crossed his arms over his chest, leaned back against the tree trunk behind him, and again fell asleep.

Danath started awake to the sound of yelling in Thalassian and a strange, eerie squawking sound. He leaped to his feet. "What's going on?"

He didn't get a verbal answer in the chaos. Running toward the source of the noise, Danath saw what seemed to him like a dozen elves piled atop something that was making the awful screeching sound.

"Step back!" he ordered. The elves reluctantly rose, dusting themselves off, while two of their fellows kept a firm grip on one of the strangest things Danath had ever seen. The intruder wore deep purple robes, now torn and stained with blood and grass. It was about the size of a man and had arms and legs, but the resemblance stopped there.

Jutting from the cowl was not a human face, but the head of a bird.

It had a long, sharp face, most of it a glossy violet beak, and slanting oval eyes that glowed yellow in the night. A cluster of feathers rose above each eye like a human brow, and these merged with the shock of red, purple, gold, and brown feathers all around the head to form the equivalent of hair. One bright eye was partially closed; the elves had not been gentle in their capture.

"What manner of creature are you, and what were you doing skulking about our camp?" Talthressar demanded.

"You're wasting your breath," Danath said. "It can't understand our language."

"But Grizzik can! He does! And he means no harm!" The creature's voice was a strange trill, but clearly understandable. Danath blinked at him.

"He's like a trained parrot—all sound, no meaning," one of the men muttered, and raised a fist to silence the bird-man.

"No, wait," Danath ordered. "Say that again."

"Grizzik! I mean no harm! I only want to know— who are you? Why have you come?"

Danath glanced at Talthressar, who shrugged, stepped back, and let Danath direct the inquisition.

"Your name's Grizzik?" At the rapid nodding, Danath continued, "Answer our questions and maybe we'll answer yours. What are you?"

"Grizzik is arakkoa," the bird-man answered, his words oddly clipped and each followed with whistles and sighs. "Old race. Oldest maybe in the world. Grizzik is curious. He means no harm!"

"So you keep saying. But why were you spying on us? How do you know our language?"

"Arakkoa is clever," Grizzik said proudly. "Smart. Grizzik followed you, listened close, learned fast! Thinks you are strange. Curious."

"Are the arakkoa friends of the Horde or their enemies?"

That produced the greatest reaction yet. Grizzik's facial feathers puffed up like a frightened bird's and he huddled in on himself. "Grizzik fears and hates them. They were not bad once. I have seen it. But now . . . ." He shivered.

Danath had seen enough of Grizzik by now to realize he was no physical threat and nodded to the elves who still held the intruder. "Give him water, and tend to his wounds," he told them. To Grizzik, he said, "Explain."

"Arakkoa are ancient people. We stay to ourselves. But! We watch peaceful draenei, primitive orcs. But who could know? Madness came to the orcs. What— we know not."

Despite his heavy robe, he shivered, feathers shifting uneasily before he made a visible effort to continue. "Orcs and the draenei are not friends—but they do not hate. They share respect."

"Whoa, whoa," said Danath, holding up a hand. "Slow down. Orcs and *draenei*? Draenei as in Draenor?"

"Draenor is the name they call the world, yes. They are proud of themselves, they named the whole world after themselves. They were strong . . . before."

"You said there was a madness . . . the orcs turned on these draenei?"

Grizzik nodded. "Yes, yes. There were once many, many draenei. They used bright light. Lived here a long time. They think themselves strong and good, no one can stop the draenei, no no. But orcs—" Grizzik made a whooshing sound and swept his arm before him. "Gone. Only a few left now. Now the once-proud draenei are hidden away."

Danath felt a chill. "The orcs . . . wiped out a whole civilization?" He glanced up at Talthressar. "Sounds like the Horde did a practice run before they came to Azeroth."

"Indeed it does. Except Azeroth did not fall to them as Draenor has. We were stronger."

"Luckier, maybe." He shook his head, his face hard. "A whole civilization of peaceful people. What a damned shame." He returned his attention to the arakkoa. "Keep talking. You said the draenei were peaceful, but also powerful, and that the orcs were primitive at first. How is it they were able to wipe out these draenei?"

"The orcs . . ." Grizzik groped for words. "Came to-gether. No longer separate."

"The orcs do have different clans," Talthressar said. "It sounds as if they were not always a unified, directed Horde."

"Long Ears is right!" chirped Grizzik excitedly. At any other time Danath would have laughed at the of-fended look that crossed Talthressar's face at the insult. "The orcs united. They grew strong, cruel. Their skin turned from—hm. From this," and he pointed to a brown feather, "to this," and he indicated a green one.

"Their skin turned color? From brown to green?" Danath said, raising an eyebrow.

"Yes! Then green orcs attacked and slayed draenei. Arakkoa said, we are next!" He pointed to the massive ruins just visible through the trees. "Auchindoun. The dead draenei sleep there. It is holy. Most—" It patted the soil.

"Most is below ground?" Danath asked.

Grizzik nodded. "Winding, below ground, yes. All dead now."

A thought occurred to Danath. "Have you been there? To Auchindoun? To these winding tunnels?"

Grizzik nodded enthusiastically.

"Do you know your way through?" Danath asked.

Grizzik nodded. "I have been down, down, many times. But . . . why do you wish to go there?"

"I am Danath Trollbane, of the Alliance," Danath re-sponded. "We have pursued the orcish Horde here from our own world, and I intend to attack them on the morrow and see them dead and their threat destroyed. They're hiding in those tunnels. I'm going to find them. We . . . could use your help."

Talthressar looked disapprovingly at Danath, but the human ignored the glare. Grizzik seemed harmless enough, and he obviously hated the Horde. If he could save them from getting lost in a maze in a city of the dead, Danath was all for it.

"Griz—I. I know a way in. A way that even the orcs who live there now do not know." He leaned forward. "I know where they live, and which passage the new orcs will pick."

Danath and Talthressar again exchanged a glance. "That's incredibly useful information," Danath said after a moment. "We—"

"Ah!" The arakkoa got to his feet excitedly, staring at the gryphons which roosted in the trees, claws digging into the branches they had chosen, heads tucked under one wing. He hurried toward them.

"Magnificent!" he whispered, reaching out to stroke the nearest gryphon along a shoulder. The beast shuddered slightly but did not wake up. Danath noticed that Grizzik's hands were more like talons than anything else, but his touch across the gryphon's feathers was gentle.

"'Ere now, what are ye doing!" exclaimed one of the Wildhammers, hurrying toward Grizzik.

"Easy, Fergun," Danath said before the dwarf tackled their potential new guide. "They're called gryphons, from our world," Danath explained to Grizzik. "Each gryphon has a rider, a Wildhammer dwarf like Fergun here."

Grizzik had reached the last gryphon in line, a magnificent beast that stood shivering as if cold, despite the fact that it was a warm night. "She grieves," he said, stroking her shoulder and back.

"'At's Sky'ree," Fergun said in a voice that was gruffer than usual. "Kurdran's mount."

Grizzik clacked his beak and cocked his head askew, peering at Danath. "Sky'ree's rider, Kurdran, was the leader of the Wildhammers," Danath explained. "He . . . he fell in battle today."

Grizzik nodded. "Ah. Prisoner. I saw him."

"Prisoner?" Danath exclaimed.

"The orcs brought a captive with them into Auchindoun. Looked like him," and the bird-man pointed at Fergun. "Red fur on chin. Blue drawn on skin. He was very loud."

Danath felt a surge of excitement. Kurdran was alive? He turned to Talthressar. "We need to rescue him."

"The dwarf knew the risk," the ranger replied coolly. "And the mission must come before personal attachments."

But Danath shook his head. "Kurdran is one of Turalyon's most trusted lieutenants. The fact that he's even alive means that the Horde realizes he knows things about our forces that they'd find very valuable— if they can crack him. We need to get him out of there before that happens. And this . . . arakkoa can take us to him."

Talthressar sighed. "Grizzik. No doubt it is dangerous for you to help us. Why do you do so?"

"It is a simple answer. You oppose Horde," Grizzik replied with a decisive clack of his beak. "I too hate the Horde, for what they have done to arakkoa, to our world."

Danath looked from Grizzik to Talthressar. The ranger nodded. It was the best chance they had—and if Grizzik did try to betray them, he'd pay, and quickly.

"Let's do it," he said.

By the time Grizzik had sketched out a basic map of Auchindoun and the various tunnels, and explained them in Common that grew clearer almost by the moment, Danath had abandoned the idea of taking a small force in to rescue Kurdran. Instead, he had a far better plan.

Now he strode down a long, dark tunnel, only the torch in his hand providing any light. Grizzik was perhaps ten feet in front of him, and Talthressar was between the two of them, neither the arakkoa nor the elf requiring additional light to make their way.

And behind Danath walked fully half the Alliance army.

"Tunnels are wide—ten Alliance-people can go together," Grizzik had assured him. "And tall. Even ogres only stoop! Draenei built them well. The explosion that destroyed central passages did not reach the outer tunnels. Still clean and dry and secure."

That had convinced Danath, especially once Rellian had gone with Grizzik and reported back on the tunnel the bird-man had shown him. "It's like the long hall in a palace," the ranger had said. "Exactly as he told us, and I saw no other movement, not even vermin."

"We will divide in two," Danath had decided. "Half of our forces will follow me through the tunnels and up into Auchindoun. The other half will attack the front, sneaking in through the temple ruins and down to distract the Horde while we approach from behind. Once we're in position we'll strike and crush them between us."

And now, less than an hour after entering the tunnel, Grizzik was stopping and gesturing toward a wide door set into the wall. "Behind this are stairs," the arakkoa explained. "They lead down into Auchindoun proper."

Danath scowled, remembering the maze the arakkoa had sketched out for him. "And you don't know where exactly the Horde will be, or where they've taken their prisoner?" he asked again.

Unfortunately, the bird-man's answer was the same as before. "I know the way into Auchindoun," he said again, "but little beyond that." For a second the shadows of his cowl gave his long, sharp-planed face a sinister cast. "My people—we were not truly welcome here. Draenei revere their dead, not appreciate intrusion. I wandered, I explored here—learned a little. Only a little, though."

Danath nodded. He'd known it was too much to hope that the arakkoa could lead him straight to Kurdran, but still he didn't relish the idea of wandering aimlessly through miles of tunnel while the Horde warriors crouched in ambush.

Grizzik reached for the door—and jumped back, beak clacking in surprise, taloned hands rising even as he crouched, as the door shifted and creaked open. Danath raised his shield and lifted his sword as well—and stopped, staring at the figure outlined in the now-open door.

CHAPTER TWENTY-ONE

It was not an orc.

It was no race Danath had ever seen before. The figure was tall and broad-shouldered, with pale blue skin that nearly glowed in the dim torchlight. Its features were strong and noble, similar to an elf's but more rugged, with smaller pointed ears and wide eyes. A row of ridged plates covered the figure's high forehead, ending just above the stern brow, and thick tentacles hung down from the jaw on either side of a small tufted beard. Silver hair swept back around the head and fell beyond the shoulders of the stranger's richly brocaded but heavily worn robes, and he held a long, ornate staff in one hand. Cloven hooves emerged below the robe's frayed hem, Danath saw, and a sweep of motion behind them told him this strange figure had a tail as well.

The figure spoke in a deep smooth voice, raising the staff before him, and its tip flared with a pale violet light that reflected in his eyes. Those eyes caught sight of Grizzik, who was cowering behind Danath, and they narrowed. He spoke again, in angry tones, and Grizzik replied in the same language.

"What is this creature? What's it want?" Danath barked at Grizzik. "He certainly doesn't seem happy to see you."

"I told him, I was leading noble warriors here, that's all."

The being turned toward them again and impaled Danath with his gaze. Then he murmured something and his staff glowed yet again. He opened his eyes and spoke—in perfect Common.

"This . . . creature . . . tells me he leads you here. What are you, and what is your goal here, among the revered dead?

Danath lowered his shield and sheathed his sword, shocked that the other knew his language, but caring more about convincing him to let them pass than in finding out how he learned it.

"I apologize for the intrusion," he told the stranger. "We would not disturb your dead, or yourself. But the orcish Horde has taken refuge in your tunnels, and has captured our friend. We seek to rescue him and to defeat them as well."

The being—Danath assumed it was some sort of draenei, since Grizzik had said this was their temple—glared at the mention of the Horde, but nodded when Danath had finished. "Yes, the orcs have invaded our tunnels," he confirmed, lowering his staff to rest its base upon the floor. "They have laid claim to the Shadow Labyrinth, the deepest part of Auchindoun and the least damaged. It is there they will have taken your friend, and there you will find the majority of the Horde forces."

"The majority?" Danath asked, leaning forward eagerly.

"Some of the orcs did not arrive recently," the draenei said. "They have been here for some years, since just before the explosion. They reside within a different tunnel." He shook his head, a mixture of anger and grief on his noble features. "They have sullied this temple with their presence for far too long."

"We'll soon fix that," Danath assured him.

"You have told me your purpose. Now tell me what manner of creature you are. Many places I have traveled, but I have never seen your like before."

"I am human," Danath replied. "We hail from Azeroth, another world—the orcs forged a portal between there and Draenor and invaded, but we have broken their army and pushed them back. Now we seek to seal the portal once and for all, to protect our home and our people."

The draenei studied him, those large eyes unblinking, and Danath knew the stranger was somehow testing the truth of his words. At last he nodded. "That is a noble goal," he stated, and stepped out of the doorway to stand before Danath. "I am Nemuraan, one of the last of the Auchenai," he introduced himself. "We were the priests of our people, and cared for the dead here in Auchindoun." Danath introduced himself and Talthressar, and both bowed slightly.

"I applaud your determination, both in rescuing your friend and in removing the Horde's taint," Nemuraan continued. "I can help you with both tasks, if you will allow it."

"I'd be grateful," Danath answered honestly. He showed the Auchenai the rough map Grizzik had sketched out. "This is all I know of Auchindoun."

Nemuraan examined the crude drawing and chuckled, though it was a bitter sound. "Did that one draw this for you, then?" he asked, indicating the arakkoa with a quick jerk of his tentacled chin. Grizzik was no longer cowering, though he was carefully staying back among the Alliance warriors, Danath noted. "He has been prowling through our halls for years," the Auchenai continued after Danath nodded, "but he knows little beyond where to search for items to steal."

"I meant no harm!" Grizzik protested. "I did not know anyone remained within Auchindoun! I never would have taken anything if I'd thought—"

"If you thought you'd get caught?" Nemuraan interrupted. "Be careful with this one," he warned Danath. "The arakkoa were ever devious, and selfish."

"He has been true to his word thus far," Danath replied, "and I believe him when he says he hates the Horde."

"Yes!" Grizzik agreed fervently, his dark eyes glittering. "I hate them all! Please please! We have a common enemy!"

"That we do," Nemuraan admitted after a moment. "Very well, arakkoa, we will start fresh as of this moment." The Auchenai turned back to Danath, taking the parchment from his hand and producing a small black stick from a fold in his robes. With several quick marks he altered a few lines, linked a few tunnels, and expanded the map considerably. "The orcs will be here," he explained, indicating one section. "Come. I will lead you to them." Without another word Nemuraan thrust the map back at Danath and turned away, starting back up the stairs, his hooves clopping on the stone floor.

Danath glanced at Talthressar and Rellian, who nodded. He took a deep breath, and followed the draenei into Auchindoun.

"Have you lived here by yourself all these years?" he asked softly as Nemuraan led them into a second wide hallway and then through a series of twisting corridors.

"There are others," the Auchenai replied, his staff raised to light the way. "Several of us survived the Horde's attack and fled into the tunnels. Other draenei joined us later, seeking refuge from the Horde's sudden onslaught. Many of them died in the explosion, and others have been lost since. Only a handful of us remain."

Danath glanced around, wondering where these

others might be, but ahead of him Nemuraan shook his head.

"You will not see them. Though you seem noble and true, it would not be wise for me to put the rest of my people at risk. They will remain hidden while I aid you, so that if you do betray me, our kind will yet continue."

"A wise precaution," Danath agreed. "I'd have done the same."

They continued to walk for some time, finally stopping at another door. "This marks the start of the Shadow Labyrinth," Nemuraan explained. "Behind it lies the Horde." He turned and studied Danath closely, his face somber yet his eyes alight with . . . anticipation? Joy? "I would aid you further, if you will permit it," he offered softly, "though I warn that the type of aid might prove unsettling to some."

Danath frowned and raised an eyebrow. "What do you mean?"

The Auchenai bowed his head. "In my keeping are the souls of all our departed," he explained humbly, hands clasped on his staff. "At times of great need I may call upon them. I would do so now—they would relish the chance to rid these halls of the orcs' foul touch."

Danath was a little shaken at the matter-of-factness with which this was presented. He knew the Horde's death knights were orc spirits placed in human bodies, so clearly spirits could survive beyond death, although he'd always been taught the dead should be left to rest in peace. But if Nemuraan was a protector of the dead, it would be all right if he asked for their help . . . wouldn't it? Danath had said to Turalyon earlier that the ghosts of the men who had fallen would fight with him when they found the orcs, but he'd been speaking metaphorically. It looked as though the ghosts of someone's fallen took such comments literally. Finally Danath shrugged. Such questions were for those of a more esoteric mind-set, and from a military standpoint he could certainly use all the help they could get.

"I am honored," he told Nemuraan. "And if it would not disturb or anger them, we would welcome their assistance."

Nemuraan nodded and bowed deeply, clearly pleased with Danath's reply, then straightened and raised his staff high. Violet light blossomed down the length of the hallway, filling it with light and awakening answering gleams all along the ceiling. These gleams grew brighter rather than dimming, their colors shifting from violet to blue to green to gold as they descended and expanded, gaining shape and definition. The one nearest Danath and Nemuraan altered to reveal a massive figure, clearly a draenei but burlier than Nemuraan and wearing ornate plate armor rather than robes, a giant warhammer across one shoulder and a long cape trailing behind him. Others came into crisp focus as well, filling the room.

And they were all staring at Danath and his men.

A wind sprung out of nowhere, rustling Danath's

cape, stirring Talthressar's long hair. A deep coldness seized Danath and he began to shiver uncontrollably. The spectral warriors advanced, beautiful and implacable, and Danath was rooted to the spot in sudden terror. Their leader extended a hand and brushed Danath's forehead with it. The human cried out as images filled his mind—young Farrol and Vann in the stables before departing. Vann's words cut off as an orc club had silenced him forever. Crouching low over his horse, living so the dead could know peace. Sky'ree, returning riderless. Bodies . . . so many of them, *my boys, my boys, I'm sorry, I'm so sorry—*

The image of the Horde, strong and armed, racing over fertile fields that were not Azeroth. Hundreds of fields, hundreds of worlds, innocent people dying as a green wave that did not belong in that place snuffed the life out of it. Moving on to the next, and the next—

"Your soul is troubled, Danath Trollbane of the Alliance," said the spirit, though his face did not move. The words were in his mind. "You grieve for the fallen. Though you have come here with grief and rage in your heart, the true reasons that drive you are good and just. Be at peace. I am Boulestraan, once known as the Blinding Light, and my army and I shall aid you in your struggle."

The cold terror faded, replaced by an odd sort of peace. Danath blinked. He looked again at the spirit and saw with a start that its eyes were pure gold, and that a flare of golden light rose from its brow as well.

"We are in your debt," Danath managed. It was difficult to force the words out, or to tear his eyes from the figure before him, and Danath wondered if this was what Turalyon meant when he referred to the glory of the Holy Light. For Boulestraan and his ghostly warriors were no longer terrifying in the least. They were glorious, golden and gleaming and beautiful. Danath realized he'd just been tested, and relief washed over him as he regarded the draenei dead hovering protectively around his men.

With a quick shake to clear his head, Danath settled his shield upon one arm. Drawing his sword, he gripped the leather-wrapped pommel firmly. He glanced at Talthressar and Rellian. "Once we're out, you're with me," he told them. "We have to find Kurdran." Turning to the men in his charge, he said, "The orcs are behind this door. They don't know we are here, and are likely expecting a dawn attack in a few hours. We have the element of surprise—let's use it to full advantage. Once through the door, attack the first orc you see. Shout and yell and kick things out of your way. We want them confused, panicked, and unsure of how many foes they face and where." He grinned. "That will leave them easy marks for our blows." The men nodded back, and raised their fists in a silent cheer. Danath raised his fist as well, the torch held high. Then he turned back toward the door, readied himself, and nodded for Nemuraan to open it.

The Auchenai eased the door handle, then slammed

the door open with surprising force, the thud of stone against stone a sharp crack that echoed like thunder in the enclosed space of the ruins.

"For the Sons of Lothar!" Danath shouted as he leaped through the opening. The door had opened onto a medium-sized tunnel not far behind a makeshift wall, and there were perhaps a dozen orcs here, lounging and sleeping and repairing gear. They glanced up, startled, as he burst in among them. Several stumbled to their feet, scrambling for weapons. But they were too slow. Danath's first blow took an orc in the throat just as it was raising its head to shout an alarm. He continued the swing around, cut another orc across the forehead, and stabbed the creature through the heart while it shook its head to clear its vision. By now several of his men accompanied him.

Then in came the glowing, golden dead, implacable and beautiful, their weapons spectral but lethal. The orcs panicked at the sight, bellowing in terror, many of them dropping what weapons they'd raised and falling to the floor, and they were quickly dispatched. Most of the orcs here had not even been fully armed yet.

"Go!" Danath shouted to his men even as the last few orcs fell. "Go! Kill every orc you see!" He glanced at Boulestraan. "Send your warriors with them," he said, and the draenei commander nodded, his spirit-warriors already splitting off to accompany Danath's men. "Nemuraan—show me to their prisoner!"

The Auchenai nodded and opened a door in the far

wall, then led Danath and the two elven rangers through it and into a shorter, narrow corridor. Grizzik followed close behind them. They passed along that and into a larger room at the end, where more orcs sat or ate or slept. Fortunately, both rangers had their bows at the ready, and arrows flew from their graceful fingers, killing several orcs before the others even realized they were not alone. Then Danath was in among them, his sword biting deep, and the screams and groans of his victims mingled with the sounds of chaos he heard from the rooms behind them, where his men were engaged in the same grisly work.

Nor was Grizzik idle. The bird-man launched himself forward in a strange gliding leap that carried him soundlessly behind several orcs, his long taloned hands darting forward and slashing one orc's throat open with a single swipe. A second orc turned, axe raised high, but the arakkoa ducked beneath the awkward blow and twisted around to the front, then pecked the orc's eyes out before shredding his throat as well. Whatever else the arakkoa was, Danath thought, catching glimpses of the quick, silent carnage, he was no pacifist.

"This way!" Nemuraan urged once the room's defenders were dead, and led them across the blood-spattered chamber to another door. The Auchenai had not attacked any of the orcs himself, though his very presence and the light from his staff had seemed to confound them and make them easier to dispatch. This new door opened onto a much smaller room, and occupying half the space was a strange wooden framework like a rough table with raised crossbeams.

Lashed to those beams was a short, muscular figure. Blood had dried in a pool around him, had caked on his flesh. He sagged, unconscious, against the restraints, and Danath, seasoned warrior though he was, stared for a precious moment in simple horror at the atrocities perpetrated on his friend.

A single heavy-set orc leaned against the wall nearby, a spiked club at its side, clearly set to guard the prisoner. It pushed off the wall as Danath came into the room, a look of surprise on its brutish face, and its eyes widened further when the elves put a pair of arrows in its chest. A third arrow struck right between the eyes, and the orc died before it could even speak.

Danath was already hacking at the ropes binding his friend. "Kurdran!" he shouted, grasping his friend. "Kurdran!"

Talthressar murmured something in his musical tongue, but he too was pale as he helped Danath lower the Wildhammer to the table. Danath was still in shock. Both of Kurdran's arms bent in unnatural ways, and his muscular body seemed to have more welts and cuts than tattoos now. His hands and feet were utterly broken, as if crushed with a club; the only sign that he was even alive was a faint rise and fall of his chest. The dwarf looked like something they'd find in a butcher's shop. What had the orcs *done* to him?

"Light . . . I don't even know where to start," Danath said, his voice thick, staring at the bloody, broken body.

"I do . . . if you will permit me." Danath's head whipped up. Nemuraan had come forward, his staff glowing. "I am a priest of my people. I would do what I can to heal him. But you should know—your friend's spirit clings to life only tenuously. I can try to heal him, or I can ease his crossing. If you would rather let him pass—"

"No!" Danath cried. "I've seen too many—please. If you can heal him, please do it."

Danath and Talthressar stepped back as the draenei extended a hand. He placed it on Kurdran's head, matted with dried blood, and lifted his staff with the other hand. Closing his eyes, the Auchenai began to pray.

Danath gasped softly as a pure, gentle radiance limned Nemuraan's form. He didn't know the words, but they calmed his heart. The glow brightened at the draenei's hand where it rested on Kurdran's brow. The radiance increased, until it was so bright Danath reluctantly closed his eyes against it.

He'd seen this before. This being from another world, this draenei, so strange in appearance to him—he was wielding the Light. Just as Turalyon did.

A grunt made Danath open his eyes. "Eh? What?" Kurdran muttered, his head tossing from side to side. "Do yer worst, ye awful beasties!" He opened his eyes and stared straight up at the blue figure bending over him.

"It's all right," Danath assured him before he could struggle, placing a hand on the dwarf's shoulder. Nemuraan stepped back, the light around him starting to fade, and smiled. "He's . . . will he be . . . ?"

"I have done all I could. He is healed, for the most part. But not all scars can be erased, nor things that are broken made as they were before."

"Who's broken?" Kurdran snorted. He sat up slowly, flexing his hands and feet, touching his body. "Heh. Dinna know I had that much blood in me." He peered up at Danath. "Ah, Danath, lad!" he said when he realized who was beside him, his broad face splitting into a wide grin. "It's ye, then, eh? And about bloody time! Not to worry—those beasties got not a word out o' me. Did ye bring my hammer?"

"He should rest," the draenei warned.

"Bah! Rest is fer the dead," Kurdran growled.

"And sometimes not even for them," Talthressar said quietly, glancing at Nemuraan.

"He's a Wildhammer," Danath said to the priest; it was the best explanation he could come up with. "I brought it, Kurdran. Here." The hammer had been on Sky'ree when the gryphon had returned, and Danath had possessed enough foresight to bring it with him into the tunnel. He handed over the weapon, and couldn't help grinning as the dwarf took the ponderous hammer and hefted it, though Kurdran moved more slowly and stiffly than before.

"Good." Kurdran inspected the hammer quickly,

then nodded his approval. "Now then, what's the plan, laddie? And who be yer friends?" A nod of his head indicated Grizzik and Nemuraan, and Danath didn't miss the revulsion that washed across the Auchenai's face at being considered in the same breath as the arakkoa.

"Nemuraan is an Auchenai, a draenei priest of the dead," Danath explained quickly. "He is one of the last of this place's guardians. You owe your life to him—he healed you."

"Ah," said Kurdran, putting the pieces together. "Thank ye, lad. The Wildhammers dinna ferget such debts." Nemuraan inclined his head graciously.

"And that's Grizzik the arakkoa," Danath continued. "He hates the orcs and guided us into this place from the forest. And the plan?" He raised his sword. "The troops are storming the tunnel. The rest will attack soon and draw the orcs' attention away. And we will find Ner'zhul and bring his head back on a polearm."

"Aye, that's a plan I'm liking. Where be this orc shaman, then?"

They both glanced at Nemuraan, who tilted his head to one side. "The most defensible room is our former prayer center," the Auchenai said after a moment. "That is where he is most likely to be found."

"Lead on, then!" Danath said, and Nemuraan nodded, taking them out of that room and down a short corridor to a wide, heavy stone door covered in elaborate designs.

"Here," he told them. "Behind this door lies the

prayer center." Grief shone from his eyes. "We would come here to pay our respects and commune with our dead."

Rellian tried the handle. "Locked," he said.

"Stand back, lad," Kurdran urged as he raised his hammer. "This may splinter some." He was still unsteady on his feet, and Danath bit back a protest. He wouldn't try to stop Kurdran; the Wildhammer needed to reassure himself he could still fight. Danath held his breath as the dwarf steadied himself, and then hurled the stormhammer at the barrier before them.

The thunderclap that sounded upon impact nearly knocked Danath off his feet. A loud crack and a cloud of dust followed, and as he waved that away Danath saw that the blow had shattered the door. Through it he could see a large round room beyond, and a mass of figures near its center. Several of them glanced up, surprise evident in their faces, but two did not—a massive one-eyed orc and an older-looking orc whose face had been painted white to resemble a skull. That had to be Ner'zhul.

Their eyes met for a fraction of a second. Then, before Danath could begin his charge, Ner'zhul said something to the one-eyed orc, turned, and slipped past him, racing through a door at the far end of the room.

"No you don't!" Danath cried, starting after Ner'zhul, but the one-eyed orc strode forward, blocking him. A long scar ran down the side of the large orc's face, and a patch covered that eye, but the other glared at Danath without fear.

"I am Kilrogg Deadeye," the orc announced proudly in heavily accented Common, pounding his chest with one hand even as he raised a massive war axe with the other. "I am chieftain of the Bleeding Hollow clan. Many humans have I slain. You will not be the last. I am charged with stopping you from passing, and so . . . you shall not."

Danath eyed this new foe carefully. He could see from the streaks of white in his hair and the lines on his face that this Kilrogg was older than he, but his body was still heavily muscled and he moved with the grace of a natural warrior. He seemed to have honor, too. For some reason, Danath was prompted to respond in kind.

"So be it," he replied, raising his sword to salute his opponent. "I am Danath Trollbane, commander of the Alliance army. I have slain many orcs, and you won't be the last. And I *will* pass!" With that he charged, shield braced before him, sword already moving in a vicious downward stroke.

Kilrogg blocked the blow with his axe, almost wrenching the sword from Danath's grip as the blade caught between the axe blade and handle. Danath did not slow, however, and his shield slammed full force into Kilrogg's chest. The orc staggered back a pace. Danath took advantage of the moment to set free his sword and swing again, this time low and to the side.

The edge clipped Kilrogg's torso just above the waist, and the Bleeding Hollow chieftain grunted as the strike drew blood.

The wound did not slow him down, however, and Kilrogg responded with an attack of his own. He slammed his heavy fist against Danath's shield, denting the sturdy metal and making Danath falter on his feet, then brought his axe around and up with an almost lazy arc that drove it beneath the shield's bottom edge. Danath had to jump back to avoid being disemboweled, and winced as the axe's back edge bashed into the inside of his shield, driving it hard away from him and wrenching his shield arm in the process.

Danath glanced up, and their eyes met. The human saw his own grudging admiration reflected in the orc's single eye as Kilrogg nodded. Each found the other a worthy foe.

The temperature suddenly plummeted, and Danath grinned fiercely. Cries rose from elsewhere in the room, sounds of not only pain but fear; once again Boulestraan's spirit-soldiers, beautiful and terrible, had come to the aid of the Alliance forces. Talthressar and Rellian were firing arrow after arrow, dropping orcs with well-placed shots. Kurdran, meanwhile, was focusing upon the orcs in the front of the room, the Wildhammer single-handedly keeping them at bay with furious swings and throws of his stormhammer, his fighting spirit unbroken although the orcs had done their damnedest to break his body.

Kilrogg noticed all this as well. He roared in rage and charged—not at Danath but at a cluster of men off to his side. The heavy axe rose and fell with lightning speed and two of the soldiers dropped, blood spattering everywhere as their fellows leaped back, desperately trying to hold their own against the enraged orc leader. The draenei spirits floated toward him with dreadful purpose, but Kilrogg evaded their attacks, concentrating his efforts on the humans instead. As fast as Danath's troops cut down the other orcs, Kilrogg carved a space through them in return.

Suddenly Danath winced. A strong droning noise was drilling in his head. What the—he looked everywhere but could not locate it. Then he realized that it was coming from the other door, the one Ner'zhul had disappeared through moments ago. And that the edge beneath the door was glowing. The sounds were a chant, Danath realized suddenly. Between the glow and the chanting, and the hairs rising on the back of his neck, Danath knew they must be working some sort of magic. By the Light, was he opening the portals right now?

"Get past them!" he shouted to his men. "Get in the next room! Now!"

But still Kilrogg blocked the way. The Bleeding Hollow chieftain was almost alone now, all his warriors cut down by the elves and dwarf and humans and draenei working together, but he showed no sign of giving up. Danath could tell that the big orc was willing to sacrifice himself to buy Ner'zhul the time he needed for whatever magic he was working.

A voice suddenly shouted from the other side of the door. Danath couldn't understand the guttural language, but he didn't need to—whatever Ner'zhul had been trying to do, he'd done. There was a faint bursting sound, and the glow under the door intensified suddenly, filling the room with light and sound. Then it faded just as rapidly and soon was completely gone, leaving the room even darker than it had seemed before.

Kurdran managed to get past the burly orc, however. Panting heavily, he swung with all his might, straight at the now-darkened door. The portal shattered with a loud crack and the Wildhammer leader kicked the fragments aside, revealing a smaller room with a rune-scribed circle set into the stone floor. The room was empty.

Kilrogg had glanced toward the door as well, and now he grinned. "You did get past me—I give you that. Well fought, but in the end, you have failed, human. My master has gone ahead to the Black Temple to cast his spell. You cannot stop him now, and worlds without end will know the trampling feet of the Horde."

"By the Light, at least you won't follow him!" Danath renewed the attack, fueled by his anger. He rained blow after blow, but each one was blocked by the wily old warrior. Kilrogg grabbed the shield with one hand, shoving it aside, and slammed his axe down with the other, knocking the sword away before it could reach his belly. Then he grinned at Danath, showing the long curving tusks that sprang from his lower lip.

"You will have to do better than that, human," the orc chided. Taking his axe in both hands, again he swung for Danath's face, then reversed direction and swung once again, forcing Danath to step back or lose his head.

On the next swing Danath ducked and brought his shield up hard. It smashed into Kilrogg's arms, forcing them up as well, and threw the orc off-balance. Then Danath thrust, his sword catching the orc in the belly and sinking deep. He was almost surprised that he'd managed it.

With a roar Kilrogg slammed his forearms down, sending the shield crashing onto Danath's head, and staggered back. He was bleeding heavily from the gut wound, but that only seemed to enrage him. Raising his axe again, Kilrogg brought it down squarely atop Danath's shield, the heavy blade sinking deep into the protective metal. He yanked back and the shield tore away from its straps, leaving Danath defenseless.

"Now we face each other blade to blade," Kilrogg told him, ripping the sundered shield from his axe blade and tossing it aside. "And only one will live to sing of the battle."

"Fine by me," Danath muttered back through clenched teeth. Taking his sword in both hands, he ran forward, straight for Kilrogg, sword held high over one shoulder. But just as the orc chieftain stepped up to meet him, Danath stopped short, using his momentum to pivot on one foot instead, one hand releasing the sword and the other arcing outward so that his strike came from the opposite side. Kilrogg's blind side.

The flashing blade took the surprised orc in the neck, slicing through his throat, and Kilrogg toppled, his axe falling from his hands as they flew up to stop the blood spurting from his wound. But the Bleeding Hollow chieftain was grinning as he dropped to his knees.

"By my blood . . . the Horde . . . lives," the orc managed to gasp out, his voice a bubbling whisper. "Ancestors . . . I come. . . ." Then his eyes glazed over and Kilrogg Deadeye toppled sideways, to land heavily upon the carved stone floor of the prayer room. Danath was panting, but lifted his sword in salute to a fallen foe.

"Well done, lad," Kurdran said, stepping up beside Danath and patting him on the arm. But Danath shook his head.

"I failed," he said bitterly, glancing down at Kilrogg's body. "He was right. He did what he was supposed to do—he gave them enough time to escape." Danath scowled and gritted his teeth. "Whatever spell they used transported them straight to some place he called the Black Temple! How can we possibly stop them now? I don't even know where this place is!"

The arakkoa turned, his eyes bright. "Grizzik know! Can take you there!"

"You know where—"

"Sir!" One of Danath's men burst into the room, followed by Nemuraan and the flowing, drifting forms of the draenei dead. "We have the orcs on the run, sir! Some of them have fled deeper into the tunnels, though!" He paused, clearly expecting a reply, and seemed puzzled when Danath did not respond. "Sir?"

Kurdran nudged Danath. "Ye're in charge, lad," the Wildhammer reminded him quietly. "Even if ye feel ye've failed, ye canna let yer troops know it, eh?"

He was right, of course. Danath nodded and straightened. Then he met the soldier's eyes.

"Let the orcs run," he said. "We know where Ner'zhul went, and we're going to follow him. We'll be making for a place called the Black Temple."

"The Black Temple?"

Danath turned at the anger he heard in Boulestraan's spectral voice, and saw the spirit glowering, though not at him. "That was once Karabor, our holiest place. But the orcs defiled it, as they defile all that they touch." His hands tightened on his glowing hammer, which was still completely clean despite the orcs he had slain with it. "I pray when you reach it, you will drive the orcs from its hallowed ground."

Danath nodded. "That's the plan. Thank you for your help. It has been an honor fighting alongside you."

"For us as well," Boulestraan replied, bowing. "You and your Alliance are noble warriors, and honorable people. I wish you well, Danath Trollbane. We go to our rest, until summoned again." Then he and his warriors faded away, leaving only soft glows behind, until those diffused as well.

Danath turned to Nemuraan. On impulse, he said, "Come with us. This is no place to live, and you can serve your people more by leaving here and returning to the world. We would even take you to Azeroth with us, if you liked."

Nemuraan smiled. "Truly your world must be a wondrous place, to have produced such a people," he complimented, "and I appreciate your offer. But no, my place is here. Our dead remain in this world—honorably laid to rest in Auchindoun, or scattered in the forest, even paving the path the orcs misname the Path of Glory. Here they lie, in Draenor, and here I stay, to tend them. The Holy Light has placed us here for a reason, and some day it will triumph over all. Until then, I rejoice in the knowledge that I have aided you, and that you and your people carry the Light as well. Go forth, and let your courage and strength drive the orcs before you like chaff before the strong wind. And who knows? Perhaps one day our peoples will indeed battle such evil side by side." He hesitated. "A favor, before you go?"

Danath nodded. "Name it."

"Do not let that one undo what the Light has wrought. A noble and fierce warrior he is to be sure, but wisdom marks a warrior as much as bravery." He indicated Kurdran, who scowled and colored slightly. In the midst of his worry, Danath managed a small smile.

"I'll do what I can—but you see how stubborn he is."

"Bah, the lot of ye."

"Come on, walking wounded," Danath said to Kurdran. "We've a Black Temple to take." And with a final nod to the Auchenai, Danath Trollbane headed back into the corridors of the city of the dead, hoping that Nemuraan's prayers for the Alliance would be answered.

CHAPTER TWENTY-TWO

"Don't worry—we're still on the right track," Khadgar felt compelled to say as the group stopped for a rest and to drink some precious water. They needed the reassurance.

They had traveled north from the orcish citadel, skirting the jagged coastline to the east. The ground had remained consistent with what they had seen near the portal itself, though less severe: cracked earth, gray, dusty soil, withered plants and trees. They had passed patches of greenery here and there, but most of Draenor was dreary and desolate and bitter.

Now the ground around them had grown more uneven, its dips and rises more significant, and wind whipped by on all sides. Most assuredly a mountain range, but like none he'd ever seen. Stone spikes protruded from the cliff walls around them, jutting outward in every direction as if the peaks themselves were hungry for blood. The rock was a dull reddish brown, too, the color of dried blood, and the sky seemed a vivid scarlet in comparison. It was one of the most un-welcoming places he'd ever encountered, and he sus-pected the shudder that passed through him had as much to do with that as with the sharp winds knifing among the spikes.

Idly, Khadgar reached out to touch the nearest spike, but stopped just short of actual contact—perhaps tempting the fates was not the best plan. "The skull is not far," he said again.

"You're certain?" Turalyon asked.

"Oh, trust me, I'm certain." He could sense its pres-ence in his head without even searching now, a dull pulse just behind the eyes that almost became visible when he squeezed them shut. Definitely close.

"Good," Turalyon replied, hefting his hammer and eyeing the spikes. "I've had enough of this place."

"I think we—" began Khadgar, but Alleria lifted a commanding hand for silence.

"Listen!"

Khadgar strained to hear, but his ears were not as sharp as an elf's. Moments passed; all he heard were the winds. And then—there it was, a sort of flapping sound, like wings, but somehow sharper than those of any bird he knew. The only creature he'd ever encoun-tered that made a noise like that in flight was—

"Dragon!" he shouted, grabbing Turalyon and yank-ing his friend down as he dove to the ground himself. Just behind him he heard an angry roar and a hiss.

White-hot pain blossomed in his arm, and even as he sucked in his breath at the agony he heard more hissing. There was a smoking hole in his sleeve, and a nasty-looking burn in his arm below that. The hissing was the sound of something eating away at the rocks below them as well. Magma. Krasus had said that black dragons spat magma.

Glancing up, Khadgar saw several small dark forms flit among the spikes and then rise and swoop back around. "Shields up!" Turalyon shouted, rising to his feet, "and weapons at the ready! They're not fully grown dragons—we can take them!"

Turalyon was right. The creatures attacking them were no larger than the horses, perhaps six feet long, but with a wingspan wider than that. They had small heads and only a few spikes along their back, and Khadgar realized that these must be an immature form. Drakes, he remembered Krasus calling them once. Yes, drakes.

"Drakes—young dragons," he warned Turalyon, raising his staff as the black drakes circled for a second attack. "Not as strong as their parents, but still dangerous."

Turalyon nodded, but his focus was on the attacking creatures. He was back in his element now, and had settled at once into the military commander mind-set.

"Archers, fire at will!" he shouted. Beside him Alleria began loosing arrows at the small, agile creatures. One of her shots took a drake through the throat, the power of her longbow propelling the shaft clean through the dragon youth's lighter scales, and the thing reared up, clearly in pain. A second arrow pierced its eye and brain, and it fell to the ground with a croak and lay still.

That heartened the soldiers, and they swung with enthusiasm, swatting at the young dragons and ducking to avoid the creatures' small but sharp claws and the fist-sized gobbets of lava they spewed. The drakes shot past them, then banked, circling back. There were fewer of them now—several of their fellows lay dead among the spikes.

Turalyon turned to say something else to Khadgar—and stopped, toppling without warning and catching himself just in time to avoid being impaled upon the nearest cluster of stone spikes. Everyone was staggering about, trying to keep their footing, as the ground itself danced beneath them.

"What in the name of the Light?" Turalyon asked, his words jarred out of him; then he was staring back and to the left of Khadgar.

Afraid to see but terrified of not knowing, Khadgar glanced behind himself.

And almost fell over from shock.

The creature pounding through—not around but *through*—the stone spikes was monstrous even compared with an ogre. It stood easily twice as tall as those giant creatures, its skin as thick and rough as rock, sweeping designs carved into its arms and shoulders. A ridge of dark spikes ran like a miniature mountain range down its back, and more spikes protruded from its shoulders and upper arms. But the face—the face was perhaps the most horrific thing of all. It resembled that of an ogre, but was far more intelligent. The creature had no tusks but its teeth were long and sharp and yellowing, its ears pointed and tufted, and its single eye glaring and glowing—and fastened on them.

"Intruders!" the behemoth shouted, the force of his cry cracking stone all around them. "Crush them!"

More figures emerged from the stone thicket to the east and west. These were ogres of the same type—and size—that Khadgar had encountered before, and they snarled and growled and laughed as they moved toward the Alliance soldiers.

"Wait!" Khadgar shouted. To his relief, the things actually paused. Thank the Light, he had the means to at least converse with them. "We meant no offense!"

"Offense? You live, that is offense!" The creature roared and continued to advance.

"Whatever you're telling him, it isn't working," Turalyon muttered. "And damn it, here come the drakes again."

Khadgar never thought he'd be happy to see dragons, but when the drakes circled back right at that moment for another attack, he wanted to thank them. The ogres and their master were completely distracted when the drakes began spitting magma at both groups, and turned their attention to the assault from the skies. They raised massive conical clubs—Khadgar realized at once that they were simply using spires they'd broken off the mountain itself.

Khadgar realized an opportunity when he saw one. "The drakes!" he cried. "Attack the drakes!"

Alleria stared at him for a moment, and Khadgar knew what she was thinking. This would be a perfect time to flee, to let the drakes attack the ogres and their strange leader for them. But Turalyon grinned and nodded; he'd gotten it. Now the Alliance members, too, focused on the flying reptilian creatures, setting to them with sword and arrows. But their efforts were feeble compared with what the ogres did to the drakes. The ogres easily smashed the beasts out of the sky and then stomped on them, crushing the immature dragons beneath their massive feet.

Their oversized leader killed a drake as well, but it didn't bother with a club—instead it simply reached up, catching a charging black drake as easily as Khadgar had once caught an apple a friend had tossed to him. The colossal beast held the drake in one hand, its thumb and forefinger pinning the young dragon's wings together as it struggled to get free. Then the beast brought the drake to its mouth, tilted its head back, and engulfed the scaled body in a single fierce bite, chewing a few extra times to get the rest of the wings into its cavernous mouth before finally swallowing.

"That was . . ." Turalyon started, but he couldn't find words to encompass what he'd just seen. He lowered his sword and lifted his visor, barely aware of his actions. "You . . . those . . ."

The creature peered at him. "Dragons came. You did

not run, but could have. You stay and fight—helped us."

There was a bit of astonishment in that earth-deep voice. Khadgar could well understand it. He was willing to bet that few had willingly risked themselves to help the ogres before. His heart lifted slightly; things were going exactly as he'd hoped.

"No, we do not run. We are not your enemies. We only wish—"

Khadgar had just drawn breath to continue to negotiate the tentative truce when the ground began to suddenly shake again, and the creature glanced back the way it had come. It hunched in upon itself, arms wrapping protectively around its broad chest, and a strange sound emerged from its hideous mouth, half snarl and half whimper. Watching it, Khadgar would have sworn this beast, which had just all but swallowed a dragon whole, looked frightened.

He shuddered to think what could scare such a thing.

That question was answered a few minutes later, when a second monstrous beast strode from the mountains. This creature was even larger than the first one, and had more stone spikes protruding from its back and arms. Its skin was redder than that of the other, its one eye so pale it was almost white all the way across, and its teeth were longer and sharper.

That white eye held great intelligence, and it fastened upon Khadgar and Turalyon and the other humans. "Who are you?" it demanded. "And why are you still alive?"

"We are only passing through," Khadgar stammered. The great being's eye narrowed in skepticism. "We aren't your enemies. Just let us go and we'll—"

"No." The finality of the single word was chilling. "If you leave, you'll speak. Speak of gronn. Speak of Gruul." The giant being thumped his chest. "Horde came. No, it's best you die. Then our secret stays safe. Gronn stays safe."

Turalyon glanced at the first creature he'd been conversing with, hoping for help, but Khadgar could tell they would not get any there. The massive being had curled in upon itself after the rebuke, looking like nothing so much as a recently punished child. And that, he realized, was exactly what it was. The second creature was its parent and this was the baby. The thought made him shudder.

"We will keep your secret! We helped the—the gronn with the dragons! This one can tell you so himself!"

The giant that had called itself Gruul scowled and glanced around, apparently only now noticing the black drake corpses scattered around the mountainside. "You're dragon-killers?"

"Yes," Khadgar answered desperately.

But Gruul was not so easily tricked. He tilted back his monstrous head, his fang-filled mouth gaping open—and laughed. The deep peals shook the walls around them and sent several small spires shattering to the ground.

"Kill baby dragons, maybe," it said, still grinning. "We do that. We do not need help. No, you die."

"Wait!" Khadgar cried. "What *do* you want help with?" They could probably take down more than drakes, if they absolutely had to.

Gruul sobered at once. "You are too weak. You cannot help."

"Maybe we can. Ask."

Gruul was silent, then he said in a somber voice, "Blackwing Greatfather."

It took Khadgar a second to figure out what Gruul meant. His eyes widened, he burst out, "Deathwing? You want us to kill Deathwing?"

"What?" cried Turalyon. "Deathwing? Here?"

"And they want us to kill him?" Alleria chimed in.

Khadgar was as shocked as they. They'd known the black dragons had allied with the Horde, and had seen several of them dart through the portal to Draenor, but he'd assumed it was only lesser members of the dragonflight, not the dragonflight patriarch . . . their "great and terrible sire . . ." himself!

"He left some black dragons behind as guards for the orcs at the citadel," Turalyon muttered. "But he brought the rest of them up here, to these mountains."

Khadgar nodded, then realized Gruul was still watching them expectantly.

He took a deep breath and drew himself up to his full height. "Yes. Of course. Do not worry—we can handle Deathwing," he told the gronn with forced assurance. "He won't be a problem for us." He did his best to ignore the stunned silence radiating from his friends and prayed Gruul couldn't see the sweat dripping off his brow, or that if he did, he didn't understand its significance.

Gruul nodded, a grotesque smile splitting his massive lips. "Good," he announced. "Foolish, but brave! Gruul likes." He peered down at them. "Now prove it." He gestured, his enormous hand lifting to indicate a peak not far away. "Deathwing," the gronn explained. "Kill. Help gronn rid the mountain of pests. Then . . . you can pass." His smile shifted down to a scowl that revealed all his fangs. "Tell no one!"

Khadgar nodded. "Agreed." He hoped his voice didn't sound quite so quivery to Gruul as it did in his own ears.

Gruul turned and began making his way across the mountainside. The massive gronn didn't bother searching for a path, he created one, his heavy feet shattering stone and leaving a wide, cracked trail through the stone spires, which broke off against his thick skin. The smaller gronn hurried to follow its parent, and the ogres—Khadgar was horrified to realize he now thought of them as "small," even though they were twice his own height—shuffled along behind their two oversized leaders. Grimly Khadgar followed. A thought occurred to him. Deathwing was here . . . and the skull was in this direction. . . . He paused for a second, closing his eyes, and then he grinned.

"What are you doing?" Alleria whispered to him as she and Turalyon fell into step beside him. "We're supposed to be looking for Gul'dan's skull, not going up against Deathwing! Do you have any idea what that dragon is capable of?"

"Yes, actually," he answered. "But he's got the skull."

"What?" exclaimed Turalyon.

"The skull is right in front of us, and so is Deathwing. We'd have had to confront him regardless, most likely."

"Wonderful. Now all we have to do is fight Deathwing to get the skull back!" She shuddered. "I'd rather face the entire Horde any day!"

Privately, Khadgar agreed with her, but he saw no other option. They needed the skull, and Deathwing had it. He was deep in thought, going over his spells in his mind, when Turalyon gripped his arm and pointed.

"Look," he said in a quiet voice.

They had reached a deep valley that led up to the peak in question, and had stopped, fanning out around the valley's edge.

Eggs. The ground was littered with them. They were about a yard long and shone from within with a pulsing red glow that revealed dark veins through the eggshells themselves—and coiled forms cocooned inside.

"That's what was in those wagons Alleria spotted!" Turalyon whispered, staring. "No wonder the dragons were flying right above them! Deathwing brought these here to Draenor! If they hatch, the black dragons will overrun this entire world!"

"Then we had best make sure they don't hatch," Alleria countered, raising her bow and nocking an arrow.

Khadgar placed his hand on her left arm and pointed. "Let's make those your first targets." The others followed his gaze and cursed softly as they saw the dark shapes winging toward them from the valley's far side.

Fortunately, it seemed that none of the largest dragons were protecting the eggs. The first fledgling dragon to approach was swatted aside by Gruul, his casual gesture slamming the small dragon into the valley's far wall hard enough to crack the stone there and drop the body in a shattered heap. The next one fell, twitching, with one of Alleria's arrows through its right eye, and Khadgar froze a third into solid ice with a quick incantation. Those three had only been the vanguard, however—a fierce shrieking arose from all around the valley, and suddenly more dark, darting forms descended.

The ogres excelled at brute force. Though smaller than the gronn, they were still large enough to wrestle a drake down and snap its long neck or bash in its skull. Many of them also proved to be spellcasters, firing bolts of arcane magic that seared through dragon wings and hide alike. The sheer number of drakes would have overwhelmed them, however, if not for aid from both gronn and Alliance warriors. Turalyon had his men using their shields for protection from the drakes' claws and teeth, then slashing at their wings; though tough as leather, the wings were still the drakes' weak spot, and once a wing had torn the creature was forced onto the ground, where it lost most of

its agility. The ogres quickly caught on to this tactic
and began tearing wings off entirely, hurling the leathery appendages aside while the now-grounded creatures were stomped flat with heavy feet. Khadgar was
reminded, with a sick feeling, of a cruel child tearing
the wings off butterflies.

At one point Turalyon muttered, "You know, I'm
not sure we're fighting the right enemy." Khadgar had
to admit these tactics were brutal, almost ghoulish, but
he couldn't argue with the results.

Gruul and the other gronn—Khadgar thought of
them both as male—had selected thick spires from the
cliffs just beyond the valley. They swung these clubs
around them with enough force to create strong winds
that buffeted the drakes, driving them back into one another and making them easier targets for the ogres and
humans. Any drake unlucky enough to actually be
within the clubs' radius was crushed instantly, and the
valley floor was soon thick with bodies.

"The eggs next," Khadgar said to Turalyon. But the
paladin hesitated, peering at one of the eggs but making no move toward it. Khadgar frowned at him.
"What's wrong?" Khadgar asked.

"I . . . dragons are sentient creatures. They think,
they feel. It's one thing to fight the drakes, but—these
are infants. Just . . . babies, really. They can't even fight
back. And we'd be butchering them."

"Turalyon," Alleria said, "Light, do I love you, not
least for that compassionate heart of yours. But these

are black dragons. You know what will happen if they're not killed now."

Turalyon nodded grimly, making yet another one of those difficult decisions any general has to make in the thick of battle.

"Destroy the eggs!" he shouted, striding to the nearest and bringing his hammer down atop it. The thick shell shattered with a loud crack, followed by a softer thud as the hammer connected with the half-formed dragon inside. Large as a medium-sized dog, the unhatched dragon had smoky red skin, and nubs where head and wings would have been. It did not move as it was attacked, save to twitch slightly. A pale reddish fluid oozed from the broken egg as the shell crumbled away and the whelp within slumped to the ground, its final shudders already fading.

The rest of the Alliance warriors quickly followed suit. Just as Turalyon was breaching the last egg and the ogres were dismembering the last drakes, Khadgar heard a loud shriek from the peak above—the same place where he had last sensed the skull. Glancing up, he saw another shadow launch itself into the air, its wings covering all the valley in darkness. Its bulk dwarfed even Gruul, who shrank back against the valley wall before growling and straightening defiantly. His ogres and the lesser gronn were not made of such stern stuff; they shrieked and fled in terror. The shape plummeted down, sunlight glinting off its skin, its long neck arched, its jaws wide. Lava burst from its throat, a torrent of glowing magma that instantly incinerated ogre, human, dead drake, shattered egg—anything unlucky enough to fall within its spray.

"Pull back!" Turalyon shouted to his men, who were already scrambling away from the monstrous apparition. "Back to the valley wall!"

They clustered there, Khadgar and Turalyon and Alleria at the forefront, and watched the gargantuan dragon alight. Khadgar gulped. He'd known the creature would be impressive, but this—Deathwing was almost inconceivably huge. The drakes they had been fighting seemed as toddlers compared with their great parent. Khadgar could barely take it all in. But one thing struck him as curious, even in the midst of his awe. The father of the black dragonflight had plates of silvery, glinting metal running along his spine. Beneath those plates were glowing lines of red, like the magma Deathwing had just attacked them with. The dragon's massive claws dug deep into the stone of the valley floor. All but his left foreclaw, Khadgar saw. That was held high and curled inward, as if injured—or holding something.

"The skull!" he whispered to Turalyon and Alleria. "He has the skull with him!"

"Nice of him to bring it to us," Turalyon muttered. "But how do we get it?"

Deathwing folded his wings behind his sinuous body and settled on his haunches. His long neck reared up and glared balefully down at them, his red eyes alight with rage.

"*My children!*" the dragon howled, his voice like fire licking at burning wood, like metal chipping bone. Along with the anger was a deep grief. "My children, murdered!" His tail lifted, slammed down, and a crack ran along the earth. "Come forward, disgusting, cowardly wretches, murderers of defenseless infants, and know torment and madness before I devour you whole! Who will be the first to be blasted to ashes?"

His gleaming eyes narrowed as they focused with dreadful intent upon Gruul. "You," he said, drawing out the single syllable so that it contained a world of promised agony, his voice dropping to almost a whisper, almost a caress, and Light help him, Khadgar knew a sharp gratitude that that terrible gaze had, for the moment, passed him over.

Yet Gruul did not quail. "I!" he proclaimed. "I am Gruul, greatest of gronn! This is my land. My mountains. And you will not take them! You go or end up like your children!"

Deathwing's roar of fury nearly deafened Khadgar. "My children!" he wailed, and the pain in his voice almost—almost—made Khadgar feel a twinge of sympathy. "Perfection incarnate . . . beautiful and defenseless . . ." The words turned unintelligible as Deathwing howled and almost flailed in his anger and grief, magma dripping from his jaws, shredding the stone upon which he stood, his flapping wings creating almost tornado force gales. Khadgar began to wish he'd listened to Turalyon's reluctance to smash the eggs.

What had they been thinking? Light, what had *he* been thinking, to stand up to this monster, this ancient, evil, terrifying vision of rage? How could they possibly defeat him?

"Oh, how brave of you!" Deathwing's grief had sharpened into scorn, less raw but no less deadly. "Such courage it must have taken, to smash shells and murder defenseless infants! A pity you will not live to brag about such a noble feat!" His wings flared out behind him and beat down again, the powerful gust they created slamming Gruul back against the wall. Gruul's ogres yowled in fear and cringed back, almost hugging the walls of the valley. Gruul would get no aid from them.

"Puny mortals! I have had many names throughout history, all of them spoken with dread: Neltharion, Xaxas, and many more. Yet you shall know me best as Deathwing, for so I am! I am the bane of life, the darkness within history, the lord of death, the master of destruction. And I tell you now, and so it is true, that this world is *mine!*"

"Never!" Gruul replied, snarling, and launched himself at Deathwing. The giant gronn slammed into the colossal dragon's chest with an impact that cracked the cliffs around them and sent rock cascading down from the fractured peaks. It drove most of the Alliance forces from their feet and even the ogres to their knees. Other dragons had appeared along the valley walls, watching their father intently, and they were forced back a step as well. But when the dust had cleared, Gruul was shaking his head and Deathwing stood unmarred and unmoved.

"Is that the best the oh so mighty Gruul can do?" Deathwing sneered, lowering his head so that his bony forehead ridge brushed up against Gruul's own thick brow. "Is that all you have?" He lifted one foreclaw, the other still closed and curled up to his breast, and held it over Gruul's head as if he were preparing to squash an insect. It was like a signal. The dragons shrieked a battle cry, sprang from their perches, and flew with lethal grace toward the humans, ogres, and gronn lining the walls of the valley. The ogres seemed to be paralyzed, staring, slack-jawed, at the winged doom.

"Sons of Lothar! Attack!"

Turalyon's voice was clear and strong, and carried much farther than it should have. He lifted his hammer, his eyes bright, and charged forward to meet the drakes. The hammer glowed as it struck the first drake square in the skull. The beast dropped like a stone.

"For Quel'Thalas!" Alleria and her rangers began firing. Battle cries rose from the Alliance soldiers, elf and human alike, and it was joined by the earsplitting roar of the ogres and gronn as they roused themselves from their terror. The dragons swooped down, heady with excitement and pride in their father, spewing magma or clamping their jaws on their enemy. The ogres and gronn seemed to remember that they had fought drakes before, and again began to pluck the creatures from the very air and rip off their wings. One ogre slammed his flapping victim so hard into the wall of the valley that a whole chunk of it crumbled, sliding slowly down in a mass of broken stone and dust, burying in its path those too slow to escape.

Khadgar kept his eyes on the battle between Deathwing and Gruul. The gronn was brave to even go up against the black dragon, but he would lose soon. The mage suspected the only reason he hadn't lost before now was because Deathwing was toying with him, tormenting the creature he believed had slain his precious, obscene offspring before dispatching him.

And when he was done with Gruul . . .

They had to get that skull from him. Had to.

Khadgar raised his staff high, and muttered words of power. The resulting lightning strike seared his eyes, blinding him for an instant and leaving afterimages when he blinked. The massive bolt struck Deathwing square in the chest and actually succeeded in jolting the dragon back a few feet. Lightning skittered along the metal spinal plating like water droplets on a hot skillet, but Khadgar realized that the dragon was unharmed.

"Well struck, little mage," Deathwing acknowledged, though his long mouth curved up in a cold smile. "But I mastered such magics millennia before your race first learned of them—you will have to try much harder than that if you wish to breach my skin!"

Gruul hurled himself into the fray once more, rousing reluctant admiration from Khadgar as the mage frantically considered what to do. Deathwing turned his attention to the gronn, weathering its awesome blows easily and batting him aside with a quick flip of his wings.

Khadgar stared at the dragon, a sickening feeling spreading through him even as the mage attacked again. He watched with horror as Deathwing shrugged off a spell that should have turned his very bones to ice. Deathwing was right. Khadgar realized he'd been an arrogant fool. There was no way to pierce that armored hide.

Armored . . .

Khadgar's eyes narrowed. Deathwing shone in the red sunlight, gleaming like dark brass or pools of blood, and Khadgar studied him.

Metal plating . . .

With gaps and fissures underneath it that glowed magma-red . . .

And it all clicked. His ice spell hadn't worked because it couldn't hope to compete with the heat Deathwing's entire body generated. The black dragon was virtually made of lava! And those plates along his spine—which Khadgar now saw were red-hot along the edges and at the joints—were holding him together.

Lightning didn't work. Fire and ice were useless. His most powerful magics, and they didn't touch the dragon. But what about one of his weakest? What about one of the first spells they taught in Dalaran, a parlor trick every apprentice could perform at will?

Hope, painful and yet intoxicating, rose inside him.

It could work—maybe. It was the last card he could play, and so play it he would. Play it he had to. But he would need to get closer. Steeling himself, Khadgar squared his shoulders and pushed forward, brushing past where Turalyon and Alleria were battling a black dragon alongside two ogres. And walked, alone, toward Deathwing.

Fortunately, Gruul was keeping Deathwing busy, and neither of the massive creatures noticed the old-seeming man who crept toward them until he was only ten paces from Deathwing's head. Gruul was struggling to escape the heavy, taloned foot Deathwing had pinned him with, and the dragon was leaning in, his long jaws opening to bite, when Khadgar raised his hands and cast his spell.

Sensing the magic, Deathwing glanced around and, spying Khadgar, laughed at him. "More wizardry?" the dragon mocked, eyes slitted like those of an amused cat. "How entertaining. Have you not realized yet that your mightiest spells cannot harm me?" But then the words of Khadgar's incantation registered, and the dragon's eyes flew wide with alarm. "What are you—pathetic wretch, I will silence you!" He turned and, ignoring Gruul utterly, bore down with terrible purpose on Khadgar.

The sight was so horrifying Khadgar almost forgot to complete the spell. Shaking his head, he rallied, and spoke the command words in a voice that shook.

A loud creaking rose from the dragon before him. Deathwing screamed again, writhing in pain, as the metal plates covering his body began to shift, bending away from him. Joints snapped and several plates fell away completely—where that happened, magma erupted as if from a volcano, gushing out and spilling onto the valley floor. The armor really had been holding Deathwing together, and as Khadgar's spell removed it, the dragon began to lose cohesion.

"No!" Deathwing, if such a thing were possible, looked utterly taken aback. He craned his neck to look at the damage, at the crunched, warped metal, the seeping magma, then turned glowing eyes on Khadgar. "You may have won this battle, I give you that. But hear this, and hear it well. *I have seen you, mage.*"

Khadgar gulped, unable to tear his gaze away.

"I have burned your face into my memory," Deathwing continued, his voice reverberating along Khadgar's bones. "I will haunt your dreams and your waking moments alike. Rest assured, I will come for you, and when at last I do, you will beg me for your death as the only respite from your terror."

His mighty wings unfurled again, his claws spasming open to release both Gruul and the skull, and Deathwing took to the air, his wings beating hard as he fled the mountains. Khadgar's legs, which had been shaking, finally collapsed and he sat on the ground for a long moment, gasping and acutely aware that he'd just been terribly, terribly lucky.

With their father and ruler gone, the remaining black dragons seemed to lose heart and focus. One of the larger creatures abandoned the fight immediately, his body covered with heavy gashes and one wing bent at an odd angle.

"Father," he cried, leaning back to snap at where the smaller gronn had his tail in a death grip. "Father, wait for me!" Spitting magma, the dragon burned the gronn's hands until he released his hold, then took off after Deathwing.

With the horror that was Deathwing forced into retreat, the ogres and the gronn seemed to go mad for slaughter. They descended upon those dragons that had not escaped in time, ripping them apart with huge meaty fists and teeth, crunching their throats, lifting the bodies to the skies, and then impaling the still-writhing drakes upon the rocky spires.

Khadgar took advantage of the confusion to grab up the skull Deathwing had dropped.

Human . . . but powerful. What great potential I sense here! But that is to be expected, is it not, from the young apprentice to Medivh? You can become stronger yet, if you have the courage to embrace your destiny. Why not become my apprentice? I will teach you that blood and slaughter are the keys to true—

"Ah!" Khadgar gasped, almost dropping the skull. Gul'dan! He gritted his teeth and shuttered his mind. Even dead, it would seem, Gul'dan was a danger. Quickly he stashed the skull in a pouch and hurried back to where Turalyon and the others still fought.

"I have the skull," he told Turalyon, finding his

friend just backing away from a dragon's death throes.

"Well done," Turalyon said. "Now let's get out of here. We retreat. Now." Their men were quickly gathered, and Alleria rounded up her rangers. The ogres and the gronn were too busy tormenting the dragons to even notice their departure.

Turalyon led them quickly back out of the mountains. "Your gamble worked, Khadgar, and brilliantly," he told his friend once they were well clear of the valley and its carnage. "We got the skull, and we dealt with the dragons—they won't be aiding the Horde again any time soon."

Khadgar thought about Deathwing's parting threat and couldn't suppress a shiver. He wasn't so sure Turalyon's optimism was warranted. Nevertheless, he nodded as if he believed it. "All that's left is Ner'zhul. Once I get that book, I can close the portal for good."

All that was left was stopping a powerful shaman, one who had the powers of the skies and the earth, from opening portals into countless worlds. Still, they'd just dealt an extremely powerful dragon a setback. Who knew, maybe they'd be able to do this after all. One thing was certain. If they didn't stop the orcs now, on Draenor . . . they would never stop them.

CHAPTER TWENTY-THREE

"Village up ahead," Ba'rak reported, leaning over with his hands on his legs as he struggled to catch his breath. Dried blood still coated his side beneath the rough bandages they'd rigged for him after Kargath Bladefist had ordered the Shattered Hand clan to abandon Hellfire Citadel. Yet Ba'rak was actually one of the least injured among their little band.

Which was why they were here.

"I'll go on by myself," Kargath told Ba'rak and the others. "I will make better time." He glanced around at the other orcs. "Heal quickly. When I return we'll set out for the Black Temple."

As he walked, Kargath wondered how it had come to this. True, when Ner'zhul had given him those orders to stay behind and delay the Alliance at Hellfire Citadel, it had been obvious the shaman did not expect them to survive. Nor was death in battle a problem for Kargath or any of his Shattered Hand orcs. But dying with honor was one thing—dying for no reason was another. And leaving Ner'zhul and the others defenseless against the Alliance would bring dishonor on them and their entire clan, even if they had died in the process. That was why, when he had seen that the Alliance had conquered the citadel and shattered all their defenses, Kargath had gathered what warriors he could find and had set out for the Black Temple itself. But he'd had fewer than he'd hoped, and many of them had been so badly wounded they hadn't even survived the first night. Now he had only a handful left, none of them uninjured.

He stalked on, a part of him noting the landscape around him. Most of Draenor resembled Hellfire Peninsula, with its cracked red ground and bare stretches. Why, then, was this region still so green? Lush grass cushioned his steps, and clumps of bushes alternated with tall trees. Nagrand had clearly not been touched by the same desolation as the rest of their world, but why?

It was ironic, in a way—the greenest, healthiest part of Draenor, and it was home to sick and weakened orcs. As he crested a low hill, Kargath saw the village spread out before him. Its tightly built walls, domed roofs, and plank porches were in the same style as most orc villages, including his own. For a second Kargath entertained the notion of bringing his warriors here, chasing out the current inhabitants, and claiming the village as their own. They could let the war pass them by—Ner'zhul did not expect to see any of them again, so he wouldn't be surprised when they never appeared. They could let the Horde go on to other worlds and live out their days here instead, tending herds and crops and battling whatever beasts lived in the forests whenever they felt the old bloodlust rise.

But no, Kargath scolded himself. He had sworn an oath to fight for the Horde. How could he live with himself—or look any of his warriors in the eye—if he did not give them his all? Besides, he thought with a shiver, claiming this village would mean facing its current residents, and he didn't think any of his warriors were up for that.

Walking down the hill, Kargath approached the village cautiously. He saw a few orcs moving around sluggishly, patches of brown against the green of their surroundings, but they hadn't noticed him yet. When he was still a hundred feet or so from the nearest hut, Kargath slowed to a halt.

"Geyah!" he shouted, breaking into a short spate of coughing as the deep breath exacerbated his injuries. "Greatmother Geyah!" The orcs he'd noticed earlier looked up, startled, then disappeared into the nearest huts. Hopefully they were summoning Geyah, Kargath thought bitterly. He doubted he had the strength for another shout right now.

A moment later the curtains over a hut entrance rustled and then were pushed aside. Greatmother Geyah emerged and stomped toward him, squinting against the sunlight. "Who's there?" she called out, her voice as sharp as ever.

"Kargath Bladefist, chieftain of the Shattered Hand clan," he replied, forcing himself to stand up straight as she approached.

"Kargath, eh? I've not seen you for many a year," Geyah commented. She finally stopped halfway between him and the huts and met his gaze. Her eyes were still violet, Kargath noted, and her long hair was still thick, if streaked with gray. She didn't look ill. Impatient, though. And the curl of her lip—was that revulsion he saw there?

"What do you want here?" she demanded, confirming his impression.

"An Alliance army has invaded Draenor," Kargath told her, his sense of urgency warring with the respectfulness his elders had drummed into him as a youth. "They've overthrown Hellfire Citadel and will be marching on the Black Temple soon."

"Eh? And what's that to me?" Geyah asked, sniffing. "Monuments to war, the both of those places. We're better off with them gone."

"I need warriors," Kargath explained, hoping he sounded confident and demanding rather than desperate. "Any orc able to fight must come with me at once."

Geyah stared at him, her eyes wide. "Are you mad?" she burst out. "This is a village of the sick, or have you forgotten that?" She studied him, and a sly grin flickered across her lips. "No, I can see you haven't—or would you rather we continued this discussion inside one of the huts?" When he shifted uneasily from foot to foot, her grin widened. "As I thought. You know who dwells here." Her grin turned to a scowl. "And now you want to add to their suffering by dragging them into your foolish war? Why should they fight? Why should any of us?" She glared at him. "You invaded the humans' world. This is the consequence."

Kargath felt his own lips pulling back in a snarl as his anger began to outweigh his fear. "We are all part of the Horde," he reminded her sharply. "We are one race, and all must survive or fall together." He studied her for a second, then switched to a different tack. "Ner'zhul says he can get us off this hellhole. If he can get to the Black Temple and hold off the Alliance long enough, he can open portals to other worlds. You could have an entire world to yourself, for you and your patients."

"What's wrong with this world?" Geyah responded. She gestured at the greenery all around them. "I like it just fine."

"This world is dying."

"Only part of it," she countered. "The part you and your fool warlocks have tainted. Nagrand is as vibrant as ever." She looked smug. "It is mag'har— uncorrupted. And so are its people. They may be sick with the red pox, even dying from it. But at least they have not been fouled by the Horde's dark magics."

"It is your duty!" Kargath insisted. "All your warriors must come with me at once!"

Geyah laughed at him then. "You want them?" she asked. "Get them yourself. Drag them out of their sickbeds and you can take them with you to your war."

Kargath glared at her, but his anger was up now and overwhelming all else, including his fear. "They don't look that ill," he said, staring past her to where many of the orcs she tended had emerged from the various huts to watch the exchange. From here he could see that some of them were limping and others were bent or bowed or hunched, but they all appeared to have the right number of limbs. And at this point as long as they could hold a club he'd take them.

He started toward the village, just as one of the figures stepped away from its hut and approached them. It was a male, a young warrior, and as he neared, Kargath could see he was tall and muscular. He was also staggering, swaying on his feet, and his brown skin was pale except where angry red pustules marred it, many of them seeping a thin red fluid that looked more like tainted tears than blood.

With a start Kargath realized he knew the youth. It was Garrosh Hellscream, son of Grom!

"What has happened?" Garrosh demanded, lurching to a stop beside Geyah. "Why are you here? Is it the Horde?" A strange look came over the youth's face. "Is it my—?" A horrible wet groan rose from his throat, drowning out his words, and then Garrosh fell to his knees, gasping as blood and bile spilled from his mouth, pouring down his chin and chest and soaking into the grass below.

"I warned you not to exert yourself!" Geyah snapped, steadying him with a hand on his shoulder. She did not seem concerned about the risk of touching him. "The pox is still upon you, and you're nowhere near well enough to leave your hut yet!" Then she glared at Kargath, a nasty smile on her face. "Do you want him to join you for battle? Are these the warriors you'd hoped to find?"

Kargath had recoiled when Garrosh started spitting up blood, and he continued to back away now. "No. They are no warriors." Disgust and despair added venom to his words. "They are not even orcs anymore—they are useless." He glared at Geyah, at Garrosh, and at the other villagers behind them. "You pathetic weaklings!" he snarled, raising his voice as best he could. "Do the Horde a favor and die here! If you can't help defend your people, you have no right to live!"

With that he turned on his heel and stalked off. There was nothing for it now but to take his remaining warriors and disappear into the hills. He lacked the numbers to make a difference at the Black Temple. Too, the more he thought about it, after being abandoned at Hellfire Citadel, Kargath felt that he did not owe Ner'zhul anything anyway. No, he would take what few soldiers he had left and find some place to hole up and rebuild. Some day they would be strong again, and then they would reclaim Hellfire Citadel and the rest of the land from there. And when he did finally die, Kargath vowed, it would be on his feet. He shuddered at what lay behind him. No matter what, he would not end up like them.

"We need to get you back to your bed," Geyah scolded Garrosh, though more gently now.

Garrosh shook off her hands. "What did he say?" he demanded in a hoarse whisper, his throat still spasming after tossing out so much liquid. "Was it—was it about my father? Is he—is he still alive?"

Geyah looked away, unable to meet the hope flickering in the boy's eyes. Was Grom alive? She had no idea. Not that it mattered. She had heard plenty about the older Hellscream over the past few years, about his savagery and his battle frenzy and his appetite for violence. He had been the first to give himself to the Horde and to Gul'dan's foul magic, she knew, and it had corrupted him utterly. Even if he still lived, he would surely be beyond redemption.

"He didn't say anything about your father," she told Garrosh now, gripping his arm again and refusing to be put off a second time. "I am sure he is still alive and well, else Kargath would have mentioned it."

Garrosh nodded and let himself be led away, his energy spent. Geyah's heart went out to him, and to all the orcs she tended here. Would they survive the red pox? Some of them, perhaps, but not all. Yet a part of her couldn't help feeling that at least their deaths would be cleaner than those of the orcs whose souls had been so tainted; the mark showed through to their very skin. She shook her head and continued walking with Garrosh, refusing to glance back to where the emerald-skinned Kargath was still marching away.

CHAPTER TWENTY-FOUR

"Ho, lads!"

Turalyon glanced up, surprised. It was overcast, and a shape had just dropped out of the heavy clouds, plummeting through the dark sky. The shout was all that stopped Alleria and her rangers from loosing arrows at the descending figure, and prevented Turalyon from ordering his men into defensive positions. Instead he stepped back and waited, hands at his side, a small smile on his lips, as Sky'ree spread her wings and swooped in for a landing.

Kurdran was already climbing down from Sky'ree's back while her talons were still digging into the earth, and strode up to Turalyon where he and Alleria and Khadgar waited. Turalyon's pleasure at seeing the dwarf was dampened, however, by the dwarf's stiff, slow gait, and changed to confusion by the strange, hunched figure that dismounted and scurried after him.

"Ah, I'm glad to see ye all," Kurdran said, clasping hands with Turalyon and Khadgar in turn and kissing Alleria's hand. "An' it were a near thing, too, for those green beasts captured me, they did."

Turalyon frowned and studied his short friend. "I'm glad you escaped."

"Nay, rescued, I was, and healed up right proper," Kurdran corrected. "The lad Danath sprung me, an' stormed their great ruin ta boot. Called Auchindoun, it were. Found ourselves a strange-looking friend there who might teach even ye a thing or two about healing wi' the Light. Good thing too—I, er, wasn't at me best."

Turalyon looked with fresh admiration at his friend. What Kurdran had said amounted to a confession of being at death's door. "I'm glad," he said fervently.

"Eh, ye'll nae be so glad about the next part. Ner'zhul got away. He and his pet death knight cast a spell tha' took them straight ta a place called th' Black Temple, an' we couldna stop them."

Turalyon sighed and placed his hand on Kurdran's shoulder. "Don't worry, Kurdran. I know you and Danath did your best. I'm grateful you're all right." He ran a hand through his hair, thinking. "Black Temple—sounds ominous. What do we know about it?"

"Nae much, but yon feathered creature here will take us ta it." Kurdran jerked a thumb at the figure who had accompanied him atop Sky'ree. It bowed obsequiously. "This is Grizzik. He led Danath into

Auchindoun, an' then Danath found his way ta me."

"Grizzik knows!" it stated, its voice high and reedy. "I will tell you of the Black Temple. I know what and where!"

"Is this your benefactor?" Alleria asked. "The one who healed you?"

"Nay, nay, that's a draenei. It does get complicated."

"Then what are you?" Alleria asked softly, and Turalyon realized her elven eyes had pierced the shadows of the heavy cowl that hid Grizzik's face.

"I am arakkoa," Grizzik answered, flinging back his cowl, and Turalyon tried not to start at the stranger's long beak and feathered hair. "We were born of this world, as are orcs. Long have arakkoa kept to ourselves. Little have we to do with orcs or draenei. Then orcs rose up, banding together, forming the Horde. They slaughtered draenei."

"Auchindoun was a draenei burial city," Kurdran explained. "So Grizzik's told me."

"And Black Temple was theirs as well," Grizzik added. "Though it was not called that then. There draenei made their last stand, and there my brethren and I, too, came to fight orcs." His eyes glittered with what Tura-lyon took for rage, though there seemed something malicious in them as well. "We failed. Though not from lack of arms. Orcs have a sorcerer, Gul'dan. He is very strong. He alters earth itself, raising a great volcano in our midst." Now his small eyes clearly blazed with anger.

"Gul'dan, eh?" Khadgar swung the sack down from his shoulder, opened it, and pulled out the skull. "Here's all that's left of him. He won't be causing you any more trouble," the young-old mage told the arakkoa before dropping the skull back inside with a quickly concealed look of relief.

Grizzik's eyes were wide. "You slew Gul'dan?" he asked, his voice a breathy whisper.

"No," Turalyon admitted. "Someone else got to him first. But we have destroyed the Horde's power and broken one of its major strongholds. Now we just need to reach the Black Temple, find Ner'zhul, and kill him as well."

The arakkoa bobbed his head. "I can show you way," he assured them.

Turalyon caught Kurdran's eye, and the Wildhammer leader shrugged. Turalyon understood—the clever dwarf wasn't sure whether to trust Grizzik either, but what choice did they have? "Thank you," he told the arakkoa. "We welcome your help." He turned to Kurdran. "We'll draw up a rough map tonight, based on Grizzik's information," he said. "Tomorrow I want you to head back to Danath. We'll decide where to meet up for the final assault."

Kurdran nodded. "Aye, lad, tha's a fine plan," he agreed. "Now, who's got ale for me, and some food? Once I'm refreshed I'll tell ye the full o' our trek, and the battle at Auchindoun."

Turalyon smiled. "I can't wait to hear it," he told the dwarf, and it was true. He caught Alleria's eye and smiled as she slipped her hand into his. Tomorrow they would begin the march again, but for tonight, at least, they could sit and drink and listen to the Wildhammer's no doubt colorful tale.

Several days later they rode between two low mountain ranges and saw a wide valley stretching out before them. Kurdran had found them when they were almost level with what Turalyon now knew the orcs called Hellfire Citadel and the Dark Portal. Grizzik had led them far farther south and then east, skirting the waters the arakkoa had told them were called the Devouring Sea. There, at the very edge of the land, stood the Black Temple, where the Shadowmoon Valley ran up against the mountains that dropped off into the raging sea. And it was there that Danath and the rest of the Alliance army were waiting for them.

Danath and the others had not been idle, Turalyon saw as he reined in. A crude but effective camp stood near the southwest edge of the valley, and thick log walls were already half-erected around it.

"Kurdran's idea," Danath said as he approached them, clasping Turalyon's hand in greeting. "He felt we'd need a place where we could keep an eye on things across the valley, and this struck us both as a good vantage point." Turalyon nodded. It was indeed that—from there they could see all the way across to the land's edge, including the massive volcano rising up in the center and billowing smoke and ash and lava in every direction.

"Aye, and it's best it were someone as didn't need ta set foot on tha' ground," Kurdran added as he joined them. "That lava's green, if'n ye canna tell from here, an' the very ground's saturated with it."

Khadgar nodded and Turalyon noticed the pained expression on his friend's face. "Fel magic," he whispered hoarsely. "The purest I've ever seen." The archmage shook his head. "I don't even want to know what sort of spells Gul'dan worked to cause this. It's a violation of nature itself—no wonder this world is dying." He frowned at Kurdran. "Keep your people as far from that thing as possible," he warned, "and don't enter the valley any more than necessary."

"Och, aye, we'll steer well clear," Kurdran assured him. "The good news, though, is that we've already scouted the valley for ye." He produced a roll of parchment and showed them the map he'd sketched out. "The Black Temple be there, at the far east end," he said, gesturing toward where a massive dark structure could be clearly seen across the valley. "An' there's no easy way out from it, either, 'cepting through this valley. It's a big horseshoe, it is, and its open end points this way."

"Any sign of Ner'zhul?" Alleria asked.

"Aye, he's there," Kurdran answered. "An' those death knights as well. Plus some orcs, though not many." He grinned. "We've got them pinned in—they'll nae be goin' anywhere."

Turalyon glanced over at Danath, who nodded. "We

laid siege to the temple as soon as we arrived," he explained. "I didn't want to risk them getting reinforcements."

"Good." Turalyon turned to the others. "We need to get over there ourselves. Khadgar, you're the key here—we need you to take out Ner'zhul and stop his spell. Alleria, you and your rangers protect him from long-range attacks. Shoot down anything that even looks his way. I'll be right beside him to take care of anything close by. We smash through their defenses, find Ner'zhul, kill him, take back the artifacts, and get the hell out. Agreed?"

"Absolutely," Khadgar agreed, and the others nodded as well.

"Good." Turalyon sighed and said a quick prayer, calling down the Holy Light's protection upon them all. He felt it pouring over them all, warm and calming, and thanked it. He clasped hands with Kurdran, Danath, and Khadgar, then turned to Alleria. She smiled bravely up at him, but she knew, as he did, the risks. Alleria. Thank the Light, they had not been so stupid as to still be shunning one another. Instead, they had found strength and comfort in each other. He folded her close for a long moment, resting his chin on her shining hair, then tilted her head up to kiss her. Pulling back, he gave her his best smile and hefted his hammer. "Let's go."

They charged across the valley, the remaining Alliance forces right behind them—only a handful of men stayed behind to guard the camp. As they raced around the volcano, Turalyon saw the Black Temple for the first time, and only his faith kept him from jerking his horse to a stop and then kicking it into a gallop in any other direction.

The place was enormous, towering over even the volcano jutting up from the valley floor. Carved of some stone that had perhaps once been bright but was now coated in ash and other foul substances that swallowed the light, it loomed like a piece of shadow given solid form, squat and ugly and dangerous, mocking the army that threw itself against its walls. Turalyon could tell that every surface was heavily carved, though he could not make out details yet, and the top of the central portion had protrusions that reminded him of a hand grasping at the sky. Even as Turalyon tried to take it all in, his horse stumbled, and he was nearly thrown as the earth rocked beneath him. Lightning, green and loud and ominous and crackling with darkness instead of illumination, shattered the skies. His horse whickered in terror and reared. Its rider was only marginally less frightened, but did his best to calm the animal.

"What's going on?" he shouted to Khadgar over the roll of thunder.

"The skies are right," Khadgar shouted back. "I fear that—"

His words were snatched away as the earth shook again and the skies flashed green.

Turalyon saw another flash, and his head whipped up.

The portion that evoked the image of a hand reaching for the skies—it was glowing.

"Oh no," he breathed, and turned to Khadgar.

"I was right," Khadgar yelled. "Ner'zhul has begun his spell."

"Can we still stop him?"

"I can," Khadgar answered grimly. "Just get me there in time."

"Consider it done." Turalyon raised his hammer high overhead and summoned his faith, channeling it into the blessed weapon. The hammer's surface began to glow, the light spreading as it grew, until it shone so brilliantly the volcano dimmed alongside it. The orcs and death knights battling before the Black Temple turned away, blinded, but the light did not sear Alliance eyes and his soldiers cheered as Turalyon galloped past them, his hammer burning a path through the temple's defenders.

Until one figure stepped out into his path.

"Your little light does not frighten me!" Teron Gorefiend called out, a jeweled truncheon in his hand. It was obvious to anyone with eyes that the death knight was lying. He had let his hood fall back and his hideous, decaying face and burning red eyes were plainly visible. That face was contorted with pain, and the body strained as if wanting to flee of its own accord. Gorefiend lifted the strange weapon he held. It glowed with a multicolored light, and that varied radiance battered at Turalyon's glow, attempting to overpower it.

"The Holy Light is all that you are not, monster," Turalyon shouted in reply, pointing the hammer at Gorefiend and loosing a burst of light like a missile. "If you do not fear it, then embrace it!"

The burst struck Gorefiend, but he swept his truncheon before him and it scattered Turalyon's attack, diffusing the brilliant white into rays of color. Then the death knight struck in turn—he leveled his truncheon at Turalyon, and a shadow emerged from its tip, engulfing the Alliance commander. Turalyon felt the darkness constrict, smothering his light and his limbs simultaneously, and fought against it, writhing to break free. Air passed beneath him and he hit the ground hard, rolling and struggling—clearly the attack had carried him from his horse, but the darkness stayed on him, pressing him down into the earth.

He gasped for air, but his lungs refused to inflate, refused to obey his commands. He'd fallen. Of course he had—he was not even good enough to stay atop his horse. What kind of general was he? His troops would die too. He'd led them straight to their deaths. Lothar would be so ashamed of him. . . .

Turalyon spasmed on the earth, willing himself to breathe, but tendrils of darkness wrapped around his chest, crushing it. Snakelike, they wound up around him, pinning his arms to his sides, forcing their way into his mouth, his nostrils, his eyes—ah, it burned! Tears spilled from tightly closed lids, but only inflamed the fire.

And so he would die, a failure, a catastrophe. All those deaths would be on his head. Those innocents in other worlds, gaping in horror as the vast green tide swept over them. The men who had believed him when he told them the Light would be with them. Light . . . what Light—where was it now, now that it mattered—

Alleria!

Dead, too, she would be, joining her family, cursing him in whatever afterlife the elves believed in. She never loved him; he saw that now. He was a toy, one she would have outlived, one she'd have moved on from. Khadgar—Kurdran—Danath—

The dark tendrils tightened. Turalyon opened his eyes, staring blankly. *I'm sorry, Lothar. I failed you. I'm not you. I led them—*

He blinked.

He led them the best he'd known how. No, he wasn't Anduin Lothar, the Lion of Azeroth. Only Lothar could be Lothar. It would be the height of arrogance to assume otherwise. He was Turalyon, and the Light *was* with him; it hadn't failed him yet, not when he had prayed with his whole heart.

Just ask. All you have to do is ask, with a pure heart. That's why Lothar picked you. Not because he thought you'd be him. Because he knew you'd be you.

Turalyon took a shallow breath, constrained by the dark tendrils, and prayed. He opened his eyes, and he knew without understanding how he knew that they were shining with pure white radiance. He looked down at the tendrils of darkness and they melted, retreated, as shadows must always, must ever retreat, before the Light. His chest heaved with a great breath and he clambered to his feet and grabbed his hammer, swinging it through what remained of the shadows.

The attack had lasted only a few seconds, though it had felt like an eternity. Gorefiend had used the diversion to creep closer, and when Turalyon could see and move freely again he realized the death knight was only a few feet away. His red eyes widened as Turalyon took a step forward—clearly he had not expected the young Alliance commander to win free so quickly, if at all—and he was not prepared for the heavy blow Turalyon's hammer struck him full in the chest. Turalyon was sure he heard bones snap beneath the worn armor, and the death knight stumbled back, though he did not fall.

"You cannot win," Gorefiend hissed through gritted teeth. "I am already dead—what is the worst you could do to me?" His truncheon jabbed forward, catching Turalyon in the stomach and doubling him over, and Gorefiend's hand brushed the back of Turalyon's helm. Instantly pain blossomed in Turalyon's head, as if a vise had gripped his helm and was squeezing it tight onto his temples and skull. Stars exploded behind his eyes and he felt the world tilt crazily around him. In desperation he swung his hammer again, a mighty

two-handed arc, and felt the heavy head strike something solid. There was a rattle and a gasp and the pain
vanished.

Blinking away spots and taking a deep, racking
breath to clear his head, Turalyon glanced up in time to
see Gorefiend stagger a step, one arm hanging limp.
While the death knight was off-balance Turalyon
lurched forward, hammer raised high. He summoned
his faith to him again, and the radiance shone from his
limbs and from his weapon, too bright to look upon as
he advanced upon his foe.

The death knight cried out, raising his hands to
shield his eyes from the radiance, which was now actually starting to make his flesh smoke and curl.

"By the Light!" Turalyon cried, praise, prayer, and
promise all in one. The light flared brightly, so brightly,
and as he brought the hammer down it did more than
simply crush the reanimated body. It cleaved through
it, the light carving an arc through Teron Gorefiend,
ripping through him until the dead flesh fell in a soggy,
reeking heap.

A horrible wailing pierced Turalyon's ears and he
staggered back, staring in horror and disbelief as the
jagged, shrieking wisp that was Teron Gorefiend's soul
twisted upward from the wreckage of his body. The
paladin lifted the glowing hammer and swung once
more, but he was a fraction of a second too late, and
the spirit was gone, shrieking in pain and frustration,
fleeing into the crackling green and black sky.

"Come on!" came Alleria's voice, startling Turalyon. His heart swelled to see her. He quickly leaped atop his horse and galloped toward her.

Riding ahead of them was Khadgar, and they caught up quickly. The death knight had been the temple's last barrier. Now they were within the Black Temple itself, and faced the long stairs winding up toward the top and the sickly light that pulsed forth from that height.

Alleria . . . Khadgar . . . Danath . . . Kurdran—damn it, they were not going to die here. With a physical shake of his head, Turalyon dispelled the last of the shadow's hold on him, gripped his hammer, and rode toward his destiny.

CHAPTER TWENTY-FIVE

Ner'zhul stood upon the roof of the Black Temple, in the center of the inscribed circle. Above him, obscured by the lowering clouds and flashes of green lightning, the great conjunction involving the Watcher, the Staff, and the Tome was reaching its peak. And as above, so below. Also below, beneath his feet, Ner'zhul could sense Draenor's ley lines crossing over and around and through him, and as he closed his eyes he could feel the entire world trembling in his grasp. This was why the draenei had built their temple here, and why it was the only place where he could cast this spell. From here he could literally tap the entire planet for the power to cast his spell.

Arrayed around him, in the larger circle that surrounded the first, were several of Gorefiend's death knights, the few warlocks who had survived Doomhammer's wrath, and a handful of his own Shadowmoon orcs. The latter group stood in the third and largest circle, facing outward, weapons raised. They were there for protection, while the others aided Ner'zhul in tapping the planet's power and performing the ritual.

They had already been casting for an entire day, since the moment the celestial alignment was right, and only the energy flowing through them kept the old shaman from collapsing from fatigue or hunger. As it was, his skin tingled and his hair danced about him as if carried high by an unseen wind.

They were nearing the end of the spell. The Alliance had crashed against the Black Temple's thick walls hours before, and were in danger of breaching its defenses at any moment. But they would be too late, Ner'zhul thought triumphantly. He raised the Scepter of Sargeras in his right hand, and the Eye of Dalaran in his left. Both gleamed brightly, inner light shining from the head of the scepter and dancing from facet to facet within the Eye's violet center. Those two artifacts focused the ley line energy, coalescing it into almost physical form, and then pulsed the strength into Ner'zhul's limbs. Now his entire body was thrumming, and he knew that he was no longer standing on the stone roof but hovering just above it as the energy lifted him from the surface.

"Now!" he shouted, touching the tip of the scepter to the center of the Eye and feeling the rest of their stored energy flash through his limbs and into his heart and mind. He knew his eyes were glowing bright, brighter than the sun, and he could see the lines of magic etched upon the world and through the air, see the souls of those surrounding him, see the connection between them and this world, and between this world and the rest of the cosmos. He could feel the curtains surrounding Draenor, separating it from other realities.

And, with a single quick, slashing gesture of the scepter, he tore through those curtains, shredding them as easily as he might slice through thin parchment.

The world shook. The ground trembled. The sky rumbled. A terrible grinding sound echoed up from far below and met an earsplitting shriek descending from above the clouds. Draenor screamed and thrashed in pain. The other participants staggered as the Black Temple shifted, many of them falling to their knees. Ner'zhul, too, staggered but managed to stay upright, buoyed by the power coursing through him.

He could feel the magic reaching across reality, like a fishing line cast into the void. It leaped forward, Draenor's own energies giving it vast momentum—and hooked onto something solid. Another world. The line grew taut, and with a twang that vibrated right through him a responding chord raced back down the line—and tore open a hole in their reality.

A rift. It was a rift. Ner'zhul recognized the feel of it, the raw power that frayed air and earth and nature, the throbbing link that bound this world to the next. Beneath the skull face paint, his lips split into a broad smile, and he closed his eyes, drinking in the heady feel of success. He had done it! He had opened a rift!

And not just one. He could sense other rifts appearing all across Draenor, like tiny bubbles emerging from the sea and bursting open when they touched the raw air, like lightning strikes from a storm that blanketed the entire planet. Each one burned in his mind like a new volcano.

He could send scouts through each rift, to report back on the worlds they found. Then he would choose the most likely and lead the Horde through to a better place. And, perhaps, to another after that. And after that as well, until his people had as many worlds as they wanted, as many as they could comfortably hold. Until each clan had its own world, if they liked. Then no one would be able to stop them.

Obris, one of the many who had been guarding the spellcasters all this time, said, *"This* is our new world?"

Indeed, what they could see through the undulating rift was not pleasant. It was not much, but enough to be disturbing: Something fluttered and loomed up, then was gone. A sickly light surged dully, then vanished. "This doesn't look like anything we—"

"Silence!" Ner'zhul cried, whirling to face Obris. "We—"

And in that moment of inattention, within his grasp, the Eye trembled. Ner'zhul frowned and clutched it harder. It seemed to writhe like a fish and before he realized what had happened, it leaped from his hand, flew through the air—

—and came to rest in the hand of a tall, broad-shouldered man with white hair and violet robes. A staff in one hand shone with power, and his eyes blazed with far more hidden deep within. A human wizard—and he had literally snatched victory from Ner'zhul's grasp.

Behind the mage stood a man in full armor, carrying a hammer that glowed with a blinding white light. Ner'zhul realized this man was not just a warrior, but akin to a shaman—except that the forces he tapped were somehow on a grander scale than a mere planet's. The elven female who stood beside them had no such magical abilities, but her face showed righteous anger. She had an arrow nocked and aimed directly at him.

Ner'zhul trembled.

How dare they?

How *dare* they interrupt his moment of absolute glory! Ner'zhul realized he felt no fear, no worry—just absolute outrage.

"The Eye will not serve you when you are dust!" he cried, and let the outrage take him. It blazed through him, pure and hot and deadly. With a cry he lifted his hands. The tortured rock and stone obeyed in agony, cracking beneath the intruders' feet. Barely in time, the Alliance intruders leaped aside, rolling to come up with weapons at the ready. But Ner'zhul was not done. Not yet. He was just getting started.

The rocks that had cracked now rose up and hurled themselves at the Alliance interlopers. Wind and rain whipped around them, snatching them up to hover helplessly in the air before slamming them mercilessly down on the unyielding stone. Ner'zhul took great pleasure in watching them suffer. It was with effort that he turned back to yell, "Through the rift! Now! Glory and fresh worlds await us!"

Obris gaped at him. "Kill the Alliance and let us gather our Horde! You cannot possibly mean that only we few will escape? What about our brothers, who fight even now? Grom and the Warsong are still in Azeroth. There are females and children scattered all over. We cannot abandon them! To do so would be the most gutless, cowardly—"

Something snapped in Ner'zhul. Something that had been holding him down, he suddenly realized. It was only now—now that he was free of guilt, of shame, of trying to still do good for his people—that he realized what a burden it had truly been. He had once accepted death as part of the cycle; then feared it; then realized he was the bringer of it, and all the heavy weight that that implied.

No more. He was free.

He didn't even favor Obris with a retort. Ner'zhul extended his hand. Lightning balled in his palm and raced in a crackling arc toward the other orc, slamming into Obris's chest with a thunderclap and hurtling him backward. He crashed into the wall and slid down, a smoking black hole in his chest. He did not rise.

Whirling, Ner'zhul turned to those around him,

who stared at him in shock. "The other orcs are lost. They have served their purpose. From this point on, all that we gain will be ours alone. I am the Horde, and I will survive. Choose me, or choose death!"

When they did not move, he growled and lifted the scepter. Now they did move, as if suddenly freed, rushing toward the flickering rift. It hovered a few inches above the roof's surface and rose to nearly ten feet. Ner'zhul went last, holding the rift open with his power and his will, then stepped into the rift himself.

He had just enough time to gasp before the rift vanished behind them.

CHAPTER TWENTY-SIX

Khadgar's head swam, but he felt warm healing energy spreading through his body. He got to his feet, swaying, and swore. The rift was just fading from view, leaving a faint afterimage like a steam trail. And Ner'zhul and his orcs were gone with it.

"... we're too late. It's gone."

"Gone? By the Light, no!" Turalyon was right behind Khadgar but apparently hadn't seen the rift. Then again, Khadgar had felt it with his other senses before he'd actually seen it. Although Turalyon too wielded great power, his facility with the Holy Light gave him no particular insight into arcane magic.

"He must have closed the rift behind him," Khadgar guessed as he and Turalyon stepped back onto the roof itself, Alleria right behind them.

"But you got the Eye of Dalaran back," Alleria pointed out. "That's important, isn't it?" Khadgar nodded. "Well, what do we do now?" She turned her head to gaze down from the Black Temple. "It looks like we're winning down there, at least."

"Any way you can follow him?" Turalyon asked.

Khadgar shook his head. "I don't know the spell Ner'zhul was using," he admitted, "or how to find whatever world that rift took him to. So even if I could open a new rift here, there's no guarantee it would open onto the same world." His attention was caught by something else, however, and he frowned, stepping forward and walking to the triple circle inlaid in the roof.

"What is it?"

"Power," Khadgar said absently. "More power than I've ever felt in any one place save Medivh's tower." He cocked his head to the side. "That's why," he muttered. "I'd wondered why Ner'zhul left Hellfire Citadel to us instead of defending it properly and casting the spell from there. But he couldn't. He had to be here. He needed the magic here to fuel his ritual."

"Does that help us any?" Alleria asked.

"I'm not sure," he replied. "Perhaps." He stepped into the center circle, and his head snapped back, mouth falling open in a silent scream. Such power! It poured through him like wildfire, igniting his veins, sending every sense into overload.

Ner'zhul was a shaman, not a mage. His magics came from the earth and the sky and the water, from the world itself. And that was what this place was, a focal point for the world's power. For Ner'zhul it would have been like tapping full force into something he had already broached repeatedly, but on a lesser scale—he would know how to handle it. For Khadgar, however, it was a completely new experience. And a dangerous one.

But Khadgar was not an archmage for nothing. He had been a promising student at Dalaran, and had learned much during his brief apprenticeship with Medivh—and far more afterward. He was a master of magic, and while this form was new, it was still magic. And that meant it was still a matter of willpower.

And Khadgar had will.

Slowly he reined in his senses, forcing the new energy down until it was merely a background hum. Then he opened his eyes—and gasped. Standing here now, flooded with the power of a whole world, he could see what he couldn't see previously.

"Oh, no," he breathed.

"What is it?" Turalyon asked.

"The rifts . . . ," Khadgar breathed, barely able to find the words to encompass the scope of it. "Ner'zhul didn't just open one. He opened many—so many, all over this poor world." They flickered and glittered, looking almost like fireflies on a hot summer evening. "The scope of this . . . I don't think Draenor can bear it. It can't hold all this. Rifts are tears—and these tears are going to rip this whole damned place apart." *And us with it,* he thought, but did not say.

Turalyon and Alleria looked at each other. As one,

they turned to Khadgar. "What do we do? And how long do we have?"

Even as he formed the words a shudder passed through the temple and the land around it. The volcano before it trembled, spewing even more of its noxious lava out into the air and creating a billowing green cloud. Then they heard a horrible crack and a deafening rumble from behind them.

Glancing over his shoulder, Khadgar watched as a mountain of rock cascaded down, literally. The Black Temple had been built up against the mountains that overlooked the sea, and those peaks were crumbling away. Most of the debris was falling into the waters, but some of it exploded toward them instead. Thinking quickly, Khadgar murmured a spell that shielded them from the onslaught, and the three of them stood untouched as rock and gravel and dust flew by on either side. A second spell protected the area directly below, where the Alliance forces were already mopping up the remaining Horde. Many of the orcs had scattered when the battle had turned against them, and the sudden avalanche only hastened their headlong flight.

Draenor, as he had realized it would be, was a beast in pain tearing itself to pieces.

And, Khadgar realized, Draenor might not die alone. "Azeroth is in danger!" he yelled over the din. "These rifts are links between worlds. And the Dark Portal is the largest and the only stable one." There was an odd silence as, for the moment, the earth stilled. Khadgar spoke quickly.

"Our worlds are connected. Damage here could leak through the portal and affect Azeroth as well!" He grimaced and stepped out of the circle, trying not to groan in dismay as his energy levels plummeted back to normal. It was like turning away from a bonfire and accepting a weak torch in its place. But he knew that to stay there longer would endanger them all. "I have to get back to the Dark Portal!"

"Do you have what you need to close it?"

"I have the skull. And the book is here, somewhere. I'll find it," he said with more assurance than he felt.

Turalyon nodded. "I'll rally the troops," he promised.

But Khadgar shook his head. "There's no time!" he insisted, grabbing his friend's shoulder. "Don't you understand? I'm sorry, Turalyon, so sorry—but if I can't shut down the portal right away, when Draenor is destroyed it could take Azeroth with it!"

He saw the realization dawn in Turalyon's eyes, and hated the grim resignation he saw accompany it. But his friend merely nodded. "We'll take gryphons," he announced. "That's the fastest way back." Then he squared his shoulders. "I will speak to the troops before we go. However short time may be, they deserve that." He extended a hand to Alleria and together they ran down the stairs.

Khadgar barely noticed them depart. He'd snatched the Eye right out of Ner'zhul's hand, but he hadn't had time to locate the Book of Medivh before Ner'zhul had retaliated. It was here, he told himself—it had to be in order for the spell to work in harmony with the three constellations. Ner'zhul had still been clutching a silver-trimmed scepter when he'd disappeared, presumably the Scepter of Sargeras. Fine—far safer for such an accursed item to be well away from Azeroth. But where was the blasted book? He needed it to finish the job, and that job had to be finished right now, before it was too late for all of them.

He extended his senses, but there was too much magic in the air for him to sense anything clearly. *The book could be right beneath my nose or miles away. Damn it!* he thought in frustration.

Khadgar caught a glimpse of movement out of the corner of his eye. He whirled, ready to defend himself. One of the bodies had moved, just a little. Its midsection was badly charred, and Khadgar realized that this was the orc Ner'zhul had attacked just before going through the portal. The one who'd called Ner'zhul a coward for leaving the others behind. Again, Khadgar was grateful he'd brought the ring that had enabled him to understand other languages, and he lowered his hands, watching closely.

The orc heaved and grunted, obviously in tremendous pain. It reached for something and, with great effort, held it out to Khadgar with an arm that shook. It was a large, heavily embossed rectangle with carved metal edges. Khadgar caught his breath as he recognized it.

The Book of Medivh.

"I am no . . . shaman. But Obris is smart enough to know . . . that this will be of use to you, will it not?"

Khadgar hesitated. The orc was a few steps away from death, but it could still be some kind of trick. "Yes," he said at last. "Why do you give it to me then? I am your enemy."

"You at least are an honorable foe," Obris growled. "Ner'zhul betrayed us. He re-formed the Horde, and forced my Laughing Skull clan back into the fold. He promised us a new start. But as soon as—" He coughed and then continued in a ragged voice. "As soon as he found safety, he fled. He and his favorites live. . . . The rest of us . . . we are nothing to him."

The eyes flashed with a final spark. "It would please me to know my last act . . . was to defy him. Take it. Take it, curse you! Take it and make him pay for his treachery."

Khadgar moved toward the dying orc and gently took the book from his blackened, bloody hands. "I promise you, Obris: We will do everything in our power to stop Ner'zhul."

The orc nodded, closed his eyes, and went still.

The vagaries of fate, Khadgar mused, quickly undoing the clasps and opening the book to glance through its pages. He remembered first seeing this massive tome back in Medivh's library only a few years ago. So much had changed since then; it felt like a lifetime. Then, he had been terrified of the book but overpowered by curiosity. Fortunately, its wards had prevented him from even turning the cover, or else the magics contained within might have destroyed him. Now Khadgar bypassed them with ease, and skimmed the book's contents with growing excitement. As he expected, the book contained details about how Medivh and Gul'dan had worked together to create the rift. Armed with these necessary details and the still-lingering power in Gul'dan's skull, Khadgar was confident he could now shut down the Dark Portal for good. But could he do so in time?

He glanced up at the sound of beating wings. Several gryphons were circling the roof, wings spread as they prepared to land. Khadgar spotted Kurdran, and another Wildhammer was gesturing to the mage. Nodding, he threw the book in his sack, handed the precious bag up, then gripped the Wildhammer's outstretched hand and swung himself onto the gryphon.

"Where are Alleria and Turalyon?" Khadgar shouted to Kurdran.

"Speakin' tae 'is troops," the dwarf replied.

"They'll have to catch up, then," Khadgar said, shaking his head. "We have no time to waste! To the Dark Portal!"

The gryphons squawked as their riders tugged on the reins, then they wheeled about and rose, wings beating hard against the wind and the weight of two passengers each. Khadgar watched the Black Temple slip away behind them and closed his eyes, his hair and beard streaming out behind him. He held the sack close. With the gryphons they would reach the portal in minutes instead of hours or days. He just hoped it was soon enough.

Alleria rested her head on her lover's shoulder as the gryphon they rode hovered over the Black Temple. She squeezed Turalyon's waist gently, giving him silent support. She knew how bleak his heart was at what he was about to do. But she also knew he would not shirk what had to be done.

"Sons of Lothar!" Turalyon cried, raising his hammer high above his head. Alleria glanced away; its light pierced the clouds gathering above, shedding a brilliant white radiance upon the entire valley, from the Black Temple behind them to the mouth of the Alliance fort far ahead. "Months ago, we came through the Dark Portal, not knowing what awaited us, but knowing that we had to come. We had to come to stop the Horde from taking other worlds as it tried—and failed!—to do with our beloved Azeroth. And the moment to do precisely that has arrived. Khadgar has what he needs in order to close the portal, but this world is in chaos. Azeroth—our home—is in danger once again. We must all do everything we can—serve as best we may—to save it, and our families we have left behind."

He looked out over the men before him, and Alleria knew he was burning each face into his memory. "I go to help Khadgar, to protect him, for I am sure there will be resistance. You . . . must hold the line here. You have never failed me yet. I know, my brothers, you will not fail me now." His voice cracked. Through the tears in her own eyes, Alleria saw that he wept.

"None of us knows what will happen. We may survive this, and find a way home, and live to a ripe old age with stories to dazzle our grandchildren. Or we may die here, with this world. And if such is our fate, I know each one of you chooses it gladly. For we fight for our world—our families—our honor. We fight so that others might live free because of what we do here, today, this hour, this moment. And if there is anything in this world or any other worth dying for—the Light knows, it is this."

Alleria stared at him. His eyes, though still filled with tears, shone now with the radiant white light. Awe shivered through her. *Bright . . . Turalyon, my love, you are so bright.*

"Sons of Lothar! The Light is with you . . . as it always has been, and always will be. For Azeroth!"

His hammer glowed brighter than the day, and many of the captured orcs nearby fell to the ground screaming as its aura burned at their eyes. Turalyon's soldiers were strengthened by the glow, however, and cheered as the gryphon rose, carrying Turalyon and Alleria after the Wildhammers, toward the Dark Portal.

"I would I could stand with them," he murmured softly. She kissed his neck.

"You do, beloved. Their hearts are filled with the Light . . . and so you are there."

★ ★ ★

The scene around the Dark Portal was utter chaos. Turalyon had told his troops the unvarnished truth—Khadgar would need defending. He just hadn't realized how much he and his friends would be defending the wizard from.

Danath, Khadgar, Kurdran, and several others had arrived before them and were fiercely fighting their way to the portal. It seemed the orcs had rallied. Ner'zhul's abrupt departure had stranded several clans on Draenor, and all of them had realized the same thing—the Dark Portal was the only stable rift, and the only one that led to a world they knew was hospitable.

Nor was the battle just on Draenor. One was raging on the other side of the portal as well—it would seem that once again, the orcs had wrested control of the portal from the Alliance. They were trying to push their way through the portal and back into Draenor, unaware of the cataclysm gripping their homeworld. The Alliance forces there were holding them at bay for the moment, but Turalyon could expect no aid. He and this handful were all that stood between the Horde and Azeroth.

But they weren't here to win a battle, he reminded himself. That was entirely secondary right now. Their goal was simply to protect Khadgar and the other magi while they closed the portal once and for all.

"Do what you have to do," he told Khadgar, who stood nearby, the other magi clustered around him.

The young-old archmage nodded and raised his hands, letting his eyes close. His staff was in one hand, the Skull of Gul'dan in the other, and he began to chant, energies coalescing and swirling around him.

The orcs outnumbered them by a significant margin, and were fighting in a frenzy, desperate to escape their collapsing world by any means necessary. The ground was trembling so violently warriors could barely keep their feet, and the battle devolved into mere brawling as orc and human swung wildly at each other, unable to concentrate enough to attack more effectively. The sky split with lightning, storms appearing and disappearing at blurring speeds, stars visible one instant and the sun the next. The planet was going mad.

Between skirmishes Turalyon caught glimpses of Khadgar. The other magi had joined in now, all of them outlined in radiance, and when he squinted Turalyon could just see the trails of energy they were pouring into Khadgar, who stood at their center. He knew his friend was absorbing all that magic, so that he could focus it upon the portal and destroy it for good.

Just as Khadgar's chanting reached a fever pitch, Turalyon heard a strange ripping sound, sharp but somehow faint as well, as if it had occurred both nearby and very far away. He had heard something similar atop the Black Temple, and after dispatching another orc he glanced around and saw a strange shimmer in the air not far from them, a short ways behind the magi. A new rift!

The earth shook beneath his feet and on pure gut instinct Turalyon leaped backward. A fissure opened where he'd been standing just a second before, widening like a hungry mouth. Cracks raced around jaggedly and then suddenly an enormous chunk of earth surged upward, carrying with it a small cluster of men and orcs, bucking them off like an unbroken steed as it turned wildly in midair.

Khadgar hadn't exaggerated. Draenor quite literally was physically tearing itself to pieces.

He was still staring at the floating hunk of earth when Khadgar raised his staff high and a beam of light shot from it to strike the Dark Portal in its center. The light was too bright to look upon, but unlike the Holy Light this was many colors all at once, swirling and dancing and shifting. It was pure magic wrought into a powerful spell, and when it struck the whirling surface of the portal he heard a sound like shattering glass. Then the Dark Portal began to crumble, its curtain of energy splitting and fragmenting as the spell unwrought it.

"It is done," Khadgar said wearily, planting his staff against the ground and leaning heavily upon it. Then he looked up and spotted one of Kurdran's dwarves, a young Wildhammer who had just hurled his stormhammer at a hulking orc that had threatened Danath. "You!" Khadgar shouted. "Take these!" He slammed the skull into his sack and thrust the unwieldy bundle at the surprised dwarf. "Take it and fly back to Azeroth! This needs to get to the Kirin Tor!"

"But sir," the young dwarf said, "are ye nae coming through yersels?"

Khadgar shook his white head. "No. We've got to shut it down here. It's the only way to make sure the damage happening here won't follow us into Azeroth."

Turalyon inhaled swiftly. So there it was, then. Khadgar had never been one to mince words and he'd just said bluntly what they'd all suspected. Only this one dwarf would make it back. The rest of them would be stranded in a world that lurched closer to nothingness by the second.

So be it.

The paladin saw the young Wildhammer hesitate, not sure how to respond, and then gasped as he saw the gleaming arc of a massive axe slicing directly toward the unwary dwarf. But before Turalyon could shout a warning, a stormhammer flashed past, striking the axe wielder with a thunderclap that rang in his ears, and axe and orc alike fell to the ground.

"Go on, lad!" Kurdran ordered, his stormhammer returning to his grasp as he wheeled Sky'ree alongside the surprised dwarf.

The younger dwarf nodded, leaning down to grab the sack from Khadgar and then nudging his gryphon with heel and knee and elbow. She responded at once, beating her wings hard and rising like a shot, then arrowing straight for the collapsing portal. But as she passed under its cracking arches, the sack flared with light, and the portal responded, the resulting glare blinding them all. Turalyon heard the gryphon shriek in pain, and the dwarf screamed as well, but he could not see what had happened to them. The terrible sounds were drowned out by a ferocious rumbling. Before he fully realized what had happened, there was a deafening crash and Khadgar was flying backward. He landed hard, blacking out for a second. When he came to an instant later, aching and barely able to breathe, he looked immediately toward the portal.

It was gone.

The giant statues that had guarded it had tumbled to unrecognizable boulders. The three pillars that had formed the gateway, that had contained the rift in glorious carved majesty, were now nothing but rubble. No sight of Azeroth remained.

They had done it. They had destroyed the rift and the portal. And now, they were forever cut off from everything they had known.

All around him, Horde and Alliance were staggering to their feet, only to feel Draenor buck beneath them again. The orcs took off, not understanding, as Khadgar did, that there was really nowhere for them to run. The portal's collapse had apparently injured Draenor further, and the upheavals grew in intensity and frequency. They were constantly jarred and tossed about as if they were a small boat on an angry sea, the ground rippling like water and the sky thicker than fog.

What an ignominious death, Khadgar thought with a hint of wry amusement. *Having one's brains bashed out by a chunk of earth.* He looked around one last time at his friends—Danath still on his feet, still fighting what orcs hadn't fled. Alleria had fallen and Turalyon was helping her to her feet, quickly wrapping linen around a nasty gash on her arm.

Perhaps feeling Khadgar's gaze, Turalyon looked up. Their eyes met for a moment, and Turalyon smiled that calm, gentle smile that Khadgar associated with the paladin. Alleria glanced at the archmage as well, and nodded her head, the bright gold dimmed with dust and matted here and there with blood. Kurdran, still hovering on Sky'ree, raised a hammer in salute.

And so it would end. Khadgar had always suspected they wouldn't survive this, but he was fiercely grateful they'd been able to close the portal and save their world. And he was equally grateful that if they had to die—which, he mused wryly, all men did—it would be here, together, fighting side by side as they always had.

A faint glimmer caught his eye.

He blinked. No, it was there—a ripple in the fabric of space and time. Another rift.

Another world. One that, perhaps, wasn't shuddering in its death throes.

"There!" he yelled as loudly as he could, pointing at the rift. "We go through there! It's the only chance we've got!"

Turalyon and Alleria looked at one another. Khadgar

couldn't hear what they said over the deafening noises of a world shaking itself to pieces, but he saw them hold each other for a moment before, hands joined, they turned to the rift.

They had all ventured forth through the Dark Portal into Draenor, but at least they'd had a vague idea of what they would find. But this . . .

Draenor's death throes continued, and Khadgar hit the earth hard. Scrambling to his feet, knees and palms scraped raw, he looked toward the rift. Salvation, or a yet worse fate? He didn't know. None of them knew.

They'd just have to find out . . . one way or the other.

Khadgar, archmage, old man, youth, swallowed hard, steeled himself, and ran through.

CHAPTER TWENTY-SEVEN

"Push on, Horde warriors! We are not far!"

Grom Hellscream's voice cut through the din, heartening those who heard it. Rexxar spun, the battle-axe in his left hand shearing through an Alliance warrior's neck and the matching axe in his right slicing down to split another warrior from shoulder to waist. Beside him his wolf Haratha snarled and lunged in, his massive jaws snapping shut upon a third warrior's forearm. Rexxar heard the distinctive crunch of teeth splintering bone and the man cried out, the sword falling from his hand. Haratha released the mangled arm and, in a lightning-fast move, sprang and crunched the man's throat in his jaws. They made a lethal team.

Off to one side Rexxar could see Grom Hellscream, chieftain of the Warsong, Gorehowl shrieking and slicing through foes. Other Warsong warriors fought beside their leader, their chants and battle cries blending together into an eerie melody of death and destruction.

Rexxar was one of the few left who wasn't from that clan, but that was not unusual for him. He didn't really have a clan. At least, not one involved in the Horde. His own people, the mok'nathal, had always been stubbornly independent. Small in number, their lives had been difficult and focused on maintaining their traditional land in the Blade's Edge Mountains, defending it against the ogres who sought to claim it. Rexxar had tried to tell his father, Leoroxx, about the Dark Portal the orcs were building; about the chance to find a fresh new world for the beleaguered mok'nathal. But Leoroxx saw only that his son was not staying where he had been born, to fight to protect his homeland. Both had the goal of helping their people; but in the end, Rexxar had followed the Horde, and been disowned for his choice. Now, it was the only family he had.

But then, he'd always been different.

Another human went down. Rexxar glanced up, his height allowing him to see over the other warriors. Grom was right—they were not far from the Dark Portal. Perhaps a hundred humans stood between him and his homeworld. Rexxar grinned and raised both axes. He was about to thin that number considerably.

Over the last few months, the fortunes of war had swung back and forth. The Alliance had penned them in a small valley adjoining this one for a short time, but could not hold the Horde there for long. The human warriors had underestimated the will and ferocity of the cornered orcs, and Grom had led his people to free-

dom. They had regrouped in a place to the north called
Stonard. It had been the first outpost the Horde had
created when they had come through the Dark Portal
originally. The swamp, though fetid and unpleasant,
held life and water, and Grom had refused to let the
orcs fall into despair. They had built up Stonard, aug-
mented it with raids on Alliance supplies, and had eventually regained control of the portal.

Back and forth the Horde and Alliance had gone.
But now, the little game was at an end. Grom had decided that it was time to return. No other clans had
come to aid them, and while they were still a fighting
force to be reckoned with—as the Alliance was discov-
ering now—their numbers were slowly dwindling,
while the Alliance seemed to breed more by the
minute. Too, there was the matter of that strange
device—the one the warlocks had tried to activate.
They had told Grom that it would create a shield to
protect them from attack and make it easier to defend
the Dark Portal. But the thing had been designed to
destroy, not to protect. Someone was ready to abandon
them here—and Grom Hellscream would not let his
people die because of another's treachery. Rexxar
wanted to be around when Grom returned and con-
fronted the one who had issued the order.

A human charged him on horseback, sword raised
high and shield set before him, but the soldier hadn't
counted on Rexxar's height. Rexxar struck the shield a
heavy blow with one axe, smashing it into the man,

while knocking the sword away with the other. As the rider was jolted from his saddle, Rexxar brought both axes up and let the man's own momentum impale him on the blades. He grinned and let loose a fierce war cry as he yanked the axes free and stepped over the dead soldier, the riderless horse turning and fleeing Haratha's snapping jaws.

Sometimes it was good to be half ogre.

Something flickered at the corner of his vision, from inside the Dark Portal. He had only seen it for a second, but he'd gotten a clear impression of lightning, rolling dust clouds, lashing waves, and shifting ground. Always before the portal had shown the other side, so he had been able to catch glimpses of Draenor during the fight. But what he'd just seen—that was not his homeworld. It was a place of nightmare.

Another Alliance soldier attacked him then, and that brought Rexxar's mind instantly back to the battle. He dispatched the warrior easily, but a handspan or two away from him another orc was not so lucky. Clad in the robes of a warlock, the orc had the green skin of most Horde members—unlike Rexxar himself, who had not joined the Horde until shortly before they invaded Azeroth. There were several warlocks here, some of them quite powerful, but their death magics took time, and things happened quickly in battle.

Two warriors attacked the warlock together, and while the orc had managed to disable one, sending him fleeing in mindless terror, the other had stabbed the warlock through the chest before a nearby Warsong warrior had caved in the human's skull with a shrieking warclub. Now the warlock staggered, one hand pressed to the blossoming bloodstain across his front, his skin already turning pale, sweat breaking out on his brow. Rexxar merely grunted and shook his head. He had little use for warlocks, and this one had clearly not been prepared for combat.

The motion caught the warlock's gaze, and the wounded orc stared at Rexxar, disgust and disdain washing across his features in turn. Then he staggered forward, his other hand palm out.

"You!" the warlock shouted. "You are not true Horde, not a true orc. But you will do. Come here!"

Rexxar stared at the warlock, too surprised to respond. What? This warlock insulted him and then expected him to help? Was he completely mad?

But then, as the warlock drew closer, Rexxar saw the green glow outlining the orc's fingers, and sucked in a quick breath as he felt a rare burst of fear. No, the warlock didn't want his help. He wanted Rexxar's life. Warlocks could leech life energy off others, healing themselves by draining another. The process had a high cost, and a severe wound could easily render a healthy orc lifeless.

And this warlock's wound was mortal.

Rexxar tried to step back but he was boxed in, the orcs and humans behind him too tightly packed for him to move. He growled instead and raised both axes, determined to cut down the warlock rather than die himself, but the orc gestured and suddenly Rexxar dropped to his knees, unbelievable agony racing through him.

"What, no longer so sure of yourself?" the warlock taunted softly, stepping up close enough that his breath tickled Rexxar's skin. Rexxar crumpled and writhed in pain, too weakened by it to struggle. "Does it hurt? Do not worry. Soon the pain will be gone." He raised his hand, slowly, deliberately drawing the moment out, and Rexxar stared as the green-limned flesh inched closer. Already he thought he could feel his energy being drawn from him, and a wave of fatigue washed over him.

A fierce snarl cut through the haze of torment and a large black blur slammed into the warlock.

"Haratha, *no!*" With the warlock's distraction, the spell broke and Rexxar could move again. But he was too late. His devoted wolf companion had shoved the warlock away, but in the process the orc's hand had touched Haratha's thick pelt. Rexxar stared, horrified, as his friend shriveled before his eyes, the powerful wolf shrinking in upon himself in an instant and then collapsing, his body turning to dust that the wind carried away.

"Ah, that feels better," the warlock remarked, rising to his feet and brushing off his robes. The bloodstain remained but he now moved without injury. "Your pet just saved your life," he told Rexxar with a nasty grin.

"Yes, he did," Rexxar replied softly, twirling both axes up and around. "But who will save yours?"

With a snap of his wrists and a roll of his shoulders the axes came arcing back down, to drive deep into the warlock's chest on either side of his head. Rexxar had put much of his considerable strength into the blows, and the warlock crashed to his knees as the impact drove him down, the axes ripping through him and leaving him to collapse in pieces upon the blood-soaked ground.

Rexxar stared at the body, panting, then turned to look at the spot where the wolf had died, the rage still roaring through him and thundering in his ears. He knelt and placed his hand, wet with the warlock's blood, on the dust for a moment.

"You are avenged, my friend," he said softly, "though I would you were still by my side." He took a breath, rose, and channeled his grief and rage into action, calling out for the Warsong leader.

Grom looked up, saw Rexxar, and waved his axe to acknowledge the half-orc. One thing Rexxar had always liked about the Warsong leader—for all his violence, Grom had always given him the same re-spect he would show any warrior. He'd always shown Grom the proper respect in turn, but right now results were more important than manners.

"The portal!" Rexxar yelled, pointing. "Something is wrong!"

Grom glanced toward the portal just as a handful of orcs staggered through. At first Rexxar's heart lifted, thinking the Horde had sent them help after all. But then he saw that these orcs were already battered and bleeding, and that they were running rather than marching—running as if fleeing something. Something on the Draenor side.

"Run!" one of them shouted as he barreled into an Alliance soldier hard enough to knock the man over, and kept right on going without even stopping to attack the prone target. "Run!"

"What is going on?" Grom demanded, and Rexxar shrugged, just as confused. They were both still staring toward the Dark Portal as the scene it framed changed from the crazed landscape of a moment before to an utter maelstrom of swirling color and then to complete darkness.

And then, it vanished.

A heartbeat later, the stone framework that had enclosed the Dark Portal, the rift between worlds, itself began to creak and groan. The sounds increased, straining, rising to a crescendo, and then the center snapped, the two massive halves toppling inward and colliding with a loud crack and a cloud of dust and rock chips. The support pillars fell next, knocked off-balance by the initial impact, and Rexxar ducked his head, pulling the edge of his hood over his mouth to avoid choking on the dust that billowed forth. Orcs and humans alike were scattering, trying to escape the confusion and the debris.

"No!" someone was screaming, and other groans and cries filled the air. For his part, Rexxar was struck dumb, staring at the rubble that had once been a gateway between worlds. The portal—gone? Didn't that mean they could never go home? What would happen to them now?

Fortunately, one orc kept his head. "We will regroup!" Grom shouted, slapping Rexxar on the shoulder. "You gather everyone on that side, I'll get them from this side! Move toward the mouth of the valley!"

Rexxar was jarred from his paralysis and nodded, hurrying to obey. He let the hood fall again once he was clear of the swirling dust. He could still feel the panic within but forced it back by concentrating on the task Grom had assigned him. Every orc he saw, he directed back toward the valley's front, and whether because of his size, or the axes he wielded, or simply because they were desperate for orders, the orcs all obeyed without dispute. By the time Rexxar reached the mouth himself, Grom was back as well, and all the Horde members still on Azeroth were with them. Most of them looked as stunned as Rexxar felt.

"Grom! The portal is gone!" one of them wailed.

"What do we do?"

"Yes. The portal is gone. And the Alliance regroups," Grom announced loudly, gesturing to where the humans were gathering in front of what had been the portal just moments before. "They think we will be easy prey. They think we will be lost, and frightened without the portal. But they will be wrong. We are the Horde!"

His glowing red eyes scanned the crowd before him, and he lifted Gorehowl. "We head north, back to Stonard. We discover what happened to our world. We tend our wounded. We survive.

"Then we'll regroup so we can face the humans on our terms rather than theirs." He growled. "The Alliance closes in. Will they take us?"

A resounding "No!" lifted from what Rexxar privately feared was the last remnants of the orcish Horde. Grom grinned, tilted his head back, opened his black-tattooed jaw, and uttered his battle cry before he charged, his people following.

That one. Grom marched up to the orc sitting huddled beside the fire as they camped in Stonard that night. He was not dusty or bloody and Grom knew all his warriors. Grom clamped his hand down on the orc's shoulder and yanked him backward, looming over the orc, whose eyes were wide with surprise. Beside Grom towered Rexxar.

As easily as if he were hoisting a child, Grom lifted the orc and held him in the air. The orc's feet kicked and flailed. The Warsong chieftain leaned in close.

"Now," Grom said softly, a deep scowl on his face. "What in the name of the ancestors happened back there?"

Shivering, the orc frantically told all he knew. The

other orcs listened. The only sound was the orc's rapid talking, the crackle of the fire, and the omnipresent sounds of the swamp at night. When he finished, no one spoke. They simply stared, shocked beyond speech.

Finally, after several minutes, Grom shook himself. "So," he growled, glaring at the others and half-shaming, half-intimidating them into looking away, shuffling their feet, and straightening up. "We prepare, then."

"Prepare?" Rexxar cried, and Grom turned to face the half-orc, half-ogre warrior. "Prepare for what, Hellscream? Our whole world is dead, our people are dead, and we're trapped here forever. Alone. What in the name of the ancestors should we prepare *for*?" Rexxar's grip on his axes was so tight Grom thought he heard the stone hafts creaking from strain.

"We prepare for vengeance for the dead!" Grom snapped, an image of Garrosh leaping into his mind's eye once more. His son and heir. *My boy,* he thought; *my boy. Dead, like all the rest.* "We're all that's left!" he insisted, rounding upon the other orcs. "*We* are the Horde now! If we give up, it means the end of everything we knew, everything we cared about! Our race will not die unless we lie down and accept death like craven weaklings! If Ner'zhul's plans—"

"Ner'zhul!" Rexxar shouted, leaning down so his face was right by Grom's. "This must be his fault! Who else could have caused a world to shatter so? He betrayed us all! He said he would save Draenor and instead he destroyed it!"

"We don't know that!" Grom insisted. "We knew he was dealing with extremely powerful magic to open portals to other worlds. Perhaps something went wrong."

"Or maybe it went perfectly right—for him!" Rexxar countered furiously. "Maybe he was just using us, all of us, our entire world, to further his own ambitions. That's what Gul'dan did, isn't it?" Many of the assembled orcs grunted or murmured or snarled agreement—everyone knew of Gul'dan's betrayal and how it had cost them the Second War. "And who trained Gul'dan?" Rexxar continued. "Who taught him? Ner'zhul! Clearly the fruit did not fall far from the vine!"

The mutterings were louder and angrier now, and Grom knew he had to stop them before the group of warriors devolved into an angry mob.

"Do you not see that it doesn't matter?" he stated, cutting through Rexxar's anger by projecting calm. "Shall we decide what we do based upon rumor and worry? Shall we pine for what could have been or fret about what might have happened? Is this how the mighty Horde behaves?" He looked from orc to orc, including them all in this conversation, and was pleased to hear the murmurs die down as they waited to hear what else he had to say.

"We have survived! We are on Azeroth, a world full of life and food and land and battle! We can restore the Horde and sweep across this world once more!"

Some of the other orcs cheered his statement, and Grom used that energy to fuel his own fervor, whipping Gorehowl around over his head so its shrieking would add a backdrop to his words.

"Yes, the Alliance is hunting us," he shouted, "and yes, we are no match for them today. But one day, and that day soon, we will be! Here we can rest, recover, and strategize. Here we will launch attacks, as we have already been doing for the last several turns of their moons. We will grow strong again. We will become the predators once more, and the humans will quake with fear!" He jerked his axe to a stop and held it still above his head, lowering his voice so his words fell softly into the sudden quiet. "And one day we, the Horde, will rise and take our vengeance against the humans with a true and final victory!"

The warriors cheered and whooped and shouted, raising their own weapons high, and Grom nodded. Pleased. They were all behind him again, all united once more.

All except one.

"You have been betrayed repeatedly, each time by another orc claiming leadership, and still you continue down that same path," Rexxar said softly, though his eyes burned with rage. "You have no reason left to fight! Before, we fought to protect our people by claiming this world for them. But they are gone! We no longer need this world! With the handful left, you could find a place the humans have never gone and claim it without shedding a single drop of blood!"

"Where would be the glory in that?" one of the other orcs shouted.

Grom nodded. "What is life without battle?" he demanded of Rexxar. "You are a warrior—you understand that! Fighting keeps us strong, keeps us sharp!"

"Perhaps," the half-breed admitted. "But why fight when there is no need? Why fight just for its own sake? That is not fighting to save anyone, or to win anything, or even for glory. It is fighting from sheer bloodlust, from love of violence alone. And I am sick of that. I want no part of it."

"Coward!" someone shouted, and Rexxar's eyes narrowed as he straightened to his full height, the twin axes rising to shoulder level.

"Step forth and say that," he challenged, his voice an ominous rumble. "Step away from the rest, where I can see you clearly, and call me a coward to my face! Then see whether I shrink from a fight!"

No one moved, and after a second Rexxar shook his head, a sneer on his heavy features. "You are the cowards," he proclaimed, spitting the words down upon them. "You are too afraid to live truly, outside the shadows of lies and promises you have been bought with. You have no courage, and no honor. That is why you cannot be trusted." The half-orc's shoulders slumped. "From now on, only the beasts will I trust."

Grom felt a mixture of emotions as he watched the towering warrior depart. How dare Rexxar abandon them now, when they most needed to stay together? At the same time, who could blame him? He was not even part of the Horde in the normal sense, for the mok'nathal were ever reluctant to leave the Blade's Edge Mountains. To the best of Grom's knowledge, only Rexxar himself had responded to the Horde's plea, to fight during the First War and then again during the Second. And what had it gained him? He had lost his world, his people, and even his companion the wolf. Was it any wonder the half-orc felt betrayed?

"No one walks away from the Horde!" someone insisted. "We should drag him back by his ears, or kill him!"

"He insulted us all!" another pointed out. "He should die for his insolence!"

"We need his strength," a third countered. "We cannot afford to lose him!"

"Enough!" Grom shouted, glaring at them all. The dissenters fell silent. "Let him go," he ordered. "Rexxar has served the Horde well. Let him have his peace now."

"And what about us?" one of the warriors demanded. "What will we do now?"

"We know what to do," Grom replied. "This world is our home now. Let us live in it fully." But even as they nodded and returned to the fire, to speak softly in voices about plans and victory and supplies, Rexxar's words returned to haunt him, and a part of Grom wondered if they would ever find that which they had lost so long ago: peace.

CHAPTER TWENTY-EIGHT

Turalyon emerged from the rift, blinking. "Is . . . is this . . . Draenor?"

They had escaped Draenor's destruction by stepping through into another world, one they could barely make sense of. Khadgar and the other magi had shielded them from the tremors passing through the rift, and once it had quieted they had returned, hoping to search for any of their comrades that might have survived. But as his eyes registered what they saw, Turalyon jerked to a halt, staring. Only Alleria's tug on his hand reminded him to move out of the way so the rest could emerge as well.

"It is. What's left of it, anyway," Khadgar said. Turalyon recognized the rubble of the fallen Dark Portal behind them, with Honor Hold and Hellfire Citadel in the distance. The cracked red earth was the same as well. But the sky—!

It rippled with color now, and ribbons of light shot

through it like multihued lightning bolts that traveled across instead of ever touching the earth. The sun had vanished and the sky was a dark red, but he could see the moon hovering high above, looking far larger than it ever had before. A second sphere, this one rosy, was low on the horizon, and a third, smaller and a bright blue, floated just above that one. Wisps like tendrils of cloud drifted here and there.

And while the earth was the same in color and consistency, not far away Turalyon saw a small wedge of cracked ground—only it was perhaps a hundred feet up! It bobbed slightly, buffeted by the fierce winds that raged all around them, but otherwise stayed in place. Other fragments floated here and there as well.

"The damage has sundered reality as we know it," Khadgar continued. "Gravity, space, perhaps even time itself no longer function properly here."

Khadgar's words were swallowed by a tearing sound beneath them. Turalyon grabbed his arm with one hand and Alleria's with the other, instinctively tugging them both back toward what had been the rest of the land.

"Fall back!" Turalyon shouted, though he wasn't sure the men could hear him over the rending of the earth or the howling of the winds overhead. "Back away from the rift!" They could see him, however, and he gestured to the west, toward Honor Hold. They ran then, all order forgotten in their panic.

And not a moment too soon. As Turalyon pulled Khadgar and Alleria along, the ground beneath their feet began to crumble. They hurled themselves toward the ground beyond, barely reaching it before the ledge behind them collapsed, chunks of rock and earth falling away. Before, the Dark Portal had been partially encircled by mountains to the east, and beyond that had been the sea. Now most of the mountains had vanished, and, shockingly, so had the waves. Only empty space waited to swallow the falling debris, as the world's remains now hung in a great yawning darkness shot through with ripples and flashes of light here and there.

"Sir," one of the men piped up. "Wasn't . . . wasn't that where the rift was?"

"Yes," Turalyon said. "It was." The rift through which they had first fled Draenor and then returned to it had indeed been on that ledge, and had collapsed when the earth beneath it had shattered, leaving behind only the remnants of the Dark Portal.

There was silence, and Turalyon sensed their growing despair. "Look there," he told them, spotting a familiar cluster of buildings a short distance away. "Honor Hold still stands. We built it to serve as our stronghold here on Draenor, and so it will be."

He turned to look at them—dusty, bloody, exhausted. "We knew when we came through we might not be returning. Light, we expected to die—but we didn't. The portal's closed. We did what we came here to do. What we do now—that's up to us. There are others still out there—we need to find them, bring them back. We'll explore. Make new allies. Keep fighting the Horde, whatever's left of it here, so they don't ever try to do something like this again. The Light is still with us. We still have a job to do. This world will be what we choose to make of it."

Alleria stepped beside him, her eyes shining. He squeezed her hand tightly. Turalyon glanced over at Khadgar, who nodded, his young eyes crinkling in an approving smile. The paladin again looked toward his men. They were still worried. Still unsure. But the despair and panic were gone.

This world will be what we choose to make of it.

"Come on," Turalyon said, and pointed to Honor Hold. "Let's go home."

EPILOGUE

"Ner'zhul!"

The orc shaman and Horde warchief cried out at the sound of his name, his eyes flicking open. At once the strange swirling nothingness all around him assaulted his senses, and he squeezed his eyes shut, hoping to force away the welter of sensation that threatened to drive him mad. Then, through the thrums and howls and cracklings, he heard it again.

"Ner'zhul!"

Blinking, he glanced around him. A short ways away—or so it seemed, though an instant later he would have sworn it was miles distant—Ner'zhul saw a dark form. It was shaped like an orc, and a longer look confirmed it, revealing green skin and tusks and long braids. Definitely an orc, and one Ner'zhul recognized as one of his own Shadowmoon warriors. The warrior did not move, however—Ner'zhul thought he saw the other orc's chest rising and falling, but in this place he could not be sure of anything.

Other shapes littered the strange maelstrom of light and shadow. All those who had followed him through the rift appeared to be here with him.

The question was, where was *here*? Why hadn't the rift led them to another world? For whatever this place might be, Ner'zhul was sure it was not a normal world. What had happened? Why was he awake and aware, while all the others were trapped in a deep sleep?

A column of light rolled past, and for an instant Ner'zhul saw echoing glimmers around each of the other orcs—and around himself. His eyes widened, then clamped shut as they overloaded from the sights assaulting them. But he knew what he had seen. They were trapped indeed—something was binding them to this place!

"Ner'zhul!" His name wafted across the strangeness yet again, but this time Ner'zhul felt something tug upon his chest and his limbs. The other orcs receded rapidly, or perhaps he was the one moving while they remained locked in place—it was impossible to tell here. But within minutes Ner'zhul was alone, the rest of his orcs only distant shadows.

And then a larger, darker shadow fell across him, and he looked up—

—into the face of wrath itself.

Before Ner'zhul hung a massive being arrayed in

heavy armor of etched blood-red metal. The figure's face resembled that of a draenei, intelligent-looking and clever, but with bright red skin and a demonic cast. The creature had short, curving horns rising from his high temples, and two strange protrusions like tentacles extending below his mouth and well past the short beard covering his chin. Several earrings gleamed, and the creature's eyes glowed a deep yellow.

And Ner'zhul knew him at once.

"Great One!" Ner'zhul gasped, doing his best to bow though his limbs were still bound somehow.

"Ah, Ner'zhul, my unfaithful little servant," replied Kil'jaeden, demon lord of the Burning Legion. "Did you think I had forgotten about you?"

"No, Great One, of course not." In truth Ner'zhul had hoped so, and after the first few years had begun to think it true. Now his heart sank as the demon lord continued speaking.

"Oh, I have been watching you closely all this time, Ner'zhul," Kil'jaeden assured him. "You cost me a great deal, you know." The demon lord laughed, a chilling, grating sound. "And now you shall pay for such failure!"

"I—," Ner'zhul began, but his brain could barely formulate words.

"You could not leave well enough alone," Kil'jaeden finished for him. "I knew that eventually you would try yet again to cast magics you were not ready to handle and did not understand. I waited, knowing that some day your own arrogance would bring you to me." He spread his gauntleted hands wide. "And here we are!" His eyes narrowed to mere slits. "You have dreamed of death. You thought to escape it. Now, my little puppet, death will be all you ever know."

Brief glimpses seared Ner'zhul's brain: Agony as pieces of flesh were torn from his still-living body; the dead surrounding him, closing in on him, their blood on his hands, his own blood coating them, a morbid union of death, life, and excruciating torment.

"No!" Ner'zhul shouted, thrashing about, trying everything to free himself from his invisible bonds. "My people still need me!"

Laughter shook the demon's powerful form, a horrible, eerie sound that made Ner'zhul's heart spasm.

"I know full well they mean nothing to you. So do not worry," the demon lord whispered, stabbing the tip of one long finger into Ner'zhul's cheek. The motion burned, sending spikes of heat and pain through Ner'zhul's flesh. "There is no saving them. Do you not yet understand? Little puppet, you cannot even save yourself."

Then he twisted that finger, the rest of his splayed hand latching onto Ner'zhul's face, and the orc shaman let his head fall back, a horrible scream wrenching its way out past his trembling lips.

He knew it was but the first of many.

ABOUT THE AUTHORS

AARON ROSENBERG is originally from New Jersey and New York. He returned to New York City in 1996 after stints in New Orleans and Kansas. He has taught college-level English and worked in corporate graphics and book publishing.

Aaron has written novels for *Star Trek*, *StarCraft*, *Warcraft*, *Warhammer*, and *Exalted*. He also writes roleplaying games and has worked on the *Star Trek*, *Warcraft*, and *Warhammer* games. He writes educational books as well.

Aaron lives in New York City with his family. For more information about his writing you can visit him online at www.rosenbergbooks.com.

Award-winning author CHRISTIE GOLDEN has written thirty-two novels and several short stories in the fields of science fiction, fantasy and horror.

Golden launched the TSR *Ravenloft* line in 1991 with her first novel, the highly successful *Vampire of the Mists*, which introduced elven vampire Jander Sunstar. To the best of her knowledge, she is the creator of the elven

Covenant: Vampire of the Mists in September 2006, fifteen years to the month after its original publication.

She is the author of several original fantasy novels, including *On Fire's Wings*; *In Stone's Clasp*; and *Under Sea's Shadow* (currently available only as an e-book) the first three in her multi-book fantasy series *The Final Dance* from LUNA Books. *In Stone's Clasp* won the Colorado Author's League Award for Best Genre Novel of 2005, the second of Golden's novels to win the award.

Among Golden's other projects are over a dozen *Star Trek* novels, including the bestsellers *Homecoming* and *The Farther Shore*, and the well-received *StarCraft: Dark Templar* trilogy—*Firstborn*, *Shadow Hunters*, and the upcoming *Twilight*. An avid player of Blizzard's MMORPG *World of Warcraft*, Golden has written several novels in that world (*Lord of the Clans*, *Rise of the Horde*) with more in the works.

Golden lives in Colorado with her husband and two cats.